Heart

of

Ice

Rose Harvey

Copyright © Rose Harvey, 2024

Published: 2024 by The Book Reality Experience,
Leschenault, Western Australia

ISBN: 9781923020696 - Paperback
          9781923020702 - eBook

The right of Rose Harvey to be identified as author of this work has been asserted by her in accordance with sections 77 and 78 of the copyright, designs and patents act 1988.

This book is a work of fiction and any resemblance to actual persons, living or dead, or locations, is purely coincidental.

All rights reserved. No part of this publication may be reproduced or transmitted in any form or by any means, electronic or mechanical, including photography, recording, or any information storage or retrieval system, without permission in writing from the publisher.

The book is sold subject to the condition that it shall not, by way of trade or otherwise, be lent, resold or otherwise circulated without the publisher's prior consent in any form of binding or cover other than that in which it is published and without a similar condition, including this condition, being imposed on the subsequent purchaser.

Cover Design by Brittany Wilson | Brittwilsonart.com

To Jordan
for being my sun, moon and stars.

Also by Rose Harvey

The Ice Flame Trilogy
Heir to the Ice Flame
Heart of Ice
Fire on the Ice

The Order Series
Robin

Prologue

It started with a wish. A young girl wept by a fountain in the palace garden, hating the fact that she wasn't old enough to be free from her wardens. Everywhere she went there was always someone watching her, either a nursemaid, a guard or a courtier, someone trying to win her parents' favour. In recent months the watchers had increased, shadowing her every movement, chastising her for the rare moments she wandered off alone. Even now, as she wept over the stone rim of the fountain, a couple of guards stood at the edge of her peripheral vision, close enough to ensure her safety but far enough away to not see the tears falling into the water. The girl rubbed her eyes, turned her face away from the unwanted audience, and hiccupped. She sat there for a while unmoving, drinking in the rare sunshine and longing for things to be different.

She was sick of her parents telling her that things would change when she got older, and that in the meantime she should continue her lessons, practise deportment and be grateful for her upbringing. There were always rules– as the palace steward reminded her constantly– and she seemed to have a habit of breaking them. The girl sighed and gazed down at her reflection in the ripples, wondering whether she would ever live up to her parents' expectations, dreading the possibility that she may end up disappointing them and all the people who relied on her to do the right thing.

A movement flickered across the surface of the water, and she glanced up to see a man reclining on the far rim of the fountain. He asked her why such a lovely young lady was crying and what could be done to make her feel better. She gazed at him in shock, for never had she seen anyone like him before. His skin was the colour of dark umber, his sparkling eyes were jet black and his hair was pulled up into a turban, encrusted with glittering rubies. He exuded warmth and security, and she felt an instant urge to move closer, to take comfort in his presence. His appearance did not seem to have affected the guards, who gazed past him, unaware of his presence. The girl didn't pause to think about the impact of this, too drawn in was she by the stranger's cajoling tone. She knew the risks of speaking with unknown people, yet with this man she felt safe, certain that he would not share her thoughts with another living soul.

In halting breaths, she told him about how trapped she felt, how she wished to be free from it all– to not have to worry about the correct posture, or table manners, or recalling mind-numbing facts from seven hundred years ago. She said how she ached from the birch rod after mis-stepping in her dancing lesson the day before and for failing to complete her sums to an adequate standard. She explained how her parents seemed to be more distant from her every day; whereas once they had been happy to leave their duties behind to keep her company, now she was shut out from their quarters and they conversed in whispers behind closed doors. She was lonely, angry at their abandonment, and hurt that she couldn't know what they were keeping from her. Perhaps if she was not the princess, she would have friends her own age to run and play with, and would feel the lack of her parents less.

And so, on that day, in that moment, she wished to escape, to be free from the constraints of the monarchy and to experience life as a normal, ordinary person. A particle of dust blew into her eye and she blinked, rubbing it away. In the time it took for her eyes to stop watering, the man had vanished, leaving no trace behind. The girl looked around, peering behind trees and bushes, but there was no sign of him. As she headed back towards the palace, she sighed and shrugged, wondering if perhaps he had merely been a figment of her imagination all along. By the next morning she had mostly forgotten about the strange encounter, and if the memory of the man crossed her mind, she considered him a fanciful daydream, brought on by the heat of the day. She had also forgotten the wish she had made.

Three days later, her life was irreparably changed. Her parents lay dead, her country was in political uproar and she was running for her life.

Chapter One

The dream hadn't changed for the past few weeks. I saw Markus' eyes widen in horror as he crumpled, his mouth opening in shock at the sight of the blood pooling around the knife wound in his side. I was helpless to go to him, stuck in the invisible bonds which kept me rooted in place.

Markus' gaze met mine and held it before gasping out, 'why?'

As he collapsed, eyes sightless and blank, I was released from my bonds and I staggered towards him. My hands reached out to hold him before I recoiled in horror, noticing for the first time the blood staining my forearms and the front of my clothing.

And, as had become the habit, I awoke at that exact moment, heart pounding and the taste of bile in my throat. I wiped my forehead and registered the cold sweat that came away on my palm. Unconsciously, my hand then went to the lucky coin that hung around my neck. Sitting up in bed, I glanced around the room, making sure that my grandfather's retainers hadn't been alerted to my abrupt waking. The pale light of dawn was filtering through the curtains around my bed as I quietly got to my feet and padded over to a pitcher of water. I filled the glass next to it and took a long draught, calming my pounding heart. The water was cold and sweet, and I felt not only refreshed after drinking, but also filled with clarity and peace. It had surprised me that, on arriving in my grandfather's kingdom, everything from water to food tasted better than it had in Scardia. For so many years I had been used to surviving on meagre fare– sometimes going days without proper sustenance– which was a far cry from my childhood where food and drink had been plentiful and abundant. Placing the cup down, I began to brush out my long red hair, reflecting on the nightmare. The ghost of Markus' crumpled figure lingered in my mind, and I flinched as I caught on a tangle.

It had been over a month since I had laid eyes on him and my heart continued to ache with resentment and anger at the unanswered questions that still haunted me. I gritted my teeth, laid down the brush and began to braid my hair ruthlessly, pulling slightly harder than necessary. It had been a godsend to focus on the war effort instead of revisiting our moment of parting over and over again. I had worked harder than ever before, pushing myself to the limits, training each day and spending time with Grandfather to catch up on all the years we had missed. It had surprised me how I thrived in this environment, enjoying the training sessions and debates, since during childhood I had never found them that interesting. Most importantly though, I relished the time I spent with Grandfather. Deprived of family for so long, it was both blessing and curse to be around him so much. I knew he was there to support me through whatever would come to pass, but it also brought regret that I had not tried to locate him sooner and reminded me of what I had lost. And yet, while most days I succeeded in wearing myself out so much that I could fall asleep immediately, my mind still dwelled on Markus in those times before waking or sleeping.

There was a sharp knock at the door, startling me out of my reverie. Without waiting for a response, the door opened and a short woman with blonde, curly hair and sparkling beady eyes entered, a pile of clothing in her arms.

'Good morning Lisette,' I said, smiling. She placed the clothes down on the bed and motioned for me to stop braiding so that she could take over. I had noticed early on that Lisette was deft with her fingers but also gentle, unlike myself. Within seconds she had tied my hair back and pinned it up so that it would not get in the way during training. She tapped my shoulder and I stood as she whipped my nightdress up and over my head. I jumped into the kid-skin breeches she had brought me and pulled on a linen shirt and tunic. Lisette began to tie up my boots and I tightened the belt around my waist, attaching my dagger in its scabbard to hang by my side. Lisette cast a quick look over me to make sure that I was presentable and then nodded her approval. She ushered me out of the door, pushing me towards the dining hall for breakfast.

I had noticed early on that routine was very important in my grandfather's court, mealtimes especially so. The Elves liked to rise early and take full advantage of the day, so it was not uncommon to see the majority of the court present at breakfast, sharing in bread and fruit, laughing and discussing their plans for the day ahead. This morning was no different, with everyone crowded around long tables, while I moved next to my grandfather at the long table on the dais overlooking the hall. He had already started eating, head bent to listen attentively to Erik, who was somehow shovelling food into his mouth and talking a million miles a minute at the same time.

'And then Stefan swung his staff like this,' he paused to demonstrate a complicated swishing movement with his free arm, 'and Elder Haycin fell backwards into the pile of horse sh…'

'I hope,' I said as I sat down next to him, 'that you're not going to finish that sentence.'

Erik turned to me, eyes wide, 'but it was *so cool.*'

'It might have been, but I don't want to hear about Elder Haycin falling into a pile of manure as soon as I start to eat,' I replied, indicating to a young Elven boy with sandy hair and bright brown eyes, who hovered eagerly at the edge of the room, watching Erik keenly. 'It looks like Stefan's waiting for you to finish so you can go to training together.' Erik spun around to wave at Stefan and then began eating so fast I was worried he would throw all the food back up again. Within a minute, his plate was empty and he stood up to go.

'Remember to invite Stefan to eat with us next time,' I said, 'and have a good morning.'

He grinned at me, 'he's worried you'll have him executed if you're in a bad mood.' I blinked, baffled, and glanced over at Stefan who turned bright red and ducked away through a doorway. I turned to Erik and he shrugged, 'you scare him.'

'*How?*' I asked incredulously. 'It's not like I've been lopping people's heads off left, right and centre since we got here. What have you been telling him about me?'

'Only the good things,' he answered sweetly, and then snorted with laughter as I tried and failed to box his ears. He dodged backwards and with a cheery wave and a skip in his step, followed Stefan.

I turned to Grandfather, 'I hope he's not been spreading too many rumours.' My grandfather's eyes twinkled with a glimmer of amusement.

'Come Nina, you also have much to do today,' he too rose and gestured for me to follow. I eyed the food in front of me longingly, grabbing a chunk of bread, some cheese and half an apple to see me through. Grandfather gave a little huff, 'if you were up earlier you would have time to eat properly.'

I grinned and took a bite of the apple, 'I'm already getting up at dawn, would you rather I get up before the sun rises?' When he didn't reply, I bit into the bread and cheese and led the way back out of the hall towards the training rooms. In a few minutes I had finished the apple and polished off the remaining crumbs just in time for training.

My grandfather's court was spread out across the upper canopy of a forest of trees, connected with platforms and woven wicker walkways. Vines and ivy crept up the walls, filtering the light through so that it was often tinged with green. If we had still been in Scardia, it would've been freezing, with little protection from the sleet-filled winds or icy mornings. However, in the Eastern Lands it was much warmer, the land lush and bountiful, and everyone seemed happier. At times it was hard to remember how different things were in Scardia, where everyone lived in fear of the Usurper's Trackers, food could be scarce and the cold of winter was an almost constant companion.

I glanced over the railing of the walkway as we crossed from the dining hall to the training rooms, taking in the long descent, the winding stairs that rose from the ground to the platforms, and the roofs of Lowton below us. I hadn't realised on my arrival how close my grandfather's court was to the ocean. Lowton was the portside town bridging the fey Elven kingdom which Grandfather ruled and the wider world beyond the Eastern Lands' shores. Grandfather had told me that many hundreds of years before, sailors from Scardia had been terrified on arriving here when they met Elves for the first time, and how that had caused an instant distrust of the strange beings. The Elves had decided from then on to have a mid-way point, which became Lowton. A town inhabited by both humans and Elves, it had grown to become a melting pot of cultures, inspiring those from even further afield to move there, such as Felshkrans from their land of rolling deserts or the reptilian Karshkans. As I gazed down, I saw Lowton's inhabitants begin to go about their daily business, street vendors opening shutters and beginning to set up their stalls along the main street.

'So you've arrived, Princess.' The harsh and commanding tone jerked me back to reality. I looked around and saw Rakael standing in the doorway to the main training room. Her hair was pulled back, highlighting the scars across her face, and she wore loose breeches with a linen shirt. Her arms were crossed and her fingers were tapping in quick succession.

'I will see you at luncheon, Nina,' Grandfather spoke quietly, gave Rakael a sharp nod and in a few quick strides had left us.

'Let's get started,' Rakael spoke again, her mouth twisted up in what I hoped was a smile. 'We can see how much you've improved since the last time you fought with staves.' My stomach dropped and I felt a lurch of anxiety. On meeting her eyes, I thought I saw a glint of satisfaction before it was gone. I swallowed, realising that this morning was not going to be memorable in a good way.

'Again.' Rakael's voice was bored. I gritted my teeth, wiping the sweat off my brow with the back of my hand. I turned back to face Jesse who was watching me intently, the staff balanced perfectly in her hands. With aching muscles, I readied myself for the anticipated onslaught.

'Now,' Rakael said from the edge of the platform, 'prepare yourself and clear your mind. You can't afford to get distracted by your emotions like *each* time before. And, one, two, three,' at each clipped word, Jesse struck and I blocked, barely managing to keep up with her quick movements. My lips pinched in annoyance, biting back a retort to Rakael's acerbic comments.

'Over, under,' Rakael drilled, and I ducked as Jesse's staff brushed over me, narrowly missing my head. 'Anticipate her,' the dry voice continued, 'stop cowering behind your staff. Stand up for yourself. Fight *back*.'

'I'm not cowering,' I growled as I sidestepped one of Jesse's blows. The staves clashed together and as the shock of the impact ran through my body, jarring my arms, I gasped in pain.

'Then prove it,' Rakael snapped, obviously losing what little patience she had. I glowered at her words and struck out, forcing Jesse to take the defensive for the first time since we started training. I struck again and again, and each time she deflected my staff. I spun around, trying to find some weakness in her defence so that I could strike her when her guard was down. She laughed as if she read my thoughts and suddenly her blows came harder and faster than before, catching me off-guard. Within seconds my parries were failing and a sneaky blow caught the back of my knees, toppling me to the ground. I hit the wooden floor with a cry of pain and glared up at Jesse and Rakael, who stepped forward and looked down at me coldly.

'Well done Princess,' she said, 'you just died.'

I spat my hair out of my mouth and rubbed my legs which were stinging mercilessly. Rakael watched as I got to my feet, using the staff to help support my weight as my legs shook uncontrollably.

'Pathetic,' she said, 'how can you expect to lead if you cannot complete a simple training exercise? Our people need you to be *strong*, not weak and spineless.' Her words cut into me, deeper than I expected them to. I'd thought I was getting used to Rakael's criticism over the past weeks, but clearly not.

'I'm *not* weak,' I spoke through gritted teeth, 'I *am* trying.' Anger pounded through me, and I felt an irrational urge to lash out at Rakael, to force her to recognise my efforts. The air began to shimmer in front of my eyes and I saw Rakael's gaze tighten with something indecipherable.

An arm clasped my elbow, steadying me. Jesse stood beside me and smiled. 'You fought well. Let's have a rest outside before we continue.' Just hearing the words helped appease my anger, and I felt myself calming down. The haze in my vision disappeared and I let Jesse lead me away from the training space. When we were outside and the fresh air caressed my sweaty face, she halted and gazed out at the twisting canopy around us.

'You can't let her get to you, Nina,' she said quietly, 'she's testing you.'

'I know,' I muttered. 'Why else is she making the training sessions harder and harder?'

Jesse shook her head, 'I mean more than physically. She needs to know that you can control yourself when things get tough. That's why she's so hard on you.'

I snorted, 'maybe– but I think she just doesn't like me.'

Jesse frowned pensively, 'It's hard to tell with Rakael. She doesn't let many people get too close after… well…' Her voice drifted and I understood what she meant. I had heard the story of how Rakael had gotten her scars– how her family were burned alive while the Usurper's Trackers watched and laughed. She had been lucky to survive, and since then her hatred and desire for vengeance had only gotten stronger. But it still irked that she took out that anger on me. Despite what Jesse said, the idea that Rakael continued to blame me for Keely's loss hadn't left me. The thought of Keely sent shame and guilt through me, and my vision clouded as memories of his cries filled my mind. A painful ache clenched in my gut and for a moment it was hard to breathe. I was brought back to the present when Jesse said,

'Nina, you should go to King Aegis at once.' Something in her tone made me blink in surprise.

'Why?'

'You're… well there's no easy way to say this,' she said, 'but you're glowing.' I glanced down at myself, concerned. I looked fine— what was she talking about? 'Please Nina,' she continued, 'just go to see him.'

I shrugged and headed towards Grandfather's rooms, confused about what Jesse had meant. However, I wasn't going to complain about cutting the training session short and getting a reprieve from more of Rakael's criticism. The wooden boards creaked under my feet as I strode away, the light breeze flicking my errant hair out of its braid so that it caught in my eyes. As I raised a hand to brush the hair away, I realised that I was shaking. Gods above, I needed to learn to control my temper— I couldn't be reduced to a quivering mass of anger and shame whenever Rakael pushed me in the training room.

Grandfather's rooms were not too far, so it did not take me too long to reach them. His receiving room was small, with a large fireplace that dominated a side of the room and a wide balcony, with a railing of woven branches and vines.

Leading off from his receiving room were two rooms: his bed chamber, which mirrored mine with open windows and a giant bed with a canopy of ivy, and another room which I had not entered. It was darker, shrouded from outside by tendrils of leaves in the doorway. I was sure that there was some form of water in there though, as I had heard the splashing of water whenever I had visited Grandfather.

I paused in the doorway to the receiving room as Grandfather's attendants bowed, raising two fingers to their forehead in respect. I smiled and stepped inside, heading towards where he stood on one of the balconies, looking out over the forest and town below.

'What brings you here so early, Wilhelmina?' On the use of my full name I halted, suddenly unsure. How had he known that I was his visitor? No one had announced me.

'I was training,' I began haltingly, 'and I needed to take a break.'

'Why?' he continued to gaze away from me, his tone unchanged– cool, distant.

'I lost my temper,' I said quietly, feeling a faint blush fill my cheeks. Gods, did he want me to relive all of that torturous morning?

'Was there a reason for losing your temper?'

'I did not appreciate Rakael's teaching method,' I grumbled, my temper starting to rekindle despite his calm questioning. 'Jesse also told me to see you,' I rushed on, keen to change the subject, 'she said that something was wrong with me.'

On this he turned, his pale blue eyes burned into mine and I felt that he saw much more than I could in my response. Grandfather beckoned me closer and my legs stumbled back into action. He watched me approach gravely and then, with a sharp gesture, his retainers vanished, disappearing with silent obedience.

'Did she say what was wrong with you?' he asked as I reached him.

'Apparently I was glowing,' I replied, 'but I'm fine. There's nothing wrong with me– I have no idea what she was going on about.' My words tumbled after each other in a rush, tripping on my tongue until they all seemed to merge together into incoherence. I forced myself to pause and give a half shrug, forcing a smile and a laugh. 'I think she just wanted me to have more time to cool down after arguing with Rakael– I'm fine, honestly.' But as I continued to hold his gaze, I felt my smile subside and the laughter fizzled away into awkward silence.

'You need to appreciate, Wilhelmina,' he said, 'that you are no ordinary princess. In you I see not only your father's pride and loyalty, but also your mother's compassion and kindness.' His words surprised me and I was rooted to the spot. I hadn't felt particularly kind or compassionate of late, and after hearing Rakael's criticism, hearing compliments threw me off balance even more. I felt like a blind novice with no idea where to place her feet on a winding road, like I kept making mistakes and when I thought that I had made some progress, Rakael would be there to cut me down and push me two steps back. Grandfather's eyes crinkled, as if he had read my mind.

'Come,' he took my elbow and guided me away from the balcony. I acquiesced and walked at his side, thinking we were going to sit down by the fire, which was where we usually sat for our discussions. But instead, he continued towards the shrouded room, pushing aside the tendrils of leaves and leading me into the semi-darkness. I blinked, eyes adjusting to the change, and gazed around at the space. Tiny patches of sunlight were able to push through the leaves that wove tightly together overhead, creating shafts of light that pierced the gloom. The room was round, with a fountain in its centre, two stone dryads pouring water out of their hands as they danced together. The water caught the light and shimmering reflections darted around the space. There was almost no furniture in this room, save some bookshelves and a stone bench along the far wall. Cushions littered the floor, and I noticed that several were leaning up against the fountain's edge, almost as though Grandfather would lean against the stone and rest there, listening to the sound of cascading water.

'You must remember,' Grandfather had let go of my arm, leaving me just inside the doorway as he propped himself against the edge of the fountain, 'that you have both human and Elven blood in your veins.' He beckoned me over and I obeyed, perching beside him, one hand trailing in the glistening water. 'Elves,' he continued, 'as you know, possess certain skills– gifts, one could say– that humans do not. Now that you are here among your family, it is possible for you to learn how to unlock these gifts within yourself.'

I tilted my head and frowned at him in confusion. 'Are you talking about magic?'

He laughed, 'that is one word for it. We Elves consider it more gifts from the Gods, mainly Helebor– Lord of the Arcane and its mysteries. Through his benevolence, the four spirits were created for each season, all of whom can wield a range of powers and choose to gift powers onto mortals. The Elves were blessed by the Lord of Spring, who I believe you have met before.'

I remembered the Lord of Spring, his shaggy hide and strange way of communicating via images in the mind. He had helped me, along with the Winter Spirit, who had urged me to find Grandfather and whose instructions I had followed.

'So Helebor bestowed gifts upon the Spirits and they in turn had the authority to grant powers to those they considered worthy?'

Grandfather nodded, 'That's right. And, since your mother was an Elf, you share in some of those gifts.'

'But how would that be possible?' I asked, 'if I had any sort of magical ability surely it would have surfaced long before now.' In my head it just didn't make sense. I was a fugitive princess, skilled in cooking and cleaning, a graceful dancer and useful with a dagger, but incompetent with almost every other form of combat and not the strongest strategist. I was too hot-headed to be a calm negotiator or diplomat. I was different in so many ways from my parents. Grandfather chuckled and tilted my face until we were both looking at my shimmering reflection. I gazed down at the face I knew so well, forehead creased in thought, green eyes flickering with worry and confusion.

'Since you were raised among humans it is no wonder that it remained dormant. Magic responds to magic, like with like and, in your case, clearly it needed to take time to thaw out before it could be unleashed. These gifts don't normally appear until adolescence anyway– the time when you change from child to adult, when you're beginning to ascertain who you truly are. Your gifts become stronger as you become more confident in yourself. While you were hiding and denying your true identity, one could safely assume that it stunted the development of your gifts.' I stared at him, the shock that his words had elicited slowly fading and being replaced with curiosity.

'So once my magic has 'thawed out' as you describe it,' I said, 'what sort of things will I be able to do?' It still seemed a bit surreal, and I watched him closely in case it was all some joke.

Grandfather patted my hand, 'that will depend,' he said calmly, 'all Elves have some basic control over natural earth magics– the ability to enhance fog or shadow for stealthy escapes, to clear rain or snow storms and to help plants grow in challenging conditions. You will learn how to scry– to have visions of events and of people.'

'Hold on,' I interjected, 'Elves have the ability to see things? To keep track of events and people no matter how far away they are?' He nodded. 'So how was it that you remained distant all of these years?' I burst out, 'if you could keep track of me through scrying?' I felt my throat clog up with sudden emotion; could it be that he had *chosen* to stay away all of these years? That he had seen what I went through and hadn't sent anyone to find me or bring me to safety?

A brief spasm of pain passed across Grandfather's face and he gripped the fountain rim until his knuckles turned white. 'You can only see people whom you have met before,' he whispered, his voice breaking, 'I had seen you in visions with your parents and was waiting for your mother to bring you to meet me in person. Then the coup happened, and once they were gone my only connection with Scardia was lost– and so were you.' His eyes were shadowed with tortured sorrow and I felt my concerns disappear in an instant. I reached out and held his wrinkled hands in mine, squeezing them in silent compassion as he continued.

'Since my beloved Lydia died,' his voice shook, 'I sent out Elves in bird-form far and wide, searching for you, but you were nowhere to be found. Those who returned spoke of the horrors that the Usurper was inflicting on the Scardian people, but we did not have the forces to oppose him outright. Supporting the Resistance was my sole hope for finding you, and when their stronghold was razed, I feared I would never get to see you at all.'

'When did you send Lisette to find me?' I asked quietly.

'She was one of the first to volunteer for the task,' he smiled, 'she had faith that a child of seven could have found a way to survive. She had known your mother only when she was a girl but loved her dearly. Only she knows what happened in the intervening years while she searched for you, but she succeeded where so many others failed and for that my heart will always be full of gratitude.'

Tears filled my eyes and I pressed a kiss to Grandfather's hands. 'I didn't know,' I whispered, 'I thought for so long that you either didn't care or were no longer alive. I was too scared to find a way across the Meridian, it was easier to hide and keep away from the ports. If the Winter Spirit hadn't told me to come…' My voice trailed off as Grandfather pulled me into a hug.

'Let's not dwell too much on the past,' Grandfather said softly, and I realised that my emotion had allowed him to regain control of his. 'There is still much for you to learn, and we cannot allow ourselves to get caught up in what might have been. Going down that path only leads to disappointment, pain and regret. The important thing is that you're here now and you're safe.'

I nodded, sniffing slightly.

'The longer you spend here, the more access to your gifts you will have,' Grandfather continued, 'and we will soon find out which spirit has bestowed particular gifts upon you, that will become evident in time. Until then, you can begin to learn how to scry, this will help you reach a place inside yourself where you can begin to control and understand these gifts. Magic flows from emotions and the more control you have over them, the easier it will be to use your gifts.'

'But I can't even control my temper,' I interjected.

Grandfather regarded me calmly, and I felt that he chose his next words with care. 'You are still young, Wilhelmina, and you've been through more than many other young women have in their lifetimes. It takes time to learn these skills and hone them, and as they start to emerge they can influence your mood.'

I nodded at his words, but then something he had said replayed in my head and I felt a tingle of dreadful realisation.

'But we don't have time,' I said gravely, 'I need to learn as much as I can before I'm eighteen and that's only six moons away.'

He nodded sadly, 'we have even less time than that, my dear, but now is not the moment to discuss it. So, since your gifts are starting to show themselves, we need to start your scrying lessons immediately.'

I wanted to ask what he meant, but something in his voice told me that even if I did, he wouldn't answer. So instead, I smiled bravely and straightened my shoulders, remembering wryly my governess telling me that a princess shouldn't face new challenges with a slouched back.

'Take a deep breath,' Grandfather said, 'hold it for three counts and then release it. Breathe slowly and focus on who you want to see. Think only about them and then look into the water.' He stood and moved to the doorway, 'I will make sure no one disturbs you; it is easier to practise without someone watching.'

I nodded and began count my breaths. After a minute I was uncomfortable and turned around, finding it easier to kneel beside the fountain rim with a cushion under my knees for comfort, almost as if I were about to pray. Facing the dancing dryads, I slowly felt myself relaxing. My breath moved in and out like the water in front of me, and time seemed to slow. The water pouring forth from the dryads' hands seemed to pause, taking an age to fall.

I hadn't even realised that I had closed my eyes, but I knew without a doubt who I wanted to see. It had been a month since we'd exchanged our strained goodbye, and my heart ached with his absence. Markus, my mind whispered, oh, please Gods let me see him. My thoughts focussed on him, my forehead creased in concentration, willing any stray thoughts away. As I breathed out, I opened my eyes and gazed into the fountain, and my hands convulsed on the stone rim. The water rippled as my breath hit it and as it stilled, an image came into focus before me. I knelt there, frozen in shock, amazed that it was working, my eyes feasting on the sight of him.

He had lost weight– that was the first thing I noticed. His black hair was longer than it had been when I last saw him, and roughly clubbed back with a piece of leather. His eyes had dark shadows under them and his face was drawn and gaunt. But despite this, his eyes flashed as he spoke, pointing at areas along a map, while gesticulating with the other hand. I couldn't hear what he was saying, but his passion was evident. On closer inspection, I realised that the map was of Scardia and the Eastern Lands, with pins jabbed along key ports. I noticed Viktor and some of the other sailors around him, nodding in agreement with what Markus was saying. Viktor's arms were folded and he watched Markus closely, a faint frown creasing his face. I moved closer until I was inches away from the water and paused, noticing for the first time the men on the other side of the table whose chainmail glinted in the low lighting. Their leader seemed to be the only one with an uncovered face, as he was asking questions. His eyes were cold and grey– reminiscent of a flat stone– and he had a thick beard that was plaited with beads. As I looked at him, a sense of discomfort filled me and I drew back slightly. There was something familiar about him, but I couldn't place where I had seen him before. He lifted a hand and Markus shook it firmly. The stranger gave an abrupt nod and departed, followed by his men. Slowly the ship's crew followed suit, casting side glances back at Markus as they left.

When he was alone it seemed that his energy drained away and he leaned over the map, hands curled into fists and eyes closed. He stood like that for a moment in perfect stillness before he suddenly lashed out, upending the table and everything on it. The map, goblets and books that had been on there before flew everywhere, landing in a mess around him. I jumped, startled, and his necklace fell out from my shirt, splashing into the fountain and causing the image to dissolve as quickly as it had appeared.

Grandfather was sitting in one of his padded chairs by the fireplace when I emerged several minutes later, having taken a moment to calm my emotions and racing heart. I felt exhausted, head aching slightly from the exertion of concentrating, and I sank into the chair next to him, warming my hands by the fire. He had summoned refreshments in the time I'd been by the fountain, and I gratefully accepted a tisane of dried thyme. He poured it out carefully into a small cup and handed it to me, watching me intently.

'Drinking herbal teas can help to cleanse the mind and soul,' he said as I inhaled the fumes and took a sip, 'I always find it useful having a tisane after scrying, it helps to restore balance.'

I nodded and took another sip. The water burned my throat but the thyme was soothing.

'What did you see?' he asked gently. When I didn't initially reply, he sat straighter, assessing my expression closely. '*Did you see something?*' he probed, and I nodded briefly in response. I didn't really want to share what I had seen– it felt like I was breaking a promise, something private.

Grandfather paused and then said, 'I assume you saw that captain who brought you here.'

The tea halted just before it reached my lips and I gaped at him. 'How did you know?'

His mouth quirked in a smile, 'it wasn't that hard to guess. I know that you both shared a… connection.' I felt myself blush, how much had Lisette communicated to him? In our time together, we hadn't raised the topic of Markus or what he represented, or how much he meant to me. However as I looked at Grandfather, I realised that he *knew*– perhaps not all, but at least the majority of what had happened while I crossed the Meridian. 'Also Erik has been very forthcoming,' he continued, 'particularly about his confusion as to why you left your captain in such a rush.'

Ah Gods, of course. *Erik.* How could I have ignored the fact that he might want to talk about Markus? That he also had questions that were unanswered?

'Nevertheless,' Grandfather said calmly, 'what's done is done and we need to move on. Now, Wilhelmina, what did you see?'

Slowly, I summarised the vision I had had. As I spoke Grandfather's brow creased, and he listened intently.

'Your powers are stronger than I anticipated,' he finally said when I came to a halting finish. 'We will need to set aside time each day to refine them. Thank you for telling me about what you saw,' he paused to smile at me, 'my advice is to not dwell too much on what you see. I know it's not that easy, but we only see a snapshot of a moment, and cannot always understand the greater picture.'

No, it wasn't easy. Ever since I had seen him, Markus' image had filled my mind and I kept wondering what had been happening at this meeting, who the strange men had been and what they had agreed to. Mainly though, my heart bled at how Markus had looked, and a part of me felt that I was responsible.

'I shall also remind you,' Grandfather's tone was now firm, 'that perhaps this captain of yours was just after one thing and nothing more. It is entirely possible that he only saw you as a means to an end, a passing amusement.' I felt coldness spread through me as I fought the urge to shake my head. 'He is not a suitable partner for the Princess of Scardia,' Grandfather continued, 'you will not be able to ally yourself to one of common birth through marriage.'

I was frozen, unable to think about what to say. His words stung but still rang true. I knew deep down— had always known— that anything between Markus and I would have been fleeting. But, oh, how I wished it could have been different.

'But now it is time for you to return to the training hall,' Grandfather said briskly, startling me out of my thoughts. 'There is much for you to learn, and as you said earlier we have little time. I will not keep you any more from your training.'

I rose and replaced the empty cup on its tray. I dropped into a curtsey, two fingers raised to my forehead, 'Thank you for your advice, Grandfather.'

'Until luncheon, Wilhelmina,' he said gently, 'remember the breathing exercises if you feel that you will lose control of your temper.'

I nodded and left quickly, my mind awash with questions and worries. As I returned to the training room, I fervently sent out a prayer to the Gods that Rakael would have moved on from staves, and that whatever new hellish training session she had concocted would help to banish thoughts of Markus for a little while.

Chapter Two

Lisette was waiting for me when I staggered back into my rooms. She bustled around me, forcing me out of my dirty clothes and into the waiting bathing pool. As I washed myself, she laid out new clothes on the bed and then came and began to rub scented oil into my hair.

My head was pounding and my eyes burning with unshed tears of embarrassment. The training session I had returned to had been brutal, Rakael had pushed me through archery and fencing and then returned to the dreaded staves. Except this time, it had been so much worse. Throughout the day, more people had come to the training hall and it became a spectacle, watching me try and fail time and time again. Jesse's words of encouragement had barely gotten me through and I had found myself struggling to breathe deeply, to calm my emotions as Rakael pushed me harder and harder. I'd felt the angry haze descend on me several times, only just containing it by biting my tongue and reminding myself that all I was going through would be worth it eventually.

By the end of the afternoon, the majority of Grandfather's guards and the new recruits— including Erik and Stefan— had been standing around the outside of the ring, watching me. They had all seen— all witnessed— my inability to win a match against Jesse and then Rakael. If Erik hadn't been there, I wouldn't have found the strength to keep getting back up. If Erik hadn't been there, maybe I wouldn't be feeling as defeated as I was now. His young face had been full of blazing admiration when he began watching me, and then it had changed to one of disappointment. In the end he hadn't stayed until it was done, dragging Stefan away from the crowd. I couldn't blame him for leaving. After all, who would want to follow a princess who was weak?

'I can't do this Lisette,' I whispered as the traitorous tears starting to fall at last. 'I can't be who they want me to be– who they *expect* me to be.'

Lisette paused in the motion of scrubbing my scalp and shook her head, wispy blond curls bobbing around her face. She tilted my head back and smiled at me, wiping the tears away with gentle fingers.

'I'm not as strong as everyone seems to want me to be,' I said bitterly, 'they want some sort of Valkyrie queen, who is wise and undefeatable. There's no way I could become that before my birthday.' She shrugged and dunked my head under. I wasn't prepared and when I rose, spitting water out and rubbing my eyes, I blinked up at her grumpily. 'You could have *warned* me you were about to do that.'

She grinned and then dunked me under again, but this time I was more prepared. The water rushed over my head, warm and scented with rose petals. I closed my eyes and allowed myself to relax for a moment, letting my screaming muscles be comforted for an instant. When my head broke the surface this time, I glanced down at my body, noticing the bruises that stretched across my skin. Some had faded to a ghastly yellowish tinge, whereas newer ones shone purplish blue. My hands were red and calloused, some blisters rubbed raw on my palms.

'I didn't realise that this was what I was signing up for when I arrived here, Lisette,' I mused as I inspected one of the new bruises on my rib cage, wincing. 'I knew that I would need to train to fight, but I didn't think it would be this intense.' Lisette clucked her tongue and raised her eyes to the ceiling as if to say 'well, what did you expect?' She began scrubbing my back, mercilessly ignoring my gasps of pain. After a final rinse, she lifted me to my feet and enveloped me in a soft towel. She led me like a child towards the bed, where she sat me down and began to massage salve into my hands.

'Thank you Lisette,' I said quietly, 'I'm grateful to have you here. I don't mean to be feeling so down, it's just that today was... particularly difficult.' My voice drifted off as I considered all that had happened. Really, it had been miraculous that I hadn't just crumpled this afternoon, especially since I had felt so depleted after scrying for the first time.

'Grandfather told me about how you volunteered to find me all those years ago,' I said tentatively, 'he said that you always had hope that I would survive.' She nodded, smiling slightly as she bent over her work. 'I wish you could tell me about where you went, all the places you searched before you found me,' I whispered, 'I'm sure that if you could speak you would have such interesting stories to tell.'

Lisette glanced up at me quickly before taking my other hand between hers. She shook her head gently and I got the impression that she was uncomfortable.

'How did you end up in Little Fleming?' I asked, 'was it just by chance? How did you have such faith in me being alive?'

She shrugged non-committedly and I fell into silence, wishing that she could answer my questions. With a brisk gesture, Lisette stood and indicated for me to get into the clean clothes nearby. As I pulled on the chemise and my stockings, she began to fasten my dress, deftly cutting off any more questions I may have asked. She pulled tight on the bodice, making me gasp for breath as the waist was cinched in.

'Careful, Lisette,' I muttered, 'everything *hurts*.'

She rolled her eyes and ignored my stifled groan as the overskirt was attached. I was pushed back down and she began to brush out my hair, carefully working through any tangles. In minutes my hair had been plaited and wound up into a coronet with some tendrils left to float by my temples. The pins jabbed into my scalp and I forced myself not to wince. Finally, I had been granted Lisette's seal of approval and she stepped back, motioning for me to step into the velvet slippers that she had whisked out of thin air.

I paused in front of the mirror on the other side of the room and gazed at my reflection in its polished surface. The dress was a rich deep red, making me seem several years older than I was. I looked more confident, more regal, and despite the afternoon's events I allowed myself to smile. Even though I felt bruised and battered, with Lisette's help I looked better than I had in years. If Markus could see me now, he might not recognise the half-starved farm girl who was haunted by her past demons. Would he like what he saw?

Lisette moved behind me, brushing off some imaginary dust from my skirts. In the distance a bell began to chime, and a cacophony of birdsong began to fill the halls. Grandfather was summoning his court to dine.

'Thank you Lisette,' I murmured as she led the way out of my rooms towards the dining hall. I followed more slowly, the brief confidence I had felt on seeing my reflection dissipating quickly as I remembered that most of the court had been watching my training this afternoon. There was a shuffling sound behind me, almost as though someone was trying and failing to move stealthily.

I turned and saw Erik who paused, uncomfortable with being caught.

'What are you doing?' I asked, surprised. He stood up properly and frowned, almost as though it was my fault that he had been seen.

'Nothing.'

I raised my eyebrows disbelievingly. 'Nothing meaning sneaking around?'

'I wasn't sneaking around!' he retorted and then bit his lip thoughtfully, 'I was just trying to practise.'

'Practise catching people unawares?'

He nodded, 'Jesse says it's useful. She says all knights need to know how to be quiet in case we need to ambush someone.'

A wave of memories flashed through me: of men in dark leather stabbing my father's guards, of arrows whistling through the air, screams of servants piercing the night as they were taken by surprise. I froze momentarily, remembering other times when I had needed to creep out of the back window of a small cottage, crawling into a small crevice in a nearby outcrop of rocks as Trackers razed the building to the ground, laughing at the cries for help coming from inside the locked doors. A haze began to descend on my vision, blurring my sight and my breathing became ragged.

'Nina?' Erik's voice was tentative and I felt his hand on my arm, bringing me back to reality. 'Are you alright?'

'Yes,' I said jerkily, 'Yes, I'm fine.'

He squinted at me sceptically. 'I don't believe you, it's like you were somewhere else.'

I smiled away his concern, embarrassed at the moment's relapse. I thought that I was getting better at controlling the memories but clearly that wasn't the case.

'I think it is useful to learn how to be quiet and stealthy,' I said, 'but maybe don't try and sneak up on me.' I forced a quick smile and ruffled his hair spontaneously, 'now, let's go to dinner. Everyone will be waiting for us.'

'I don't want to sit with *her*,' Erik said suddenly as we reached the entrance to the dining hall.

'With who?' But as I said the words, I followed his glare and saw who he was talking about. Rakael was sitting on Grandfather's right-hand side, the spot where I usually sat. She and Grandfather were deep in conversation, heads bent over together in quiet discussion.

'What's betting she's regaling him with stories about this afternoon,' I muttered bitterly. 'Telling him how I'm a terrible student who can't win a match.'

'That's not true,' Erik snapped, moving his glare from Rakael to me. 'You're good at a lot of things. You're a great rider, you can use knives better than *she* can and you're a lot kinder too.'

'Try telling *her* that,' I smiled, touched at his words.

'Besides it wasn't fair this afternoon,' he continued, 'she hadn't been training all day but you had.'

I gripped his shoulder in silent gratitude, feeling the anxiety that my performance in the training hall had shamed him melting away. 'Come, Grandfather's waiting.'

People had noticed our arrival and a quiet murmuring filled the room. I felt eyes on me but kept walking, ignoring their curious glances and whispered comments. When we sat down at Grandfather's table, he and Rakael looked up. Rakael's mouth pursed in a tight pinch and she gave a brisk nod in my direction. Grandfather patted my hand absentmindedly and then turned back to her, keeping their conversation private.

Erik shot Rakael another glare and then began to pile his plate with roasted meat and vegetables before digging in. Clearly his resentment towards Rakael would not be allowed to interfere with his appetite. I grinned and followed suit, taking large mouthfuls of the steaming pork and vegetables in front of me. Gradually the quiet murmurs around the room began to increase in volume as the courtiers decided that watching me eat was not that interesting after all. I began to relax, enjoying the rich food and drinking deeply from my goblet of mead.

'But she isn't ready,' Rakael's low hiss reached my ears, 'we need more time.'

Grandfather's voice rumbled in a quiet response and I heard Rakael sigh impatiently. 'Only a week? Make it two and we might have a chance.'

Grandfather grunted something and she sniffed, 'fine. But don't go expecting any miracles Aegis. She still has a lot to learn. We'll do our best to have her ready by then.'

I waited to hear more, but it seemed that their conversation was over. A shiver of trepidation ran through me, what had they been talking about? Glancing at Erik, I knew that he hadn't heard Rakael's words, he was blissfully enjoying his second helpings of dinner already. I followed his lead and returned to my plate, although the taste of the food was suddenly not as good as it had been. Curiosity and anxiety churned through me, making it impossible to focus on the meal. What had they meant? What was happening in a week? When would I find out about it?

The next day dawned bright and the sparrows decided to wake me early, flitting through my room with sharp trills, urging me to rise and greet the sunrise. I hadn't slept well, the usual dreams of Markus now including a man with eyes the colour of stone standing behind him in the shadows.

There was a tap on my door. I looked up, surprised, and saw Jesse, already dressed and ready to begin the training for the day. I almost groaned, it was too early to be put through the same tortures as yesterday. She grinned as if she could read my mind, her green eyes dancing in merriment.

'Don't worry Nina, I'm not here to challenge you to a rematch,' she said, 'I need you to check in on that scholar friend of yours. He's not been seen in several days and Rakael's starting to worry. It seems you're the only one with the power to make him return to the world of the living.' She grinned as if she had made the funniest joke in the world.

I scowled. 'In other words, Rakael just doesn't want to go herself and I'm now the messenger?'

'Pretty much,' Jesse shrugged. 'Make sure he's alive and then your grandfather wants you to meet him at the stables.' With a brief wave, she turned and vanished, leaving me falling back onto the pillows with a groan. Ah well, there was no use delaying the inevitable.

Muttering oaths about how Rakael should do her own investigating, I got changed and stumbled out of the door.

Dylan was in the library when I found him. Since Grandfather had sent some retainers to collect his equipment, Dylan had usually been holed up in one of the antechambers off the library, which allowed him space and quiet to conduct his research and commune with his spirits in peace. Surprisingly, this seemed to have wrought a change in his attitude and now whenever we saw each other, he was more reserved and cordial than he had previously been. Erik scoffed at his behaviour, claiming that now Dylan knew my true identity he was vying for my approval for when we retook the kingdom. However I didn't quite believe this, feeling that Dylan was just more comfortable surrounded by his familiar books and belongings and that, so long as I wasn't disturbing him constantly, he could be more civil.

I knocked on the door and Dylan's voice called out, 'Come in.' I opened it and almost gagged at the smell. For some reason he had a bowl of powder which reeked of rotten eggs in front of him. He was crouched next to it, a pair of scales next to him, weighing out the powder into different quantities.

'Watch where you step,' he said absentmindedly, his attention fixed on the powder in front of him. I promptly checked the floor and, sure enough, it was littered with maps, parchment, scrolls and books. I smiled despite myself— it seemed that messiness was a staple of Dylan's life. 'Just put the tray down by the door,' Dylan continued, his gaze not leaving his task. I glanced down and saw an untouched plate with last night's meal still on it.

'It looks like you haven't finished your dinner,' I said wryly.

'Ah, Your Highness,' he jumped, 'my apologies. I didn't realise…' His voice trailed away as his hand slipped on the scales and some of the weights tumbled onto the ground with a soft thunk.

I could have turned and left then, satisfied that he was still alive, but I was curious. As I made my way towards him, I picked up one of the books strewn on the floor, admiring the runic markings that were spread across the page. Dylan had seemed to forget my presence and was muttering to himself, pouring different powders together and crushing herbs in a mortar and pestle. He added a pinch of herbs to the mixture and then sat back, waiting expectantly. I looked at the mixture too, wondering what on earth he expected to happen. When nothing did, he leaned forward, prodding the powder with a tentative finger. The powder remained still, and he huffed in disappointment, picking up a nearby scroll and following some of the runes with a dirty finger.

'What are you doing?' I asked and he paused, turning to face me. He looked exhausted, his monocle was grimy and coated with dusty powder and his hair was in desperate need of brushing. He smelt as though he hadn't bathed in a while and his clothes were crumpled beyond recognition.

'I've been trying to figure out one of the Karshkan alchemical marvels,' he said dejectedly, 'but it isn't going as well as I'd hoped.'

'What is it supposed to do?'

He stabbed the scroll with his finger, 'it *says* that it's supposed to create something worthy of the Gods themselves. Something wonderful and majestic, that can make mortals tremble in fear.'

I quirked a brow at him, 'so you don't actually know what it does?'

He huffed again disdainfully but didn't deign to reply. I chuckled, 'why create something when you're not even sure what it does? It sounds a bit too dangerous for me.'

'King Aegis has commanded that I make myself useful while I stay here,' Dylan said with a touch of his old hauteur, 'and since I cannot return to the Lord of Winterdale, I am able to use King Aegis' library to find anything that might be useful for the Resistance.' He shook his head slightly, 'I didn't expect to find so much here. This Karshkan mixture is only one of many, but it's proving particularly difficult to get the quantities right. None of the others have been this complex.'

'Maybe have a rest?' I suggested, 'you look like you've not had a proper sleep for days. Eat something, have a bath…' He glanced at me in surprise, as though he had forgotten he had such mundane needs and I stumbled on, 'you can't expect to work efficiently when you're not looking after yourself.'

'But time is running out,' he muttered, eyes darting around the room at the other books and scrolls, 'I need it to be ready…'

'You *need* to rest,' I interrupted and when he seemed about to argue, I swiftly said, 'consider it a royal order.'

He sighed in acquiescence and smiled reluctantly.

'Fine,' he grumbled, 'but I'll rest *only* for a little while and then I simply must get this to work.'

I left him on the floor, pleased with my success. I wondered what other discoveries he had shared with Grandfather and why he felt that time was short. Questions filled my mind, piling on top of the ones that had sprung up during last night's dinner, until my mind felt like it was overflowing. Luckily, I was able to go and see Grandfather now– maybe he might clarify what was going on.

With eager steps, I hastened away from the library towards the winding staircase that led down towards the ground. I dodged around courtiers passing by, the light breeze whipping my hair as I took the steps two at a time, eager to see Dolce and escape– albeit briefly– from Grandfather's court. On one of the far platforms, I saw Stefan and Erik practising to shoot under Rakael's steely gaze. I could tell from Erik's stiff posture that he had not forgiven her for yesterday, but then Stefan said something and he laughed, relaxing in an instant.

'Careful, Your Highness!' I turned back and realised that I'd nearly hit one of Grandfather's guards.

'Sorry!' I gasped, stepping nimbly to the side and dodging past him. I made sure to be more vigilant as I continued down the stairs, trying to measure my breaths as I raced onward. I'd not enjoy the climb back up, but at least I could enjoy the descent.

The Elven stables were at the base of the stairs, where Dolce had been moved after Grandfather's men brought us to the court. Grandfather was waiting patiently for me, sat atop a bay horse with Dolce next to him.

'Good morning Nina,' he said as I bobbed a curtsey. 'We have much to do today.' He gave a sharp gesture towards the guards who melted away into the nearby trees. Without another word he began to move off, towards the road to Lowton. I pulled myself up into Dolce's saddle and nudged her to follow him. Once he knew I was behind him, he began to trot briskly, and I urged Dolce faster to keep up.

Lowton was not too far from the stables, and I was surprised that Grandfather was leading us in that direction. Since my arrival I had not been into the town, having been reminded consistently by Rakael that the Resistance did not want it well known that I was here. She had said that there was no point in giving the Usurper a definitive reason to attack the Eastern Lands, since he could not be certain of my location unless I made it blatantly obvious. I had agreed with her– it was one of the few things on which we were in accord.

'Grandfather, where are we going?'

Instead of responding, he turned off the road and led us into the forest, pushing through the underbrush. We rode in silence for about half an hour, until we reached a clearing surrounded by tall birch trees, their pale trunks glistening in the morning light. He dismounted and helped me down. I dropped to the ground and tied Dolce's reins loosely to one of the nearby branches.

The grove was quiet, there was no birdsong, no buzz of cicadas or soft whistling of the wind through the leaves. Instead, it was peaceful, silent as though time itself was paused. And in that stillness, I felt something, almost like the moment before you gasp in anticipation, as though something was watching, waiting.

'What is this place, Grandfather?' I wasn't surprised that my words came out as a whisper, it seemed wrong to speak too loudly. He drew out a blanket from the saddlebags and lay it on the ground, then he reached back, pulling out a small bowl and a box decorated with mother of pearl. He knelt down and began to fill the bowl with items from the box, some sticks of sandalwood, dried rosemary and sage, a sprig of lavender and some dried rose petals.

'Today we will call upon the Gods,' he said quietly, 'they prefer isolated, private locations where nature is glorious in her bounty. Join me.' He indicated a spot beside him and I obeyed, sitting cross legged next to the bowl. 'We need to give them an offering, to let them know that we seek their counsel.'

'Why?' I asked, 'what do we need to ask them?'

He turned to me, his blue eyes clouded in thought. 'We need to know which spirit has blessed you. Your powers are starting to grow and you will need to learn how to control them.'

It felt like a big leap, from only learning to scry yesterday to trying to discover what particular gifts I had. I felt my breathing hitch momentarily but I wasn't scared, I wanted to know more.

'Here,' he said, 'put your hands over the bowl.' I did as he asked and then looked at him expectantly. 'Now close your eyes,' he continued, 'breathe deeply like you practised yesterday. Will a flame to life.'

I did as he said, trying to not feel silly for leaning over the bowl. My brow knitted in concentration as I began to breathe deeply, taking in the scents of the offerings and the soft grass beneath me. I visualised a flame catching on the stick of sandalwood and then moving slowly along to the rose petals and lavender. As I imagined it, I could feel a flickering beneath my hands, and smelt a faint tinge of burning.

'Excellent Wilhelmina,' Grandfather breathed. 'Look at what you have accomplished.'

I opened my eyes and saw with faint surprise the flames that filled the bowl, sending wispy tendrils of smoke up towards the sky. A movement to my side made me turn and I blinked as Grandfather held up a pin, its point glinting in the sunlight.

'The final ingredient is an offering of blood,' he said, 'it only needs to be a drop.' Slowly, I held out my hand and he pricked my finger, causing a teardrop of blood to fall on the flames. I gasped and pulled away as the smoke flashed scarlet and began twisting into strange shapes. The smoke whirled around faster and faster, whipping up a small storm of heat which crackled and burned with energy. I felt it rise up and surround me, and I lost sight of the birch trees, Grandfather and the horses. Heat swirled around me and I saw a laughing face with sparkling eyes and a turban encrusted with rubies.

What's this, little Princess? he crowed, dancing around me, weren't you happy with your wish? Don't you want to know what you can accomplish once your powers are freed?

I reached out as he disappeared into the smoke, and I was burning, consumed by the flames from the bowl. I opened my mouth to cry out in terror, but no sound came out. The ashes from the fire rose up, filling my nose and blocking my throat. The pain was excruciating, and I writhed, twisting as I tried to break away from the flames. Tears began to fall down my cheeks in terror and I fell backwards, wondering why Grandfather didn't help me, why he didn't interfere. The flames crackled and then vanished as a chill began to descend on the grove, causing my breathing to catch with the sudden change in temperature. I batted my arms and legs to make sure that there were no flames left, shivering as the cold set into my bones.

'You poor child.'

Her voice sounded so familiar and I looked around, relief flooding through me. I realised that as soon as Grandfather had begun talking about the seasonal spirits, I had hoped she would come back, that she would guide me again.

'My lady,' I knelt at her feet, too shaken by what had just happened to stand. Her pale hand tilted my chin upwards until I was looking at her, gazing into her eyes which were an icy blue. 'What is going on?'

'You are changing,' she said gravely, 'your powers are growing. Until now, your grandfather thought you might only have similar gifts to the other Elves, but today will prove him wrong. He wanted to summon the Gods, to find out which spirit blessed you with gifts.' She smiled slightly, 'he will be surprised with the results.'

I was confused, and looked up at her mutely. I didn't know how to phrase my questions into words, but she seemed to understand me all the same.

'Stand, child.' With surprising strength, I was pulled up and felt the crackle of frost beneath my feet. 'Walk with me.'

Silently, I walked by her side. Her robes were light and silvery, embroidered with snowflakes of every shape and size. She was barefoot I noticed, untouched by the chill.

'There is not much time, Wilhelmina,' the Winter Spirit murmured, 'soon you will leave this place and face new dangers. Lord Niall suspects where you have gone and he is seeking you out, it will not be possible for you to remain in hiding for much longer.' We paused by the edge of the grove and I watched a flurry of snow begin to fall around us.

'The time is coming for you to stand up and regain your birthright,' she continued, 'but before then, you need to use your powers to your advantage.' She put her hands on my shoulders and turned me to face her, 'once you control those gifts you will become more powerful than you had ever thought.' She spoke urgently, 'remember to be calm and steady like the tide, for high emotion will make your powers lash out and possibly hurt others. Once you find the calm in the storm, you will be able to use them to your advantage.'

I didn't quite understand– it felt like she was speaking in riddles.

'What powers do I have?' I managed to ask. The Winter Spirit assessed me for an instant before answering,

'You have been given gifts by two seasonal spirits, that's very rare. The last time a mortal was blessed by more than one spirit was when Edward Lightbringer ruled Scardia.' I held my breath in anticipation, eager to hear what she would say next. 'The Lord of Summer has been watching over you since you were a child, it seems,' she mused quietly, 'his fancies and desires burn bright and hot, like the fire you lit earlier. He can be both vindictive and benevolent and is not one to be crossed. Those who he bestows with gifts are always instruments of change– whether for good or bad.' Her fingers brushed my hair, touching the white streak that stood out against the red. 'But I also watch over you.'

Before I could say anything, she was gone in a flurry of snow, leaving no trace behind. I blinked and looked around, suddenly back on my knees beside the bowl which still smoked with burning sage and rosemary. I swayed and then felt a hand steady me. Turning, I saw Grandfather, his face blanched with anxiety. On seeing me he gasped and leaned back slightly,

'What happened Nina?'

'I saw her,' I said quietly, 'The Winter Spirit. She was just here…' My voice trailed off as I glanced around the grove, searching for the frost or snow that had been there moments before. Grandfather was watching me carefully now.

'What did she tell you?' he asked.

'She said that two seasonal spirits have given me gifts,' I said slowly, 'but I don't know what the gifts are.'

'Two?' His voice was a thin whisper. I nodded. He gave a strangled laugh and before I knew it, he was hugging me tightly. 'You have been blessed indeed, my child.' He cried, 'wait until we announce it tonight. We must celebrate.'

'But I don't know what gifts I have,' I said into his shoulder.

Grandfather squeezed me tightly, 'they have already started to show themselves.'

I blinked at his statement, confused. What did he mean?

'Who would have guessed that the Lord of Summer and the Winter Spirit would both bless you,' his voice was shaking with emotion. At this I pulled away.

'How did you know it was them?' I asked.

Grandfather smiled, eyes shimmering with unshed tears.

'Only the Lord of Summer would make you have such an affinity with fire,' he said, 'but the Winter Spirit has also marked you as her own.' He stood shakily and went over to his saddle bags, withdrawing a mirror and handing it to me. 'See for yourself Nina.'

I took the mirror with trembling fingers, suddenly afraid of what I would see.

Remember to breathe in and out, as steady as the tide. It was almost like the Winter Spirit had whispered it into my ear and I obeyed, calming my irrational fears. I closed my eyes briefly and then glanced down; my mouth dropped open in shock.

The face that looked back from the mirror was still me, but different. Her red hair had flecks of gold through it and the white streak had grown, becoming even more prominent. Her ears were no longer round, like they had been that morning, but pointed like Grandfather's. Her cheekbones seemed more prominent; her eyes more almond-shaped— dear Gods!

'My eyes,' I choked out, 'what has happened to my eyes?'

Grandfather smiled and stroked tears away from my cheeks. I hadn't even realised that they were there until he rubbed them off.

'Your magic is starting to develop,' he said quietly, 'your Elven blood is starting to regain its affinity to the powers of nature, and it seems that the Lord of Summer and the Winter Spirit have given it a push.'

'But my eyes!' I gasped, 'my hair, my ears, how…'

'You are beautiful,' Grandfather said, 'you are growing into the queen you are meant to be.' I just sat in silence, unsure how to respond and wondering what other changes I would notice over time.

Chapter Three

'But they're *blue*,' Erik stated belligerently. 'How are they blue?'

'You seem to be overlooking the other changes,' Jesse grinned, pointing at my ears. 'Although I like the new look, it's very regal.' I shot her a glare and she chuckled, holding her hands up in jest.

'I have often read tales of those who met the seasonal spirits,' Dylan mused, 'but cannot believe you actually met one.'

'She didn't just meet one, she was blessed by one,' Erik shot back.

'Two,' Dylan said, 'and the difference is incredible. Just wait until you can harness your powers…'

'She will need to control her emotions before that can happen,' Rakael's sour voice interrupted, and I glanced up to see her hovering in the doorway.

'That depends on whether you can leave her alone or not,' Erik muttered under his breath. Stifling a giggle which I masked as a cough, I looked back down at my reflection in the back of my spoon, at my eyes which burned with an icy blue flame. Only this morning they had been green, now they were reminiscent of my mother and Grandfather. The more I looked at them, the more I liked what I saw.

'I wish I could have seen them,' Dylan's voice was twinged with envy, 'all these years I've communed with them but never before have they made an appearance.'

Erik and I exchanged a quick look, remembering all too well how Dylan had tried communing with the spirits on the crossing of the Meridian. I had to cough a little louder to cover up my laughter.

Rakael moved closer, arms crossed as she watched us. 'Maybe if you spent less time dreaming and failing to get the spirits' attention, you would have made more progress with your mission, scholar.' Her words sliced the air and I saw Dylan stiffen. He blinked owlishly, wiped his monocle and put it in his pocket before standing rather shakily.

'Most, uh, insightful of you, Mistress Rakael,' he said hollowly. 'I should return to my experiments if you will excuse me. Your Highness.' He gave a short jerky bow in my direction and then hastened away. I watched him leave, anger and indignation rising in me as I turned to Rakael, but Jesse spoke before I could.

'There was no need to be that harsh, Rakael,' she said bluntly, 'he's barely slept, the poor man. So what if he has multiple interests, he has been working day and night to give you what you ask for.'

'He cannot afford to be distracted,' Rakael snapped, 'none of you can. You especially Princess.' Her finger jabbed in my direction and I felt a cold fury spread through me.

'We have been doing the best we can,' I retorted, 'although nothing any of us does seems to meet your oh-so-high expectations.'

Rakael stepped closer until we were nose to nose, her scars twisted grotesquely as she scowled at me. 'Don't forget Princess,' her voice was low and hard, 'the Usurper has had years of training. His Trackers are raised on violence and learning the art of war. They will crush you in an instant,' her fingers snapped in front of my eyes, 'if you are not vigilant and do not remain one step ahead of them at all times. Until you can fight as well as they can, until you can outsmart them, you will not be ready. He has waited many long years to make an example of you and if you are caught…'

'Rakael *stop*,' Jesse interrupted, pulling her away. 'There is no need to be like this.'

'There is *every* need,' Rakael snapped, her voice verging on manic, 'we only have a week until they arrive and she is not ready.'

'A week until who arrives?' Erik piped up, eyes wide.

'Yes, who?' I asked, remembering Rakael's discussion with Grandfather the night before.

'Rakael,' Jesse hissed, 'pull yourself together.'

It seemed that her words had a magic effect on Rakael, who regained her usual cool composure quickly.

'What I mean is,' she said, 'that we don't have a lot of time for relaxing. Our Princess needs to become strong– she needs to be able to match the Usurper and win.'

I didn't like being referred to as if I wasn't in the room, before I could speak up however, a cool voice spoke from the doorway.

'I believe you have made your point Rakael. Now if you do not mind, I should like to speak to my granddaughter alone.'

I looked up and saw Grandfather and felt a wave of relief. Rakael dipped her head in recognition and strode away, Jesse following behind. Erik lingered, unwilling to follow them.

'Erik, why don't you go and check on Dylan?' I said, 'I'm alright. Go on.'

He looked from me to Grandfather and squared his shoulders, before saying, 'Rakael shouldn't be able to speak to us that way. It's not right.' With that he fled, obviously worried that Grandfather would chastise him for speaking up.

'He's not wrong,' I added, 'why is she like that? Why does she hate me so much?'

'Rakael is many things,' Grandfather said gravely, 'but everything she does is– in her eyes– necessary to create a stronger Scardia. Her story is her own to tell, but she will keep you safe and guard you with her life. Her personal feelings towards you will not come in the way of her duty.'

I shrugged, it felt like I was more of an inconvenience to Rakael. 'She's not going to turn me into a warrior,' I stated bluntly, 'no matter how hard she tries. I won't be able to change that much.'

'She is hard on you so that you will become tougher,' Grandfather took my arm and we left the dining hall, walking towards his rooms. 'You would do well to learn from this.'

I looked at him, astonished. 'There's only so much I can take, Grandfather, and I don't like it when she treats others the same way.'

He nodded slowly. 'I will speak with her if that would appease you.'

I blinked, and then inclined my head. 'Thank you.' It may not make her treat me any differently but if it stopped her snapping at others, I would be grateful. As we entered Grandfather's rooms and sat down in front of the fire, I allowed myself to change the subject and asked,

'What did she mean when she said we only had a week? Who is coming here?'

Grandfather was quiet for a long time, staring into the flames for so long that I began to wonder if he had heard me.

Then he said slowly, 'the Resistance and my forces alone are not enough to take on Lord Niall and his troops. We need to have allies. That is why we have reached out to our brethren, the Dark Elves, from the mountains. They are sending an envoy to meet us next week, and if they are impressed with you, we may be able to gain their support for our cause.'

I had not heard about any Elves who lived in the mountains, and sat mutely for a few minutes, racking my brains as I tried to remember the tales my mother had told me.

'Their timing is inconvenient,' Grandfather continued, 'we had hoped we would have more time. You have barely begun to tap into your gifts and have only been training for a month.'

'So these people are coming to inspect me?' I asked, 'and if I impress them, we are guaranteed their help?'

Grandfather's eyes were shadowed as he turned to me, 'they are powerful, Nina. With their soldiers, we would have a strong chance of overthrowing Lord Niall once and for all.'

I pondered that for a moment, but really there was not much to consider. If Grandfather said we needed their support, I would do whatever it took to get it.

'What will I need to do?' I asked quietly. 'I can't work miracles, but I'll do my best to be ready.'

Grandfather took my hands in his and sat beside me. 'Train with Rakael each morning, do whatever she tells you.' He ignored my grimace and continued, 'and in the afternoons we will work together to develop your control of your gifts.'

The next few days were tough to say the least. I'd thought that I was training hard before, but Rakael seemed to have new ideas about ways to torture me. Mornings were greeted with exercises that tested my agility and endurance, until I felt like my muscles were on fire. She tested me with blades and bow, snapping out instructions in her usual curt tone. Thankfully her usual barbs seemed to have stopped for the moment, which I supposed I had to thank Grandfather for. I was barely given a moment of respite and was constantly aching with tiredness. She showed me new ways to dodge blows, how to use my slighter height to my advantage and to roll out of an attacker's hold. When I eventually succeeded in evading her blows and successfully toppled her to the ground, I could have sworn that a small smile flashed across her face. It was gone in an instant, but I felt greater pride in that moment than I had for many days. Her response of grabbing my ankle and yanking my feet out from under me, causing me to crash down next to her quickly dissipated my sense of accomplishment.

I would have hoped that the afternoons would be less tiring, however Grandfather had other plans. We often spent the afternoons with an hour of meditation, before he would ask me to practise scrying. I had become quite adept at it, and it took less time for the image to form each day. On my request, a large shallow bowl had been brought to my chambers so I could practise as the night fell. As I had developed, I was able to hear the sounds of the scenes I witnessed, although with Grandfather watching I had not seen Markus again. When I was alone in my room however, I allowed myself to watch him going about his daily activities, barking orders and sharing a mug of ale with his fellow sailors. He still looked gaunt and drawn, and each time I saw him left me with a painful ache in my heart. In turn, this only drove me to practise more in the hopes of ignoring the reminder that he was able to go on living his life without me there.

As well as scrying, Grandfather had shown me how to conjure light and shadow, although I had struggled with this exercise. When I had tried it had only resulted in a faint dimming of the light, however when it came to encouraging a fire to start, I was more confident.

'You have an affinity with fire my dear,' Grandfather said on the afternoon before our visitors would arrive. I was sitting cross legged in the grove of birch trees, tempting sparks from our fire to twist in a dance. The flames followed my fingertips, swaying upwards and leaving the kindling behind. For an instant the ball of fire hung in the air, spinning gently, before I guided it back to the ground.

'It's easier than I expected,' I said quietly, 'it just feels more natural, like it's become a part of me.'

Grandfather nodded, 'that is how it should be. But beware of your gifts controlling you, it all…'

'Is dependent on emotion.' I finished for him, 'I *know*. You've told me many times, Grandfather.'

He chuckled. 'I just don't want you to get ahead of yourself, Wilhelmina. These powers can be as dangerous as benevolent.'

I was silent for a moment, and then asked,

'What gift did the Winter Spirit bestow? It's pretty obvious what the Lord of Summer gave me, but I still haven't figured out what she did.'

Grandfather touched the white streak in my hair briefly, 'I think,' he murmured, 'that her gifts will show themselves in time. I would hazard a guess that your ability to scry is enhanced by her, you already demonstrate much more control than that of an ordinary novice.'

The flames flickered and died in front of me and I rose to my feet, leaning against Dolce who was grazing nearby. She nickered in acknowledgement before returning to her meal. I patted her neck thoughtfully, my mind now moving to what would happen the next day.

'Do we know when our guests will arrive tomorrow?' I asked tentatively, trying to keep my anxiety out of my voice. Between Grandfather and Rakael's training over the past few days, it had only reinforced to me the need for the meeting tomorrow to go well. I didn't think I could face them if I didn't please our guests, or at least Grandfather, who seemed particularly tense about the meeting. I thought Rakael wouldn't be too surprised if I didn't impress them, but I felt that Grandfather would be disappointed. I couldn't bear the thought of letting him down.

'They will arrive when they arrive,' Grandfather answered calmly and I almost rolled my eyes at his ambiguity. 'We should return,' he continued as he mounted in a fluid motion, 'there is still much to prepare.'

When we returned to the Elven court it was chaos. Courtiers and servants sped back and forth in a flurry of movement as I paused at the top of the stairs to regain my breath.

Grandfather was quickly inundated with guards and courtiers asking him questions and he led them away, striding towards the reception hall. I was left on the stairs, until one of the passing servants noticed me and with a panicked cry pulled me in the opposite direction.

'You must get ready Your Highness,' she stammered, half dragging me to my rooms. 'There is very little time to prepare you.' As we arrived at my rooms, the waiting hands of several attendants took over and led me inside. I blinked, surprised to see at least four servants in my rooms. I was used to only having Lisette take charge of me. Lisette shooed the other attendants into the bathing room and began to lead me after them.

'What's going on Lisette?' I asked, confused. She shook her head and gestured for me to get into the waiting bath. I undressed slowly, watching her tap her foot impatiently. 'Why is everyone so frantic?' I pressed, 'it isn't until tomorrow when...' My voice trailed off and then I froze, one shoe half untied. 'They haven't come early, have they?'

She nodded curtly and made frantic motions for me to hurry up, and when I didn't move fast enough she took over and I was pushed none too gently into the steaming bath.

'They were sighted not half an hour ago, milady,' one of the other attendants said, 'they should arrive before nightfall.'

'How many are coming?' I asked curiously as Lisette began to scrub the dust and grime off me.

'We don't know milady,' the servant murmured demurely, 'the birds came with news and it was relayed directly to Elder Haycin. He did not share much beyond the order for us to prepare the court in all due haste and to make sure that you are presentable.' I nodded slowly as I considered her words.

It seemed that a lot more than usual needed to be done to get me ready for dinner that evening. Not only was my hair rinsed and oiled with rose-scented perfumes, but my arms and legs were shaved, the attendants careful to not draw blood. My nails were trimmed, filed and polished. Two attendants began to work on my hair, making my skin break out in a familiar tingle when they used magic to dry it before brushing it out and pinning it up. When Lisette began to ruthlessly pluck my eyebrows, I grit my teeth and shut my eyes, silently cursing Grandfather's guests for arriving early, for having to be put through this beautification process. I was still not comfortable with other people around me while I bathed and dressed, but any awkwardness I felt was alleviated by the way they treated the tasks with such normality.

'What do you think, milady?' One of the attendants finally asked and I allowed myself to look in the mirror.

My dress was a peacock blue, tapered in at the waist and embellished with gold thread. A necklace of sapphires lay coolly against my skin and the matching earrings swung in the light evening breeze. I stood tall, shoulders back and head high, the flickering light in my eyes changing colour to reflect the darker blue of my clothing. A diadem of gold was placed around my forehead, glinting in the light from the setting sun.

'Thank you,' I murmured to my attendants, gazing mesmerised at my reflection.

'You look pretty,' Erik's voice came from the doorway. I turned and smiled at him, taking in how he was looking particularly clean in the dark tunic of a page.

'Thank you,' I said, 'you look particularly dashing yourself.'

He grinned awkwardly and then rubbed the back of his neck, pulling on his collar.

'It's a bit scratchy,' he admitted, tugging on the wool. 'But Stefan said we need to be dressed all fancy tonight.' His face twisted comically, as though he couldn't think of anything worse than having to wear formal attire. No doubt he would prefer to be in his training gear, wrestling with Stefan or some of the other pages in the training hall.

'Have you come to escort me?' I asked as Lisette sprayed me with rose perfume.

'King Aegis asked me to get you *personally*,' his chest puffed out with pride and he held out his arm. 'He said that I needed to bring you to the great hall.'

I smiled and tucked Markus' necklace into a small pocket that had been stitched into the lining of my bodice. Lisette pursed her lips disapprovingly but I ignored her and took Erik's arm and said, 'then we shouldn't keep him waiting.'

'I wonder what the Dark Elves will be like,' Erik whispered excitedly, 'I've heard they're excellent fighters. Stefan told me that his uncle once saw them ambush some raiders, he said they were in and out without a trace, leaving only bodies behind. He said that he'd never seen anything like it.'

I shivered, trying to push the image of dead raiders out of my mind. If these visitors were as deadly and skilled as Erik said, what chance did I have at impressing them tomorrow? I'd be knocked out in an instant, disarmed within thirty seconds of a fight against them.

'Stefan said that they haven't been seen in years,' Erik continued, 'he said there was a disagreement many years ago and the two courts have barely spoken since.'

'Did he say what caused the disagreement?' I asked, my curiosity was piqued.

Erik shook his head, 'apparently it was kept quiet. But don't worry, if they decide to attack, I'll protect you.'

Erik took my silence as acceptance and puffed up again with pride.

'I'm going to be the best protector in the realms,' he declared and I smiled, amused.

'I'm lucky to have you at my side,' I said.

'I know,' he replied brightly.

Our conversation was brought to an abrupt halt as we reached the audience chamber. Candles flickered around the edge of the room, illuminating the Elven court who were standing in silence. Grandfather was seated in his throne, resplendent in robes of blue, a silver crown of twisted leaves on his brow. He looked up at my arrival and raised a hand in welcome.

'My friends, allow me to present my granddaughter: Princess Wilhelmina Constantina Fiordlasher, Heir to the Ice Flame.' I felt myself stiffen and stood tall, leaving Erik behind and stepping towards the group of four men in front of Grandfather. As I approached, I took in how they were covered from head to toe in black leather armour, masks covering their faces. They stood confidently, their gear making it impossible to gauge their reactions. I wondered if my anxiety showed in my face and schooled my features into a small smile of welcome.

One of the men stepped forward and bowed low, reaching out for my hand. I dropped into a low curtsey, raising my left hand to my forehead and placing my right hand in his gloved one. As I stood, he pressed his masked lips to my knuckles. I suppressed a shiver, unsure if it was of fear or anticipation, and moved to sit beside Grandfather who had been watching the silent exchange closely.

'We have heard much about your granddaughter,' one of the masked visitors said, his voice sounding raspy from lack of use. 'Even in the Underdark stories reached us of her.'

'It was a blessing when she arrived,' Grandfather said calmly, 'we awaited her coming for many years.' I shifted uncomfortably in my seat, and then stopped when Grandfather caught my eye. 'We bid you welcome to our halls,' he continued, 'my people will see to any requests you may have. We have prepared a feast to celebrate your arrival, if you would follow me.' He rose and swept out of the room, his courtiers bowing as he passed.

The man who had taken my hand reached out again and I tentatively accepted it, still slightly unnerved by his mask. Unlike the rest of their outfit, the mask was silver, closely fitted around the face so that nothing was revealed. The eyes were obscured with a dark mesh underneath so it was impossible to tell what colour they were. He was silent as he led me after Grandfather, the remaining members of his party following close behind. He was the same height as I was, and I cast him sideways glances, trying to find a distinguishing feature– the colour of his hair, the shape of his eyes, anything– but was unsuccessful.

The dining hall had been festooned with glowing lights and garlands of flowers, draped elegantly along the ceiling so that it was like we were in a flowery grotto. My companion pulled a seat out for me beside my grandfather and then sat on my other side. The other masked men followed suit, placing themselves on Grandfather's other side. I noticed Rakael and Elder Haycin sit at the far end of the table and watched them begin to engage our visitors in conversation.

I realised that I probably would need to do the same with my companion, and half turned towards him, wondering how to begin. There was something disconcerting about trying to converse with someone who you couldn't see. I opened my mouth about to speak and then paused, not sure about what to say. Thankfully a servant chose that moment to fill my goblet with wine and I took a sip. My companion did not seem to notice, but was watching the proceedings around the hall, as the courtiers began to eat and the lilt of conversation filled the room. I took another gulp of wine, grateful for the short reprieve.

As I replaced the goblet, a thought struck me and I looked at my companion closely. How was he going to be able to eat and drink through the mask? But almost as soon as the thought entered my mind, he reached up and unhooked the lower half of his mask, placing it carefully next to his plate. If I had been hoping that this would show the lower half of his face though I was wrong. He seemed to have a woollen balaclava on underneath, revealing only a narrow space for his mouth.

He turned to me and I realised that I had been staring in what could be considered unflattering rudeness. I glanced down at my own plate, feeling the familiar heat fill my cheeks as I blushed.

We were silent for the first few courses, he seemingly too preoccupied with eating through the mask and I with awkward embarrassment. Eventually I garnered the courage to speak and asked, 'Did you have a pleasant journey here?'

He paused, a spoon halfway to his mouth before saying rather bluntly, 'you don't speak all evening and the first thing you can think of is *that*?'

I blinked, surprised. He snorted at my expression and then said, 'All right, I'll play along. We have been travelling for five nights to reach this place. We had to travel over land and down the coast. It's not easy when you can only travel during nightfall.'

'Why did you only travel at night?' The words were out of my mouth before I could stop them and I took another hasty sip of wine, hoping I hadn't come across as rude.

'You don't know much about our kind, do you?' he said wryly. 'We live in the Underdark, in the Ombre Mountains. For us the sun is a deadly force. It blinds and burns away all reason.'

'So you've never been out in daylight?' I asked, confused. He chuckled brittlely.

'Of course I have, Princess. But we need to wear protection otherwise we will be vulnerable.'

I considered his words. 'So that's why you wear masks,' I mused, 'but doesn't it get claustrophobic?'

'When you've been raised in tunnels, claustrophobia is a sign of weakness,' he answered shortly. 'Besides it isn't too bad once you get used to it.' With a sharp motion, he reattached the base of his mask, and I watched, fascinated despite myself. He continued, 'We have been waiting a long time to make your acquaintance, Princess. Your grandfather's missives were not the most detailed, I must admit. I understand you have not been in his court for long?'

I noticed the change of conversation and felt slightly awkward again. I didn't want to talk about myself and I didn't know what Grandfather had told them about me.

'That's right,' I managed, realising belatedly that my goblet was empty as I lifted it to my lips. 'I only crossed the Meridian a month ago.'

'A dangerous crossing,' he mused, 'the ship we got passage on had also recently made that journey. The crew mentioned a sea monster that terrorised them.'

It was as though a shard of ice had pierced my heart, slowly spreading through my body until I was numb. I couldn't breathe, the noise from the laughter and chatter around the room was suddenly too loud.

'Are you alright, Princess?' the visitor's voice cut through the haze that had begun to cloud my vision, laced with concern. I nodded, taking deep breaths to steady my racing heart.

'I'm perfectly well, thank you,' I murmured, 'it just seems coincidental that our journey also had a similar experience.

Perhaps that is a regular occurrence for ships crossing the Meridian.'

'Perhaps,' he said, his voice devoid of any emotion.

'Wilhelmina,' Grandfather interrupted, and I turned to him, relieved to have a reason to end our conversation. 'You are to lead the dancing, my dear,' Grandfather continued before saying to my companion, 'perhaps his lordship would lead you out.'

'With pleasure, Your Highness,' my companion said smoothly. 'Shall we, Princess?'

I plastered a smile on my face and nodded, placing my hand in his. His gloved fingers gripped mine and led me out onto the platform for dancing, which stretched above the twinkling lights of Lowton. There were no musicians, but a lyre, lute and reed flutes played a soft, lilting tune as they hovered in mid-air. The rest of the court watched as my companion and I stopped in the centre of the dance floor. I felt the steady gaze of Grandfather and Rakael, closely examining my every move. Erik was muttering something to Stefan, glancing distrustfully at the other visitors who had remained seated beside Grandfather.

'So, you're a lord,' I said as the opening chords of the dance began and I sank into a curtsey. I realised suddenly that I had not asked him for his name.

'Indeed,' he bowed and then swiftly pulled me up, spinning me out before I could manage a reply. My skirts whipped out, slapping my legs as I stepped back and forth, following his lead as our hands met time and again across the space between us. He turned me, drawing me in until we were inches apart, and I felt my breath catch. Before I could identify the feeling that rushed through me, he moved away and the welcome distance was back between us. I noticed faintly that other couples had joined us on the dance floor and felt a moment's relief as I realised that we were no longer the centre of attention. My companion seemed to recognise this and chuckled, lifting me as we spun around. I clung onto him for dear life, trying to ignore the exhilarating rush that rose in me, coaxing a smile of pure enjoyment to my lips.

The last time I had danced like this was with Markus. It felt almost sacrilegious to enjoy dancing this way with another man, and the icy feeling began to return. Now that I had remembered him, Markus' face filled my mind, and my pleasure in the dance began to slip away. How could I enjoy dancing with someone whose face I couldn't even *see*?

My partner's grip tightened and I wondered if he could see the change in my eyes because he pulled me in again, until I was too close for comfort. His hand reached around my back, not letting me lean away, keeping me pinned in place. We moved in unison, stepping to the side and around, seamlessly matching the rhythm of the flutes. The tune increased in tempo and he lifted me again, my skirts flying out as I spun around. As I returned to the ground, he held me still for an instant longer than was necessary and I could have sworn that he was about to say something.

'Who are you?' I whispered, wishing that I was able to see his face properly.

'You can call me Aidyn,' he answered just as quietly, before the music faded away and he clicked his heels together and bowed formally.

'Thank you, Princess Wilhelmina,' he said, 'that dance was most enlightening.'

He moved away and I watched him for a few seconds, pondering the sense of trepidation that his words had caused.

'May I have this dance, milady?' I blinked and accepted one of the other visitor's hands as he led me into a minuet. I wasn't paying close attention to this dance however, and my eyes followed the dark figure who bowed to my grandfather and then left with one of his armoured companions, striding out of the hall without a backward glance.

Chapter Four

The dancing continued for another few hours, and it was at least half as long afterwards before I was able to slip away and return to my rooms. I was not in a mood for small talk, and barely said two words as my attendants spoke rapturously about the visitors.

'You should've seen the way they danced,' one stressed to Lisette, who was taking out my hair pins, 'they were so mysterious in their armour. They'll have to give their support. King Aegis looked so proud of you, milady.'

I remained quiet until only Lisette remained, my other attendants giggling and twittering like sparrows. I sat on my bed, gazing aimlessly at the space in front of me, reliving the evening's events. I still felt cold, confused by the conflicting emotions which continued to flow through me.

'There's something about these visitors that's strange, Lisette,' I murmured once the attendants had gone, 'those masks are scary, how can I feel comfortable around them?' She shrugged and stroked my hair, trying to comfort me. 'When we danced, I thought of him.' My eyes met hers and held her worried gaze, 'of Markus, I mean. For a second I forgot about him, and then I felt terrible, like I was doing something wrong.'

Lisette shook her head and held me close, as tears trickled down my cheeks.

'I miss him, Lisette,' I whispered, 'I don't know what I did to make him so angry with me, but I miss him. I wish he was here instead of the Dark Elves.'

Lisette held me tightly for a moment and then held out a handkerchief which I accepted gratefully. She patted my shoulder and gestured for me to get into bed as I wiped my face and blew my nose. I obeyed like a child and crawled into the sheets, watching her snuff out the candles and leave the room, with a final, worried glance in my direction.

I lay there for a while, tossing and turning as sleep eluded me. Eventually, I sat up with a huff and rolled out of bed, picking up my scrying bowl and kneeling on the floor near the open windows. The moonlight filtered down, and I urged a small flame to life, hovering above me, banishing the creeping shadows. I took a deep, shuddering breath, hands covering my face as I focused.

'I need to see him,' I breathed, looking down at the shimmering water. Sure enough, Markus' image appeared and my hands gripped the bowl painfully.

He was laughing, the shadows under his eyes seemed to have faded slightly since the last time I'd seen him. Around him were his crew, joking raucously and drinking deeply from the tankards of ale in front of them. They were seated around a large table in a tavern, and judging by the empty jugs before them, had clearly been there for quite a while.

'Easiest job we've had to do in a long time,' one of the sailors crowed loudly, his tankard sloshing as he hit it down on the table. 'Maybe we should get into the habit of ferrying wealthy nobs around.'

'They didn't seem that high and mighty,' another interjected, 'they weren't afraid to get their hands dirty. Helped out with delivering that last shipment on the way too.

I wonder what they needed to do in Lowton, it's not a common place for people like them to visit.'

'It doesn't matter,' Markus said, 'they paid well. Not to mention the gold pieces they gave for us to wait around for them. Whatever they're here for, they aren't intending to stick around for long. I don't blame them.'

'Yes, a couple of days of shore leave should do nicely,' another sailor grunted, 'got an eye on a wench to help me through that.' He nodded at the barmaids who were watching the group with interest, 'looks like that one's interested in you Captain.' I followed his gaze and my stomach twisted as I saw the brunette leaning against the bar, her dark eyes watching Markus invitingly.

No, I thought, please Gods, no.

Markus grinned and toasted the barmaid who gave him a sultry smile and moved over, her hips swaying. 'Perhaps.' His tone was casual and I felt my eyes fill with tears again. The barmaid reached out and took his hand in hers, leading him away from the table and the guffaws and bawdy jokes of his companions. The barmaid grinned up at him coquettishly and traced his cheek before whispering something into his ear. As Markus smiled, I cried out, smacking the bowl away from me, a ray of sparks shooting from my fingers.

I leaned out of the window, breathing the night air in shakily, trying desperately to control the simmering flames that crackled around me. The flames reached up towards the sky in a swirling pillar, flickering out like a bright torch into the darkness. My hands were clenched so tightly that I had sharp moons indented deeply in my skin. I wanted to scream, to throw my head back and wail until the ache in my chest was gone. Instead, I took another breath and released it so that the flames gradually dimmed, before vanishing altogether. It hurt too much to see him with someone else, especially since I didn't know why he had sent me away. Could it be like Grandfather had suggested and that all Markus had wanted was to sleep with me?

I had thought that the night we shared together was special, that it had meant something similar to him as it had to me, but his coldness the next morning and his curt cruelty in dismissing me suggested otherwise. Perhaps Grandfather had been right after all.

I gazed out at the distant lights of Lowton which flickered in the darkness and felt a numbness start to spread throughout my body. The past month I had cried, punched my pillow in anger and asked myself over and over what I had done wrong.

'If he's moving on, maybe I should too,' I murmured. Like a sleepwalker, I stood there for a while longer, until the chill became unbearable and I returned to my bed. Before I tried to sleep, I lifted off the necklace he had given me and which I had worn each day since we parted, and placed it on the bedside table. I felt the absence of its familiar weight but turned away, fervently hoping that I would soon find the oblivion of sleep.

It felt like the scene had been waiting to play in my mind as soon as I fell asleep. The figures were familiar: men with dark armour and helmets that covered their faces, save for a tilted slit over their eyes. A bull's head was painted on their chests in red, all too reminiscent of the blood that had been spilt for the Usurper. They drew in around me, cutting off all potential exits until they were circling me, laughing. Their weapons hung loosely in their hands, apart from the point of one spear which prodded me as they called out taunts and jibes.

'Stop, stop, *stop!*' I cried, trying to dodge the jabbing point. The Trackers pressed closer and I was pushed down into the ground, failing to bat away the spear. It kept poking me, traces of blood beginning to soak my dress. The sight of it incited the Trackers further, and they crowded in, converging on me in a swirl of blades, which struck harder and faster.

I screamed and woke up, thrashing in the bed sheets. Lisette jumped backwards, eyes wide with concern, a damp cloth in her hand. I blinked, taking a few seconds to realise that I was safe in my bedchamber and that the prodding I had felt had been Lisette trying to wake me up. She held out a glass of water, which I accepted gratefully with trembling hands.

'Nina?'

I looked up to see Jesse in the doorway. She was already dressed and ready for the day, making me wonder what time it was. Surely I hadn't overslept?

'Your grandfather has requested that you prepare yourself for training immediately,' she said, 'the Dark Elves want to watch you in action.' Her reassuring smile did little to appease the creeping anxiety that was filling me, exacerbated by the nightmare I had just had.

'I'll be out shortly,' I croaked.

'Are you alright?' she asked, her brow creasing in worry as she took in my expression properly for the first time, 'you look *terrible.*'

Lisette clicked her tongue and bustled towards Jesse, as if offended that she had made such an observation.

'I brought you something to eat before training,' Jesse added quickly as she was hustled outside. 'I hope you're alright...' Lisette gave her a firm push, whipping the small platter of fruit and cheese out of Jesse's hands, '...I'll see you soon!' She tripped away down the hallway and we were left in silence.

Lisette stepped back, seemingly pleased with herself for dispatching our visitor so efficiently. She put down the platter and began to pull out my training gear. I groaned, flopping onto the pillows, feeling like doing anything except training. My head was pounding and my muscles ached as Lisette coaxed me to sit back up.

'I don't want to go, Lisette,' I said quietly, 'I feel like I'll just crumple, I don't feel well.'

She gave me a short, assessing glance and then placed the platter in my lap, gesturing for me to start eating as she left the room. I didn't really feel like eating either, but forced myself to swallow a few mouthfuls of sliced apple. It didn't do that much to stop the nausea that hovered at the back of my throat. I groaned and took another gulp of water, hoping that that would settle my stomach.

I made it through a few more pieces of apple and some grapes before Lisette returned, a tray with a steaming pot balanced between her hands. She poured out a cup and handed it to me, and I breathed in the comforting scent of chamomile tea. The tea did what the water hadn't and my nausea slowly faded.

Lisette moved me to sit on the edge of the bed and began to brush and plait my hair, tying it securely with a ribbon. She noticed the coin lying next to the bed but didn't comment, for which I was grateful. Like a child, she urged me to change and tidy myself up, watching as I splashed my face with water and finished off the tea and breakfast. In far too short a time I was ready to go to the training hall, but still I loitered after

Lisette had left, unwilling to start the inevitable pain I knew the training session would cause. I hovered in the doorway for a moment longer, and then strode back to the bed and grabbed the necklace, pulling it over my head and hiding it under my clothes.

'I need all the luck I can get,' I thought to myself, while traitorously welcoming its familiar weight back against my skin. After all, there was no reason why I couldn't still wear Markus' gift, even if I was decided against watching him through the scrying pool again. I was determined to move on, but there wasn't any harm in keeping the necklace close, was there?

'You seem very pensive, Princess.'

I whirled around, reaching automatically for my mother's dagger that rested in its sheath at my side. My visitor laughed and I relaxed slightly, walking towards the doorway.

'Isn't it inappropriate for you to be here?' I asked the masked figure who lolled indolently against the wall. 'My quarters are off limits for visitors.'

'They probably are,' he said, 'but I was exploring the hallways and got lost.'

'How convenient,' I muttered.

'Yes, it was rather,' he answered smoothly. 'Because that means that I got to run into you, which is quite a pleasant surprise.'

'Did Rakael send you?' I asked bluntly, not believing for a moment that he had actually gotten lost or that his coming across me was accidental. 'It's a bit rich of her to send you to bring me to the training hall.'

'Rakael?'

'The leader of the Resistance,' I clarified.

'The one with the scars?' I nodded.

He shrugged, 'I haven't spoken with her. Not personally at any rate. But no, she did not send me to find you.'

I raised an eyebrow in an attempt at looking haughty. From his chuckle, I figured that I didn't succeed. 'How did you get here without being followed?' I asked, curiosity getting the better of me. There was no sign of his companions in the hallway and it struck me as odd. From the way at least one had always shadowed him last night I found it strange that they would allow him to be left alone, especially in a new environment.

Aidyn shrugged again, 'I thought I was going back to my rooms and took a wrong turn. If my presence offends you, I'll leave, although I think I'd probably get more lost.'

'It would make more sense to help you by showing you the way back to the hall,' I said after some deliberate consideration. 'Then I wouldn't run the risk of you getting lost around my quarters again. I suppose I *could* show you the way, one can't leave a poor, helpless stranger in need.'

'You are most obliging,' he said and I heard the catch of laughter in his voice. 'Please lead on, my lady.'

I drew myself up with imagined haughtiness and condescended to lead the way down the hall, ignoring his chuckle as he fell into step beside me.

'I apologise for my abrupt departure last night,' he said, matching me stride for stride. 'It was a tiring journey and I do not particularly like to travel.'

'Are you feeling better this morning?' I asked, 'I hope the dancing didn't keep you up too late.'

He shrugged again. 'It was no louder than the parties we have at home, so it didn't bother me. There was something I saw that kept me awake for a while though.'

Even though I did not turn, I could feel that he was looking at me closely.

'Oh?'

'There was a light,' he mused, 'not for long, but it looked like flames. It lit up the sky and chased the shadows away.' His tone had become tinged with wonder and I glanced at him, slightly confused by his words. 'You see,' he spoke quickly, 'where I'm from, it isn't, I mean…'

'My lord,' a sharp, raspy voice interrupted him and Aidyn cut off, leaving an awkward silence between us. I looked around to see two of his companions before us and shivered despite myself. It really was disconcerting how they all wore those masks. When I was just with Aidyn it was slightly bearable– his conversation intrigued me and he had even made me laugh on occasion– but his companions were a different story.

'I see you found the Princess Wilhelmina,' his companion continued coldly, 'we have been waiting for you both to join us. It is time for the demonstration to begin.'

I felt a wave of dread wash over me. It was clear from this man's tone that he fully expected me to disappoint. I wondered how much Rakael had told him.

'We shouldn't keep them waiting,' Aidyn said calmly, and followed his companions in silence until we reached the training hall. I baulked then, taking in the majority of the Elven court who were gathered around a space in the centre of the room, the visitors seated next to Grandfather on a raised dais. The Elves were talking amongst themselves, and I spied Dylan, Erik and Stefan in the crowd. Dylan looked particularly out of his element, and Erik pulled on his arm, pointing to me and waving.

I wanted to turn around and run all the way down to the stables, leap on Dolce's back and get as far away from this horror as soon as possible.

'It'll be alright,' Aidyn whispered, giving my hand a reassuring squeeze, 'good luck.' I sucked in a breath, partly from fear and partly from surprise that he was holding my hand. I looked at him searchingly, wanting to see through the mask to gauge his expression.

'Aidyn *come*,' his companion snapped, and together they strode towards the dais, Aidyn standing behind his companion who took the seat of honour next to Grandfather.

Jesse materialised, as if out of nowhere, and drew me to the side, casting a glance at Rakael who was stretching on the edge of the circle.

'You took your time,' she muttered, and I detected a similar thread of anxiety to mine. 'We haven't much time to warm you up, come on, start stretching.'

Together we stepped outside the doorway so that we weren't in full view of the spectators.

'Why are there so many people?' I gasped as I began to stretch.

'It's not often Dark Elves visit the court, I think,' Jesse replied, 'I think most of them are there to watch them. They've seen you fight already but this is more important.'

I blanched and she continued quickly, 'but try to view it like a normal fight, Nina. You have to trust yourself and your instincts, you're better than you give yourself credit for. Even if they don't choose to support the Resistance, we can still find support elsewhere.'

'Thanks Jess,' I muttered sarcastically, deepening the stretch and leaning down towards the ground. 'But it's all very good to *say* it's not that important, when everyone else seems to believe the contrary. I mean anyone and everyone seems to be here, *that's* not intimidating at all.'

'Nina,' Rakael's voice interrupted my deep breathing and I peered up at her from the floor, startled that she had used my name instead of her habitual 'Princess'.

'It's time to get started.' She must've been nervous too, her usual abruptness was not there and she seemed almost human.

'Give her a minute to stretch, Rakael,' Jesse said.

'We don't have time,' Rakael replied, her usual waspishness returning slightly, 'our visitors are getting *bored*.'

'Then let them get bored,' Jesse retorted, 'she needs time to warm up.'

'The Chief Counsel to the King of the Dark Elves begs to disagree,' Rakael grimaced, her mouth twisting with distaste. 'I don't like it any more than you do, but we need to start before he decides that our cause isn't worth supporting.'

'He would do that?' I asked, aghast.

'He seems to be that way inclined, yes,' Rakael said grimly. 'Now come on.' She gripped my hand and pulled me to my feet, leading me back into the training hall. I followed, Jesse close behind, her presence giving me a faint sense of support. Touching the coin against my chest briefly, I drew comfort from its familiar weight, breathing deeply to calm my nerves.

Rakael paused in front of the dais and gave a short jerky bow to Grandfather and the Dark Elf Chief Counsel. Her jaw was clenched and I figured she probably disliked having to obey the whims of the Dark Elves. I inclined my head slightly at Grandfather, whose expression was inscrutable, giving no clue as to whether he was concerned or pleased with how proceedings were playing out. I highly doubted the latter.

'Have Your Lordships got preferences about what you would like to see?' Rakael's tone was steely but still with a modicum of civility.

'Entertain us for today,' the Chief Counsel said, waving a hand. 'If we feel we need more demonstration, we will send one of our own into the ring.'

Rakael straightened and nodded curtly. She turned to me and murmured, 'remember three taps when you concede. Fight like we have practised and think fast.' I was so nervous that I only managed a croak in reply. She gave a brief, crooked smile which might have been in an attempt to make me feel better but it didn't really work.

I saw the movement out of the corner of my eye and reacted just in time, dropping and rolling away, jumping back to my feet as Jesse advanced. Her blow had almost caught me unawares, but now I watched her closely, hands raised as we circled each other. She struck again and I jumped away, retaliating with a punch which she dodged.

There was an audible yawn from the dais. I frowned, forcing myself to not get too distracted as I pushed the attack, striking harder and faster, dropping down and sweeping Jesse's legs out from under her with a kick. She fell and I held her down until she tapped my shoulder three times and I released her.

I helped her up and Jess grinned at me, panting slightly. 'Good one, Nina,' she said. I felt a rush of pride and smiled back.

'Again.' The Chief Counsel's raspy voice cut through the approving applause from the audience. 'Make it more interesting this time.'

Rakael stiffened slightly and then forcibly relaxed. I watched her, perversely enjoying seeing her get riled up by the visitors.

'Knives,' she bit out, 'prepare yourself Princess.'

My hand hovered over the blade at my side, drawing it out as Jesse advanced, slashing in a wide arc. I skipped back, and then realised that Rakael was also approaching, her dagger raised and ready to strike. I gasped and deflected Jesse's next blows, twisting to face both of them so I wouldn't be taken by surprise. Rakael struck downwards, aiming for my legs and I blocked her, the clang of metal-on-metal sounding out around the room.

I sensed Jesse's movement and rolled sideways, grimacing as her strike caught my shoulder. There was no time to care about the momentary pain however, as Rakael advanced and I parried, grunting as she kicked the back of my knees and I fell. My dagger slashed her side as I landed, not drawing blood but cutting through her leather vest to the tunic underneath. I braced my landing and jumped back up, watching them circle me warily. My shoulder was starting to sting but I ignored it, focussing instead on deflecting Jesse's next strike, jumping away from her and then meeting Rakael's blade, which narrowly missed my neck. I twisted and struck out, throwing Jesse off balance slightly. I pressed my advantage, ducked under her retaliating blow and slipping behind her, pressing my dagger against her neck. She tapped my shoulder thrice and I released her, now entirely focussed on Rakael, whose movements almost mirrored my own.

Rakael feinted to the side and I responded too late, barely blocking the blade that ended up grazing my brow. Blood began to blur my vision but I didn't have time to wipe it away, as Rakael pushed her attack, the blade in her hand a whirl of silver. My blocks became less effective and she toppled me with another kick. As I fell, I twisted and pulled her down with me, so that we both lay panting on the ground before she leapt up and straddled me, knife pressed none too gently against my throat.

'Yield Princess,' she growled.

'Only if you do,' I retorted, spitting the blood out of my mouth. She blinked and then looked down at my dagger, which was aimed directly for her gut.

Rakael's mouth quirked in a spasm that could have been called a smile. She stood and lifted me up. 'Get cleaned up, Princess,' she said coolly, 'we still need to demonstrate your other skills.'

Lisette was standing on the sidelines, a bevy of attendants waiting with her. I stumbled towards her and allowed the Elves to bathe my brow and shoulder. One held a hand over my wounds, there was a brief heat and then the stinging ache was gone. Lisette cleaned away the blood and sweat from my face and forced me to sit and drink some water. On the dais, Grandfather and the Dark Elves were in discussion, and the remaining audience seemed to settle back into soft conversation. Erik and Stefan were speaking excitedly, and Dylan listened, although his eyes seemed to have misted over, clearly not paying close attention to the proceedings. Most likely he was thinking about one of his alchemical experiments or his research on the spirits. Lisette gave me a gentle squeeze and pushed me back towards the ring with a supportive smile. I sighed and returned to Rakael and Jesse, who were waiting for me by a rack of potential weapons; it was going to be a long morning.

I supposed, in hindsight, that it could have been worse. It most certainly couldn't have been much better, considering I performed as best I was able. Let it never be said that I did not try, I thought wryly, as I spooned fragrant chicken soup into my mouth.

Rakael and Jesse had done their best to provide an adequate demonstration of all my fighting skills. I had been put through rounds of archery, sword fighting and the dreaded staves. Thankfully that last one had been quick. I had barely lasted fifteen minutes before falling to one of Jesse's blows. Apart from that, I thought I had done reasonably well with the archery and fencing. It was clear to all who watched that I was not a born soldier, but I was able to defend myself adequately enough, surely that would be sufficient for the Dark Elves.

Our visitors had withdrawn to their chambers after the demonstrations were over and they had not emerged since. I wondered if they were deliberating whether to make a decision early, or if they would choose to stay longer.

'You did well, Nina,' Grandfather murmured at my side, his voice penetrating my thoughts. 'I am proud of the progress you have made.' I smiled at him and he added, 'I know that Rakael is also impressed with your development.' That was a nice, albeit surprising, addition and I felt warmth spread through me. Grandfather's eyes crinkled and he patted my hand paternally.

'By the time I'm your age, I'll be better,' Erik piped up confidently, twirling his spoon like an imaginary sword.

'That's fine with me,' I laughed, ruffling his hair. 'You're the one of us who wants to be a knight after all.'

He batted my hand away and then caught Stefan's shifting glance from across the room. The two friends shared a look and seemed to understand each other perfectly, both rising to sneak off and play. Knowing Erik, they would probably practise with their blunted swords in the training room until one of the sword masters came to hasten them to bed.

'Good night, Nina,' Erik said quickly, 'Good night, King Aegis.'

Grandfather gave a wave of his hand and Erik was off, slipping between the tables before we could change our minds about letting him go. In another instant he and Stefan had vanished.

'May I be excused as well, Grandfather?' I asked, filled with a strong desire to find somewhere quiet to be alone.

His gaze perused my features for a moment and then he said, 'you may, but don't stay up too late, child.' I nodded gratefully and also departed, following in Erik's footsteps until I reached the entrance hall. It had been such a trying day, I longed for sleep but knew that it would elude me, much as it had last night. Besides it was still early, the sun had barely begun to set, the sky still alight with glowing hues of pink and blinding orange.

My feet led me towards the staircase, and I allowed myself to run down, enjoying the feeling of the exertion, laughing as the evening breeze caught my hair and skirts. Down and around the staircase I went, getting dizzier and dizzier but not slowing my pace. The ground rushed up faster than I wanted, and I paused at the base, reorientating myself.

I walked into the stables, staggering slightly as the dizziness abated. Dolce's stall was not far and she nickered in welcome as I approached, snagging an apple from a bucket near the doors. She began to devour her treat as soon as I held it out, and I stroked her neck gently.

Dolce had completely recovered after the sea voyage here; her coat was glowing with a healthy sheen again and she had been eating well. I leaned against her neck, breathing in the scent of hay and sighed, releasing some of the tension that had been built up for so long. Dolce bumped my hand with her head, searching for more apples, whickering softly. I stood there a while longer, stroking her until she gave up on trying to find another apple and decided that the hay was far more appetising.

The sound of footsteps interrupted my quiet reverie and I looked up, abruptly brought back to the present. Erik entered the stables, with one of the masked Dark Elves beside him. He didn't look particularly comfortable and hurried to my side.

'He asked me to find you,' Erik whispered urgently, 'I thought you might be here.'

I latched Dolce's stall shut and put an arm around Erik, holding him securely at my side. He was trembling slightly, and I was confused. What had happened to make him like this?

'Aidyn?' I asked, 'what are you doing here?'

'I presume you mean *Lord* Aidyn,' the man replied with a slight sneer and I knew instantly that I had made a mistake. 'Since we have not been introduced, I will not expect an apology from you *this* time. But he is the reason I came. He wants to see you. Come.' He reached out and drew me forward, leading me towards the doors. His grip was tight and I struggled to pull free, uncomfortable with his closeness. He ignored my attempts and strode on, heading towards the forest.

'Where are we going?' I demanded, trying to ignore my rising panic.

'He came out here to meditate,' the guard responded shortly, 'Your grandfather knows that you are going to meet him.'

This partially answered my question, but also sprouted half a dozen more. Why was Aidyn meditating outside the court? Had Grandfather told him about the grove? Why did he want to see me particularly? And why, by the Gods, was this man pulling me along so damned *fast?*

He tugged again and I stumbled, crying out as I hit the rocky ground. Erik helped me up and then let out a terrified squeak. I looked up and felt myself freeze.

Erik's eyes were wide, quivering as the man's thick arm wrapped around his neck, a small sharp blade inches away from his face.

'Don't scream, Princess,' the man hissed, 'or this one pays the price. Now get up, nice and easy.'

I obeyed slowly, raising my hands to my shoulders. He let out a cackling laugh and we continued walking through the undergrowth. I kept my eyes focussed on the path ahead, thinking furiously of what I could do. I had left my trusty silver knife back in my chamber and cursed myself, I couldn't risk Erik getting hurt.

We walked on for a short while, the man's heavy breathing loud to my ears. The sky began to darken as night started to fall.

'It's cowardly to draw a knife on a child,' I said suddenly, 'you should take me instead.'

'And lose my chance to get you to do what I want?' he sneered, 'nice try Princess, but it won't work. This one should be grateful that I didn't hurt him more. Not like his little friend.'

Erik whimpered and I glanced back, horrified. What had happened to Stefan?

'Who are you?' I asked, 'you're monstrous.'

He laughed again. 'If you think you can appeal to my better nature, don't even bother. I don't have one.' His blade traced a line along Erik's cheek, cutting in deeply. He flinched and I watched, speechless as the blood began to trickle down his face.

'Consider this a warning, Princess,' the man growled, 'next time it's his neck. Now *move.*' I turned back shakily and walked on, taking deep calming breaths. What could I do?

I was so caught up in my thoughts that I didn't notice the tree root until my ankle was caught and I toppled again, but this time my foot wrenched and I cried out as I sprawled forwards.

'Get up,' the man snapped.

I lay in a heap of skirts and turned, pulling my ankle free from the root, wincing in pain. Then as I looked up at him, I had an idea. My hands gripped my ankle that was already starting to swell, and as I gazed down at my leg, I urged the darkness to descend faster. Erik cried out as the shadows spread, casting the world around us into an almost impenetrable gloom. The man cursed and there were the sounds of a scuffle and a sharp yelp.

'Erik!' I gasped, swaying to my feet. I heard a heavy body crash to the ground and felt the flames rise from my hand, as if they had been waiting for me to call them to life. Erik stood above our attempted abductor, kicking the dagger away from the man's grasp. He had clearly waited until the man's grip loosened slightly before attempting to break free.

'Come here,' I said, and then leaned heavily on his shoulder when he came to my side. The flames in my hand danced and I flung them at the man on the ground, scorching the earth around him. His mask and balaclava caught alight and he pulled them off, screaming. Another ball of flame filled my hand and I lifted it, ready to strike if he came any closer. I had no sympathy for this man and watched him writhe in pain. When he sat up, I took in his features in shock, thrown by a sense of familiarity. Mocking stone-grey eyes met mine, wide cheekbones with a scraggly beard that was woven through clay beads.

'So, the little girl has learned some new tricks?' he snarled, 'Our king will be most interested to learn that.'

'Who *are* you?' I asked, as Erik and I began to back away. He laughed and the sound made me shiver.

'I thought you would be more intelligent than that, Princess,' he said. 'But for a runaway child, I suppose you didn't have many chances to improve your education.'

Erik tugged on my arm, and I realised that I had stopped moving.

'You're not really a Dark Elf at all, are you?' I whispered through numb lips, the flames in my palm rising higher.

'Their armour is useful,' he grinned, revealing crooked teeth. 'No one guessed that one of their own had conveniently gone missing. I made sure he didn't go quickly though, he needed to know exactly what pain was before I let him breathe his last.' He cackled again and I felt nauseated.

'Nina,' Erik whispered, 'we need to get out of here. Let's *go*.' He sounded as terrified as I felt.

'You can try to run, Princess,' the man laughed, the sound deranged, 'but you won't be able to hide forever. We will always find you.'

The flames shot off my palm towards where he lay and we escaped, the darkness swallowing up the screams that filled the air. I couldn't run properly, my ankle sending spikes of pain up my leg. Erik helped me remain upright, urging me on.

'Look, Nina,' he said suddenly, 'torches!'

Sure enough, there were torches in the distance and I could hear voices calling out.

'It's King Aegis,' Erik muttered and then called out, 'We're here! We're over here!'

I leaned against a tree, drawing shaky breaths as the voices drew closer. Erik was standing near me, shoulders hunched and silent tears running down his face.

'I wouldn't have made it out without you, Erik,' I murmured, reaching out and grasping his hand. 'I didn't know what to do.'

'I led him to you,' Erik said harshly, 'he hit Stefan over the head and told me that if I found you, no one else would get hurt. I didn't know what to do, no one was around and there was blood everywhere. I couldn't…'

'Shh,' I murmured, pulling him closer and holding him against my side. 'You did the only thing you could. Don't blame yourself for what happened. Besides, you managed to knock him down. I'm proud of you.'

He buried his head into my shoulder, sobs racking his slight frame and I held him there, rocking him back and forth. His blood soaked my dress but I didn't care, it was already covered in dirt stains and torn from the undergrowth.

'Nina!' Grandfather sounded desperate, his voice cracked as he reached us, the torch in his hand shaking. He embraced both of us, 'You're all right. You're all right.'

'What happened, Nina?' Rakael's voice pierced the air, and I looked up to see her, Jesse and a small group of Elven guards a few paces away.

'I think he was a Tracker,' I managed, 'we left him back there.' I pointed and Rakael nodded, leading the group onwards, drawing weapons from their sheaths.

'Let's get you home,' Grandfather said, stepping back and placing a handkerchief to Erik's face. His movement made me lose my balance and I gripped the tree harder, gasping in pain as I fought to stay upright.

'She's hurt.' A new voice cut in, and I turned to it, as the shrouded figure emerged from the darkness.

'Aidyn?' I asked, wavering slightly, leaning away from the masked man.

'Princess Wilhelmina?' He stepped forward, and this time I recoiled despite myself. 'What's wrong?'

'The man who took us was wearing your mask,' Erik said coldly, glaring at Aidyn.

I lifted a hand to my forehead, wondering why the world was suddenly starting to get fuzzy.

'She's not well,' Aidyn's voice sounded like it was coming from the end of a long tunnel.

'Get away from her!' Erik cried out, and I reached out to comfort him but the darkness rose up to greet me before I could reach him.

I must have only been out for a short while. When I came to, I was in someone's arms, heading back to the court. I tilted my head, realising that Aidyn was the one holding me.

'You're awake,' he said, 'good. That friend of yours should be able to relax now.'

'Nina,' Erik's face appeared near my own, the bloody gash garishly contrasting with his pale skin. 'Are you alright? Can you walk?'

'I can try,' I said thoughtfully, and Aidyn stopped to put me down. I tried to move forward but buckled before I could take more than two paces.

'You shouldn't be walking on that,' Aidyn's tone was clipped and for the first time I wondered if he was angry. 'Let me take you.' Before I could respond, he had lifted me up again and I wrapped my arms around his neck automatically.

Erik fell into step beside us, 'your grandfather has followed the others. They were going to bring the Tracker back and find out what he knows.'

'Your friend explained,' Aidyn said quietly, 'that this man had taken the armour of one of my companions.'

'Yes,' I replied, 'he killed him and took his armour. I don't know how long ago it was though.'

'It is regrettable,' Aidyn said tightly, 'he had a family. I knew them well. They will mourn his parting even more since we will not be able to give him a proper burial.'

We had reached the road and began to make our way towards the staircase back to court when suddenly Erik gave a loud cry,

'Stefan!' He sprinted ahead and hugged his friend, who was waiting anxiously at the base of the stairs. A group of servants and courtiers were around him, and on seeing us there was an uproar.

'Aidyn,' I whispered before they converged on us, 'please stay with me a while.'

He nodded and his grip tightened marginally. We were soon encompassed by a crowd of servants, who tried to pry me out of his arms.

'King Aegis has requested that I deliver Princess Wilhelmina to her chambers personally,' Aidyn spoke with a quiet authority which silenced the crowd immediately. 'Please go and prepare her maid. This young man also needs medical attention.' He indicated Erik with a jerk of his head and then strode up the stairs, leaving the servants behind us speechless.

I rolled my eyes, 'they'll be talking about that for days now.'

He shrugged, 'let them. It doesn't matter.'

I was quiet for a moment and the silence stretched out. I didn't want to think too much about what had just happened and sought to distract myself by filling the silence. I looked at Aidyn, shivering inadvertently at the polished silver mask that covered his features. It made me think of the Tracker, of how easily he had infiltrated the court and found a way to lure me away. He had so nearly succeeded.

'Why do you wear masks?' My voice broke the silence, as I watched Aidyn closely.

'Not a fan of them, are you?' His voice was tinged with humour before becoming serious again, 'although considering what happened tonight, I can understand why.'

'Not particularly, no,' I said grimly, 'I know you said you wore them during daytime to protect yourselves from the light, but it's nighttime. It seems more like a defence tactic, what are you trying to hide?'

'So that's where your mind automatically jumps to is it?' he snorted. 'Very trusting.'

'I've not had many other options in my experience,' I said coldly, 'Trust is difficult to earn and all too easy to break. Look at tonight— that Tracker was able to infiltrate your party and none of you were any the wiser.'

'You're right there,' he said quietly, 'my apologies. I know all too well how it can be difficult to trust those around you.'

'So why do you continue to wear the mask?' I pushed, 'it's hard to develop any trust for someone when you can't see their face.'

'Don't you trust me, then?' His voice was a mere whisper and I pretended not to hear it.

'I mean hypothetically.'

'Of course,' he murmured.

'You haven't answered my question,' I persisted.

'In our culture,' he finally replied, 'it is not common to see one without a mask on. I believe it was not always the case, but long ago it became the normal practice. Even if we take off our masks we are covered, it is just how we are raised.'

I felt like there was more he was not telling me but felt it would be useless to press him any longer.

'How were you able to find us?' I asked instead. 'And why were you with Grandfather?'

He chuckled briefly. 'You are full of questions, Princess. Maybe I have a few of my own.'

'Like what?'

'Like why on earth you went with that man into the forest? What tale did he spin to make you think it was alright to leave the safety of the court?' His tone had turned sharp and angry.

'Well firstly,' I counted off the reasons on my fingers, 'he told me that you had requested my presence and wanted to speak to me.' He convulsed briefly but kept walking, taking long strides. I continued, 'secondly, he was armed and we weren't. He threatened Erik and I wasn't prepared to lose him.'

'I want you to know that I would never ask you to leave the court. I know that it is not safe for you,' he said. I blinked, speechless for a moment and he pressed on. 'In regard to your questions; I was the one who found the young boy incapacitated in the training room. When I brought him around, he began babbling about a conspiracy to kidnap you. I found some servants to take care of him and went straight to your grandfather and we gathered a group of guards to follow you.'

'How did you find us then?' I asked curiously.

'There were some flashes of light from the forest that your grandfather said would guide us to you both.' He paused, 'I assume that was you?'

I didn't answer. We had reached the entrance to my chamber and Lisette was hovering, her face drawn with anxiety. She gestured for Aidyn to put me down and he helped me into a low chair.

He clicked his heels and bowed, 'I must leave you now, Wilhelmina. My companions will need to hear about the fate of our comrade. We will need to conduct a search of our own.'

Lisette curtseyed and then began to pull back the bedsheets. He turned and began to walk away.

'Aidyn?' My voice sounded shakier than normal, perhaps the shock was starting to settle in. He paused in the doorway and turned back, waiting patiently for me to speak. 'I think, under the circumstances, you can call me Nina.' I managed a watery smile. 'And, thank you.'

He bowed again and departed, leaving me to be fussed over by Lisette, who clicked her tongue in horror at the state of my dress as she tended to my cuts and bruises. I hopped to the bed and lay down, and my ankle was wrapped in linen and raised onto some cushions. Lisette forced me to drink a strong but bitter tisane and within moments the pain began to fade. My eyes grew heavy and I allowed myself to sink into a deep, and thankfully dreamless, sleep.

Chapter Five

I awoke abruptly, and realised that the sun was almost half-way across the sky. The late morning was warm and the sweet scent of flowers tinged the air. I stretched and felt the twinge of pain from my ankle jolt through me. My yawn became a quick gasp and I sat up as Lisette came to my side, fluffing the pillows and arranging the covers so that I could sit comfortably. Another maid appeared almost instantaneously with a breakfast tray and another steaming tisane. As I began to pick at the fruit on the tray, Lisette lifted the pot onto a side table and began to pour out a cup for me. I sniffed in the scent of thyme and smiled, taking a grateful sip. For a moment all was peaceful bliss, but then Erik crashed through the doorway, panting. He still bore the wounds from last night, but now the gash across his face had been cleaned and I could see it properly. It had clearly been tended to by a healer, for it already looked like it was several days through the healing process. It stretched from his temple to chin, and I knew deep down that he would be forever marked, just like Rakael. I bit my lip, it had been my responsibility to bring him with me across the Meridian, my responsibility to keep him safe and now, because of me, who knew how many other scars he would end up getting?

'You're awake,' Erik gasped in between heaving breaths, 'at last.'

'Good morning to you too,' I murmured, as I began to work my way through some apple slices.

Erik ignored me and sailed on, 'everyone's in an uproar. There were search parties looking all night and they just came back with the Dark Elf guard's body.'

I felt a mixture of sadness and bittersweet relief, mourning the pointless tragedy of a man losing his life but also feeling glad that at least now he could be returned home. I remembered how Aidyn's voice had tightened with pain when he had said that the man had had a family. I understood that feeling all too well.

'But that's not all,' Erik began to pace, 'they didn't find *him*.'

'What do you mean?' I asked automatically.

'I mean– by the Gods you lit him on fire,' Erik continued bitterly, 'how hard can it be to catch a man who's on *fire*?' Coldness gripped me and I felt my hands shaking on the teacup. I took a large sip to steady myself and watched Erik closely.

'He got away?' My words came out as a thin whisper. '*How?!*' My vision began to blur slightly and I felt the faint rush of magic responding to my emotions. Lisette reached out and took the cup away as it was starting to shake. She gripped my hand with hers, the warmth anchoring and calming me.

'I don't know,' Erik cried, too caught up in his own anger to notice my reaction. 'That's why they had people searching all night, Rakael just got back in and said all they found was his bloody *mask*.' He kicked one of the rugs in frustration. 'The Dark Elves aren't happy either. Their Chief Counsel,' he spat out the last words, 'is saying that King Aegis' court is incapable and it's a waste of their time to stay any longer. He said that it was your fault that we got captured yesterday.'

The cold fear returned with a vengeance and Lisette made a sharp sound of pain. I turned to her and noticed that her hand had blistered.

'Oh Lisette,' I pulled my hand away from hers, 'I'm so sorry... I didn't mean...' She waved away my concern and thrust her hand in the pitcher of water that stood on the nightstand. Erik had paused in his pacing and was looking at me in shock,

'Gods, Nina,' he said.

'I didn't mean to,' I snapped, and then felt ashamed. 'I can't control it at times,' I moderated my tone and reached for my tea again, noticing that my hand was still trembling. 'It's getting harder to control when I'm surprised or...'

'Scared?' he asked quietly.

I blinked, and then nodded. 'Since when did you get so wise?'

He grinned sheepishly and shrugged, 'I'm not a child anymore. I've heard the Elves talking about magic, I know all sorts of things now. You'd be surprised at some of the things the other trainees will talk about.'

Lisette clicked her tongue disapprovingly from the side of the room and Erik rolled his eyes. 'How's Stefan?' I asked, keen to change the conversation away from what else the trainees discussed in their downtime. I was sure it would be something I didn't want Erik to be hearing.

Erik's expression clouded slightly, 'he's alright. He just got taken by surprise and I think he blames himself for what happened.' He looked down at his feet, 'but I still think it's partly my fault too.'

'It's not either of your faults,' I said, reaching out a hand and drawing him into a hug. 'Please don't think about that anymore. It's just like the Usurper's Trackers to play on people's weaknesses.'

Erik nodded jerkily. I looked over his head at Lisette, whose hand was still in the pitcher, watching us closely.

'Lisette, can you go and find out what is happening with the Dark Elves?' I asked, 'and get someone to take care of your hand. I'm really sorry.'

She nodded and departed, leaving Erik and I alone.

'Erik,' I said gently, 'I must go and speak to them. I can't let the Dark Elves leave yet. We need to have their support for our cause, if they leave, I don't think we'll be able to face the Usurper. We just don't have enough people.'

'You don't want *him* to leave either,' Erik said bitterly, moving towards the windowsill and looking out at the forest. I sat in the bed, mute and slightly surprised at his sudden change of tone.

'I saw the way you looked at him,' Erik continued, 'it wasn't that long ago you were looking at Markus the same way.' My breath caught somewhere in my throat and my gut twisted. Erik turned back to me, 'I liked Markus. He didn't hide behind a mask or keep secrets. He took care of us.'

I didn't say anything, recognising that he was finally saying what he had probably held in for the past month.

'Why can't Markus help us?' he said moodily, 'I'm sure he would know a lot of people from his travels who could support our cause. We don't *need* the Dark Elves.'

'We do, Erik,' I said, swallowing the painful lump in my throat, 'and besides, Markus probably doesn't have an army who could support us.'

'As a matter of fact,' a curt voice interjected from the doorway, 'it no longer matters.'

Erik and I both turned and saw Rakael, who looked exhausted. Her face was drawn and pale, with dark rings under her eyes and scars more visible than usual.

'What do you mean?' Erik and I asked simultaneously. Rakael raised an eyebrow and said,

'They've left. We won't be getting their support.'

It was like I had been winded. 'They… left?'

Rakael nodded, 'their Chief Counsel had the gall to blame you and your grandfather. As if any of us could have foreseen what would happen.' She shook her head, 'now we need to regroup and think about what to do next. Rest up Princess, we'll need you to be on your feet soon.' She turned and paused for a moment, before adding over her shoulder, 'don't blame yourself. The Gods clearly didn't want this alliance to go ahead.' With that she left, and I gazed blindly after her. Her words lingered in my ears but didn't do much to halt the wave of guilt and disappointment wash through me.

'I didn't really think they'd leave,' Erik said, 'I'm sorry, Nina.'

'It's alright, Erik,' my voice was flat and numb, 'but I think you should go and find Stefan. Make sure he knows that I don't blame him for last night.'

Erik nodded and followed Rakael. As his footsteps receded, I let out a shaky breath and tried to calm myself. They said that I shouldn't blame myself, but I had been the one who needed to impress the Dark Elves. I was the one who should have convinced them to support my cause, without them I wasn't sure what would happen. Even though I had lived on the run for so many years– unsure about what the future held or what would happen– since finding my grandfather and the Resistance I had embraced knowing about what the next steps would be. I liked knowing that there were plans in place for facing challenges, but so much had relied on the Dark Elves' support.

I also felt bereft that they had left so abruptly– I would have at least liked to try and convince them to stay. And, I admitted to myself, I was upset that Aidyn had left without saying farewell. I had wanted to get to know him more. Erik's accusations filled my mind, and I fell back onto the pillows with a groan, covering my head with my arms in a lame attempt to keep the thoughts at bay.

A knock startled me, and I peered through my arms at Lisette, who now had a bandaged hand that was holding a letter. She approached me and brushed my hair away from my eyes, wiping away the tears that had begun to trickle down my cheeks.

'It's not my fault, is it Lisette?' I asked quietly, 'Grandfather doesn't blame me, does he?' Even though I knew deep down that I had done everything I possibly could, I still needed to be comforted. Lisette smiled gently and shook her head, and then took me in her arms and gripped me tight. We stayed like that for a few moments until I noticed the letter that was on my nightstand.

'What's this?' Lisette smiled and stood, taking the breakfast tray away quietly.

I looked at the letter curiously, not recognising the slanted penmanship. I noted that there was an imprint of a bird in the wax seal and broke it carefully, unfolding the parchment. My eyes scanned the letter, taking in the short message quickly.

Princess,

We must return to the Underdark. I fear that our comrade's death precipitated matters and my fellow councillors are keen to return home for the funeral arrangements to begin. I must apologise for our hasty departure and can only hope that we will meet again one day under less trying circumstances.

There was no name to sign off save for the letter 'A'. I reread the letter several times and then refolded it in my lap, pondering his words. It wasn't a proper farewell, but at least he had thought to leave a note. It made their departure slightly easier to bear and it made me feel that Aidyn at least hadn't wanted to leave so abruptly.

The rest of the day dragged, except for when Grandfather came to visit me mid-way through the afternoon. He looked older than usual and as he sat beside me, I registered the wrinkles around his temples that seemed deeper than they had been before.

'Wilhelmina,' he said, taking my hand in his. 'I understand that Rakael has already told you about our guests.'

I nodded.

'We did the best we could, my dear,' he continued heavily, 'we had no way of knowing that a Tracker would come into our midst.' He closed his eyes for a moment and rubbed his brow, 'I must admit, a part of me does not blame them for wanting to return to the Underdark so quickly. Their accusations about our lack of security were not wrong; I have been perhaps too lax in watching over you. The court is not as safe as I had thought.'

'Nowhere is truly safe, Grandfather,' I murmured, 'I think that you have done the best you can. It seemed like the Chief Counsel had made his mind up about whether to approve or disapprove of me before they even arrived.'

Grandfather sighed, 'there was always that risk. Dark Elves are not raised like us. It is a shame, I had hoped… well,' he patted my hand, 'it does not matter now.'

I was curious about what he meant but did not want to press further. Instead, I hugged him, 'don't worry Grandfather. Rakael will come up with something, I'm sure.'

He laughed, 'you remind me of Lydia when you say things like that.' He leaned back and gazed at me, 'every day you are more like her. She would be proud of you my dear, just like I am.'

His words filled me with warmth, and I smiled.

'How are you feeling after last night?' he asked, concern shadowing his tone.

'My ankle is still tender,' I replied, glancing down at my wrapped foot. 'It's hard to stay in bed and not be able to do anything.'

Grandfather smiled, 'I would have thought you would like some rest, you've been working constantly since you arrived.'

I didn't answer, not wanting to admit that the main reason I liked working hard was so that I wouldn't be alone with my thoughts. The day had felt like an interminable torture. Left without anything to distract myself I had lain in bed staring at the woven roof, pondering everything that had happened since I left Scardia. I hadn't even been able to scry, the pitcher and basin of water were too heavy for me to easily carry back to my bed. Perhaps my distaste at being idle showed on my face because Grandfather chuckled.

'I will send the healer to you for your ankle,' he said as he rose, 'he will make sure that you can be on your feet soon. Your presence has been missed today.' I smiled, and then as he moved away the question I hadn't asked came out before I could stop it.

'Will we see the Dark Elves again? Do you think there's a chance that they might return?'

He paused, taking in the folded letter on my bedside table and my anxious expression. 'Perhaps, Wilhelmina. But I do not think that they will return here, it is rare for them to leave the Underdark. I will keep hope in my prayers though, and recommend that you do the same.'

I nodded, slightly disappointed. Again, I was left alone and I gazed around glumly. For a while I practised moving a ball of flame from one hand to another, twisting it into different shapes. The sound of footsteps finally brought an end to my reverie, and with a crackling sizzle, the flame was cast into my water pitcher. Only a faint trace of smoke remained as the healer entered, Lisette following close behind.

'Your Highness,' the healer bowed, 'King Aegis ordered that I have a look at your ankle.' Without another word, she bent over my foot, massaging it and twisting it at certain angles, making me wince. Her brows were furrowed in concentration, and a warmth flowed through my foot, burning hot and then receding. When she tilted my ankle now there was no longer any biting pain, merely a slight tenderness.

'You should avoid riding and excessive exercise for a couple more days, Your Highness,' the healer said as Lisette helped me up and led me to the bathing chamber. It was so good to get back on my feet without limping that I almost didn't hear her next words. 'King Aegis would like you to keep resting in your chamber tonight. He asked me to inform you that your usual routine will resume from tomorrow.'

I groaned and dunked my head under the bath water. When I resurfaced she had disappeared and Lisette clicked her tongue disapprovingly as I struggled to not roll my eyes.

'It's just been so boring having to rest, Lisette,' I complained, 'there's nothing to *do* and no one to talk to. I've been losing my mind with boredom all day and then I finally am able to walk again, and I'm confined to my room.'

She gave me a look that seemed to say that some people would give anything to have a day in bed doing absolutely nothing.

'I'd rather you than me,' I muttered under my breath as she began scrubbing lavender oil into my hair and then pushed me under, effectively cutting off my tirade of complaints.

When I had been scrubbed to within an inch of my life, ruthlessly dried and dressed in my nightgown, I found myself, now seated on the window seat, able to watch the distant lights of Lowton glittering. Lisette deposited a salad of sweet leaves and vegetables and several thickly buttered slices of bread beside me with a decanter of wine. I eyed the wine, wondering if I would manage to drink the whole decanter on my own.

It was a lot more interesting being able to see the world outside the window. I could see Elves making their way towards the dining hall, and a group of guards riding towards the stables. Already I could see that there was increased security, more soldiers were stationed around than there had been previously.

I didn't have much of an appetite and picked at my food, sipping on the sweet wine pensively. When I had finished, I lifted my pitcher and scrying bowl beside me and poured the water out. I ran my hands around its rim, calming the ripples and feeling the patterning around the edges. I closed my eyes briefly, steadying my breathing, and thought about the Dark Elves, picturing them in my mind.

I opened my eyes and looked into the water, noting the images that were starting to appear in front of me. The room was small and cramped, with three hammocks set up along the walls. A porthole looked out onto dark water, speckled with salty spray. The Dark Elves were kneeling on three points of a star that had been chalked onto the floorboards. The fourth point was empty, and a small bowl of incense was burning in the centre, smoke rising in spiralling tendrils.

'Erthor, King of the Moon, guide Gaelen to your embrace,' I recognised Aidyn's voice, 'let him join you in night eternal. May he watch over us from the night sky and may your luminescence keep him safe until we meet again. Keep his daughter Yve and son Callum safe in your glow.'

'Guide him to eternal night,' the other two Dark Elves intoned.

There was a slight movement and I watched Aidyn removing one of his dark leather gloves. The hand that was revealed was pale, almost translucent in the moonlight.

'Gaelen, I will not rest until he who took your life has lost his,' Aidyn withdrew a knife from the sheath at his side and pressed it to his palm, 'as Erthor is my witness and judge, I swear it shall be done. Blood of my blood, brother of my soul, you will be avenged.' His blood fell into the bowl, mingling with the incense as a cloud covered the moon, casting the room into shrouded darkness.

'Blood of my blood, brother of my soul, it shall be done,' the others repeated, their own blood merging with Aidyn's. The lit incense extinguished and soon only the faint smoke remained. Aidyn pulled his glove back on and thrust the dagger back into his belt.

'I need some air,' he growled and left his comrades kneeling in prayer. The image shifted, following him as he traversed the hallway, striding past sailors who moved away to avoid him. I recognised the sailors; I recognised the hallway. I had even recognised the room in which the Dark Elves had been conducting their ritual.

Aidyn climbed onto the deck and leaned against the railing, gazing out at the moonlit ocean.

'I must admit, I didn't expect your party to be ready to depart so soon.' A lazy voice interrupted the night, but Aidyn didn't turn around. I wondered if he had known that he wouldn't be alone, if he had expected the captain to be on deck still.

'I assume you found what you wanted.' I followed the voice and saw Markus at the helm. A mixture of emotions filled me and the water began to shimmer as I tried to calm myself again.

'Our trip was cut short,' Aidyn replied.

'It certainly was,' Markus said, 'a week or so, you told us. Some of my men were expecting longer shore leave. Luckily, we were all on board when you arrived.'

I gritted my teeth, remembering all too well how he had been celebrating his shore leave only two nights before.

'There were pressing matters which forced us to depart early,' Aidyn's tone was cool.

'If that's what you call a dead body, so be it,' Markus shrugged.

Aidyn stiffened slightly at his words, and then said, 'we must return him to his family. There are necessary rites we must follow.'

'Are we going to need to bring you back afterwards?' Markus asked, 'we have several other jobs to run but could be convinced to stay in port if required.'

'No,' Aidyn said quietly, 'we will not be returning any time soon. But there may be need of your services in the future. I will send word if there is.'

'Very well,' Markus sounded relieved. 'We might linger a little while, just in case. Shore leave is always a good way to lift the crew's morale.' I clenched my fists and the lamp beside Markus flared, before sputtering out.

'What the…' Markus muttered, lifting the lamp off its hook. 'It must have blown out.'

Aidyn had turned and watched him relight the lamp.

'What business did you have in Lowton anyway?' Markus asked, 'it's not every day that we have multiple people wanting to visit that place.'

'We barely had time to achieve what we set out to do,' Aidyn said thoughtfully, 'but we definitely found something of interest.'

'Like what?' Markus managed to relight the lantern and shut the glass door.

'A flame,' Aidyn murmured, looking back out at the waves. Markus raised his eyebrows but held his tongue. The wind picked up and I almost missed Aidyn's next words, which were spoken so softly that Markus couldn't hear them. 'Miss me already, Princess?'

I gasped and the image dissolved, the masked man and sea captain vanishing as quickly as they'd appeared, the bowl simply water once more. My heart was pounding and I poured another glass of wine, draining it in three swift gulps. I drank the next glass more slowly, looking back out at the moon and pondering how Aidyn had realised that I was there.

Chapter Six

I hadn't slept particularly well. It might have been the decanter of wine which I had finished before falling asleep, or it might have been the queasiness caused by the wine that kept me awake. Most probably though, it had been because for the first time, someone had been aware of my presence whilst scrying and that knowledge had scared me.

The morning sun was too bright, my head throbbed and Lisette's raised eyebrows at the empty decanter did nothing to improve my mood. Furthermore, I discovered on leaving my room that a guard was stationed outside, and he followed my every move. I was desperate for breakfast and ate more than usual, treating myself to eggs and topping my bread with liberal amounts of butter and a dusting of salt flakes. Grandfather didn't comment on my newfound appetite, but Erik was less discreet, staring openly as I shovelled bread and eggs into my mouth.

'I thought princesses were supposed to be dainty,' Erik muttered, and I cast him a black look.

'I haven't eaten properly for a day,' I grumbled, 'I'm *hungry*.'

'You could still use cutlery,' he said, as he devoured his own breakfast.

'You're one to talk,' I retorted. 'You always eat like this.'

'I'm not a princess,' Erik grinned, clearly enjoying how easily I was responding to his baiting this morning. I wanted to throw something at him to wipe the smug smile off his face, like a kipper, but instead refrained and took a long sip of tea.

'We must discuss what our next steps are this morning, Wilhelmina,' Grandfather said, 'Jesse and Rakael will be waiting for us in the library. Join us there when you have finished.'

He pushed his empty plate away and rose, striding away and leaving us in temporary silence.

'I wish I could come too,' Erik said pointedly, 'but I need to help out in the armoury with Stefan.'

'Mhmm,' I took another bite and spilt some egg down my front.

'Good thing those Dark Elves didn't see you like this,' Erik muttered under his breath.

I shot him a glare and drained my teacup, standing abruptly. 'I knew I should've thrown a kipper at you.' He spluttered and I ignored the curious glances that were cast in my direction as I left. The guard who had followed me to breakfast rose from his own table and shadowed me again, walking at least three steps behind. I was reminded all too well of my childhood, with guards and nursemaids constantly watching my every move. The feeling was irksome, and it made me uncomfortable to be so closely scrutinised again.

The library doors were open and when I entered, several faces turned to me. I went to stand beside Grandfather and nodded at his council members, Elder Haycin, Rakael, several other Resistance members and, strangely enough, Dylan. Dylan looked particularly out of place and by the way he kept cleaning his monocle against his jerkin, he was aware of it. I smiled at him to try and alleviate his anxiety, but he was glancing down at the table and the range of documents that were spread out over it.

'Wilhelmina,' Grandfather said, 'we have been working out who else we can turn to for support in our endeavours.'

Rakael leaned forward, eyes burning with intensity. 'Losing the support of the Dark Elves was a setback, a *big* one,' she said bluntly, 'but we have got some other leads who may be able to assist.'

'Like who?' I asked. Rakael spread out the map on the table, pointing to the different locations as she spoke.

'For one, we can rely on some Karshkan support with our weapons.'

'They have developed some incredible concoctions,' Dylan cut in excitedly, 'I have already sent a missive to my colleagues at the Larshka's Conservatory. They have created an oil that, once lit, will burn hotter and longer than any other. There's a poison that can slow the body and mind, leaving a victim incapacitated for days, or their potion that can remove unwanted memories. Not to mention their elixirs…'

'Yes, yes,' Rakael snapped curtly, waving away Dylan's interjections. 'You will have time to go into more detail about those, Dylan, in good time. Jesse, let her know what you've come up with.'

'We can get support from the Wood Elves in the Velkranian forests,' Jesse said, 'they are strong archers. Unfortunately, you cannot expect support from Velkra's Queen herself, she is too self-absorbed to get involved with wars. She will support the Usurper, mainly because he has visited and complimented her many times while he has been on the throne. But that doesn't mean that we cannot get help from Velkra. I have some gypsy friends who owe me a few favours.'

'Hold on,' I held up a hand, 'how can gypsies help us?'

Jesse grinned, 'gypsies can go anywhere. They travel all over the world, it's one of the easiest ways to sneak into a city. Guards recognise the gypsy caravans and let them through. They're well-known performers, it can be a good way to get a small task force into the Palace.'

'I find it hard to believe that the Usurper will let gypsies into the Capital,' I said. 'I thought that fewer people were allowed in and out.'

'True,' Rakael said. 'It is still a work in progress, Princess.'

Privately I thought it was still a significant work in progress but didn't want to critique it anymore.

'We cannot rely on Felshkar either,' Jesse continued, 'there are too many issues with the Southern mercenaries and slavers, so all the Felshkran tribes are facing their own problems. I have some friends in the Deep, but considering Scardia is half frozen, I don't think they will be able to send much support.'

'The Deep?' I looked at Grandfather, but it was his councillor Mayflower who answered my question.

'Mer-people, Your Highness.'

I blinked, I had always thought tales about Mer-people were folklore.

'Don't forget,' Rakael said, 'we also have our Resistance base in the West of Scardia. When the time comes for us to fight, we will have extra soldiers there.'

'We still face the problem,' Grandfather interjected, 'of not having enough people to combat the Usurper. His army of mercenaries, Trackers and Velkranian soldiers are highly trained and ruthless.'

'Scardia's people will fight,' Rakael said firmly. 'They just need to know when.'

'And how many of Scardia's people will fall in that fight?' I asked quietly. 'They've been beaten down for years, we have had poor harvests and they have been terrorised by Trackers. They are farmers, not soldiers.'

'You don't understand Princess,' Rakael said brusquely, 'sacrifice is a part of war.'

'I think,' Grandfather said, 'that our first move must be to contact our Velkranian and Karshkan allies. It will take them time to reach Scardia, perhaps several months.'

'They will need to meet at the Resistance hideout in the West,' Rakael muttered. 'The sooner we let them know, the sooner we can begin rallying the troops.'

She bowed to Grandfather, jerked her head at me and left with the other Resistance members, barking out orders as they departed.

Dylan hovered awkwardly and then said, 'with your permission, King Aegis, I will send word to my colleagues. I will need more materials from them.' Grandfather nodded and waved him away, Dylan bobbed a bow and trotted away, picking up some scrolls of parchment as he left.

'Surely there are more allies we could call on,' I mused, 'if we rely on the Scardian people it'll be a massacre.'

'We still have time,' Grandfather said reassuringly, 'my Elves will also fight at your side.'

'We will do our best to protect you, Your Highness,' Elder Haycin bowed his head.

I thanked him, not wanting to remind them that Grandfather's troops were also small in number. The many years of war between Elves and Scardians had affected them badly, and as Elves aged more slowly than humans, many of the children who had been born since the war ended were still young.

My concern must have still shown on my face, because Grandfather took my arm and led me away. The waiting guard at the door fell into step behind us, but with Grandfather beside me I didn't feel as uncomfortable.

'Don't you think this is a bit excessive?' I asked, jerking my head back to indicate our shadow.

'Not in the slightest,' he said gently, 'I don't want to run the risk of losing you again. The other day was too close.'

I squeezed his arm. 'I'm fine, Grandfather. You don't need to worry.'

'I do, Nina,' he murmured. 'You are too dear to me– too important to lose.'

I didn't know what to say to that.

'I think you should be careful though,' he continued, 'I fear that Rakael's desire for vengeance may be too strong.'

'I just don't want more innocent people to die,' I muttered.

'You are both right,' Grandfather mused, 'the people will need to choose to make a stand, but it is still important to remember that they are people, not pawns in someone else's game.'

I laughed darkly, 'they've been pawns in the Usurper's game for a long time, Grandfather. I think he knew that if he made them suffer, I would suffer.'

Grandfather nodded, 'Lord Niall was always a vicious boy, who grew into a vindictive man. He once wished to marry your mother, you know. I didn't grant my permission, and arranged her marriage to your father. I don't think Lord Niall ever recovered from that insult.'

I gazed at him, shocked that I hadn't heard this before. 'He wanted to marry Mama?'

'Indeed,' Grandfather sighed. 'But I sensed in him his power, the danger of it spiralling out of control. I didn't want Lydia anywhere near someone like that.'

'He was blessed by the seasonal spirits too?' I asked, 'which one?'

Grandfather eyed me keenly for a moment and then said, 'the Lord of Summer.'

The Winter Spirit's voice filled my mind as I remembered her words: He can be both vindictive and benevolent and is not one to be crossed. Those who he bestows with gifts are always instruments of change, whether for good or bad.

'The Lord of Summer blessed me too,' I mused. 'Why would he want two people with his gifts to fight each other?'

'That, I fear, only he would be able to answer,' Grandfather said. 'But all we can do from now on is prepare you for that moment.'

It should have been easy to settle back into our previous routine of training, but I found myself uneasy as the weeks turned into a month. I had reached the point where I could successfully disarm my opponent, twist out of an attacker's grasp and shoot a target through the neck at a hundred paces, but I still couldn't completely distract myself. The afternoons now also included an hour-long lecture on topics ranging from farming techniques and legal contracts to the appropriate way to stand during a ceremony. I was reminded all too well of my childhood, although now at least I found the majority of the lectures interesting or practical. In those moments I was able to forget temporarily the increased security, the additional guards who shadowed my every move and the worry lines that now seemed permanently etched into Grandfather's brow.

Erik was all too happy to return to his daily routine, and now proudly showed off his new scar to anyone and everyone. The shock from the abduction had faded and it had turned into a dashing tale of how Erik saved me from multiple Trackers, who he had fought single-handed while I lay on the ground, weak and feeble, with my injured ankle.

I didn't have the heart to tell him that everybody, except for the youngest initiates, knew that the tale wasn't true. It was too good to see him smiling and laughing again, and the anger he had shown the morning after the event seemed to have disappeared. He had told me at least three times that all famous knights had battle scars and that it was something to be proud of. I just privately hoped that he wouldn't be getting any more any time soon.

I hadn't tried to scry on Aidyn since the night he left, I was too afraid that he would sense my presence again. Instead, I practised my scrying by watching people who I had met over the years and tried to find out more about what was happening in Scardia. I watched the inn at Little Fleming regularly, hoping that the travellers who passed through Mrs Jenkins' bar would have news about the Usurper and his movements. The news I gathered from these observations was minimal, travellers or farmers preferred to complain about the poor harvest and how the winter frost had been slow to recede, even though Summer had begun. Occasionally there was a Tracker who appeared, shrouded in dark armour, chainmail clinking as he drank from an overflowing tankard. He was gruff and taciturn, and whenever he was present, all the other bar patrons avoided him, lowering their conversations or just turning and leaving the bar on seeing him. Mrs Jenkins always wordlessly filled his tankard herself, sweaty face pinched and wary. I noticed wryly that she hadn't been able to find replacements for myself or Keely in the time since we had been gone and wasn't surprised. From what I saw she hadn't changed, and I was relieved that she was not able to bully another barmaid.

There were a few snippets of information that I heard which I passed on to the Resistance and Grandfather, but they were few and far between. The Usurper had amassed a large mercenary force from Felshkar and had signed a trade agreement with them to allow payment to be given through labour. Apparently, anyone who was too outspoken now was chained and sent off to the distant southern land, never to be heard from again. Travellers told how the nobles had become proud of their slaves, making examples of them in the Capital for all to see, highlighting how even those in high positions could fall. Clearly, the Usurper's penchant for torture and mutilation had rubbed off on his court.

The idea of slavery made my stomach turn. I would remove myself from those visions abruptly, gasping and sweaty. Lisette had figured out when I would be scrying and now would bring a strong peppermint tisane to help calm me down after these sessions. When she found me hunched beside the bowl one evening, retching after seeing a former priest's remains in a hanging cage, she was determined to ensure that she would be there to calm me after each vision. I appreciated her presence on those nights, and found comfort in knowing that soon we would receive word of reinforcements of our own. My nightly prayers to the Gods consistently begged for a means to stop the Usurper. Sometimes Lisette would kneel beside me, head bowed in silent prayers of her own, but often I would wait until I was alone to quietly voice my requests.

As well as scrying, I rode to the grove each week, often with Grandfather and our retinue of guards. Each time, I hoped that the Winter Spirit would reappear and offer guidance. I meditated, cross legged in the centre of the clearing, calming my mind from the turbulent thoughts that kept racing through it. Yet while I worked on developing the natural magics which Grandfather talked me through, the Winter Spirit did not reappear. As the weeks dragged on, I began to lose hope that I would see her again.

The night the letter came was much like all the others. The dining hall was full of the sounds of chatter and laughter, with floating reed flutes playing in the background. A guard came up to Grandfather and whispered something urgently in his ear, and I watched as he rose hastily to his feet and excused himself. The guard then went to Rakael and she quickly followed him out of the hall. Erik was also watching them closely and whispered, 'what do you think is going on?' I shook my head, uncertain. 'Do you think we finally have news?'

'Perhaps,' I murmured, aware that several other courtiers had noticed Grandfather and Rakael's abrupt departure. Glances were being cast in our direction and I looked back down at my plate, pretending to nonchalantly eat my meal. Inside though I was full of conflicting emotions, excitement at something potentially changing and unease at whether that change would be good or bad.

'Come on,' Erik urged, pulling on my arm, 'let's go and find out what's going on.'

I acquiesced and let him lead me out of the room. 'You do know,' I said, 'that we may not be welcome. They didn't ask for us to join them.'

Erik snorted, 'You're the princess, I think they'll agree that you should be aware of what happens.'

I didn't argue and let him lead me towards the main hall. It didn't take us long to notice the flurry of activity up ahead, and I wondered why so many people were busy. As we approached, I saw Rakael barking orders to several Resistance members, Jesse standing at her side. Grandfather was nowhere to be seen, but when Rakael looked up she beckoned me over.

'Good, Princess,' she said briskly, 'I thought I would need to send someone for you. We are needing to move out at dawn for the Ombre Mountains. The Dark Elves want to meet. Prepare your gear and say your goodbyes, we need to leave before sunrise.' With that, she turned and strode off, instructing several guards on finer details as she went.

Jesse smiled at me and added, 'make sure you *do* have a good night's rest, Nina. Rakael is determined to leave at dawn with a small group.' She took Erik's hand and gave it a firm shake, 'Until we meet again Erik. I will see you at daybreak by the stables, Nina. Sleep well.' She followed Rakael and left Erik and I standing speechless in the main hall, struck dumb by the change in events.

When my brain began to work properly again and I could process what had just been said, I realised that I was angry. Why did Rakael think it was alright to give an instruction without any context? What did the Dark Elves want and, for the love of the Gods, *why* did we need to go to the Ombre Mountains? I thought that their Chief Counsel had made his thoughts clear when they left.

'Why did Jesse say goodbye to me?' Erik asked, 'what did she mean that you needed to say goodbye? I'm coming too, right?'

I barely heard him, I was already storming off towards Grandfather's chambers. Elves and guards moved out of my way as Erik and I cut through the hallways, determined to get more information and answers.

Grandfather was sipping honey mead from a silver goblet when I rushed into his rooms, Erik close on my tail. He was sitting in one of his chairs beside the fireplace, a folded letter in his hands.

'What is the meaning of sending us to the Ombre Mountains?' I asked without preamble, 'I thought the Dark Elves had no interest in helping our cause.'

'Perhaps one day,' Grandfather murmured into his mead, 'you will learn how to enter a room with appropriate decorum, Wilhelmina.' But I was too riled up to feel any shame at his rebuke.

'Rakael said that we must leave at dawn, without any other information,' I began to pace in front of the fireplace, 'I'm not a child anymore, Grandfather. I deserve to know what is happening. If it is to do with me regaining the throne— my *life*— I shouldn't be left out of these sorts of discussions.'

'Sometimes,' Grandfather mused, 'you remind me all too well of your mother. She had similar things to say when she realised what your father's father and I had planned with her wedding.'

'But surely you can do something, tell me what's going on,' I said desperately. 'All I've heard is that I need to be ready to leave at dawn in a small party and…'

'And I'm not included!' Erik piped up, 'I should be going with Nina. A knight's duty is to protect.'

I turned to him, 'That's very sweet Erik, but I agree with Rakael on this decision. You'll be much safer here.' I didn't know much about the Ombre Mountains, but I assumed that the journey there would not be easy. I couldn't bear the thought of Erik getting injured again.

'But we need to stick together,' Erik argued, fists clenched.

'It's not up for discussion,' I snapped, rubbing my eyes as a headache began to throb in earnest.

'Why not?' he yelled, his face turning red. 'It's not like you're my *real* sister, you can't tell me what to do!'

It was like he had slapped me. I halted in my pacing and stared at him, taking in the stubborn set of his jaw and mutinous gaze.

'You can't go because you are too young,' Grandfather interjected, 'and Nina will be in a calmer state of mind if she knows that you are safe. See what happens when she is upset.'

He waved a hand in my direction, at the sparks that were crackling in the air around me. Erik glared at us both and stormed out, slamming the door behind him.

'I'm sorry,' I apologised automatically, 'I shouldn't've lost my temper so quickly.'

'Another thing that you will need to keep learning to control,' Grandfather sighed. 'You need to prepare for your journey, but first you should see the missive they sent tonight. Apart from that, we don't have much more to go on— they do prefer to be discreet.'

He gestured for me to sit down beside him and I did so, taking with slightly trembling fingers the letter that he had been holding. As I opened it, I realised that the seal was familiar.

'A phoenix,' Grandfather said as he noticed my gaze. 'A symbol of one of the noble houses in the Underdark.'

I traced the image with the pad of my thumb and then opened the letter. The handwriting was unfamiliar and formed jagged symbols across the page. I scanned them, taking in only part of the meaning but not comprehending the overall message.

'Why did they write…'

'In the Ancient Tongue?' Grandfather smiled, 'probably because they did not want to run the risk of it falling into wrong hands. What can you understand from it?'

I blinked, trying to remember some of the lessons I had taken when I was a child.

'It mentions a meeting under the dark of the moon and something about a ship. I can't figure out much else.'

'You have done well,' Grandfather said, 'many cannot read the Ancient Tongue. It is only seen in its written form now, all those who could speak it are long gone.'

'Mama said it was the language of the Gods,' I recalled. 'But what does the rest of it say?'

He smiled and took the letter back, smoothing out the creases in the parchment.

'They have arranged passage for you and a guide will meet you near the Ombre Mountains. They invite you to the Underdark, for their royal family to assess you. Clearly there has been some debate about whether your cause is worthy of their support, for there is an impasse in their Council.'

'And they would not come back here?' I asked.

'Considering that one of their own died while here, it is highly unlikely,' Grandfather confirmed wryly. 'I think that this is the best way forward, Nina. You are no longer as safe here as I had hoped. The Dark Elves have a strong force who can protect you if needed. From what they say,' he indicated the letter, 'they are interested in you and will treat you as a guest. According to my sources, they have not shown any interest in supporting Lord Niall, which bodes well for us. If you are with them, there is less chance of him locating you.'

'But what about you?' I took his hand in mine, 'I don't want to leave you.'

'I knew that this time would come,' Grandfather smiled, 'I will remain here, making sure that our allies are gathered and ready for the fight to begin.'

'I will miss you,' I said quietly.

'And I you, my dear,' he replied. 'But I will be watching over you with the Gods' grace.'

'Will I be able to sense when you're watching?' I asked, 'will I know?'

'You will know in here,' he touched his chest, over his heart, and then continued, 'I have prepared for you to be disguised when you depart. Those going with you will have aliases ready and will ensure that you are safe.'

I nodded and stood, preparing to take my leave.

'And do not worry about Erik,' Grandfather said as he rose and pulled me into a tight hug, 'I will make sure that he doesn't get into any trouble. Once he calms down, I am sure that he will realise that it is best for him to remain here.'

I nodded, not trusting myself to speak through the sudden onset of tears that began to trickle down my cheeks. Grandfather held me for a few moments longer and then released me, blue eyes crinkling into a knowing smile as he wiped my tears away.

'Remember that no matter what happens with the Dark Elves,' he said, 'to be yourself. You were born to be a queen, do not let them forget that.'

I curtseyed, fingers raised to my brow and lowered my gaze, back straight.

'I won't, Grandfather,' I murmured.

'I will bid you farewell in the morning,' he said, 'now go and get some rest. Lisette will take care of your belongings and will go with you.'

I nodded and left. The hallways were still full of people bustling around, preparations being made and as I headed towards my rooms, I felt many eyes following me.

Lisette was in the midst of packing when I arrived, and I noticed that she had already filled two trunks. I was surprised by how many things I owned now, having lived for so long with only enough to fit in a set of saddlebags.

'Don't forget to pack your own necessities, Lisette,' I said as I helped her fold some nightclothes. She clicked her tongue and indicated for me to leave her alone, and so I leaned back on the window seat, watching her quick, fastidious movements. It didn't take her long to finish, and I sent her away, urging her to see to her own needs and let me prepare myself for bed alone.

When Lisette was gone, I gazed around my bedchamber, surprised at how I was going to miss it. This room had become a sanctuary during my time with the Elven court, and I would miss looking out over the forest and Lowton in the distance. I picked up the now well-read letter Aidyn had left behind and traced its words. It seemed that the Gods had been listening after all, and I was being offered a second chance. This time I would do everything I could to ensure I won the Dark Elves over.

I knelt, bowing my head and sending out a prayer of thanks to the Gods. I asked for safe passage and for them to watch over Erik while I was gone. I hoped that Erik would forgive me for leaving him behind.

When I had finished my prayers, I stood and put the letter into one of the trunks and settled into my bed for the last time. Tomorrow would finally bring the change that I had been waiting for, and it was both an exciting and terrifying prospect.

Chapter Seven

Lisette woke me early, when the sky was still dark and the birds had not yet awoken. Still half asleep, I allowed her to dress me in a burgundy travelling dress and my father's cloak. My hair was braided and tied back in a coronet under the hood and my silver dagger was sheathed on my thigh. A breakfast tray of fruit had been prepared and I picked at it, feeling too queasy with nerves to have much of an appetite. Lisette watched over me like a mother hen, making sure that I ate something before allowing me to move. She indicated for two servants to take my trunks down to the stables and led the way.

There was a small gathering at the stables to see us off. Two wagons were being laden with crates and trunks under Rakael's watchful eye. Grandfather was at the front of the group, along with Elder Haycin and his council members. Stefan and the other trainees were also there, but I couldn't see Erik in the crowd.

'There you are, Nina,' Jesse called as she tightened the straps on one of the wagon horses.

Rakael turned at her words and ushered the servants to keep loading the wagon next to her. 'Good timing, Princess,' she said, 'we are just about ready to go.'

Lisette and I walked over to them and I paused in front of Grandfather.

'Travel safe, my dear,' he murmured, 'may the Gods bless you and the Lord of Spring watch over your journey. I look forward to when we will see each other again.'

Behind him, the assembled Elves bowed to me, fingers raised to their foreheads and I reciprocated the gesture. When I stood up, I asked, 'where is Erik?'

Grandfather shook his head sadly, 'he did not want to say farewell. He is still angry.'

I felt my chest tighten but nodded, biting back the pain that filled my heart. I would have liked to say goodbye, to let him know that I was sorry for what I had said and that all I wanted was for him to be safe.

'He will come around, Princess Wilhelmina,' Elder Haycin said quietly, 'just give him time. We will watch over him while you are gone.'

'Thank you,' I said, turning abruptly so that they would not see the tears in my eyes. Lisette gripped my hand and led me onto the wagon. I baulked before getting in, twisting around to Rakael, 'Where's Dolce?'

She regarded me coolly, 'the horses have already left. One of our riders went ahead with them. They will join us at the next leg of the journey. For now, we will be travelling as a group of merchants.'

She pulled herself up into the driving seat and handed the reins to the guard next to her. Reluctantly I allowed Lisette to nudge me into the back of the wagon, where she and Jesse joined me. To my surprise, Dylan vaulted into the spot beside me, pushing a rucksack full of rolled up scrolls and clinking jars into one of the free gaps between the trunks. For once he looked like he had slept, and his face was alight with excitement. Our driver, who was one of my usual guards, flicked the reins and the wagon began to jolt forwards. I watched Grandfather raise his hand in farewell and waved back, scanning the crowd in the hope of seeing Erik appear, until we turned in the road and the farewell party was no longer in sight.

'Do you have everything you need, Dylan?' Jesse asked casually as we moved away, 'Rakael will not be happy if we need to turn back. She wants to depart with the morning tide.'

'Yes, yes, yes,' Dylan answered impatiently, 'I've triple checked against the list she so thoughtfully provided.' A touch of disapproval coloured his tone and then he looked at me and clarified, 'I was given a list of what to bring. Rakael seemed to think that it was necessary.' He sniffed disdainfully.

'She didn't think the rain stick was important, no,' Jesse grinned, and I could tell she was enjoying herself.

'She clearly doesn't understand that the spirits require the rain stick to bless our journey,' Dylan said pointedly. 'Just because she is not a believer in their power doesn't mean that she should dismiss them entirely.'

Jesse rolled her eyes and met my inquisitive gaze, recognising the question that I didn't want to voice. 'He's one of the few who knows about the Dark Elf culture,' she said bluntly, 'he can read the Ancient Tongue and is a hazard to himself if left unsupervised.'

I held back a laugh as Dylan spun around, outraged. 'I am perfectly capable of handling myself, thank you Jesse Rider.'

She shrugged good naturedly and grinned at me. Dylan huffed and sat back, arms folded in pointed disapproval.

'Well, we're lucky to have you joining us then,' I said, 'although it is surprising that you're leaving your books for this.'

'I didn't really have much of a choice,' he grumbled and then perked up as an idea came into his head. 'But this means that I will get the chance to study the Dark Elves and perhaps learn more about the Sigilium stones.'

'Or you could work on finding something that will help the cause,' Rakael interrupted from the front of the wagon, her voice terse. 'Don't forget that your first duty is to supporting your people, scholar.'

Dylan glared at her back and I made sure that when I spoke it was low enough for Rakael to not hear. 'Hopefully you will have time to do both, Dylan.' He gave a small, grateful smile in response.

We settled into silence, and I watched the forest pass us by, slowly thinning out until we had entered the outskirts of Lowton. By now, the sky was beginning to show the grey light that precedes sunrise. The town was starting to awaken around us as we rolled through the cobbled streets. I kept my face averted, hood up, but I could hear the sounds of early morning market stall owners beginning to set up their wares. Several voices called out greetings to our wagons as we passed and Rakael and our drivers replied in kind. The sound of gulls soon filled the air and I could smell the salty spray of the ocean. It was only when we had halted at the docks that I belatedly realised that we would be travelling by sea for the first leg of our journey. The Dark Elves had after all made part of their trip by boat, so it made sense that we would also be following the same route. But dear Gods I hoped we wouldn't be using the same vessel.

'Jess,' I whispered urgently as Rakael and the guards began to get down from the front of the wagon, 'which ship…'

But she had already jumped down and was starting to lift down the trunks with Lisette. Dylan eyed me closely and I felt myself flushing with embarrassment.

'I have been guaranteed discretion,' I overheard Rakael muttering to one of the Resistance guards, a man who I had seen before but never actually spoken to. 'He's done some work for us in the past and always been reliable. But keep your eyes open for anything.'

'Are you coming?' Jesse asked me as she lifted down another trunk. 'We need to get aboard before there are too many people about.'

I swallowed painfully, 'yes, I'll be just a second.' Dylan followed her, his rucksack clutched in one arm like it was a child. He turned and held out a hand to me. I took it, touched by the gesture, and stepped down cautiously. When I was standing at the roadside, I made sure that my face was well and truly hidden. The wind was biting and pulled at my hood, trying to flick it back, but I held on tight.

'Let's go,' Rakael said abruptly, and she began to lead the way down the dock towards a ship that was all too familiar. I stopped moving and Lisette bumped into me. She glanced at my expression, looked at our destination, and then wrapped an arm around me and drew me onwards. She nudged my face lower and led me, guiding me around the sailors who were heading towards the wagons to assist with the trunks. My heart was pounding, and as I approached the man at the end of the dock I wondered if he would know I was there. Would he recognise me?

'Ah, Captain,' Rakael's voice called out, 'I'm glad you got our message. We will need to depart as soon as possible.' I heard the jingle of coins and a grunt of satisfaction.

'Very good my lady. I'll have my men show you to your quarters. We don't put on any fancy airs for anyone, no matter their station.' The voice was terse and sharp, much like it had been months before. I squeezed my eyes shut and cursed silently. The Gods clearly had a sense of humour.

'That suits us just fine,' Rakael said smoothly, and I wondered what story she had told him. 'How long would you say…'

'Oh heavens above,' Markus' irritated voice interrupted, 'what in the hells are *you* doing here?'

I froze mid-step and then realised that he wasn't speaking to me. I lifted the edge of my hood and peeked up, watching the scene.

'I didn't think we would have the good fortune of transporting the Scholar of Winterdale again.' Markus' tone dripped with sarcasm.

'Captain,' Dylan said stiffly, 'how pleasant to see you again.'

Markus snorted and then turned back to Rakael, 'the price just went up.'

During the ensuing argument, Lisette pulled me on board and we followed one of the sailors who led us to the two main passenger cabins. I stood shaking in the room, shocked that I had passed him and he hadn't known. A part of me had wondered if he would sense something– anything– but no, it seemed that discussions regarding the price of passage had been the only thing he could think about.

Lisette wrapped me in a warm hug and rubbed my back gently, calming the turbulent feelings that being in Markus' proximity had raised. When we heard footsteps coming down the hallway, I drew away and turned to look out of the porthole. There were a few heavy thuds and some trunks were deposited by the side of the door.

'By the Gods those were heavy,' Jesse's voice gasped, 'what on earth have you got in there?'

I shrugged, 'Lisette wouldn't let me help with packing. Ask her.'

'Very funny,' Jesse said wryly as Lisette smiled.

'Did we need to choose *this* ship?' I asked quietly as Jesse came to stand next to me, already beginning to set up the hammocks.

'I wondered if it was the one you took from Scardia,' she replied, 'once the captain saw Dylan, he didn't look happy.'

No, I couldn't imagine that Markus was happy. Dylan hadn't exactly made the passage over the Meridian easy for anyone.

'I guess I hoped we would be using a different vessel,' I murmured as a sailor entered with two more trunks balanced on his shoulders.

'I must admit,' Jesse said, 'I can see why there was *something* between you both. He's quite appealing, if you like rough sailors.'

I shot her a glare and she bit back a laugh, 'Sorry. I just don't see how you and he, well…' Her voice drifted off and she looked away.

'What we may have been is something that cannot be possible,' I said, wishing that my stomach would stop twisting in knots at the thought of the 'what ifs'. 'How did you know, anyway?'

She shot me a comical look, 'Erik. And it was clear that you were working hard to take your mind off someone.'

'Who doesn't Erik tell?' I muttered and then registered everything she had said. 'Was it that obvious?'

Jesse shrugged unhelpfully. 'I think only to people who knew, besides,' her mouth twisted into a mockery of a smile, 'I know what it's like to focus on something else in the hope that you will forget someone.'

I wanted to ask more, but at that moment Rakael stomped into the room and shut the door with a sharp click.

'I am never,' she growled, 'going to bring that damned scholar anywhere. Ever. Again.'

'How much did you have to adjust the price?' Jesse asked, moving away from me and perching on one of the hammocks.

'I managed to convince that *man*,' Rakael said curtly, 'to only accept double the initial price. He wanted triple.'

'Well, we're lucky you could negotiate it down,' Jesse said soothingly, 'did he say how long it would take to get to the Lagoon?'

'Lagoon?' I asked, 'what Lagoon?'

Rakael sighed, 'the Karoni Lagoon is the furthest we will be able to go by sea. From there we will need to cut through to the Ombre Mountains. It should only be a few days, weather permitting. The Dark Elves should send someone to meet us when we arrive.'

'Don't you think the ship's crew will suspect something?' I pressed, 'they've already taken the Dark Elves back and forth and now we go coincidentally to the same location.'

'They are paid not to notice anything,' Rakael said oppressively, 'but I don't want to take any risks with you, Nina. You need to stay in here for the whole trip. Jesse and Lisette will make sure you get meals.'

The indignation rose in me, but a cowardly part of me was privately glad to hide in the cabin for the journey. If I stayed here, Markus wouldn't know I was on board.

'We will spread the word that you are ill,' Rakael continued, 'nothing contagious but something that leaves you fatigued enough to be a recluse.'

'Well thanks,' I said sarcastically, 'I can tell you put a lot of thought into it.'

'We need to keep you away from prying eyes,' Rakael said bluntly, 'and the less you are out and about the easier that will be. Do I have your word that you will stay here?'

I nodded and turned back to the porthole, not wanting to ponder too much on how the next few days would go.

'Jesse, we need to make sure everything is safely in the hold,' Rakael continued, 'Lisette, I have volunteered you to assist in the galley. Apparently, we need to help on the boat as well as pay double the required amount to compensate this captain.' She sniffed disdainfully and left, followed by Lisette and Jesse.

When the door shut I let out the breath that I hadn't been aware I was holding. I pressed my head against the thick glass and gazed out, trying to figure out what was happening through the sea spray. It looked like the ropes were being cast off from the dock, but I was too far away to hear the shouting I knew would be coming from the helm.

It was going to be a long few days, I thought bleakly. Yes, I was hidden away from the crew and captain in this room, but I would most likely be alone, bored out of my mind and unable to escape. I doubted Lisette had packed any books for light reading during the voyage, but perhaps Dylan would have something I could borrow to pass the time with. After all, he had had a rucksack bursting with scrolls and books. Surely there would be something in there that would help pass the time.

I waited a few moments, did I check if he was next door now, while the sailors were on deck, or did I wait until later?

But now the idea was stuck in my brain and by the Gods I had never been very patient. I moved to the door and leaned against it, listening closely. Everything was quiet and I gathered that now was as good a time as any. I opened the door gently and peered into the hallway, noted approvingly that it was empty and ducked out and into the men's cabin.

There were less trunks in this cabin, and I realised that the majority of our baggage must be in the hold. Luckily, Dylan's rucksack was there, leaning against the wall. I edged closer and opened it carefully, seeing with delight that several tomes were wedged underneath the tightly wrapped scrolls. I opened them and my sense of victory fell away, as I skimmed through page after page of runes. Dejected, I replaced them in the bag and left it where I had found it, moving back into the hallway to head back to my cabin.

I didn't hear anything, but I sensed a movement out of the corner of my eye as I opened my door. I turned, curious, and saw Viktor, a large bag of produce in his arms on his way to the galley. Luckily he wasn't looking in my direction, but his presence was enough to startle me to step inside and shut the door quickly.

I barely had a moment to calm myself because a loud commotion soon filled the hallway. I couldn't quite hear what was being said but recognised Rakael's voice, crossly arguing with a male one. Heavy footsteps moved closer and I stepped away from the door quickly, just before it was abruptly opened and a slight figure was thrust inside, stumbling and falling onto the floorboards.

'We cannot turn back now,' Rakael was snapping angrily.

'The Captain doesn't like stowaways,' the sailor growled from next to her. 'Extra mouths cost more to feed.'

I didn't watch Rakael turn on the sailor, but instead knelt beside the crumpled figure on the ground. His eyes were tightly scrunched up and my heart dropped.

'Erik?' I whispered, lightly gripping his shoulder, 'by the Gods, what are you doing here?'

He flinched at my touch but I held on, gently tugging him to sit up and face me. As he lifted himself up, I noticed that he gripped his stomach, and his face was red and swollen. I was reminded suddenly of the first time I had seen him, a beaten down waif with nowhere to go and no one to protect him. My hand shook as I touched his cheek and he winced.

'What happened?' I asked, dread slowly spreading through my veins. He didn't say anything, just shot a swift, frightened look at the sailor before glancing back at the ground. The dread turned to fury and I rose to my feet, trying to control the anger that was desperate to be unleashed. I wanted to make the sailor pay for what he had done.

The door slammed and Rakael turned to us, breathing heavily.

'A brilliant idea, Erik,' she said furiously, 'what possessed you to *do* such a stupid thing? Thanks to you, we've now got to triple the cost of our passage and you've caused a scene. The captain will be hearing about this and then he will have *questions.*' She glared at him and I stepped in-between them quickly.

'Haven't you seen what that sailor did?' I demanded, 'look at him.'

'I saw everything,' Rakael said curtly, 'Erik had decided that it would be a good idea to hide in one of our storage crates and when he was caught, he tried to put up a fight.'

'He hit me first,' Erik mumbled.

'You snuck onto the ship after being explicitly told you were to stay with the other trainees,' Rakael spat out, 'you've put us in a difficult predicament and don't think I'll forget it.

If I hadn't vouched for you, that sailor would have been well within his rights to toss you overboard.'

'I'll make sure he doesn't get into any more trouble,' I interjected.

'Keep him out of sight,' Rakael's tone was icy, 'if we weren't in a hurry to reach our destination before the new moon, I would send him back. If he causes any more trouble on this voyage, I'll toss him overboard myself.'

'You won't touch him,' I snarled, stepping closer until we were nose to nose. 'Don't even think of it.'

'Don't test me, Princess,' she retorted, 'you know as well as I do that where we are going is not a safe place for a child. We cannot risk him causing more trouble.'

'He won't,' I said coldly, 'but you won't hurt him.'

She sniffed, tossed a small bag onto the ground beside Erik and left. I paused for a moment, amazed that she hadn't argued further.

I turned to Erik and eyed him closely. 'You shouldn't have snuck aboard, you know,' I said and he glared at the floor. 'But I must admit,' I continued, sitting down in one of the hammocks, 'that I'm glad you're here.'

He turned to me slowly and said, 'you're not angry with me?'

I chuckled, 'of course I'm angry. I told you not to come and you came anyway. Rakael is right in saying that the Ombre Mountains and the Underdark will be dangerous.'

'But?' Erik prompted, sitting next to me cautiously.

'But,' I smiled despite myself, 'I think I'm angrier with that sailor who hit you.'

He hung his head again and said, 'he heard me moving. I couldn't stay still any longer and he opened the crate and I couldn't move.' His eyes were shadowed, lost in the past and I took his hand, anchoring him back in the moment.

'I know what it's like to be caught off-guard by the demons in our memories,' I murmured softly, 'but we can't let them control us. That's something I'm still learning to do myself.' He looked at me and nodded. 'But for now,' I continued, 'you can keep me company. I thought I'd be dying of boredom over the next few days stuck in this cabin alone.'

He gave a small smile, rolled his eyes and I laughed, relieved that he was starting to return to his usual self.

'How did you sneak away?' I asked curiously, 'it must have been hard to get past the guards.'

He shrugged, 'They weren't paying too much attention to the crates that had already been packed. I just waited until they had gone and then pulled one of the empty crates over to the pile of filled ones. I lifted up the lid and got in.' He grinned, 'I needed to curl up really tightly though, and then I just had to wait and hope that they wouldn't notice that there was an extra crate.'

'You can't have been expecting to stay in the crate for the whole trip though,' I said, and he shrugged again.

'I knew I'd need to come out eventually, but I thought I could last a bit longer.'

I eyed him sympathetically, 'I'm guessing you got in the crate and realised that you would be bored senseless with nothing to do?'

'I brought this,' he mumbled, withdrawing my well-read book of Scardian lore from his bag. I traced the familiar title as he said, 'I thought that you hadn't told me all the stories yet and it didn't feel right to leave it behind.'

'I think you would be able to read the stories yourself now,' I replied. 'You don't need me to teach you to read anymore.'

He shrugged, 'you read much faster than I do. The words still get stuck in my head sometimes.' I smiled and took the book into my hands, flicking it open to one of my favourite chapters: the tale of the Winter Spirit. Even though I knew the tale by heart I still read from the page, knowing that Erik was following the words as I voiced them and, for the first time since we boarded Markus' ship, I felt calm.

Chapter Eight

I was grateful when, later in the day, it was Lisette who brought us our midday and evening meals instead of Rakael. She gave Erik a sharp glare and shook her head, which he responded to with a sheepish grin and shuffling feet. I wasn't surprised to see that the fare was meagre, a simple bowl of soup and hard biscuits to soak it up. Erik finished his food in half the time it took me to do so, and eventually I let him finish mine as well. My anxiety grew throughout the day as I wondered when Markus would hear about the stowaway boy. Surely he would come to find out what had happened personally? He had always been invested in knowing what was going on aboard his ship.

Jesse and Rakael joined us as the sun set, Rakael pointedly ignoring Erik and he resolutely did the same. He seemed relieved when I suggested that he go into the men's cabin and set up his hammock, and left almost immediately. As the door shut, Rakael relaxed marginally and lay down, arms folded, staring at the ceiling.

'Erik's presence makes keeping the Captain oblivious to our task significantly more difficult,' she finally said, almost as though we had been mid-conversation, and I blinked in surprise. 'He's already requested to visit the "stowaway",' she sighed, 'and considering his persistence, I won't be able to keep him away for much longer.'

'If he recognises Erik,' Jesse asked quietly, 'what happens then?'

'He will recognise him,' I said resignedly, 'he would recognise both of us, he was like an older brother to Erik on the trip over– Erik idolises him. Once he realises that Markus is the Captain you were talking about, I'm certain he'll want to see him.'

'I thought you would have told him whose ship we were on,' Jesse said, surprised.

I shook my head, 'I think he might suspect, but there are some new crew members, such as the sailor who found him, so he wasn't recognised.'

My forehead creased as I thought about what would happen when Markus found out Erik was on board. He would have so many questions and would demand answers and– my stomach twisted painfully– he would surely know that I was here too.

'If only you had been discreet on your trip over the Meridian,' Rakael sighed grumpily, and I felt myself flush in angry response.

'*You* were the one who chose this vessel to take us to the Karoni Lagoon.'

'And how was *I* supposed to know that you had been indiscreet with the captain?' Rakael retorted, and I felt my blush deepen.

'We need to come up with a plan,' Jesse interrupted, 'bickering and arguing isn't going to get us anywhere.'

'Let me sleep on it,' Rakael said curtly, 'It's been a long day. I'll be thinking more clearly in the morning.'

Jesse nodded slowly and rolled into her hammock, 'All right.' She yawned, 'on that note I think we should all call it a day and sleep.'

I was tempted to get into my own hammock and sleep too, having woken up so early I was tired. However, I had been stuck inside the cabin all day and was desperate for a moment outside its four walls. Lisette met my eyes from across the room and I knew she could sense my discomfort. She gestured for me to sit beside her, and I obeyed. Together we looked out of the porthole and watched the sunset fade, the faint colours turning to darkness as night fell.

By the time the sky outside was dark, Rakael and Jesse's breathing had become heavy and slow, and I knew that they were asleep. Lisette rose quietly and handed me my cloak, indicating in the gloom for me to put it on. As the hood fell around my face, Lisette opened the door gently and we stepped out into the hallway. She led the way, finding her way with surprising surety in the darkness, and soon we had reached the hold.

The hold was packed with crates, even more than there had been on the trip across the Meridian. The stall where Dolce had been held during our first crossing was filled with wooden boxes, piled one on top of another.

'Thank you, Lisette,' I murmured, 'I just needed to get out of that room.'

She smiled at me, bobbed her head and held up one finger with sudden sternness.

'I have one hour?' I guessed and she nodded, made a gesture to indicate that she would return, and left.

I breathed out and sank down, leaning against the crates in Dolce's former stall. I had known it would be pointless to hope that I could go on deck– there was always at least one sailor up there keeping watch– but the sense of being confined was overwhelming. I crossed my legs and closed my eyes, breathing deeply and slowly, allowing my mind to clear and calm.

The silence around me was peaceful and I allowed my eyes to open gradually and observed the single tendril of flame rise up off my palm. It rolled around my forearm in lazy circles, twisting and encasing me in a flickering glow. I missed being able to scry, to distract myself with what was happening elsewhere. But since I couldn't practise that magic, I made do with what I was able to accomplish in a tight space. It took a lot of concentration to make sure the fire didn't touch any of the crates or walls, the last thing I wanted was to be responsible for setting the ship aflame.

The flame moved from my arm and began to dance in the space before my eyes and I watched, enthralled, as it responded instinctively to my thoughts. I allowed it to form images, from a galloping horse to a fish, to a bird whose wings stretched out wide as it flew around the space. I studied it closely, noting its long-plumed tail and sharply curved beak. As I watched, I recognised it as the image that had been pressed into the wax on Aidyn's letter.

There was a gasp and hurried footsteps moved towards my location. It was Lisette, who made hasty gestures for me to follow. The fire bird hovered a few instants longer and then flew towards my chest. I froze in shock as it disappeared into me and I felt a jolt, akin to the sensation of placing one's hand either into a flame or icy water. The hold was cast back into darkness and Lisette reached for my arm and led me none too gently away. As we climbed back into the main hallway, which was faintly lit by lanterns, Lisette's wide eyes searched my face. She gripped me and glanced over me, as if making sure that I was alright.

'I'm *fine*,' I whispered, 'Honestly, Lisette.'

Her eyebrows drew together in a frown and she watched me with concern. I realised that my free hand was holding my chest, right over the spot where the bird had disappeared. The shock had begun to seep away, but I was left with confusion about what had happened.

'Have you ever seen anything like that before?' I asked her quietly, and she shook her head.

'Excuse me ladies,' a voice called from behind us. 'Is there anythin' I can do to assist you?' I didn't recognise the voice but dipped my head as the man approached.

Lisette shook her head, making to lead me on, but then she froze, gazing at something over my shoulder. Her grip on me tightened, warning me not to speak.

'Emerson, why aren't you at your post?' A familiar voice cut in, and I felt myself sway slightly.

'I thought I heard something below, Cap'n,' the sailor answered.

'I will check on it,' Markus answered, and the sailor moved away. I looked down, keeping my face averted. Lisette's fingers were biting into my arm painfully and I tried not to wince.

'I wouldn't recommend wandering around the ship after nightfall,' Markus said coolly, 'I will escort you back to your cabin.'

Lisette gave a sharp nod and pulled me hard so that I nearly stumbled. A different hand clasped my other elbow, steadying me and I gave a small bob of my head in thanks.

'You must be the bedridden patient,' Markus said wryly, and I could feel his eyes inspecting me. I gave another short nod. 'Well, make sure that you don't cause us any trouble and we won't have any problems.' He continued curtly as we made our way towards the cabin door.

When we reached the door, I held my breath as Lisette opened it and slipped inside.

'Perhaps we will see each other again,' Markus said casually, 'if you are feeling well enough to leave your cabin.' I inclined my head again and made to move inside, but he caught my wrist, pausing me. 'Have we met before?' he asked quietly, so that only I could hear him.

I shook my head, pulling the hood closer so that it covered most of my features as he twisted me to face him. For the first time in months, I looked into his eyes and held my breath, waiting for him to recognise me.

Instead, his eyes scanned mine and then he looked away, confused. 'Forgive me,' he muttered, 'I thought… but clearly, I was mistaken. Good night.' He gave a short bow and stepped back, and I watched him depart, stunned. A hand reached out from the cabin and yanked me inside, shutting the door and cutting off my last sight of Markus heading away.

'He didn't recognise me, Lisette,' I whispered, as she began to prepare for bed. I was astounded, unable to fathom how he hadn't known instantly. 'How did he not know me?' I murmured, more to myself than Lisette, who clicked her tongue at me impatiently.

I sank into my hammock but did not sleep easily. Seeing him had brought back all of the memories and feelings that I had tried to suppress; all the pain, anger and hurt. But also the wonder, the thrill, that had once been there whenever he was nearby. When sleep finally did come, it was disrupted by dreams and bad memories.

When I awoke, I was alone. I didn't mind and washed myself with the leftover water and soap which had been left in a corner of the room. I shivered and dressed quickly, pulling on the same dress that I had worn the day before. Lisette might raise her eyebrows in disapproval, but I was used to wearing the same clothing while travelling, and the idea of wearing the finery I knew she had packed did not seem like a good one. Almost as if she had known I was thinking about her, there was a tap at the door and Lisette entered.

She picked up the cleaning supplies and looked at me closely. I could tell that she was wanting to make sure that I was alright after the previous night, the strange incident with the fire bird and then the meeting with Markus.

'I'm fine, Lisette,' I said calmly, wondering why I seemed to keep repeating the same thing, while feeling such a plenitude of emotions. She sniffed as if she could tell I wasn't being completely honest, but nodded and left, shutting me back in the cabin.

I began to do some stretches and exercises, which were just about possible within the tight space. I may not be able to practise fencing or archery, but I could at least make sure that my body would be ready to continue training once we arrived in the Underdark. Who knew what tests they would have for me to prove myself once we arrived?

By the time Erik came in, I was well and truly wishing that I had put on my tunic and breeches. He watched me struggle to push myself up from the floor and then joined in effortlessly. I sat up, disgusted at the ease in which he was able to do it, wiping the sweaty strands of hair out of my eyes.

'Don't stop just because I'm here,' he joked, and I rolled my eyes.

'I'll have you know I've been doing this for a lot longer than you have this morning,' I retorted, 'Give it a half hour or so and you might start to feel like I do.'

'I doubt it,' he smirked.

I sighed and rolled my eyes again, 'why did I not let you get tossed overboard?'

'Because you knew that I needed to come along?' Erik said, and I chuckled.

'In hindsight, I'm surprised that I didn't expect you to find some way to join us,' I said.

'All knights need to go on quests,' he replied, and I had to bite back another laugh.

'I thought you needed to focus on training and becoming a squire before thinking about knighthood,' I replied, trying and failing to keep the teasing note out of my voice. He didn't answer and I pressed on, 'after all, it's important for key values to be instilled in the squires. Such as honesty, loyalty, *patience*,' I ticked them off on my fingers, watching him out of the corner of my eye, 'and don't forget of course, the ability to follow orders and instructions.'

'Anyone can follow orders,' he muttered, 'but if they're *stupid* orders…'

'I thought knights were supposed to follow their monarch's orders *no matter what*,' I grinned and poked his shoulder on each word. He swiped my hand away and sat up opposite me, pushing his hair out of his eyes. I was relieved to see that the swelling from yesterday had gone down and there didn't seem to be any bruising.

'I don't like Rakael,' Erik said bluntly, 'And we need to stick together.'

As I met his gaze, I recognised that on this he was resolute, no matter what happened, he would stay with me. The thought both warmed my heart and made me worry; what if I couldn't protect him and the unthinkable happened?

'You can't stop me from coming with you,' he continued, almost as though he had read my mind. 'It's my job to make sure you're safe.'

I could have argued with him. I could have pointed out that there were many others– older, better trained and more experienced– who could protect me better than a pre-adolescent boy could. But I didn't. I didn't want to push him away anymore. I might not entirely like that he was walking into danger, but at least I would be at his side.

I held out my hand for him to take. 'Promise? We'll stay together throughout this, no matter what?'

He grinned and shook it. 'Deal.'

'How charming,' a sarcastic voice said from the doorway, and I looked up to see Rakael, one of her guards beside her.

'What do you want?' Erik scowled at her. She clucked her tongue in disapproval.

'Manners, Erik. I need to speak with you, come.' She walked out and indicated for him to follow. He looked at me, eyebrows raised in disbelief at her commanding tone.

'Try to stay on her good side,' I urged quietly, gesturing for him to stand up. 'She *is* the leader of the Resistance after all.'

He rolled his eyes and got to his feet, 'see you later.'

'Bye,' I murmured as the door shut behind him. I looked around dispiritedly, and then an idea struck me. If I was going to be alone for a while, then there was no harm in seeing if I could conjure the fire bird again. After all, if I had managed to keep the magic contained last night then I would be able to do so again. There had been something about it that entranced me, and I wanted to know more about it.

My heart was beating faster in anticipation as I straightened my back and rested my palms on my knees. I closed my eyes, picturing the flame in my mind as I willed it into existence. There was a flickering warmth and when I opened my eyes the flame was dancing in the air, hovering in front of my chest. My forehead creased in concentration and it began to change, forming a small sphere which gradually rotated around and around.

'You have come a long way, child.'

I almost lost control of the flame. It dipped down towards the floorboards before I reclaimed my equilibrium and it rose again to levitate in front of my eyes. Taking a calming breath, I turned and saw the Winter Spirit, standing beside the porthole. Her luminous eyes crinkled with amusement and she smiled.

'My lady.' I was grateful that my voice managed not to quiver or break in surprise. 'I didn't expect... I thought I wouldn't see you again.'

Her smile widened and she moved beside me, brushing my hair maternally away from my face. The skin she touched stung from the cold and soon turned numb.

'I have been watching over you,' she said, 'watching you push yourself day after day to become what you are expected to be.'

'My grandfather and the Resistance have been eager to train me,' I replied cautiously, uncertain from her tone whether she approved or not. 'I have been doing my best.'

'I know, Nina,' she said, tilting my chin upwards towards her. 'But you are still human. You have made much progress in a short time and your magic is starting to reveal its true nature.' She indicated the sphere which had started to morph into different shapes again.

As we watched, it changed into a smaller version of the firebird from the night before. It spread its wings and swept around the room, flickering with ethereal light.

'It seems that the Ice Flame is not so easily snuffed out,' the Winter Spirit said softly, 'no matter how hard Lord Niall tries to do so.'

'Is that bird the Ice Flame?' I asked, unsure. In all my memories, the Ice Flame had burnt behind the throne in the palace. It hadn't extinguished when my father died, as I lived on. As far as I knew, it continued to smoulder in the Throne Room, the ever-present reminder to the Usurper that he was not the true ruler. How, then, could it be here?

The Winter Spirit laughed, a light, tinkling sound that seemed out of place coming from her. 'No, child. It is merely an extension of the Ice Flame. The Lord of Summer's choice of gift for you was intriguing to say the least. It is an unstable gift, which many in the past have tried and failed to tame. But you have been developing your control day by day, it is only the beginning of the evolution of your powers.'

I felt a small tingle of pride at her words and smiled. There was a sharp burst of warmth on my shoulder and I realised that the firebird had perched there. It wasn't heavy and surprisingly it wasn't lighting my clothing aflame. The Winter Spirit reached out and touched the bird's head with the tip of her finger and I felt a strong vibration through the bird's taloned feet. The sensation continued rising intensely so that it was almost painful.

'What did you do?' I asked as the bird gripped tighter and I sat, paralysed, as the vibrations sent wave after wave of painful intensity through me.

She smiled but didn't immediately reply. Meanwhile I was trying to remain calm, to not focus too much on the new sensations.

'You will need additional protection in the Underdark,' she said finally, just as I was on the verge of asking her again. 'The Dark Elves are a powerful force if they support you, but there is a long history of them fighting amongst themselves. Only a leader who is strong and has a sharpened wit and cunning can successfully lead them and earn the respect of each major House.'

I made a mental note to ask Dylan to sit with me and explain everything he knew about the Dark Elves' hierarchy. I didn't want to pester the Winter Spirit with such questions, but it would be important to learn as much as I could before we arrived at the Ombre Mountains.

'They have been fighting amongst themselves for many years, and only recently have formed an alliance under the leadership of their current King. You must make sure to win his favour as there are sure to be those amongst his court who favour Lord Niall.'

'Has he sent envoys to the Underdark as well?' I asked uneasily. The bird's talons tightened imperceptibly on my shoulder, and I felt slightly comforted.

'You should expect that he has,' the Winter Spirit said gravely. 'Be careful who you trust when you're there, Nina. Follow your instincts.'

I opened my mouth to ask another question, but she held up a hand to silence me.

'I have protected you as best I can,' she said, 'Lord Niall's followers will not be able to harm you so easily now.'

'What have you done?' I asked again, noting that the persistent shocking current was now fading slightly in intensity. Yet I still felt strangely energised and alert, my heart pounding as if I had been running fast down a steep hill.

'I have merely unlocked *my* gifts to you,' she murmured, her body beginning to fade away into the aether.

'But…' I began, but then cut myself off as the Winter Spirit smiled enigmatically and vanished, leaving me yet again with more questions than answers.

'I wish *you* could tell me what she did,' I muttered to the firebird, as it tossed its head and began to circle the room again. I watched it, brow slightly creased in concentration as I urged it to return to perch on my outstretched arm. I was so focussed on the firebird that I didn't immediately notice the sounds from outside, and it wasn't until the door crashed open that I reacted, jumping in surprise. The firebird morphed back into a sphere as I lost control; it flared and then absorbed back into my chest, leaving me winded.

'*Witch*,' a deep voice cried, and rough hands grabbed me, yanking me harshly to my feet and dragging me away. I felt dazed and unable to focus on what was happening around me.

'I told you these people were trouble,' another voice grunted as another pair of arms grabbed my upper arm, pinching far too tightly as they pulled me on. 'No good, the lot of 'em.'

'Let me go,' I cried, trying to break out of their grip, but they only pulled harder and one slapped me across the face. The impact was enough to twist my head to the side, my ears rang and my vision clouded for a moment as the sharp pain made my eyes swell with tears. I blinked them away, not wanting to show weakness, and looked up at them. One was the sailor who had found Erik. The other was large and beefy, and I remembered him from our original voyage across the

Meridian. He had barely spoken to me, but had patiently taught Erik how to tie a range of nautical knots; I hadn't thought he would be the sort of man to do this.

'Shut up, witch,' he growled, and I realised that he didn't recognise me.

'I told the Captain, Elves are bad luck,' the other sailor spat on me and I scrunched up my eyes. I heard the sound of a door opening and frowned in concentration. There were two loud yelps and then I was toppling backwards, twisting and landing in a crumpled heap on the floor. There were a few gasps and then Rakael's angry voice said,

'What is the meaning of this? How dare...'

'Explain.' Markus' voice was equally angry.

'She's a witch,' one of the sailors said, 'caught her practising dark magic. She's bad luck. All those Elves do is bring destruction and suffering on those who go near 'em.'

'She attacked us first,' the other sailor added, 'burned us, she did.'

'I won't have your fellow passengers attacking my men.' Markus said coldly to Rakael, and I felt myself tense, furious that he was believing the sailors' lies.

'Perhaps they lied about her sickness so that we wouldn't find out that she was practising dark magic,' the sailor continued, his voice rising with maniacal energy. 'We should make an example of her, we should teach them all a lesson.'

'Your crew's bigotry is overwhelming, Captain,' Rakael snapped.

'I thought that this crew was supposed to be discreet,' Dylan's voice interjected with the bluster that I now recognised he used to hide nerves. 'How can you treat ladies this way?'

'Usually we are,' Markus said coolly, 'but we don't take too kindly to liars or witches in our midst.'

'But Markus…' Erik's voice piped up, before being abruptly silenced, possibly with one of Rakael's sharp glares.

'That fiend is not a lady,' one of the sailors who had brought me in growled.

'You should choose your words with more care,' Rakael said repressively, 'you do not know of what you speak.'

'I will not allow my men to be assaulted on my ship,' Markus answered doggedly.

My heart clenched and I felt the cold fury start to take over. My vision blurred and I felt the familiar energy tingle through my veins. So, he thought I was a witch now? I would make him regret that.

I finally had the strength to stand and face him properly, vaguely registering that the room was half full of people: Rakael, Erik, Dylan, Markus, Viktor and the Resistance guards and sailors. They stared at me, some with fear, others with wonder. Rakael looked both angry and resigned, but Markus' expression was inscrutable. Our eyes met and held, and I couldn't see a sign of recognition in his dark eyes. My chest felt empty and hollow, and the disappointment only heightened my emotions.

'So, it's true,' Markus murmured.

'You should be on your knees,' Jesse's voice spoke from the doorway behind me.

'I'm not kneeling to a witch,' one of the sailors muttered.

'She's not a witch,' Erik snapped, scowling at the sailor in question.

'She's an *Elf*,' the sailor retorted.

'She is your rightful queen,' Rakael said, pinning the sailors with a steady glare. 'You should be showing her due respect.'

Slowly, reluctantly, the sailors behind me sank to their knees, as did the others in the room. Markus was the last one to kneel, his expression still giving nothing away. As the room fell into silence, the heat haze dissipated and I felt the magic withdraw.

'Your men are not to share what they have seen here,' Rakael ordered Markus, 'her presence is to be kept secret.'

'I am aware,' he said curtly, his eyes fixed on the streak of white in my hair.

'You will be well compensated for your silence,' Jesse added smoothly, 'on the condition that your men no longer slander or manhandle the Princess.'

Rakael glanced at her, clearly unhappy with having to part with more gold, but nodded in acquiescence.

'You heard her, men,' Markus said, 'get back to work.'

The sailors left, grumbling and muttering amongst each other, casting me surreptitious glances which varied from guilty to distrustful. The Resistance members followed suit, perhaps to dissuade the sailors from sharing what they had learned with the rest of the crew.

Jesse patted my shoulder gently, and murmured, 'I'll get Lisette to take care of you.' She flashed a small grin and departed, indicating for Dylan and Rakael to join her. Erik came to my side, eyes wide as he scanned my face.

'I thought you were going to lose control,' he whispered, and then paused as Markus stood and walked towards us.

'Where is your sister, Erik?' Markus asked him, gripping his shoulder, knuckles white.

Erik blinked and glanced from Markus to me and back, before finally registering that Markus did not know me.

'She's… ah…' he began, but I interrupted.

'Dead.'

And it was true. The frightened girl Markus had known on that sea voyage, the one who was constantly running and scared to face her demons, who hadn't known the true depth of her potential power, was gone. The person I was now could not afford to dream about living the life of a farm girl named Karliah. She could not allow herself to fall in love with a captain, whose temperament changed with the tide.

Markus froze for a moment, and I saw a flicker of shock in his eyes before the familiar mask was back. He looked at Erik, who would not meet his gaze.

'I protect Nina now,' Erik said quietly, 'Karliah's gone.'

I felt a rush of gratitude. Markus stepped away abruptly, pulling his hand away from Erik's shoulder and moving to the table which he leaned against, palms down.

'I apologise for the way my crew treated you, Princess Wilhelmina,' he said, and I felt relief that he was changing the subject. 'I will make sure that for the remainder of your time here, you will be left alone. We will not spread word of your presence.'

'Thank you, Captain,' I replied and moved to the door, Erik at my side.

'If I may,' he said jerkily, 'I would like a private word.'

I paused and nodded for Erik to go ahead. Erik raised his eyebrows, shrugged and left, heading back towards the deck.

'Please shut the door,' he said and I did so, albeit unwillingly, before facing him. 'The boy might have told you that we had previously met.' Markus' voice was hard. 'I knew both him and his sister.'

'He had mentioned it,' I said uneasily. I didn't like spending any more time than necessary in his presence and couldn't be sure whether or not he truly did not know me.

'She was looking for family.' He continued. 'I believe that you also have family in the Eastern Lands.'

'I'm sure many people do,' I replied.

'Tell me how she died.' He demanded, still facing away from me, and I caught the edge of bitterness in his words.

I didn't know initially how to respond. But once the lie had been told, I couldn't take it back unless I wanted to explain everything. And, by the Gods, I didn't want to do that.

'Tell me,' he bit out, fists clenched on the table.

'She was killed,' I said, the old familiarity of telling untruths coming back to me like an old friend. 'She was caught by a Tracker.'

'I didn't think Trackers were in the Eastern Lands,' Markus said slowly.

'This one was looking for me.' At least in this I was truthful. 'She got mistaken for me. We have similar hair.'

'Hers was redder,' he spoke quietly, as if to himself. 'She kept it under a scarf, but it was red.'

I didn't know what to say to this.

He paused, perhaps realising that he had spoken aloud and then said, 'thank you for telling me.'

'It's best not to talk about it in front of Erik,' I murmured. 'The loss is painful.'

'I understand,' he replied. 'I suggest that you return to your cabin, Your Highness. I'm afraid we don't have much in the way of seeing to your comfort, we are a small vessel…'

'You don't need to put on airs and graces,' I interrupted quickly, 'I understand.'

My hand was on the door handle when his voice sliced through the air, 'wait.'

I heard him stride over and then his hands were on my shoulders, spinning me around until we were inches apart.

'Strange coincidences– all of this– but the strangest thing is that I feel like I know you.'

'You don't,' I whispered, suddenly terrified of the look in his eyes as they searched mine.

'I think you're lying,' he breathed. 'I think you have been lying for a long time.'

I pulled away, the familiar urge to run away kicking in too late. He smiled wryly as my back hit the door and I knew there was no easy escape this time. Then his hand reached out and pulled something around my neck. My heart dropped into the pit of my stomach as the copper coin on its threaded cord was lifted and dangled tauntingly before my eyes.

'I think,' Markus moved closer and his breath made me shiver, 'that you know exactly what I mean.'

I shook my head, unable to speak to confirm or deny his words. He chuckled softly and then his lips were on mine, kissing me like he had all those moons ago. I responded instinctively as his arms circled me, pinning me against the door. It felt almost as good as I had remembered.

But then my brain began to work again, and I was reminded of what had happened in the last months. Of the way we had parted. Of how he had eyed the barmaid in the scrying bowl. Of how there was no way I could love a man who I could never be with.

I pulled away, twisting my head to the side, gasping, 'no. Stop.'

He paused and then began to shake with cold, derisive laughter. 'I knew it.' Abruptly, he removed his arms and stalked back to the table. I watched him uneasily, trembling slightly.

'I admit, I was thrown off at first by the physical changes,' he waved at my face, 'not to mention the magic. The girl I knew was not like that, I told myself. She wasn't perfect but at least she was *human*.' He eyed me dispassionately, 'I barely recognise that girl anymore. Although she *was* quite an adept liar, she convinced me of things all too easily. But then I realised I was nothing but an amusement, a fool in her game. And I am nobody's fool.'

I watched him, stunned. I couldn't fathom what he was saying, couldn't understand how he had misinterpreted my feelings so badly.

'She was never honest,' Markus' voice was bitter. 'Not even with a new face was she honest. It seems that some things never change.'

'Markus…' I began, unsure of what I was going to say but knowing that I needed to say something.

'Oh, it's Markus now, is it?' He laughed again, and it pierced my heart like icy daggers. 'Forgive me, Your Highness.' He bowed mockingly.

'I know you're angry,' I whispered, 'But I can explain.' He smiled coldly.

'Angry, Your Highness? Of course not. I merely like knowing what the rules of the game you like to play are.'

I was starting to get angry now. '*You* kissed *me*. And you acted like there was nothing between us. You sent me away like I was a… a…'

'Everything you told me was a lie,' he spat, his mask now breaking to show the fury he had kept hidden.

'You made me feel like nothing after that night,' I hissed, crossing my arms to control the urge to go over and slap him. 'How was I to know that you were someone who I could trust? Do you have any idea what it is like to live day by day, not knowing if you will be caught or discovered and handed over to the Trackers? You have *no idea*.'

'I guess you'll never know what would have happened if you had told me the truth,' Markus said brusquely. 'You never took the *chance* to find out.'

'I guess not,' I snapped back, 'because, Gods help me, when you do discover the truth, all you can do is rain recriminations down on me.' He stared at me, eyes flashing. 'I don't know why it matters anyway,' I continued, voice rising hysterically, 'because once you got what you wanted, you were all too keen to get rid of me. And then you could sleep with whoever took your fancy. It *clearly* meant little to you, since you moved on so quickly. So it seems, in the end, the joke was on me, because I believed– albeit foolishly– that what happened between us actually *meant* something.'

It seemed that I had temporarily shocked him into silence. Satisfied that I had the final word, I spun and left the room, slamming the door behind me and racing back to my cabin where I allowed my tears to fall.

Chapter Nine

I don't know how long I cried for, but by the time I was done, I lay in the hammock, completely spent. It was then that Lisette came to find me, a basin of water and cloth in her hands. I sat up mutely and let her clean my face, staring blankly ahead until she cupped my cheeks and forced me to look at her. I didn't need to say anything because I could tell that she knew. Her eyes widened in concern and she enfolded me in a hug. She held me tightly and I began to feel the shock start to wear off and a warmth spread through me, easing the numbing cold that had set in as soon as I slammed Markus' door.

'He said I was playing a game with him,' I whispered brokenly, 'he said that I wasn't even *human.*' Lisette tensed slightly and continued to rock me gently back and forth, like I was a young child. 'Am I so changed?' I wondered aloud, 'I knew that we would not be able to be together but, deep down, I suppose I hoped that there might be a way.'

Lisette sniffed and caught my eye as if to say that I should stop dreaming and move on. She raised her eyebrows sardonically and motioned towards me, taking in everything from my puffy eyes to the coin necklace that I had been unknowingly twisting back and forth in my hands.

'Do you think I deserve this?' I asked her quietly, 'that I brought it on myself? Or that I need to go through this to become stronger?'

She quirked her head, reminiscent of the budgerigar that she had been for so long, and I was shaken by the truth that I saw in her eyes. She thought that I should be strong, that I had begun to change for the better and that I should remember this moving forward.

'But how can I act like nothing is wrong when I feel like this?' I burst out, gripping the coin so hard that my knuckles turned white. 'How can this pain be a *good* thing?'

She took my hands in her own and squeezed reassuringly, helping me to understand that no matter how long it would take, I would eventually be alright.

There was a sharp tap at the door and without a by your leave, Rakael and Jesse entered. Lisette let go of my hands and began to take charge of my hair instead. I appreciated that she stayed, feeling that I was too emotionally drained to be able to deal with Rakael's usual grim energy on my own.

'Well,' Rakael sighed, sinking down onto her own hammock, 'I suppose I should be grateful that the captain is happy to keep your presence on this ship a secret. Tobias and Leif were kind enough to persuade the crew to be discreet when we leave.'

I almost asked outright who Tobias and Leif were, before realising that they were two of the Resistance guards who were in our party. Seeing as the Resistance guards had barely spoken to me during the past few months, I was not surprised that I didn't know their names.

'I must admit though,' Rakael continued, 'that your demonstration in the captain's quarters was not helpful. Half of his crew are now convinced that you're a witch and the other half seem to believe that the Scardian heir is a Goddess of some sort.'

'Well, she has been blessed by two of the seasonal spirits,' Jesse cut in, mouth curved in a grin. 'We could use that to our advantage.'

'But our original plan of being discreet has crashed and burned spectacularly,' Rakael said bitterly.

'Figuratively speaking, of course,' Jesse interrupted flippantly, 'personally I'd rather Nina wait until we are off the ship before setting it aflame.'

'I'll keep that in mind,' I said, biting back a laugh.

'It isn't funny, Jesse,' Rakael snapped.

'Rakael,' Jesse sighed and stretched, 'We're going to arrive at the Karoni Lagoon within a day or so. There's no use worrying about what has been done. You should be thinking about how to win over the Dark Elves. They're the reason we're here, after all.'

'You're right,' Rakael said, her voice renewed with blazing energy. 'Nina, you need to spend time with Dylan before we arrive. He might actually prove himself useful by sharing what he knows about the Dark Elves with you instead of reading those dusty scrolls of his.'

'Why hasn't he been keeping me company since we started on the voyage then?' I asked, 'considering I was shut in the cabin the whole time.'

'He was continuing his research for the Resistance,' Rakael said repressively, and I knew there was no use in asking for more information. 'But since he has not been successful so far in those endeavours, he should focus on helping you to prepare for your presentation to the Dark Elf court.'

'I *am* curious to see what the Underdark is like,' Jesse mused, 'In Velkra we don't have many tales about Dark Elves, but from what I've heard in King Aegis' court, it sounds like few outsiders are welcomed there. Receiving an invitation is a rare opportunity.'

'Indeed,' Rakael said, 'And we cannot squander it.'

'We won't,' Jesse said calmly, catching my eye and shooting me a quick grin, 'so long as you remember to give Nina space to win them over. She can't work her magic— literally and figuratively— with you constantly being on her case.'

Rakael huffed in reluctant agreement, which I supposed was the best I was going to get from her. I nodded in thanks to Jesse who shrugged as if to say that it was no problem. I was grateful though, I would be more comfortable if Rakael didn't take it upon herself to push me to my limits.

'Well, we should probably go and send Dylan in,' Rakael finally said, grunting as she got to her feet. 'It's nearly time for lunch so we should head to the galley. Come on Jess.'

I didn't bother to ask if I could join them, I didn't want to go to the galley and be stared at by the sailors. I particularly didn't want to see Markus anytime soon.

'Will you bring my lunch to the cabin please, Lisette?' I asked as she finished twisting my braided hair and pinning it back. She patted my shoulder in agreement and left, leaving me alone for only a moment before Dylan entered, wiping some invisible dust off his monocle.

'I understand that I am now to play the role of tutor,' Dylan said stiffly, 'which in usual circumstances I would not have an issue with, however I do not appreciate being ordered around by *that woman*.' I just looked at him, fully aware that he was only complaining because Rakael was not there.

'You don't have to if you don't want to,' I finally said, when it was obvious that he was waiting for me fill the silence. 'But I would like to not look like a complete idiot when we arrive in the Underdark. It seems you're the only one with the knowledge to make sure that does not happen.'

He preened, affecting nonchalance, but I knew he was pleased with the compliment.

'I suppose,' he said carefully, still looking down at his pristine monocle, 'it couldn't hurt to give you a few pointers. A bit of contextual knowledge so that Scardia is justly represented, and so you don't become the laughingstock of the Ombre Court.'

I waited for a moment as he pondered that idea and then implored, 'please Dylan.'

'Using manners makes all the difference,' he sniffed, putting the monocle back into his waistcoat pocket.

I rolled my eyes, 'You just wish Rakael had asked you instead of ordering you around.'

'Who wouldn't?' he asked, as he sat down on one of the trunks, leaning against the wall. I nodded, conceding his point.

'What has Rakael been asking you to find?' I probed, and he sighed dramatically.

'As many formulas as possible to use in the coming war. She expects me to recreate them, but I'm merely a passable alchemist. I can decode what is in the Karshkan language, but it is hard to put their knowledge into practice. And since she learned that I can read the Ancient Tongue, she wants me to find older formulas. Nothing I find is ever enough, it seems.'

'I understand that feeling,' I said quietly. 'But once she's got what she wants, she should let you go on with your research, shouldn't she?'

He laughed hollowly, 'I am starting to believe that she will never be satisfied. I think she's obsessed.'

Considering how he had talked about his Sigilium Opiatus and his studies on the Sigilium stones, I thought it was pretty contradictory that he thought Rakael the one to be obsessed.

'At least you can take a break from that now, though,' I reasoned, trying desperately to get the conversation back on track. 'Surely what you know about the Dark Elves cannot be explained all in one afternoon.'

'That will depend on how much you would find useful,' he said, eyeing me critically as if appraising my intellectual capabilities. I met his gaze and held it firmly.

'Nina,' a small voice came from the doorway, 'I have your lunch.'

It was Erik. He looked curiously at Dylan and came in with two bowls, placing one before each of us.

'You can stay if you like, Erik,' I said, gesturing for him to have a seat, but he shook his head quickly.

'I'm helping on the deck. I'll see you later.' He grinned and then ducked out, skidding away down the hallway in his eagerness.

'I suppose,' Dylan said as we began to eat, 'you know the story of how the world came into being?'

I nodded slowly, 'the Gods created the land and blessed the seasonal spirits with the task to make it flourish.'

'But do you know how it began?' Dylan pressed and I frowned, trying, but failing, to remember.

'I might have forgotten,' I admitted in between mouthfuls.

'The world used to just be darkness. Erthor, King of the Night, was the only God at that time. He reigned in an eternal night for centuries, until the loneliness became too much for him to bear.'

'Isn't Erthor also the God of the Moon?' I interjected, and then held up my hands in apology as he frowned at me.

'Originally,' he said doggedly, 'he was the King of the Night. But as he became lonelier, he created the moon as a means to find some company in the darkness. When the moon was full, he searched far and wide for a companion, but was unsuccessful. Months passed, with the moon reflecting his shifting moods of hope and despair, darkening and rising in a continuous circle.

'But then, after nigh on a year of searching the land in his domain, he succeeded. He found a stone which resembled the form of a woman. He laid a hand on it and the stone melted away to reveal a living maiden underneath. She was called Sybilla, and Erthor fell in love with her on the spot.

'Their love for each other flourished as Sybilla grew with child. However she did not live through the birth, and was lost. Alone with a weak and needy infant, Erthor's pain and grief at his wife's demise were unbearable and he begged for her to be returned to him. His prayers set her ablaze with holy fire, and she was reborn. However, Sybilla was no longer the same. She could not touch him, and the flames that engulfed her blinded Erthor. Bitterly, painfully, the two lovers separated, taking turns travelling through the sky one after the other, the only time they could meet was at twilight, where they would exchange their child back and forth.

'With Sybilla becoming the Sun Goddess, the world was changed and life began to grow, bringing with it new Gods and Goddesses and later on, the Seasonal Spirits.'

'Which God was their son?' I asked thoughtfully, feeling a sense of familiarly on hearing the tale.

'Lionus, God of the...'

'Dead,' I finished for him, shivering slightly.

'Anyway,' Dylan continued, 'in order to understand the Dark Elves, it is important to know about how the world began. For you see, Sybilla was a Dark Elf. The Dark Elves were the only inhabitants in Erthor's Kingdom, and they continue to worship him as their Father and Creator. The other Gods pale in comparison to Erthor who, for them, represents more than just the moon and night sky. They value his thirst for vengeance, his cold cunning and secrecy. In their society, he is a symbol of what every Dark Elf should strive to be.'

'Hang on,' I said, holding up a hand to pause his train of thought. 'Dark Elves used to be all over the world?'

'At least Scardia and the Eastern Lands,' Dylan said, 'But when Sybilla became the Sun Goddess, some of the Dark Elves began to worship her in secret. She became a symbol of what they wanted their lives to be— lives where they could live in the light and not be blinded. Some of her followers were blessed with the ability to see in both night and daytime, and they shared their knowledge with the future generations through the Sigilium stones. However, over time they joined the majority of the Dark Elves who were unable to cope in the daylight and moved underground.'

'That's what you're wanting to learn about while we're in the Underdark, isn't it?' I asked, trying to remember correctly. Dylan nodded, his enthusiasm palpable.

'The stones tell the histories of the Dark Elves, in particular the sect of Sybilla. They were ostracised for many years by the followers of Erthor, and there were many wars across the generations between the two factions— the two Houses. When Lionus became the Lord of the Dead, another faction was born and soon there were three vying for control and for the favour of their Gods.'

'So that's why there has continued to be so much dissent between the Dark Elves over the centuries?' I said slowly.

'Whoever leads has power and has proved the dominance of their God?'

'That's right,' Dylan replied, 'but it's not just that. The Dark Elves will only follow a leader who has proven to be strong in mind and body, who has demonstrated cunning and skill across all areas. There are always contestants for the leadership, and it changes regularly. The current King has retained the throne for five years, which is significantly longer than many before him.'

I reflected on that, remembering how I had been told similar things before. I wondered about Aidyn, whether he was like the other Dark Elves, and which sect he belonged to. I recalled our conversations, how he had spoken about darkness and the wonder that had filled his voice whenever he talked about light.

'Do you know the real reason why they wear masks?' I asked suddenly, and Dylan blinked in surprise.

'There are some things that are not written down,' he said slowly, and I realised that he was remembering my interactions with Aidyn too. He was watching me closely and I felt myself flush. 'I think,' Dylan mused, 'that some of your questions are best kept for Lord Aidyn.'

If I hadn't been blushing before, I most certainly was now. I glanced away, wiping my suddenly sweaty hands on my skirts in a useless attempt to distract myself.

'You know,' Dylan continued, 'I thought you were interested in the captain. You were certainly close on the voyage over. And then when we were taken to the Elven court, you pushed yourself so hard that it was obvious you wanted to forget *something*.' I kept my eyes on my skirts, mortified. 'But when the Dark Elves came to court, that first night, something changed. There was something different about you.' I looked at him then, incredulous. 'I mean,' he continued thoughtfully, 'it was only for a short time, considering they barely stayed a few days. But you didn't seem as sad as you had been before.'

'I'm amazed,' I interrupted, 'how you could notice all of that while you were closeted away in the library for days on end.'

'I left occasionally,' he waved a hand superciliously, 'and I am blessed with keen observation skills. I don't need to always be around to know what's going on.' With that enigmatic statement he stood, picked up our empty bowls, and left, shutting the door with a soft click and leaving me blinking in surprise.

To my relief, the remainder of the voyage passed relatively smoothly. I stayed in the cabin, receiving meals via Lisette or Erik, as Dylan spread a range of scrolls out across the floor, referring to them as he spoke. I was grateful that Dylan seemed mainly to be in a good mood, although at times he seemed frustrated that I did not immediately know the answers to questions as soon as he asked them. He had even consented to teaching me some more of the runic symbols of the Ancient Tongue, and lent me a small notebook with his notes on the runes and their meanings for me to practise further.

Sometimes Erik would join us, listening with interest to aspects of Dark Elf history and lore, such as the Two Hundred Year War which had almost decimated the Dark Elf race. His eyes had brightened and he had leaned closer, drinking in the tale and asking a range of questions from the types of weapons used and the number of daily casualties, to the tactics that the leaders of the Erthor faction used against the followers of Sybilla. Eventually though, Dylan had lost his patience when the interruptions became too regular, and Erik was told that he could either sit and listen or leave. Erik, sticking his nose in the air rather pugnaciously, declared that he hadn't been that interested anyway– which we had all known was an outright lie– and stormed off to the deck where he apparently helped Markus at the helm. I had bitten my tongue when I found that out, determined not to say anything that might spoil his enjoyment. He had sensed my discomfort though, I was sure.

When he wasn't quizzing Dylan about the Two Hundred Year War, he was asking me why Markus and I were not speaking, or even interacting with each other. I got the feeling that Markus, like me, was avoiding answering these sorts of questions, but I didn't want to be the one to explain to Erik why we weren't talking. Let Markus be the one to admit that he was bitter at not being told about my identity, that he didn't approve of my magic or the changes I had undergone while living with my grandfather. Perhaps he might articulate it better for Erik than he had with me, but I doubted it.

'Nina?' Dylan's voice interrupted my thoughts and I was brought back to the present, where I noticed that he had begun to pack up the scrolls.

'What is it?' I asked, wondering what I had missed.

'We've been summoned to the deck,' he said, tying one of the tightly wound scrolls with some twine. 'I think we might nearly be at the Karoni Lagoon.'

I felt excitement spread through me, after being aboard this vessel for several days I was all too ready to leave. I wanted to get ashore, feel the fresh air again and stretch my legs properly. Most of all I wanted to leave Markus, and the tension that seemed to fill the boat, behind.

'You should probably put your cloak on,' Dylan said as I helped him with the scrolls, 'just to be safe.'

I nodded and when the last scroll had been returned to his pack, reached into my trunk and withdrew my cloak. The familiar weight of the hood fell around my face and I kept it low so that I was shrouded as I followed Dylan out to the deck.

It felt bizarre on deck and I was struck by the salty air, still warm from the afternoon sun. Dylan and I moved to the railing, taking in the shoreline, the white sandy beaches and rocky outcrops, dense shrubbery and palm trees spreading out like a green tapestry before us. My eyes closed for a moment, relishing the sensation of being outside the close confines of my cabin, hands gripping the wooden rail as the spray of the water stung my cheeks.

'Look Nina,' Erik cried excitedly as he joined me at the rail, 'look at the water.'

I followed his pointed finger and gasped; the Karoni Lagoon was unlike anything I had seen before. The aquamarine waters were crystal clear, so one could see the coral beneath the surface. Brightly coloured fish darted back and forth, flitting in and out of the reef and I wanted nothing more than to join them.

'Lower the anchor!' Markus barked from the helm, reminding me that we weren't alone on deck and that the majority of the crew and passengers were there as well. I stiffened slightly, and determinedly looked out at the lagoon, noting the mountain ranges in the distance. The sky was tinged with the vibrant oranges and pinks of sunset, the clouds making colourful patterns which stretched out across the horizon. Dispassionately I thought that in any other scenario this scene might have been considered romantic, but when I cast a surreptitious glance at Markus, he was ignoring me. The weight in my chest became leaden and I looked back at the shoreline, biting my lip.

'Do not be sad, little princess,' a voice whispered in my ear, 'I'll make sure you get everything you wish for.' The breath was warm, the scent of spices filled my nose, and I jumped, turning to see who was speaking to me. But there was no one there, save Rakael and Jesse, who were discussing next steps in an undertone and not paying me any heed.

'I'll be watching, little princess,' the voice spoke into my other ear and I twisted, scanning the deck, searching desperately for the speaker. Erik looked at me quizzically.

'Are you alright, Nina?' he asked. Dylan glanced over, his expression tinged with curiosity.

I nodded slowly, feeling on edge. The voice was familiar, and I took a deep breath, remembering all too well the flashing dark eyes and wide smile of stark white teeth. There was a soft chuckle and a warm breeze lifted my cloak, sweeping it and my dress around my ankles, carrying the scent of spices and summer heat away towards the shore.

'You look like you've seen a ghost,' Erik pressed.

'I'm fine,' I muttered, 'I just thought… I heard… something.'

My gaze flicked across the waters of the lagoon, wondering if I would be able to see the Lord of Summer laughing at me. But there was nothing, only the gentle splash of the water and distant sound of gulls.

'We'll need to go ashore by rowboat,' Rakael's voice cut in. 'The ship needs to stay out in the deeper water.'

'We're not disembarking tomorrow?' Dylan asked, surprised. 'It'll be night soon.'

'Perfect for us to get ashore and set up camp while we wait for our guides.' Rakael said, 'besides, I want to get off this ship sooner rather than later. Ah, Captain,' she continued, directing her next words behind my shoulder. 'Can your men please assist with loading our trunks in the boats so that we can start to go ashore?'

'Of course,' Markus answered curtly. 'You might want to oversee the unloading yourself to ensure nothing is damaged.'

Rakael nodded stiffly and strode away, snapping at her henchmen to follow.

'How many times have you been here, Markus?' Erik asked as Rakael's footsteps faded away.

'Rarely,' Markus answered, 'Our usual trips don't normally take us to locations this remote.'

It was awkward standing by the railing with him behind me. I stepped away, avoiding his gaze, and sidestepped around him.

'I'm going to make sure we're all packed,' I muttered to no one in particular before I fled. I couldn't get off this ship soon enough. Jesse left with me, matching my pace and thankfully keeping silent. However, when we reached the cabin it was to find Lisette finishing the packing.

'I guess there wasn't too much to do anyway,' Jesse murmured to me, 'considering that we didn't spend long enough on board to properly unpack.'

'I suppose so,' I sighed, watching as Lisette wrangled Viktor and another sailor into carrying the trunks onto the deck using sharp, direct gestures. It really was amazing what she could accomplish without having to use her voice.

'How are you feeling?' Jesse asked when the room was empty. 'The last few days can't have been easy.'

I shrugged, not particularly wanting to talk about it. What could I say? Jesse seemed to understand and squeezed my shoulder gently, before picking up the end of one of the trunks and indicating for me to lift the other. Together, we carried it to the deck in silence.

On seeing us emerge with a trunk in our hands, some of the sailors hurried over to assist. I noticed Markus and Erik leaning against the railing, Markus watching the scene unfold coolly, not making a move to come over. I passed my end of the trunk to one of the sailors with a murmured thanks and tried to ignore the awed expression he gave me as he took it from my grasp.

'We could probably go ashore with these,' Jesse said, indicating the rowboat that had been half filled with trunks.

'Then we could find a spot to set up camp,' I said, nodding.

'My idea exactly,' she replied. 'Come on, we will need to thank the captain before we take our leave.' She caught my expression and raised her eyebrows. 'We still need to be respectful, Nina. It'll be over and done with before you know it.'

Reluctantly, I followed her across the deck and dropped into a swift curtsey, keeping my eyes lowered.

'We wanted to bid you farewell, Captain,' Jesse was saying, her tone breezy and calm, 'thank you for giving us safe passage. We appreciate your discretion.'

'Thank you,' I managed through my clenched jaw.

'I'll be happier once your party has paid for that discretion,' he said coldly, and I felt the anger rise again. Was payment all he could think about? Was there nothing else he wanted to say?

'Rakael will make sure of it,' Jesse said smoothly, 'have a safe return voyage.' She strode away towards the rowboat.

'Say goodbye, Erik,' I said, pulling my cloak tighter around me against the chill I suddenly felt.

'He doesn't have to,' Markus said, one hand on Erik's shoulder. I froze, my eyes rising to meet his properly for the first time.

'What do you mean?' Erik asked, also caught off guard.

'There's a place for him on the ship,' Markus said gruffly. 'He's got the makings of a fine sailor.'

I couldn't breathe. I tried not to show the pain that was gripping my heart, biting back the objection that immediately rose to my lips. Instead, I took a steady breath, looked at Erik and said with surprising composure, 'Erik? It's up to you. The choice is yours.'

He stared at me, wide eyed. 'I could stay if I wanted to? And you wouldn't be mad?'

I shook my head, keeping my breathing slow and even while I tried to control the howling emotions inside me.

'But if I stayed,' Erik turned from me to Markus, 'she wouldn't be able to join us.'

Markus shook his head. 'You're old enough to be able to make your own choices, Erik.'

Erik paused, and the wait for him to speak seemed to stretch into eternity.

'I do like being at sea,' Erik said finally. 'But Nina needs me more. I made a promise.'

He took my hand and I let out the breath I hadn't realised I'd been holding. Markus' face showed no emotion, but I gripped Erik's hand tighter anyway.

'You're sure?' he asked abruptly, and Erik nodded. 'Then I suppose there's nothing left to say except goodbye.' Markus held out a hand and Erik shook it, 'travel safely.'

'You too,' Erik replied and then he hefted his rucksack and followed Jesse. For a moment, Markus and I watched him go before the awkward silence became too much to bear. Instinctively, I reached into my bodice and pulled the copper coin out on its cord of leather. I let it dangle in the light and then held it out to him, forcing myself to meet his eyes.

'I think it's time that I returned this to its rightful owner,' I said softly, 'I'm told it's supposed to bring luck to whoever wears it. You might need that.'

His jaw clenched. 'It was a gift,' he said gruffly, 'throw it overboard if you don't want it. I don't care.' With that, he strode off below deck and I watched him leave, biting my lip to stop the sudden tears that burned my eyes from falling.

'Nina, come on,' Jesse called from the other side of the ship as Erik began to climb down the rope ladder to the rowboat. 'We need to go.'

I watched the coin swing on its leather and then with careful precision I tied it to the helm.

'This will be a fresh start,' I muttered to myself as I left the coin behind and descended the swinging rope ladder. Two sailors pulled on the oars and began to navigate towards the shore. Even though a part of me wanted to go back and retrieve Markus' coin, I forced myself to remain in the boat as we drew further and further away.

Chapter Ten

The waters that we passed through were calm and it was easy to see right down to the coral reef below. I stared, entranced. Scardia was very different, with its glaciers and icy lakes which were always cold, even in summer. I wasn't used to seeing coral reefs or tropical fish, although I had read about them back when I was a child in the Palace.

'Look Nina,' Erik was equally awed, and I followed his gaze to see a majestic sea turtle, its weathered shell glittering as it dove back underwater towards the depths. It ducked in between the vibrant coral and sea grass like gossamer, moving almost as if in a strange dance. Several long silvery fish joined in, flitting in and out of the rocky hollows and darting around the turtle as it circled towards the shore. It came close to the surface again and I reached out, wanting to touch it.

'Keep your hands out of the water,' one of the sailors snapped as he heaved on the oars. 'Don't want you touching the mystera.'

'The what?' Erik asked.

'That's mystera,' the sailor grunted, indicating to the fine strands of sea grass which were scattered throughout the reef, undulating with the tide.

'What's wrong with it?' Jesse asked curiously, peering closer at the grass in question which seemed to be perfectly harmless.

'It's what happens when something touches it,' the sailor shivered. 'Drop something in and you'll find out.'

'The fish have been moving in and out of it alright,' Erik mused, and then he reached into his pocket and pulled out a pebble, a bundle of string, some old cork and a handkerchief.

'Erik,' I began, stumped, 'why…?'

'You never know when you might need things,' Erik interrupted, pre-empting my question. I bit back the urge to say that all the items he had, save for the handkerchief, were worthless. Instead, I watched as he hefted each item in his hand, weighing them carefully, before gently dropping the pebble overboard.

Jesse, Erik and I watched as the pebble sank towards the ocean floor. However, it never made it more than halfway, for as soon as it touched the mystera there was a flurry of movement. Snakes emerged from the crevices and hollows in the reef, striped yellow, red and black, speeding towards the pebble and catching it in a writhing ball. Their scales glinted in the light, and I watched in fascinated horror as they fought for the stone, tearing into each other as they tossed it back and forth.

'Just imagine what would have happened had you decided to go for a swim,' the sailor muttered, pulling harder on the oars to create some distance between us and the sea snakes.

'But it seemed so peaceful,' I said quietly, 'it was so beautiful.'

He snorted, but it was Jesse who spoke, 'sometimes the things that are most beautiful are also the most dangerous.'

'Aye,' the sailor nodded, 'there are lots of monsters out there that hide behind a beautiful face.' His companion, who had been silent all this time, chose that moment to engage in the conversation.

'Like sirens,' he spoke hollowly, 'they'll rip out a man's heart and soul they will.'

'That'd be why the captain never sails to Velkra on the western sea,' the other sailor said, 'we don't want to find ourselves anywhere near the Isle of Setkey.'

'Setkey?' I asked, and Jesse gasped.

'That's where the sirens can be found?' she said, 'I had heard stories, of course, but never realised they were so close to Velkranian shores.'

'But what most folks don't know,' the sailor continued, 'is that sirens aren't just confined to the shores of Setkey. They can shapeshift...'

'Don't be an idiot,' his companion scoffed, 'that's an old wives' tale and you know it. Them sirens are confined to Setkey, they can't leave without convincing a ship to take them aboard, and considering that either the ships avoid the area, or the sailors are lured to an early grave because of the sirens' thirst for blood, well...' his voice trailed off.

'I suppose they can't escape their own natures then,' Jesse mused. 'They want to escape Setkey but are lost in the urge to kill when a potential saviour comes their way.'

'It's sad really,' I said quietly, 'being caught in a situation where you want to leave but cannot.'

The sailors looked at me like I was insane.

'It's crazy talk like that that'd have people choosing to sail to their deaths,' one of them muttered, 'sirens are monsters. That's all there is to it.'

We fell into silence again, and before I knew it, the boat was scraping onto the sand and we stumbled out onto the beach, helping the sailors to heave the boat higher up onto the shore.

'Erik, Nina, help me with these trunks,' Jesse said, and in a rather motley fashion we carried them up to where the grass and sand merged, and palm trees provided some shelter.

'Thank you,' I said to the sailors, who shuffled their feet and gave quick bows of their heads, before pushing the rowboat back out to sea and beginning their slow progress back to the ship. I could see another rowboat on the way, laden down with several other large trunks.

'Well, let's start to think about getting some kindling together,' Jesse said brightly, glancing around at the shore. Erik immediately sprang into action and began a search for driftwood. Jesse and I exchanged a look and laughed, before joining him.

I focussed on finding stones to put in a large circle, while Jesse and Erik competed over who could find the most wood. By the time the second rowboat had been unloaded and the third boat was on the way with Rakael and Dylan in tow, I had finished laying out the firepit and Jesse had conceded defeat to Erik. Jesse began assembling the kindling and then looked at me expectantly.

'Nina?'

I closed my eyes and summoned the flames, which caught on the twigs and flickered in the evening light.

'I'm hungry,' Erik said, plopping down next to me and adding some more wood to the fire. I glanced at Jesse, realising that we didn't have any sort of supplies with us. She gestured at Rakael in the distance.

'I'm sure Rakael will have thought of something,' she said reassuringly. Erik snorted, clearly not having much faith in Rakael's planning.

It turned out that he was partially right. All Rakael could spare was some meat jerky, which was so dry it was painful to eat. And then, when all the boats had been unloaded and we were gathered around the fire, she began to designate guard duty.

'Nina and Erik, you can take the first watch,' she said, 'then you wake Lisette and Dylan at midnight. They will then wake Tobias and Leif. Jesse and I will take over from them.'

I didn't mind having the first watch, and settled down with Erik beside me, as the rest of our companions gradually fell asleep. When Rakael's breathing had finally become heavy, Erik spoke,

'Did you want me to stay with Markus?'

My hand froze as I reached out for another piece of driftwood and then slowly added it to the fire.

'I wanted you to make the choice yourself,' I replied quietly. 'I didn't want you to feel like you had to stay with me.'

He pondered that for a moment and then said, 'this trip was different. It wasn't like last time. I thought that when he knew who you were it might make things better. But it didn't, it only made things worse.'

I sighed and stood, moving to lean against one of the palm trees on the edge of the firelight. 'I think things were already rather bad between us, Erik. What happened wasn't something that could just be resolved easily with a conversation.'

It could have, I thought treacherously. If Markus had listened. If he hadn't immediately judged me.

'What did happen?' he pushed. When I didn't answer immediately, he became exasperated. 'You say you want me to make my own decisions but then aren't honest with me. I'm not a child anymore.'

I half smiled, reminded of myself when I had argued with Grandfather not a week ago.

'I always try to be honest with you, Erik,' I said softly, 'But some things are painful to talk about. We argued, we said hurtful things and I don't think either of us can move past that. Markus finding out who I was just reinforced his belief that I'm a liar and that I always was one.'

Erik scowled, 'that's not true.'

'It's not wrong.' I looked up at the sky, chuckling wryly. Up above us, the faint twinkle of stars was beginning to shimmer against the vast darkness. 'On our trip over I wasn't honest with anyone– not you, certainly not Markus. But I can't see how things would have been different if I had been, it's hard to be yourself when you've hidden who you are for years on end.'

'I know,' Erik murmured, and I glanced at him, noting the hollowness that had filled his eyes.

'But at least we can be who we want to be now,' I said and was grateful when his shadowy memories were banished.

'Obviously,' he said, 'I can't be a knight if I'm learning to be a sailor. Besides, a knight needs to protect those in need.'

'Which is me, I suppose?' I laughed, and then quietened when the noise made Rakael turn and grumble in her sleep. Erik nodded and I grinned, before gazing back up at the sky. There was no moon tonight, so the starlight flickered even brighter against the shadows.

'What do you think the Underdark will be like?' Erik asked, keeping his tone low to not wake our companions.

'Dark,' I replied, and he snorted.

'No, really,' he said, 'Everyone keeps talking about how it'll be dangerous, but no one seems to know for certain.'

I thought about that for a moment, but all I could say was, 'I don't know. I think we'll just have to wait and see.'

We drifted off into our own private thoughts, and I continued to watch the sky light up with stars which winked down at us from their position in the heavens. At midnight, I woke a sleepy Lisette while Erik prodded Dylan awake, before we settled down beside the fire. Erik fell asleep almost immediately, but I took longer, finding it difficult to relax on the ground after sleeping in a bed for so long. When sleep finally came, it was dreamless and seemed to only last a moment, so when I opened my eyes it was to see the dawn light stretching above me.

'Good, you're awake,' Rakael said as she glanced over and saw me. 'We need to prepare to leave. Our guides are here.'

I blinked and rubbed my eyes, groaning slightly as I sat up and felt the muscles ache in my back. 'Our guides?'

'They arrived halfway through the night,' Jesse said, helping me up. I dusted the sand off my skirts and glanced out at the ocean, which glittered invitingly in the morning light. The bay was empty, no ship was moored out to sea and I felt a stab of pain. Markus was gone.

'We'll be leaving soon, Nina,' Jesse said, bringing me back to reality. I looked around, taking in the scene around us.

A large wagon was being loaded with our trunks, Leif and Tobias were stacking them in the back and tying them in place with thick cord. There were less trunks than there had been when we left Grandfather's court and I pondered that for a moment, wondering why some of them might have been left behind. There was a loud snort from the front of the wagon, and I saw a pair of horned oxen harnessed to it, pawing at the ground impatiently. There was a soft push on my shoulder and a nickering sound. I turned and saw Dolce, her large eyes liquid pools of affection as she butted me again with her nose, searching for sugar lumps.

I laughed and stroked her, checking for any injuries or damage from her journey overland. She looked just like she had the last time I had seen her, and I rested against her neck, feeling complete for the first time since we left for the Underdark. Dolce continued to sniff at me, searching for a treat and then gave up, snorting dejectedly and flicked her mane in my face in disgust.

'When did the horses arrive?' I asked Jesse, who was taking care of her own mount, a golden stallion with a white blazing star on his forehead.

'Christoff brought them just before dawn,' she said, waving at one of the Resistance guards who was kicking sand over the remnants of the fire, masking any evidence of us being there.

'Nina,' Erik interrupted, pulling on my arm. 'They're here.'

I blinked and turned away from Dolce, noting that our guides had emerged from behind the cart in quiet conversation with the Resistance guards and Rakael. Dylan was hovering to one side, watching them eagerly. Despite the morning heat that was already starting to make my dress stick to my body, they were dressed in the usual black leather, their masks glinting silver.

'I still don't like those masks,' Erik muttered uneasily, and I didn't blame him. Even though I had been expecting to see them, the Dark Elf masks were still scary to behold, the way they clamped around one's face with a wide gaping mouth and round eyes that only showed the dark mesh of the balaclava underneath. It reminded me of the day we had almost been captured by the Tracker. I could tell that Erik was thinking the same thing from the way he unintentionally stiffened as one of the Dark Elves looked up and noticed us staring.

Lisette pulled on my arm and I looked away, allowing her to lead me to a copse of trees where I could change in privacy. She folded up my crumpled dress and gestured towards a small bowl of sea water and a faded bar of soap, indicating that I should hurry. I washed myself hastily, scrubbing and rinsing myself with a rough cloth. While I wiped myself down, Lisette replaited my hair and pinned it up. She clicked her tongue and pulled a shift over my head, which was quickly followed by a leafy green dress. The bodice was tightened with sharp tugs and I rolled the stockings up, before fastening up my shoes. I reached for my cloak and Lisette handed it over, giving me a quick inspection to make sure that I was decently dressed, and then emptied the bowl of water, rolled up the soap in the damp cloth and led the way back to the group.

I felt refreshed, despite the speed in which I had gotten ready, and smiled at Erik, who had lifted himself up into the saddle of one of the mounts. He grinned back until Dylan sat up behind him and then grimaced in annoyance.

'You chose to stow away,' Dylan said stiffly, as he eyed the cart with unconcealed longing.

'And you could choose to ride in the cart,' Erik retorted, shifting uncomfortably.

'Perhaps that is a good idea, Dylan,' I said. 'You don't look particularly happy up there.'

'Very well,' he sniffed, but the relief belied his aggrieved tone. He dismounted hastily and made his way over to the cart, where Leif and Tobias were finishing their preparations.

'Nina,' Rakael called from across the clearing, 'come here and meet our escorts.'

I obeyed her summons, realising that she was standing with the two Dark Elves. The three of them watched me approach and when I reached them, I bent into a curtsey, raising my hand to my forehead as I lowered down.

'Thank you for your assistance in escorting us,' I said, keeping my gaze aimed at their booted feet.

'It is an honour, Princess,' one replied, reaching out with a gloved hand to lift me to my feet, before bowing swiftly. His tone was light, amused and I recognised it immediately.

'Aidyn?' I asked, peering at him curiously. He dipped his head in acquiescence.

'But of course,' he said, 'our King asked for people to retrieve you from the Karoni Lagoon and I couldn't resist.' There was a soft cough from the other Dark Elf and I turned to them. Aidyn glanced over and said quickly, 'ah, how remise of me, my apologies. Princess Wilhelmina, please meet Alex, one of my oldest friends. They are one of the finest navigators in the Underdark and will make sure that we reach the Ombre Mountains safely.'

'What's your role then?' I asked, biting back a smile and nodding a greeting to Alex.

'I'm tasked with making sure we don't get ambushed or meet an untimely demise on the way,' he quipped.

'Lord Aidyn jests,' Alex interrupted, their voice low and clear. 'It is customary for a member of nobility to form part of the welcoming party whenever we have visitors. If, on the off chance, we face danger on the way to the Underdark, no doubt he will prove himself useful in a fight.'

'We are grateful for your assistance,' Rakael said smoothly, 'shall we be on our way?'

'Indeed,' Alex said, moving towards one of two black horses who had been tied to the side of the clearing. They leapt up onto one's back and moved towards the oxen and the cart, where Lisette and Dylan were perched atop the trunks and Leif and Tobias sat at the front holding the reins.

'Of course,' I murmured to myself.

'What?' Aidyn asked.

I looked at him quizzically, 'isn't is a bit dramatic to have black horses as well as black outfits?'

He chuckled as he walked me back towards Dolce, whose white flanks contrasted spectacularly with his own mount. 'Perhaps you're right,' he acknowledged and then he boosted me up into Dolce's saddle. 'Were you surprised to see me, Princess?' His tone had changed, it was now thoughtful, sincere, and I was thrown by it.

'Yes,' I replied truthfully, choosing not to say that I had hoped I would see him again when we reached the Underdark, and a part of me had been looking forward to that.

'Nina,' Erik cut in, glancing back and forth between Aidyn and I, 'we should get going.'

He urged his horse forward and Dolce followed automatically, pulling away from Aidyn. I looked back and saw him moving to his own horse and nimbly settling into the saddle. He pulled alongside Jesse, but I couldn't hear what they were discussing. Ahead of Erik and I, Rakael and Christoff were riding with Alex, the cart lumbering behind them.

'It feels so good to be back on dry land,' I murmured, raising my face to the sunlight and enjoying the warmth. Erik didn't reply, but just stared moodily ahead. I peered at him, 'what's wrong?'

He shrugged, 'Nothing.' I could tell he was lying but he didn't say anything else and I didn't press, realising that he wasn't going to explain further. Our horses pushed forward through the shrubbery leaving the beach behind, the cart following a track that Alex alone seemed to know.

Chapter Eleven

As the morning continued, the heat intensified and soon we were swatting away winged insects as they buzzed around our faces. The beach had been left far behind, and the palm trees thickened around us, surrounding us with ferns and shrubbery. The ground was no longer sandy, but dark earth twisted with vines, so the horses had to move slowly so as to avoid tripping. Sweat trickled down my brow and I wiped it away, wishing desperately for some water or something to eat. My stomach ached with hunger, and it wasn't made better when I heard Erik's rumbling too.

'We'll stop soon for a break,' Aidyn's voice interrupted my reverie. I turned so quickly that I pulled a muscle in my neck and winced.

'Don't do that,' I grumbled, rubbing my neck.

'Do what?' he asked.

'Sneak up on people like that,' I said. 'At least give some warning or something before you speak.'

He chuckled, 'my apologies.'

He didn't sound the least bit apologetic, and I couldn't help rolling my eyes.

'How long will it take to reach the Ombre Mountains?' Erik asked pointedly, peering over at us.

'It depends on the oxen,' Aidyn shrugged, his mask flashing in the sunlight. 'The forest is only the first stretch of the journey.'

'Forest?' Erik scoffed, glancing around at the thick underbrush and hanging vines. I followed his gaze, noting how moss climbed up the trunks of the trees, and that despite the heat there was dampness in the air that hummed with the croaking of frogs and buzzing of insects. It was the complete opposite to the pine forests in Scardia, or to the tall birch and evergreen forest around Lowton. While it had been warm at Grandfather's court, it had never been humid like this.

'I think it's quite beautiful,' I murmured, as palm fronds brushed against my skirts. 'There's nowhere in Scardia like this.'

'Apparently it's similar to Karshka,' Aidyn said, 'But we don't have the same swamps that they do.' I glanced at him, surprised and he laughed. 'Just because I've been raised underground doesn't mean I didn't receive an education, Princess.'

I blushed, embarrassed and looked away.

'He probably received more of an education than you did, Nina,' Erik chose that moment to pipe up again and I glared at him.

'I daresay that might be true,' Aidyn said smoothly, 'although I think we both learned different things. An education is not only gleaned through reading and studying books.'

'Of course not,' Erik agreed, 'I've learned more from Elder Haycin than from books.'

I tried to hide the pang of hurt his thoughtless words caused. 'But at least learning from books is still an option,' I said, my tone perhaps a touch too bright because Erik gave me a funny look.

'Elder Haycin was impressive,' Aidyn recalled, 'he was very courteous towards us when we visited. His skills were highly regarded, although I think our trainers in the Underdark would be able to give him some competition.' He turned to Erik, 'I'm sure that you will find training with them a novel experience during your stay. Although, a word of advice if I may,' he paused for an instant and then said, 'don't look them in the eye and don't show weakness.'

'Why can't I look at them?' Erik asked, his previous distrust faded and replaced with curiosity.

'It's a sign of disrespect to our Elders,' Aidyn replied. 'They consider eye contact from someone of lesser rank highly disrespectful. No matter what your birth, when you start to train you are considered the lowest of the low. Only through hard work can you earn their respect and your place in society.'

'What happens if you aren't a strong fighter?' I asked.

'Then you will never make it far in Dark Elf society,' Aidyn said bluntly. 'But that doesn't mean you cannot earn acclaim for yourself in other ways. For those of us who are born into the noble families however, there is no choice. We must succeed in all areas to honour our family name. Any who fail are cast out.' His tone turned bleak, but only for a moment.

'Has anyone ever failed?' Erik pressed and I watched Aidyn, caught up in Erik's curiosity.

'Of course,' he replied, 'More than you would expect. But if you are raised a certain way, the expectation to succeed becomes a habit. My siblings and I know little else.'

'You have siblings?' I don't know why it surprised me. For some reason I had never thought about it, and I wondered why I hadn't asked him before.

He nodded but didn't expand beyond saying,

'you might be introduced to them when we arrive. They are curious to meet you.'

I wondered if he had told them about me and then chided myself for getting carried away with selfishness. In all likelihood they were merely curious based on what their Chief Counsel had shared from their time in Grandfather's court.

'You'll impress them, Nina,' Erik said quietly, 'I know you will.'

'I'm sure the court will be coming up with all manner of trials for you to prove your worth,' Aidyn said unhelpfully. I frowned at him and he chuckled. 'I can assure you that it should not be anything life-threatening, Princess. Think of this visit as an example of every Dark Elf's rite of passage into adulthood.'

'Thank you,' I said sarcastically, 'that makes me feel *so* much better.'

'I'm sure it does.' It sounded like he was smiling, but one could never be sure.

'What sort of trials are there in a rite of passage?' Erik asked, 'then she can make sure that she's ready and can guarantee that she will succeed.'

I coughed to hide my laugh, 'if it's that easy, pray do tell.'

'I doubt it will be easy,' Aidyn shrugged, 'and unfortunately, I cannot tell you more. Each trial is different for everyone.'

'Then tell us about yours,' Erik demanded, 'Since you won't help Nina start to prepare.'

'Erik,' I chided and turned to Aidyn, 'You don't have to if you don't want to.'

'I get the feeling that I don't have much of a choice,' Aidyn whispered, leaning closer to me so that Erik couldn't easily hear.

'Then I suggest you call for us to stop for our midday meal,' I replied under my breath, 'if food is involved, Erik will leave you alone.'

'A good idea,' he replied and then urged his horse forward, cutting away towards Alex and Rakael. Within moments we had come to a stop, and Erik and I dismounted, stretching out our aching muscles. I tied Dolce to one of the low hanging branches nearby and left her to graze contently on the springy underbrush. The ground was soft and damp as I made my way towards the others, who were passing around a gourd of water and Rakael's favourite jerky. Erik scrunched his nose up at the fare but took it reluctantly, and I followed suit.

'I can't wait until we have a proper meal,' Erik muttered to me, looking sourly at the strip of jerky. 'This isn't enough.'

'We'll have more time to eat when we reach our campsite,' Rakael snapped, 'we need to be focussed on reaching our destination, not complaining about food.'

I raised my eyebrows at Erik and then took the gourd from Lisette. The water was cool and refreshing, but with a slightly bitter aftertaste. I handed it to Erik and he gulped it down, emptying it in moments. Luckily, he had been the last one who needed to drink, otherwise whoever would have been waiting for the water would have been left disappointed.

'We should keep moving,' Rakael said brusquely, gesturing for the guards to resume their posts and mounting her horse. 'Lead the way, Alex.' Alex gave what I considered to be a rather mocking bow, and with lithe grace mounted and began to lead the procession again. I stuck the jerky in my mouth and pulled myself back into Dolce's saddle, untying the reins and urging her onward. Erik followed suit, munching on his own piece of jerky, grumbling under his breath about the lack of proper food.

Aidyn was still at the front of our party, keeping Alex and Rakael company, chatting with the guards, their laughter carrying back to us over the cart. Dylan was leaning back against the trunks, a book in his hands and his monocle flashing as he focussed on his reading. Lisette seemed to be relaxing for a nap, her head resting against Dylan's shoulder. Jesse stayed behind us, disappearing from time to time as she rearranged branches and kicked over earth, hiding some of the traces of our passage. It seemed to be a rather thankless job, and I was privately grateful that I wasn't the one doing it.

As we journeyed on, I felt a strange peaceful sensation spreading through me and my hunger pains began to subside. The sun passed its zenith and began to sink across the afternoon sky, the heat making us feel sluggish and lazy. The cart and horses plodded on methodically, and I began to feel my eyelids drooping with tiredness.

'We're nearly there,' Alex called out and I looked up, the sleepiness I'd been feeling fading away. We were descending a steep hill, so dismounted to lead the horses and oxen down. My feet slipped in the earth, struggling to find something to grip onto as we moved. Roots twisted everywhere and I was reminded of that night in Grandfather's forest where I had tripped and fallen, twisting my ankle in the process. I didn't want a repeat occurrence here. I couldn't afford to be injured when we arrived at the Underdark.

Erik reached out and grabbed my arm, steadying me, and I smiled at him gratefully. I took another step and felt the jagged support of rock helping me to keep balance as I made my way downwards. I didn't allow myself to look further than where to next place my feet, leading Dolce behind me, moving even more slowly than we had been before. It seemed like it took forever to get down the hill, and I was surprised that the cart hadn't slipped once. When we were finally on flat ground again, I allowed myself to look up and take in our surroundings.

Before us stretched a small lake, with a waterfall crashing into the water on the far side. It came over a rocky cliff and rose back up towards the forest trees, which sprawled in an uneven tangle across the clifftop. The shore was mostly clear; moss-covered rocks and earth stretched from the water's edge to the tree line. It was peaceful and calm, a small oasis in the heart of the forest. I gazed around, taking it in, noting the wild orchids that were growing around trees and rising up from ferns, and the hanging vines that swung gently in the light breeze.

'What do you think?' I turned to see Alex beside me, their head tilted to one side, assessing me.

'It's beautiful,' I replied honestly, 'this place… there's nothing like this in Scardia.'

They nodded silently and moved away, instructing the guards on how to set up the campsite. They pulled out some bedrolls and a cooking pot from the cart.

'Come on, Nina,' Erik said, following on. I was about to go with him when Jesse came to a stop beside me, gasping from the climb.

'I'm not even going to try and cover that up,' she growled, casting a dark gaze back up the hill at the skid marks and scuffed earth from the cart, hoof marks and footprints that stretched up the hillside.

'Let me,' Aidyn said, stepping forward. He stretched his hands back and forth, before holding them up towards the hillside. There was a rustling and flurry of motion, as the earth moved, vines knotted together and spun across the ground, twisting into new shapes that covered all trace of our progress.

Jesse stared, saying in a stunned and rather annoyed voice, 'you couldn't have done that earlier?'

Aidyn lowered his hands, shaking them before putting them into his pockets. 'You didn't seem to need much help,' he shrugged. Jesse snorted in disgust and strode away, her horse cast Aidyn a dirty look and followed, flicking its mane as it stalked after her.

'I didn't even think of doing that,' I admitted, feeling ashamed that I hadn't offered to help Jesse either. He fell into step alongside me as we followed the others.

'You're still developing those skills,' he said, 'King Aegis said you had only been learning magic for a short time when we last met. I wouldn't expect it to be something you would automatically think of. When one hasn't used magic for most of their life, it's hard at times to suddenly adjust to using it.'

I nodded slowly, 'that makes sense.'

'Nina,' Erik called out, racing over to me, 'Alex said we could go hunting. We'll be able to have proper food for dinner tonight.'

'That's great,' I said, although I didn't particularly want to join them on a hunting trip.

'Lisette and Dylan will stay and help to set up camp,' Rakael said as we joined them by the cart. 'The rest of us will go with Alex.'

'I might stay as well,' I said quickly. She looked at me closely, clearly unsure about letting me remain behind.

'I can watch over the camp,' Aidyn said quietly, 'I won't let any harm come to them.'

Rakael paused for a moment and then nodded curtly.

'We'll aim to be back before sundown,' she said, opening one of the trunks to reveal weapons inside. She reached in and grabbed a bow and a quiver of arrows. 'Let's move out.'

She and Alex strode off, Erik not far behind, talking excitedly about what potential game they might find. Jesse and the guards followed more sedately, leaving us to take care of their mounts and the oxen as they disappeared into the trees.

'Do you think they'll find something to hunt?' I asked as Aidyn and I tied the horses to one of the low overhanging trees near the lake edge, removing their saddles and rubbing them down. Lisette and Dylan were setting up the bedrolls and preparing a firepit, although Lisette cast beady glances in our direction from time to time.

'Alex is a good tracker,' Aidyn said, 'With any luck they will find something for us. If not, we can always try our hand at fishing in the lake.'

I smiled as I began to brush out some of the twigs that had gotten caught in Dolce's tail. We fell into companionable silence as we worked, and I found myself relaxing into the familiar routine of caring for Dolce and the other horses. I was almost disappointed when we had finished.

'Come on,' Aidyn said, 'we might as well try to catch something in the lake. Just in case.' I followed him as he broke a long branch off one of the trees and opened one of his saddlebags. From inside, he pulled out a small leather pouch and a bundle of fine string. He handed me the pouch and perched himself down on one of the large mossy rocks beside the lake, one booted foot propped up. There was a flash of silver as he cut through the string, tying it around the end of the branch.

'Are you going to help at all or just watch?' His tone was amused and I blinked, surprised.

'What can I do?'

'Get a hook out and attach it to the end of the string,' he said, testing the knot and then handing me the branch. I sat down opposite him, the moss cool and damp as I crossed my legs on the rock, spreading my skirt down over my ankles. He wasn't paying attention, and moved to kneel by the base of one of the trees, his gloved hands rummaging around in the dirt.

'Are you tying up that hook?' he asked, not turning back and I looked down at the pouch in my hand. Tentatively, I opened it up and located a small hook, its sharp edge threatening to stab into my finger as I pulled it out. It was hard to attach the hook to the string, reminding me all too well of the times when I had threaded needles. I bit my tongue as I focussed on it, wetting the string with my tongue to make it pass through the small hole more easily. After a few attempts I succeeded and tied a knot, feeling rather proud of myself.

'Here,' Aidyn said, reaching over my shoulder and removing the hook from my grasp, 'Loop the string around like this and then back, through and pull. Now you try.'

I did my best to replicate the motions he had demonstrated, and soon another knot was on top of the first one, only this one was stronger and tighter.

'We need to make sure there's some bait,' Aidyn said, reaching down to a small pile of fat worms that he had put down beside the boulder on which I sat. Carefully, he threaded several on and around the hook, effectively covering the sharp point, before casting out the line and propping the branch up behind the boulder. 'All we have to do now is wait.'

He held out a rather grubby gloved hand and helped me to my feet and over to the campsite, where Lisette was stacking some damp wood which kept collapsing and Dylan was leaning back, a book in hand, half reading, half directing her. I could tell from Lisette's pinched expression that she was reaching the end of her tether and that Dylan's form of assistance was anything but helpful.

'Let me,' Aidyn interrupted Dylan and took over from Lisette. 'Maybe we could prepare something to drink,' he suggested and she nodded, collecting the cooking pot and filling it from the lake. She dropped it beside the firepit and looked at me expectantly. I obliged and squatted down next to Aidyn, who had successfully stacked the kindling. This time conjuring the flame took more work, and I had to focus harder and longer as the fire tentatively began to burn. The dampness of the wood was particularly unhelpful and I sat beside it for a while, keeping the flames ablaze through sheer willpower.

'It's surprising that we need to have a fire in this heat,' Dylan mused, swatting some insects away with his book. 'It's already hot enough.'

'You'll be grateful for it come nightfall, scholar,' Aidyn said. He had perched himself back on one of the lakeside boulders, keeping an eye on the makeshift fishing rod. Lisette shot Dylan an exasperated look and added some more wood to the fire, prodding it with unnecessary force. I couldn't deny that I too would rather not be stooped over the fire, already sweaty and hot from the tropical air, which was now only worse. I looked at the waterfall and the lake, longingly wishing I could go for a swim to cool off.

The flames crackled as I relinquished control and leaned back onto my bedroll. I unclasped my cloak and rolled it up, tucking it away. Next went my shoes and stockings– despite Dylan's splutter and raised eyebrows– but I didn't care too much.

I padded over to my own saddle bag and pulled out the small book of runes Dylan had given me on the ship, before making my way to sit on the mossy bank. Ignoring the scandalised looks Dylan cast my way, I rolled my skirts up to my knees and dipped my feet into the water.

It was wonderful. I settled myself more comfortably and relaxed, stretching my legs out and moving my toes back and forth in the water. I opened the book and began to flick through it, tracing the detailed drawing of the rune and then checking its meaning. Dylan's handwriting was slanted and difficult at times to decipher, becoming an illegible scrawl whenever he got excited, which unfortunately was rather often. However, his drawings of the runes were clear and precise, and contrasted completely with his roughly written notes.

I had reached a page where I had turned the book to one side, hoping that it might provide some assistance with interpreting Dylan's handwriting, when I felt Aidyn settle beside me.

'What are you reading?' he asked, his arms clasping his knees. 'Looks painful.'

I bit back a snort. 'You're not wrong. It's Dylan's handwriting. I'm trying to decipher it.'

'Why don't you just ask him?' he asked reasonably.

'He would probably go off on a long monologue which I'm not really in the mood to hear,' I admitted.

'Very possibly,' Aidyn said, 'Can I be of assistance?'

'Go ahead,' I said, handing over the book.

'You're learning the Ancient Tongue?' he asked, flicking from page to page.

'Trying to,' I replied. 'Dylan gave me this to help with translating the runes. I won't ever know them all, but I remember some. My mother taught me to read some of them when I was a child, but I think I've forgotten most of them now. It was long ago.'

'What was your mother like?' His tone was strangely pensive.

'She was everything I wanted to be,' I said quietly. 'I miss her every day.' The silence stretched out between us and then I asked, 'what about you? Tell me about your mother.'

'There isn't anything to tell,' he said, still studying the pages in his hands. 'I never knew her.'

'Why?' He had my full attention now and I watched him. He had gone deathly still at my question, and it took a while before he answered. When he did it was in a calm, measured tone which didn't seem quite right.

'We never knew our mother,' he said, 'my siblings and I. The Breeders are kept separate. They do not interact with the rest of us. We do not need to know, it is easier to become what our fathers want us to be if there is no maternal influence.' He sounded bitter and detached.

'What do you mean by Breeders?' I asked, racking my memory for anything Dylan might have told me but coming up with nothing.

'After the Two Hundred Year War, there was a restructuring,' Aidyn said, 'many of our fighters had been women. The leaders saw it as a necessity to keep the others safe and segregated. They were tasked with repopulation. When our numbers were once again strong, the leaders didn't change the system back. They found it easier, I suppose. The new fighters who were raised away from their mothers were more susceptible to persuasion. More easily moulded. Each generation some females are taken aside and join the ranks of Breeders. Many consider it an honour.'

I couldn't hide the revulsion on my face and looked away, slightly sickened. I couldn't think of anything worse.

'If we're lucky, we can be married off,' Aidyn continued, and I detected the anger in his voice. 'But for most of us, we are fated to remain in the Underdark.'

'I'm sorry,' I said quietly. He looked up, surprised.

'Why?'

'It sounds like a lonely way to live. I remember my parents together before the Dark Time. Theirs was a love match,' I smiled at the memory, 'a political one too, but they loved each other. I'm sorry you didn't have something like that when you grew up.'

He shrugged. 'Dark Elves don't believe in love matches. It causes too much disorder. After all, wasn't your parents' demise brought about by a suitor of your mother's? Love can drive people to do cruel, horrific things.'

I blinked, and then nodded, 'but it can also be the cause of happy memories. I always hoped that I would have something similar one day.' I thought about my parents, Grandfather and Erik. I remembered that night with Markus, back when I had been Karliah who could run away with a sea captain and not face any consequences. Before the hurt and the pain and the anger, there had been love, even if it had been fleeting. 'But I don't think that will necessarily happen.'

'How do you know?' he asked and I looked at him surprised, but I didn't answer. I didn't want to tell him about Markus; it didn't feel right somehow. And while I felt that he was understanding about most of the things I had mentioned already, I wasn't so sure that he would be about this. I glanced away again and my eyes fell on the book in his hands.

'Did you manage to translate Dylan's writing for me?' I asked, desperate to change the subject.

He followed my gaze and handed it back, shaking his head. 'Unfortunately not. But the rune you wanted to read was "Karmuus".'

'Karmuus?'

'It means passion,' he said, folding his arms back around his knees and looking away.

'Oh,' was all I could think of saying. 'Thank you.'

'It's no trouble,' he replied absently. We fell into silence again and I watched the waterfall, the ripples on the lake spreading wider and wider until they reached my toes, which peeped up on the surface. I noticed him out of the corner of my eye watching my feet as they dipped in and out of the water.

'Don't you want to join me?' I asked, 'The leather must be hot.'

'It's fine,' he replied, but I highly doubted that he was being honest. I'd told a few falsehoods in my time and knew the signs.

'Liar,' I smiled. 'You must be sweltering.' He didn't answer. 'Surely you can take off your boots at least,' I probed. 'If not, I'll just assume you're disfigured or something under there. A monster with scales and claws perhaps?'

He huffed and began to pull off his boots. 'What part of us being burned by the sun is too hard for you to remember?'

'I don't quite believe it,' I found myself saying, a satisfied grin stretching across my face. It disappeared when he cast his boots to the side and revealed black stockinged feet under his leather breeches. 'Of course you're wearing *black* stockings,' I muttered, and he chuckled.

'Disappointed?' he asked, before dropping his feet into the water beside mine.

'What are you doing?' I said, sitting up straighter. 'You'll be soaked.'

He shrugged. 'They'll dry off easily enough.'

'If you say so,' I said, not mentioning that in the humidity it might take a while for clothes to dry properly. My attention was caught by Lisette, who had stood up by the fire and moved to our fishing rod which had started to jerk sporadically.

'It looks like we caught something,' Aidyn mused, watching her casually from my side.

'Aren't you going to go and help?' I asked, surprised that he had put all this effort into making the fishing rod and was now just sitting back and watching.

'She's got it in hand,' he replied, as Lisette pulled a silvery fish up onto the shore. 'She seems to know what to do.'

Indeed, she did. We watched as she began to scale and gut the fish by the lake's edge, before she threw the line back out, fish entrails now on the hook instead of worms. She beckoned Dylan over and he brought her a plate from the cart, onto which she placed the raw fish. She left the knife by the rod, and carried the fish closer to the fire, covering it with some thick leaves.

'Good thing we didn't go and help,' Aidyn said, 'I'm not particularly good at preparing the fish once it's been caught. I usually let Alex take over at that point.'

I laughed softly, 'I have some experience in that area. But I would hardly call myself an expert like Lisette.'

As if she heard me mention her name, Lisette glanced up and smiled, before bending over the cooking pot and ladling some of the water into some mugs. She brought them over, and I realised that there was dried mint at the bottom.

'Thank you, Lisette,' I said as she handed me my mug, and Aidyn dipped his head in thanks as she gave him one as well. She gave me a quick, assessing look as if to check that I was alright and when she was satisfied that I was, returned to the fireside and sat beside Dylan who was still reading.

I took a sip, not realising how thirsty I was. The tea was hot and stung the roof of my mouth, but I didn't care. Aidyn had placed his mug down to the side, letting it cool down perhaps, and continued to observe the lake.

As I watched him, it reminded me of those weeks ago when I had seen him in the scrying bowl and I found the courage to ask, 'how did you know I was watching when you were on the ship?' I felt embarrassed at my words, realising once I'd said them how bad it sounded, and I felt myself blush.

He picked up a stick and began to poke it into the water, the ripples spinning around and around, not answering for a while. Then he said, 'when one is raised around magic, one can sense it.'

'But how did you know it was me?' I pressed.

'You made the lantern go out,' he said quietly. 'Not many Elves can manipulate elements while they are scrying.' He looked up at me, 'But then you didn't scry again after that. Why not?'

'Why not?' I repeated, caught off guard by his question. 'I felt like I was invading your privacy, it didn't feel…' I searched for the word, 'right.'

He waved a hand in dismissal, 'Don't lie, Princess.'

I paused. Opened my mouth and then closed it when I couldn't think of anything to say.

'You were curious,' he continued softly, 'that I can understand. But don't try to say that you were invading my privacy.' He laughed hollowly, 'you didn't see anything I wanted to hide.'

'You knew I was watching the whole time?' I asked, mortified.

'Of course,' he said, shrugging again. 'But if it *had* been something private, you wouldn't have seen anything.'

'What do you mean?' I breathed, my words a mere whisper.

'When you have practised magic for a long time,' he said, poking at the water again, 'it's like you can shield yourself. Like how you can bring on smoke or shadow to cloak your movements, except in this case it prevents people from scrying for you.'

'I'd never had anyone noticing my presence before,' I murmured, hoping that the blush had started to fade from my cheeks. 'It scared me that you knew, that you sensed I was there.'

'I half expected you to attempt it,' he said, just as quietly, 'after we left the way we did.'

'You didn't even say goodbye,' I replied, not knowing why it mattered so much but needing to say it out loud.

'I left you a note.'

'A note?' I let out a dry laugh, 'Your note made me even more confused than I already was. I felt like it was my fault that your Chief Counsel decided to leave. That I had shamed my grandfather and his court by not being enough to impress the famous Dark Elves.' My tone turned bitter, and I looked away from him, blinking away the angry tears of humiliation that sprang into my eyes.

'Our Chief Counsel is hard to please,' Aidyn said. I watched as his reflection stretched out an arm to comfort me, hovering it above my shoulder for a moment before pulling it away awkwardly. 'He rarely approves of anyone, let alone an outsider. But on our return the rest of our party told our King about you and piqued his curiosity.'

I didn't reply, not trusting myself to speak in case I said something that I'd regret.

'It's an honour he has bestowed,' Aidyn continued, 'and you cannot deny that you are in great need of support, Princess. As it stands, the Usurper outnumbers your Resistance ten to one and he has Scardia's full arsenal at his disposal.'

It rankled that I couldn't disagree, for he spoke the truth.

'I, for one, am glad that the King saw fit to overrule the Chief Counsel's decision,' he said and this time he took one of my hands in his, holding it carefully, as if it were a butterfly. I looked down at our hands, mine pale with a light dusting of freckles in his dark gloved one, the remnants of soft earth still stuck to the leather. It was too intimate and I froze, wanting to pull away as my heart began to hammer a sharp staccato in my chest. Finally, I managed to draw my hand away to support my mug of tea, which shook slightly in my grasp.

I avoided Aidyn's steady gaze, glancing back at the campsite where Dylan and Lisette were resting contentedly. The afternoon seemed to have become too warm, and I stretched my legs out further in the water, trying to cool myself down. In a desperate attempt to distract myself from the tension that now shimmered between us, I said,

'When I was scrying, I saw you and the other Dark Elves doing some kind of ritual. I haven't seen magic like that. What was it?'

He pulled away and I knew that I had inadvertently pushed too far. He stood, water streaming onto the bank, and collected his boots and the undrunk mug of tea.

'The others have returned,' he said abruptly and moved away, leaving me on the riverbank, feet still stretched out in the water and feeling oddly bereft.

The hunt had been partially successful. They returned with two birds, which were large and round with bright red feathers. Erik explained to me that they had been roosting in one of the trees when Alex shot them down in rapid succession. He grumbled that the rest of the party hadn't really been needed and took over the job of fishing with Leif, even though they only succeeded in catching two more fish before sunset.

I was left to myself, and not particularly wanting to socialise, I watched the rest of the party. Rakael and Christoff were checking and sharpening the weapons while Jesse and Tobias practised some unarmed combat. Jesse's skirts hampered her movements slightly, but Tobias seemed to be averse to attacking a woman, so she used his gallantry to her advantage until she had him laid out on his back, gasping for air. Lisette checked on me several times, occupying herself with my hair which had gotten tangled and sticky in the humidity, and then collecting my empty mug and taking it back to my bedroll.

On the edge of the clearing, Alex and Aidyn stood to one side, in quiet conversation underneath the shadow of the trees. I tried not to watch them too often in case they noticed but couldn't help that my gaze kept sliding in their direction. They were bending over something, but from my position I couldn't see what it was.

Lisette patted my shoulder and I turned to her, eyebrows raised in a silent question. She pointed from herself to me and then at the waterfall. I smiled and nodded, getting to my feet and following her. We made our way around the edge of the lake, the thick moss cushioning my feet, leaving behind faint imprints as we walked on. The waterfall drew closer, the sound intensified and soon all I could hear was the crashing of water against rock as the spray hit my face.

Lisette paused here and began to take off her own shoes and stockings, placing them carefully to the side. She reached out and held my arm, leading me closer to the rocky edge until we were standing on a stone ledge that jutted out from the cliff face. We edged our way around, trying not to slip on the wet rock as we moved behind the waterfall and were shielded from the view of the campsite. Behind the waterfall was an opening in the rock face, hiding another pool which was calmer. Lisette pulled the soap bar out of her pocket and began to strip off down to her shift, sinking into the pool and swimming away. I copied her and gasped as I entered the water, the cold a sharp contrast to the warm humidity. There were voices from behind us and I ducked under the surface, diving away from the noise and feeling the sandy bottom of the pool. When I resurfaced, I saw Rakael and Jesse had joined us.

'This was a good suggestion of Alex's,' Jesse said as she paddled up next to me. 'I wouldn't have guessed this was here. There I was thinking we would not be able to bathe properly until we arrived in the Underdark.'

I was about to reply but Lisette handed me the soap instead and it took all my concentration to not drop it.

'I could stay here forever,' Jesse continued blissfully, floating beside me and gazing up at the rocky ceiling. It glistened with green and blue light, as the crash of the waterfall cast dancing shadows on the walls. I was about to answer her and pass on the soap when it slipped from my grasp, sinking down into the depths of the pool. I took a deep breath and dove again, stretching out my hands underwater to search for the small bar. I felt something brush against my fingertips and grasped onto it, lifting it closer to my face so that I could see it properly.

It was heavier than I expected and as I opened my eyes, blinking in the water, a fuzzy shape solidified in my vision. A wide gaping hole of a mouth, sharp teeth and two empty eye sockets in a smooth, pale skull gazed back at me. I dropped it in surprise, kicking up the sand in an effort to get away. Something slippery brushed against my toes and I reached down to grab the soap bar, propelling myself back to the surface in haste.

I spluttered and gasped, pushing the soap at Jesse and swimming to the edge of the pool, clambering out onto the rock on shaky legs.

'Are you alright, Nina?' Jesse asked as she treaded water, green eyes concerned.

'I saw… there was…' I couldn't get the words out properly, my heart was still pounding from the sudden shock.

'What is it?' Rakael asked from where she was relaxing with Lisette. 'Are there eels in the water or something?'

Jesse grimaced, 'I hate eels.'

'No,' I managed to get out, 'I think someone died here. There was a skull. It looked human.'

Rakael blinked and then said calmly, 'I'm sure it's nothing to be concerned about. It might have just been someone who got lost and drowned. Or an animal might have brought remains here at some point.'

I didn't want to say that I found it unlikely that an animal could have brought its prey here and so just nodded, shivering.

'I wouldn't worry about it, Nina,' Jesse said reassuringly, 'you don't know how long it's been there.'

I bit my lip and nodded again. 'I suppose you're right. It just was a shock, that's all.'

'Understandably,' Jesse said, 'although I am glad it wasn't eels that you saw. I hate eels.'

I perched on the stone ledge, watching them swim back and forth, but reluctant to join in. No matter what Rakael and Jesse said, it didn't feel right to swim where someone had died. After a while Lisette joined me, and when Jesse and Rakael were ready, we got dressed again and made our way back to the fireside. It seemed that the men had taken advantage of our absence by swimming in the lake, and they were happily dripping around the fireside laughing and joking. Even Dylan seemed a bit more cheerful than usual, he was speaking to Alex, gesticulating something with his arms.

It appeared that the only ones who hadn't partaken in an evening swim were our two guides, who remained slightly aloof. Aidyn was hunched over a wide bowl, kneading a muslin pouch back and forth in the water, which had turned a murky brown. I padded over to the fireside and sat next to Erik, who was cooking the fish fillets Lisette had prepared over the fire. Tobias was taking charge of the bird, and the smell of roasting meat teased my empty stomach, which had survived for over a day on a few pieces of dried jerky. My mouth watered and I crossed my legs, watching the meat cook with agonising slowness.

'We have something we would like to share with you over the meal,' Alex said when we had all found our places by the fire, and Dylan paused in his discussion. 'There is a tradition of welcome amongst our people when newcomers visit us. We all partake.'

I glanced at Dylan and he gave a small, reassuring nod. Rakael took out her pipe and lit it, blowing the smoke up over the fire. Her eyes were fixed on Alex in an unreadable expression.

'What is it?' Erik asked curiously, as Aidyn placed the wide bowl into Tobias' hands, wrapping the muslin pouch up in a cloth and stowing it away.

'Kava,' Alex said, 'crushed from a root in these forests and blended into a drink. It allows us to welcome newcomers with an open mind.'

From all I had heard about the Dark Elves, they didn't seem to be very open minded, but if Dylan was nodding in agreement with Alex's words, I wasn't going to question them.

'Traditionally, the men drink first,' Alex continued, as Tobias lifted the bowl to his lips and drank. It was passed around the circle of us and the men drank, Dylan's face tightened as he took his sip and then it was in Erik's hands. He lifted it up and gulped, before passing it to me.

The bowl was quite heavy, the liquid had a faint pungent smell. I held my breath and drank, before passing it quickly to Jesse, trying not to gag as I swallowed. It tasted earthy and gritty and I didn't really like it. Rakael, however, seemed to relish it, closing her eyes and drinking deeply when it was her turn. The bowl was passed around several more times, before and after the meat was cooked and shared. Each time the bowl came around I forced myself to partake, feeling that if I did not it would be considered rude, as no one else was refusing to drink it. And as the night continued, I found myself relaxing, laughing and smiling more than I had in weeks.

For a while it seemed as though everything that had weighed me down was no longer important. It didn't matter that the Usurper and his Trackers were searching for me. It didn't matter that Markus and I had parted for a second time on bad terms. It didn't matter that when we reached the Underdark I would be pushed to my limits in unknown trials. Nothing mattered in this moment because I was happy, and life was good.

Erik was reenacting one of his favourite tales with Jesse's help, and I laughed as he stumbled back and forth, losing my balance and collapsing against someone's shoulder. A gloved hand reached around to steady me, and I realised I had fallen against Aidyn. I couldn't remember him moving next to me, but as the night had progressed the others had changed places regularly, joking and breaking out into raucous song. Unlike the rest of us, Alex and Aidyn didn't laugh too loudly or join in the loud conversations. The only exception they made was to remove their masks for the kava and meal, the dark balaclavas still eerie, but significantly less so.

'Are you alright, Nina?' he asked quietly as I lolled against his shoulder. I nodded, breathless from laughing and my head spinning from the light and the noise. My eyes were heavy and I began to feel sluggish. The fact that he had finally acquiesced to my long ago request to call me Nina barely registering in my mind. 'Here,' he said, 'I thought you might like these.' He pressed some orchids into my hand and I smiled, trying to focus on their white and pink petals.

'Thank you.' I breathed in their sweet scent and then murmured, 'this place is beautiful. But it's not like home.'

'Tell me about it,' he said, his arm around me an anchor as the world began to spin in earnest. I shut my eyes and told him about Scardia. I told him about the Lightbringer Mountains, the Capital and the Palace with its formal gardens. I mentioned the rolling fields and thick pine forests, and how winter spread like a white blanket across the land for many months. My mouth curved into a smile as I remembered the Hoarfrost, the mighty glacier that stretched from the mountains in the north to the sea. The Ice Throne was made of the Hoarfrost and that was where my ancestors had been crowned for centuries. The legends said that the Ice Flame which burned behind the throne was hotter than the sun itself, but it would not melt the Hoarfrost. I recalled how my father had said that only those of royal blood could touch the flames without suffering the wrath of the Gods. I spoke until I fell into a deep sleep, lying in the comforting warmth of the fire and Aidyn's arm, and breathing in the sweetness of orchids.

Chapter Twelve

I had a troubled sleep. My dreams were full of empty skulls and coral snakes, which struck out at me as I reached out to touch jewelled shells on the ocean bed. Masked faces loomed over me, and hands pulled me this way and that, tussling over who would carry me away. I heard cries and horses in the distance, and I could have sworn I heard a budgerigar chirp. I moved in and out of near consciousness, the world around me blurred and hazy when my eyelids opened, and when I rocked myself back to sleep, I fell back into the land of bad dreams.

The Trackers moved in and out of the masked faces, the imprint of the bull's head glowing on their armour, which then turned into a burning firebird that circled my head again and again. I cried out, reaching for it to save me from the Trackers and it encased me in flames. I looked through the firelight and saw the masked men standing mere feet away. Their masks fell away as the light from the fire hit them, revealing harsh, grotesque features underneath. They might have once been human, but their skin was puckered and misshapen, red raw and oozing, as if a butcher and a blacksmith had collaborated in creating a hideous monstrosity. The men's eyes rolled with feral malice and their pointed teeth gnashed as they approached, clawed hands reaching for me. I screamed, stumbling backwards.

One by one they leapt forwards, pushing through the flames until they grabbed me and held me down. I flailed, fighting with everything I had to escape their grip. I kicked and pushed, trying to dislodge myself from the sharp grasp. The flames around me died as my eyes opened, seeing nothing at first but shadows.

'Hold still, Nina,' Aidyn's voice grunted, and I realised that both he and Alex were holding me down. I paused in my struggle, confused and disorientated.

'What's going on?' I asked, glancing around and managing to make out the shapes of the rest of our party. The fire had gone out and I couldn't hear the waterfall. 'Where are we?' I asked, rising up onto my elbows and blinking to try and see through the gloom. I felt terrible, my mouth and throat were as dry as parchment and my head ached as if I had drunk too much of Grandfather's honey mead. I took a breath and concentrated, but could only manage to create a small flame, which flickered in front of me.

'She's thirsty,' Alex said, handing a water gourd over to Aidyn, who was still kneeling beside me. I looked around groggily, taking in the rock and solid earth around us.

'Where are we, Aidyn?' I repeated, more firmly this time.

'Here, drink,' he said, lifting the gourd to my lips. I drank, gulping down the water and then scrunching up my nose at the bitter aftertaste. Aidyn handed Alex back the gourd and helped me to lie back down. 'I'm sorry,' he whispered, his mask starting to shimmer in front of my eyes. 'It has to be this way.'

The flame I had conjured flickered and died as heaviness began to spread through me again. I struggled but couldn't find the strength to move.

'Aidyn,' I breathed, terrified, my voice sounding as if it came from the end of a long tunnel, 'what have you done?'

I never heard his answer, for sleep chose that moment to pull me back under, and I was lost again in the realm of bizarre dreams.

I came to slowly. A candle was glowing on a table beside the bed in which I lay, casting a warm glow around the room. I sat up, unsure about how I had gotten there or where I was. The walls were draped with tapestries of dark green, embroidered with silver thread. In the corner of the room was a washstand and a mirror, my trunks stacked alongside them. My hands shook as I looked at them, noting that I was still wearing the same gown as I had the night before. A vase of white orchids had been placed next to the lantern and as I gazed at them, fuzzy memories slowly came back to me. I got up abruptly and pulled on my boots, tying the laces in a rush. I needed to find Erik and Lisette. I needed to make sure that everyone was alright and figure out where we were. I needed to find Aidyn and demand an explanation.

I was halfway across the room to the door when it swung inwards and Lisette entered with Rakael on her heels, shutting the door behind them.

'Good, you're awake,' Rakael said briskly, 'we need to get you dressed.'

'I'm sorry?' I asked, 'What's going on?' Lisette was following Rakael's instructions, pushing me to sit back on the bed and undressing me without a bye your leave. Rakael was rummaging through one of my trunks, before deciding on a gown of peacock blue embellished with golden thread.

'This one,' she said, pulling it out and handing it to Lisette. 'She wore it the first time the Dark Elves came to King Aegis' court. It will be fitting to wear it again.'

'Stop!' I cried, pushing away Lisette's hands as they began to reach for my hair. I glared at them, crossing my arms belligerently. 'I'm not letting you do anything until you explain what is going on.'

Rakael sighed impatiently. 'We have arrived, Nina. We reached the Ombre Mountains and are now in the Underdark.'

'*What?!*' I was incredulous. 'But we still had a way to travel, we only left…' My voice trailed off as Rakael rolled her eyes.

'We weren't awake for the journey, Princess,' she said, reverting to the tone that she often used when she felt I was acting naïvely. 'According to *Dylan*,' she ground her teeth, 'the Underdark's location is a closely guarded secret, and it is some sort of custom for visitors to be drugged on arrival. He didn't seem to think it was information that should have been shared with the rest of us. Or with you, it would appear.'

I looked from her to Lisette, stunned. Lisette gave me a nod of confirmation that what Rakael was saying was true.

'I'm never going to drink kava again,' I muttered and Rakael snorted.

'It wasn't the kava they drugged, Nina. It was something in the water.'

'The water?'

'My guess,' Rakael said, picking out a pair of golden slippers from another trunk, 'was that whatever they put in the water took effect after we had drunk the kava. I've had kava before, and it didn't make me pass out.'

'How long were we out for?' I asked cautiously, nails biting into my forearms.

'Several days, most likely,' she replied, shrugging. 'There's nothing we can do about it now. We are well and truly in the Underdark and have no way of getting out without help. I won't deny that I don't like it.' She gritted her teeth together and let out another huffing sigh and I could feel her indignation, barely contained. 'But it seems we have no choice now except to do what King Aegis planned.' She fixed her gaze on me and assessed me critically, 'we need to make sure you are presentable for the Dark Elves' King.'

It felt like everything happened around me and I was observing from outside of myself. I was disconnected from what was going on in the room, watching dispassionately as Lisette dressed me, brushed out my hair and placed the heavy sapphire necklace around my neck. The golden diadem that I had worn last time rested on my head, and as I looked at my reflection in the mirror, the sense of control I had felt over the past months slipped away.

'I don't like this, Lisette,' I whispered to her as she dabbed sweet perfume behind my ears.

'Come on,' Rakael snapped, striding to the door and barking out some orders.

Lisette pressed my hands with hers, and I drew strength from her, squaring my shoulders and following Rakael. When I exited the room, I saw the rest of our party, looking surprisingly sombre; I supposed I wasn't the only one who hadn't been comfortable with falling asleep beside a fire one night and waking up in an entirely new place. Dylan and Erik were off to the side, and they joined me as Rakael led the way down a dimly lit tunnel built into the rock.

'Nina,' Dylan began, stumbling over his feet as we tried to keep up with Rakael's pace. 'I swear I had no idea…'

'I'm surprised you didn't share what you knew about the welcoming ceremony,' I interrupted coldly. If he had told me, perhaps I wouldn't be feeling as angry as I was, or as betrayed.

'I didn't know the full extent of it,' he spluttered, 'I swear.' His eyes were wide and pleading and I couldn't stay angry with him despite myself.

'Promise me that you won't keep things hidden in the future,' I said, 'I don't want to be surprised like this again.'

'Surprised is one word for it,' Erik muttered, 'I knew there was a reason I didn't trust them.'

I couldn't argue with Erik, even though I didn't particularly like his tone. He reminded me of Markus and the way his face had turned cold and hard when he told me that I was no longer human. It reeked of prejudice and distrust, and although I didn't blame him for not wanting to trust the Dark Elves after this, a small part of me urged that I should not judge so hastily.

The tunnel turned and descended, until it opened into a vast cavern, that stretched out into darkness. Flickering lights spread out before us, some were lanterns, while others were hovering bugs that glowed pale blue and green. There were plants that radiated with coloured light, just enough to illuminate the path that led towards a large, circular structure which rose up towards the ceiling. It was majestic, the stonework carved to depict a range of scenes and figures. It was almost like some of the temples I had seen in Scardia, but this was more extravagant than any temple I had seen before. Gargoyles and demons glared down at us as we approached, their visages frozen in grotesque horror.

'That's their amphitheatre,' Dylan whispered to me, 'it's so much larger than I thought it would be. It's traditionally the heart of the Dark Elf court. The scrolls say it can hold thousands.'

'It must be very old,' I murmured as we approached, noting how the stone steps were worn and hollowed from many years of use. As we moved closer, a whispering sound filled the air, almost as if wind was blowing through a forest of trees. However, looking around at the plants, I couldn't see any that looked anything like trees. The noise seemed to be coming from inside the amphitheatre.

'Come on,' Rakael's voice sounded shaky. 'They're waiting for us.' The dusty ground underfoot gave way to the stone steps as we walked through a shrouded entranceway, our shoes clacking loudly on the black marble floor. The atrium around us was filled with polished dark mirrors, so we were reflected many times over. Masked faces appeared from the shadows, the mirrors making it difficult to tell where the Dark Elves were standing.

'By the Gods,' Tobias muttered under his breath.

'Shh,' Jesse whispered to his side. Together we all walked on until we reached the end of the atrium and entered the arena. The whispering sound intensified and then died immediately, the hushed silence sending chills through me. I glanced up and gripped Erik's hand tightly. He looked at me and then followed my gaze, eyes widening as he took in the row after row of stone benches, which went up and up until those in the back row were merely dark, shadowy blurs. The silvery masks caught the pale blue light, and I felt a twinge of fear as they all stared down at me, tracking my every movement as I followed Rakael towards the balcony at the far end of the arena.

It seemed as though time slowed as we approached, and I saw a Dark Elf who must have been their king; his body was encased in silver, and he was sitting on an obsidian throne. Beside him were a bevy of other Dark Elves and I scanned them quickly, wondering if Aidyn or Alex were amongst their number, not that I would be able to tell them apart anyway. When there were so many Dark Elves around, it was impossible to distinguish one from the crowd.

One of the Dark Elves bent and whispered into the silver one's ear as we came to a halt, looking up at the balcony. Another one called out in a harsh voice, 'you are in the presence of King Lysander, Lord of the Underdark and the Shadow Realm, Uniter of the Three Sects and Holder of Erthor's Favour. You *will* bow and show your due reverence, newcomers.' I recognised the voice as that of the Dark Elf Chief Counsel. He sounded just as sour and arrogant as all those weeks ago when he was visiting my grandfather's court. Rakael didn't argue, but bent into a bow, and the rest of us followed suit. I raised my fingers to my brow and lowered my head, curtseying low and trying to stop my hand from trembling.

'Rise.' The order was delivered in a deep, baritone voice that sounded like it was used to giving orders and being obeyed. I kept my gaze down towards my golden slippers, the weight of over a thousand stares burning into me.

'You are Rakael Minschke?' the deep voice boomed, 'Leader of the Scardian Resistance?'

Rakael lifted her head, eyes flashing and when her voice rang out it sounded strong. 'I am.'

'You come with a proposal from King Aegis, I believe?' the king demanded, opening a tightly bound scroll and perusing it carefully.

'Indeed, Your Majesty.' Rakael said, inclining her head. Lisette shifted beside me, and I glanced at her curiously.

'State your proposal,' he said, rolling the scroll back up.

'King Aegis proposes an alliance between the Dark and High Elven kingdoms.' Rakael's back was ramrod straight and I could sense her tension, but her voice remained steady. 'He proposes that, should Your Majesty approve, an alliance be formed through marriage between his granddaughter, Wilhelmina Constantina Fiordlasher, Heir to the Ice Throne of Scardia, and one of your sons.'

I went numb and swayed, but Lisette and Erik grabbed each of my arms, holding me firm.

'Don't show your emotions,' Jesse whispered under her breath to me, and I blinked at her, too shocked to think clearly.

'Did you know about this, Lisette?' I murmured, lowering my eyes again in a semblance of what I hoped was female modesty. I felt her fingers grip me tightly and I knew that she had.

My mind spun and I struggled to breathe, the tight corseted bodice feeling even more restrictive than normal. When I was able to focus on the world around me again it was to hear the king say, 'we shall need time to consider this proposal. The Princess Wilhelmina will need to prove her worth through the Ancient Trials first.'

Rakael bowed again, 'As you command, Your Majesty.'

The king's gaze turned to me. 'Come closer, Princess Wilhelmina.' He raised a hand, and a number of stones broke away from the walls of the amphitheatre, creating a temporary stairway leading up to the balcony. Lisette gave me a subtle push and I began to climb the steps, shooting Rakael a swift glare that let her know that she would be explaining to me later exactly what she and Grandfather had proposed. I didn't have time to contemplate the pain of realising that

Grandfather had agreed to this and not told me, but that wasn't something I wanted to digest in public.

The steps were just wide enough for me to stand on and I had to focus on placing one foot in front of another in order to not lose my balance. I glanced down at the ground, which was drawing further away and swayed slightly, before a gloved hand reached out and grasped mine, helping me to climb over the balcony's banister.

'You look beautiful, Princess.' It was Aidyn. His voice sounded as shaky as I felt, as if he was unsure whether I would rail at him or smile. Remembering that all eyes were on us and knowing what Grandfather would say, I forced a small smile and thanked him. Then I turned to the king, whose silver body armour was even more impressive and intimidating up close. I dropped into another curtsey, noting the detailing in the silverwork and how the pieces were finely tied together. He observed me closely and then, when I rose to my feet, he stood and moved over to inspect me. He circled me, two advisors beside him, and their whispered comments made me hold myself even more stiffly.

'Her hips are narrow for childbearing,' one said.

'Her chin is very prominent,' the other muttered, 'her eyes are adequate, I suppose, but her mouth is too generous.'

'She is an acceptable height,' the king mused. 'Do you enjoy reading, Princess Wilhelmina?' he shot at me.

'Yes, sire,' I replied, trying to keep the tremble out of my voice.

'Can you ride?'

'Yes, sire.'

'Have you ever travelled to the continent?' His voice changed its timber, and I realised belatedly that he was speaking Felshkran, the language of the desert plains to the south of Velkra.

'I have not,' I replied in the same tongue, 'as a child I learned to speak the languages of Felshkar and Velkra, but my education did not last for very long.'

'Of course,' the king said. 'And you dance and sing, I assume?'

I nodded slowly. 'I am a better dancer than musician, I'm afraid.'

'Disappointing,' one of the councillors muttered. 'Can you embroider and weave, Princess?'

When would I have had time for weaving and embroidery over the past ten years? I had experience with sewing and needlework but had never done it for pleasure. Something probed at the edges of my mind, and a sharp pain began to pierce my temple. Images flashed before my eyes, memories that I couldn't control spanning the years of my life, playing out on fast forward in front of my eyes. My parents dancing below in a crowded ballroom while I watched from the top of the stairs, just out of sight. Keely tending to an injured puppy with brown, floppy ears. Erik crouched on a deck, slick with seawater while Markus lifted me into his arms. The pain intensified and the memories began to focus on Markus: us dancing in the galley, me leaning my head on his shoulder, our lips meeting as he pressed me against the door to his cabin.

The councillor reached out and lifted my chin, and his voice filled my mind, terrifying me.

'Are you untouched, Princess?'

I forced myself to remain still, taking deep breaths as the indignation boiled inside me. What right did they have to ask such things? What were they doing? I hadn't prepared myself for this sort of onslaught and my head pounded.

'Is this really necessary?' Aidyn asked, his tone reflecting the anger I couldn't show. 'She's been through enough just reaching this place, must you subject her to your interrogation now?'

'You are right, Aidyn,' the king stepped back, his councillors following with less enthusiasm. 'Forgive us, Princess Wilhelmina. It has been a long time since we had outsiders amongst us.'

The pain in my temples withdrew and I inclined my head, not trusting myself to respond. It was taking all of my willpower to not reveal the turbulent sea of emotion that was threatening to be unleashed.

'You are welcome in our court,' the king said. 'My son will lead you to our banquet hall for the feast.'

'Son?' I croaked, the sensation of being poleaxed was becoming all too familiar now.

'Come on, Princess,' Aidyn murmured, taking my arm and looping it through his, allowing me to lean against him. I hadn't realised how unsteady on my feet I was, how drained I felt after being questioned.

'I thought,' I muttered through a forced smile as we passed the Dark Elf councillors, 'that you were a Lord. Not a prince.'

'I'm not a prince,' he said stiffly. 'I am not royal through birth, but chance. And if my father is killed then I will revert to being a member of my House, potentially not even a Lord, if the following ruler decides it. You seem to forget that we don't inherit through birth, Princess.'

I felt sick. First, I had been drugged. Then I had found out my grandfather was bartering me off like a prize heifer. And then, to top it off, Aidyn had not been honest about who he was.

'Why didn't you tell me who you really were?' I asked numbly.

He laughed, 'That's funny, coming from you, Nina. Wasn't it only recently that you began to go by your own name again? Didn't you hide your identity for years, living under different pseudonyms? It's hypocritical of you to accuse me of being dishonest.'

He had a point, but I didn't care overly much by then. We had left the Dark Elf Council behind and were making our way down a winding stairwell of black marble, and from the sounds around us, it seemed as though all the other spectators were also leaving their seats and heading out en masse. It was easier to talk amidst the sounds of the crowd's movement, even if we couldn't see them.

'I have only ever been myself with you,' I snapped. 'A fact that I am starting to regret now.' He had the audacity to laugh again. I glared at him, 'I don't see what's so funny. Not only have you lied about who you are, but you also drugged us. How can I trust you after that?'

'Technically, Alex put the herbs in the water,' he said, and I clenched my jaw furiously. 'We didn't have a choice, Nina,' he continued, lowering his voice as we exited the stairwell and joined a throng of Dark Elves who were filing out of the amphitheatre. 'You don't understand the rules which we need to abide by. One of the reasons we have managed to avoid so many outside conflicts is because no one knows where the entrance to the Underdark *is*.'

'That didn't stop Dark Elves from having centuries of in-fighting,' I retorted. 'Just because you're hidden doesn't mean your people have avoided war.'

'Do you think I'm not aware of that, Princess?' he asked curtly, manoeuvring me through the crowd, ignoring the stares as the other Dark Elves realised who I was and paused to watch us pass. 'I happen to believe that connections with the outside world will not necessarily spell disaster for my people, but our elders and councillors have strict rules. No newcomer may learn the route, no matter who they are.'

'It wouldn't stop a Dark Elf sharing the secret of how to find the Underdark,' I replied. His grip on my arm tightened and then relaxed as he led me down the steps to the amphitheatre and turned to the right, moving quickly across the packed earth. Glowing purple plants grew in small clusters along the edge of the path, but he didn't allow me any time to inspect them more closely.

'You don't understand.' I had struck a nerve, his voice was cutting and harsh, much harsher than I had ever heard before. 'The Underdark is a reflection of Erthor's kingdom. It's against our sacraments to divulge his secrets or to work against his desires. He tasked the Dark Elves with watching over his lands and we guard that secret with our lives. No matter what happens between the sects, there is one common agreement, one consensus: that we keep Erthor's kingdom safe and secure.'

He spoke with fervour and such conviction that I could almost understand why he and Alex had done what they did.

'You could have just explained that we needed to be put to sleep for the remainder of the journey here,' I muttered grumpily, and he snorted.

'And you would have taken the draught willingly? None in your party would have fought, or argued or resisted giving up control?'

I opened my mouth to agree and then stopped myself. Rakael would have put up a fight, as might the other Resistance guards. Erik would have argued, and I would have tried everything in my power to not lose control of myself. I thought the only one of us who would actively agree would have been Dylan, who would have considered it an experiment.

'You don't have to answer,' Aidyn said, 'but perhaps you understand why we didn't say anything. Very few people would actively trust openly so soon into an acquaintance.'

I nodded thoughtfully. Satisfied, he led me on, the procession of Dark Elves following behind us, some holding small lanterns which swung back and forth. I looked ahead and realised that we were heading towards another dark tunnel mouth.

'The Underdark stretches through many tunnel systems,' Aidyn said as we entered the darkness, and his arm temporarily became my main guide. Soft light began to follow us, sending the shadows to cower and writhe on the walls as we passed. Despite the flickering lanterns behind us, Aidyn led me on so that we were on the edge of the light and dark, teetering back and forth as we walked onwards. He turned and led me down a side passage to a dark river, where a range of boats were tied up to a dock. Wood creaked underneath our feet as he helped me into one of the boats and stepped in behind me, pushing us away from the dock with a fine willow pole. I glanced back as he punted us away into the darkness, at the faint lanterns on the dock as the other Dark Elves began to pile into the other boats, jostling each other for space on the small crafts.

'Do you need some light to see where you're going?' I asked Aidyn, as we cut through the dark waters.

'That would be most helpful, Princess,' he said, 'thank you.'

'You're welcome,' I said, conjuring the small flame to hover above the front of the boat, providing just enough light so that Aidyn could see the river up ahead. I sat back in the cushioned seat, admiring the curved wooden bird on the bow, its neck reaching down towards its chest in the water, the wings spreading along the sides of the boat. It looked like a swan but with a shorter neck, wide eyes and a sharp beak. There was a plume on its bent head that I thought looked vaguely familiar.

'The phoenix,' Aidyn said quietly, noticing where my attention was fixed. 'It symbolises rebirth and change. It's the guardian of our House, our sect.'

'Which sect do you belong to?' I asked, 'there are three aren't there?'

'You've been revising your lore,' he murmured, a smile lacing his words. 'Which one do you think the phoenix represents?'

I pursed my lips, thinking back to what Dylan had told me on the voyage. 'Potentially the followers of Lionus– Lord of the Dead. Or, Sybilla, the Sun Goddess.'

'Not Erthor?' he queried.

'I don't think the moon represents rebirth or change,' I replied. 'To me it's more lonesome, more solemn.' I glanced back at him, 'so which House does the phoenix belong to?'

'Sybilla,' he said, gazing ahead at the point where the wooden phoenix's beak broke the surface of the water, inches below my ball of fire. I trailed a hand in the water, which was icy to touch, and thought back to how he had spoken about light and fire. He had always seemed almost reverent, as if it had been something holy.

Something under the water's surface shifted and I withdrew my hand. A shadow moved underneath our craft, but the water was so murky that it was impossible to tell what the creature was. I caught sight of the jagged point of a tail break the surface before the creature dove back down into the depths. The ripples caused by its rapid descent lapped against the dark riverbank. The light from my fire caught the edges of coloured stones embedded in the walls so that as we moved on, flickers of deep blue and green danced in the corner of my eyes. It felt magical, and like we were the only people around, although by now I could hear the movement of other boats behind us and quiet conversation from the other Dark Elves.

Aidyn hadn't spoken again, and the pole moved back and forth in his grasp until we pulled up alongside another dock, as the river left the tunnel and entered another cavern. He alighted and secured the boat to the dock, before holding out a hand to help me disembark. He kept hold of it as we departed, the flame I had conjured flickering away into nothingness as he led me up a stairway lit with glowing fungus. In his gloved hand my own was pale and wan, eerily so in the dim light, but his grasp was warm and filled me with a sense of security.

'Where are we going, Aidyn?' I asked as we climbed the stairs, our footsteps reverberating and echoing. 'Your father mentioned a banquet, but where is it?'

'He wants to put on a show for you and your party,' he replied, 'and we have arrived.' We had reached the top of the stairs and looked out over a vast space, the river we had travelled on winding around the land before us. The cavern's base was scattered with stalagmites that strained up towards the stalactites above, covered with the strange glowing fungus. Amongst the clusters of stalagmites, round tables were interspersed, already piled with plates of food.

'Each sect eats separately,' Aidyn indicated three different points around the cavern, 'but we will eat at the King's Table.' He pointed across the expanse to a raised platform, surrounded by a railing of twisted metals, located almost precisely in the centre of the room. At the base of the raised platform an ornate dance floor of polished marble stretched out.

As we approached the platform, the sound of pipes and whistles began to fill the air. I glanced around, searching for the musicians, who were small, misshapen creatures, suspended in a cage up amongst the stalactites, hovering high above the dance floor. The cage they were in rocked gently from side to side, hitting the stalactites with rhythmic thuds. It was a long way up. It would be far for them to fall if the cage suddenly gave way.

'They offended my father,' Aidyn said, his voice blank and emotionless as he followed my gaze. 'They're some of the cave dwellers who share the Underdark, but their kind do not always show appropriate respect.'

'Remind me to stay on your father's good side,' I muttered, 'did they do something terrible?'

'I doubt it,' he answered.

'Then their punishment seems a bit extreme,' I said cautiously.

'On the contrary, it's a light sentence,' Aidyn replied, looking away from the caged musicians. 'They should be let out of there after a month.'

'A month?' I gasped, shocked. 'A month's imprisonment for a minor misdemeanour?'

He chuckled wryly and shook his head. 'Princess, you've been studying our culture, although clearly not enough. Think about everything you have learned about my people. We are not like humankind or even your grandfather's court. We are custodians of the dark, of unreachable lands and of the night's secrets. It is not our way to be compassionate or kind, those emotions allow weakness and lead to death.'

I blinked at him, confused. 'But then how does that explain you?'

It seemed that I had rendered him temporarily speechless, so I continued. 'You're not like the others, you care.' I was grateful that the light was dim so he wouldn't see my blush. 'When that Tracker took Erik and I and you found us, you made sure that I was safe. You took care of Stefan when he was knocked unconscious. I don't truly believe you can be callous as Dylan says Dark Elves are supposed to be.'

'You have not known me for very long, Princess.' His voice was tight, and it reminded me of my own, many months before when I had pushed Markus away, feeling that he was becoming too close. It was the tone I had often used while in hiding, and it struck me as strange that it was now being used towards me by someone else. It was now I who wanted to know more, to push beyond what he said and uncover who he really was. This realisation was both stunning and frightening and I glanced away from his masked face, suddenly uncertain.

We had reached the steps up to the King's Table and ascended, his hand still gripping mine so that I wouldn't slip. When we had climbed onto the platform, he released me and moved to stand by the railing, watching the procession of Dark Elves behind us, lanterns bobbing as they filed away towards their different eating areas. I saw the other members of my party approaching us, and behind them came a litter draped in heavy cloth.

'My father likes to make an entrance,' Aidyn muttered under his breath. 'He will do his best to outshine your grandfather's hospitality. He thrives on competition.'

'It sounds like you don't,' I commented, leaning on the twisted rail beside him.

'Competition is a way of life,' he said bluntly. 'You must always strive to be better than your opponent.'

'Life isn't always a battle to fight,' I murmured, the compulsion to reach out and lay my hand on his arm was strong, but I resisted. 'There are hardships and challenges but there are good times too. Light and dark.'

'You might change your mind after being here for a while,' he said, and there was something in his tone that I couldn't quite place. Regret? Shame?

'Well considering the main reason I am here is to try to gather support for reclaiming Scardia, that might not be a bad thing.' I said lightly, 'As you said yourself, the Usurper is a formidable opponent.'

'Your Grandfather planned a political alliance,' Aidyn said thoughtfully, 'I assume he told you about that.'

I held myself very still. 'Of course.'

He chuckled wryly, 'I thought not.'

'I'm sure he had his reasons.' I wasn't sure why I was defending Grandfather, except that I felt I was the only one who had the right to be angry with him.

'He probably didn't say anything because he didn't want to have you argue it.' I flinched slightly and Aidyn touched my arm gingerly. 'Forgive me,' his voice was contrite now, 'all I meant was that you are outspoken, there's no denying it. You don't strike me as the sort of woman who would accept a marriage arrangement blindly.'

A heaviness settled around my heart and I said, 'I can't expect to have a marriage like my parents', they were the exception. It's more important that I do what's necessary to help Scardia.'

'Even if it meant marrying someone you've never met?' he asked, voice hard.

'If it was necessary.' I said firmly, watching Rakael striding across the dance floor towards us. Her expression was harsh and grim, and I could feel her tension from a distance as she stared at Aidyn and I, brows knit together.

He regarded me for a moment and I avoided his gaze, not wanting to admit that deep down I resented being offered in marriage, like something to be bartered. Especially by my grandfather, which I never would have expected. Most of all I didn't want to let Aidyn know how much this news had thrown me. I was still digesting it and hadn't quite understood how I could have been ignorant of it for so long.

'Was that why the Dark Elves originally came to my grandfather's court?' I asked quietly, knowing that as soon as my companions arrived, I wouldn't be able to ask these questions. 'It wasn't really out of any interest to support the Resistance's war effort?'

'Well,' Aidyn said uncomfortably, 'partially. We *were* curious about you, but the prospect of forming an alliance through marriage had been mentioned, yes. I don't think my father was seriously considering it though until we returned.'

My mouth tightened. So, they had known. They had all known except me, the one who would be married off.

'That was why I went to King Aegis' Court,' Aidyn continued, almost as if he were speaking to himself. 'I wanted to meet you. Talk to you. Understand who Scardia's lost princess was.' He had my full attention now and I stared at him, hating the mask for making it impossible to read his expressions. 'You weren't what I expected.' He finished, returning my gaze, his gloved hands enfolding mine once again. I held my breath, waiting for him to continue, but the silence stretched out between us, full of unspoken words and questions. My heart was beating fast again, the faint tingling that I had learned to associate with magic was running up and down my arms.

'Nina!' Erik's voice broke through the moment and I pulled away, jumping in surprise. 'We were wondering where you were.'

'I'm fine, Erik,' I said quickly, moving to his side. 'Aidyn just brought me on ahead, that's all.'

'I thought you would come back and join us so we could all go together,' Erik muttered, casting a suspicious look at Aidyn. The other members of our group were glancing around, taking in the long table piled high with food and the Dark Elven councillors who were moving to stand behind the high-backed chairs.

'Father.' Aidyn's voice rang out, and we turned to see King Lysander, his silver armour creaking as he paused at the top of the stairs. We bowed as he passed us and sat in the central chair. Two Dark Elves assisted him with removing the silver helmet, revealing the familiar balaclava underneath, except this one was woven with silver thread, decorated with delicate moons and stars.

'Sit,' he commanded, and we sat around the table, eyes wide as we looked at the plates in front of us. It was overly extravagant, with piles of fruit, stuffed birds and fish and tureens of braised vegetables stretching out across the tablecloth. There was more food than I expected we could eat in a week, let alone one meal. I could almost hear Erik's stomach rumbling and felt hungry myself, hardly surprising since I had been unconscious for several days. No wonder I felt weak.

Aidyn pulled my chair out for me and sat to my right, while Erik claimed the spot on my left. It seemed that everyone was waiting for the signal to start eating, and chatter from around the great cavern fell silent as the king held up a hand. Some attendants lifted a small chest, releasing a swarm of white butterflies, that fluttered around the room, their wings bright flashes of soft light.

'Lunar moths,' Aidyn whispered in my ear, 'blessed with Erthor's light.'

'Begin.' King Lysander boomed, and as one, the Dark Elves unhinged the lower half of their masks and removed them to eat. Many moved in unison, their motions mimicking each other so that it was hypnotising to watch.

'Eat, Nina,' Rakael said from further down the table. Her tone implied that I was being impolite having not already filled my plate. I frowned, reaching for some of the vegetables.

'Here, let me,' Aidyn said, serving me some of the fish and then ladling the vegetables onto my plate.

'Thank you,' I said, trying hard not to watch the other Dark Elves eat through their masks, taking minute bites of food at a time. It still struck me as odd and restrictive, a custom that I was sure I would never understand fully. To my left, Erik was staring at the king's silver armour, following the detailing with his eyes as he ate. I saw images of the sun and moon merging in the silver, stretching out across the breastplate. His armour clinked as he moved, and I wondered how heavy it must be.

'I trust that my son has been amusing you, Princess Wilhelmina,' he said suddenly, and Aidyn stiffened beside me.

'He has been very welcoming, Your Majesty,' I replied carefully, wondering how the king thought his son had been amusing.

'Tomorrow, you will take her on a tour, Aidyn,' he said brusquely. 'She will need to acclimatise to our realm before the Council tests her further.'

'As you wish, Father,' Aidyn replied, and if it hadn't been for the way he was holding himself like a tightly wound spring, I would have thought nothing was wrong.

'You will accompany him, of course, Princess Wilhelmina.' The cold voice of the Chief Counsel interjected, as he looked at me from across the table.

'Of course she will,' Rakael spoke up.

The Chief Counsel sniffed haughtily. 'The rest of you may participate in the General's practice drills. And you,' he shot a glance at Dylan, 'I understand have requested access to the Archives. Unfortunately,' his tone dripped with condescension, 'without a guide, you will be unable to access them. They are located deep within the Underdark and I'm afraid we cannot spare...'

'I will take the scholar.' Alex's low tone came from the other end of the table, and the Chief Counsel turned towards them, clearly annoyed. Alex ignored him and looked at Dylan, whose face was alit with excitement, like a child rewarded with a long-awaited treat. 'It will take a few days to reach the Archives, but we will make sure to return before the Princess needs to leave.'

'Very well then,' the Chief Counsel snapped, displeased. 'But do not think of taking anything scholar. King Lysander does not treat thieves with mercy.'

'Thank you, of course not... it's an honour,' Dylan spluttered, blinking owlishly in surprise.

'Dylan is not a thief,' I interrupted him, 'he will act respectfully.'

If I could have seen the Chief Counsel's expression, I'm sure I would have felt the full force of his glare.

'I have no doubt,' King Lysander said courteously. But there was a hardness behind the words, and I felt a tremor go through me.

'I still believe, Sire,' the Chief Counsel said, 'that the Princess' trial should begin sooner rather than later. She proved herself adequately prepared at our last meeting in King Aegis' court.'

'She is ready,' Rakael added, and I clenched my hands in my lap, trying to control the anger of being spoken about as if I were not present.

'Perhaps,' King Lysander mused, 'But it would be good manners to give her a day's grace. Then we shall see what she can do.'

I felt an ominous sensation creeping down my spine. Whatever these trials would entail, I was sure that I didn't want to partake in them. I laid down my cutlery, my appetite gone.

'Aidyn,' the king barked suddenly. 'The Princess is finished. Dance with her.'

All eyes were now on Aidyn and I, and I felt awkward under the scrutiny. I didn't like the way that the king commanded his son and it made me wonder how much of this Aidyn actually wanted. Did he feel like me— like a pawn being manipulated and pushed around in a game?

'Come on Nina,' Aidyn murmured, and I could feel his embarrassment. 'Please.'

I took his offered hand and had never felt more grateful to leave my dinner companions behind. The music swelled around us, and I noticed other couples from the tables down below were already out on the floor, in two snaking lines as they danced a stately minuet. Aidyn didn't speak as we joined the end of the line, and I held my tongue for the first few measures, counting the steps in my head as we moved back and forth, turning and swaying, our hands meeting demurely palm to palm.

Finally, I couldn't hold back anymore, and as we stepped shoulder to shoulder, I said quietly,

'I'm afraid I don't particularly like your father.'

'You are so quick to make a judgement, then?' he asked, as we took two steps forward and then four back before twisting away into a figure eight movement. I danced with another Dark Elf for a measure, before we switched partners again and Aidyn was opposite me once more.

'I don't like your Chief Counsel either,' I said bluntly as we circled each other.

'At least you have more reason to dislike him,' Aidyn replied. 'You only met my father today. It doesn't seem right to judge him so quickly.'

I didn't know how to explain that I didn't like the ominous feeling that I had had when his father looked at me, or the way he spoke as if I were something to be seen and not heard.

Aidyn seemed to sense my thoughts, for his grip tightened on my hand and he said, 'you must remember, Nina, that this situation is not normal for our people. I cannot remember the last time there were outsiders in our halls. My father is merely ensuring that protocol is followed.'

The music drew to an end and he bowed to me, before another Dark Elf asked me for the next dance. Aidyn drew away, standing on the edge of the dance floor, watching from beside the stairs to the King's Table. I danced with multiple partners, never being given names or asked questions, but treated with almost reverent grace as I moved across the floor. My companions soon descended and joined in the revels, and I noticed Lisette and Dylan dancing beside Jesse and Tobias. Rakael was beside Aidyn, talking gravely, Christoff and Leif hovering behind her like bodyguards. Erik led me through one measure, a slightly pained expression on his face as he tried to remember the steps.

'Jesse said I needed to practise,' he said grumpily, 'you know I hate dancing.'

'Remember that knights need to have courtly manners as well as swordsmanship skills,' I smiled, valiantly ignoring the jab of pain as he stepped on my foot. He muttered something under his breath but managed to get through the remainder of the dance without forgetting any major steps. Afterwards he skulked away, peering around for others his own age but not being able to find any amongst the sea of masks. Finally, he moved to stand sulkily by Aidyn and Rakael, scrutinising Aidyn through narrowed, distrustful eyes.

'Princess Wilhelmina,' The cold voice was like sweetened treacle. 'Might I have the honour?'

The Chief Counsel led me into the throng for a slower, more sedate courtly dance which forced us to hold ourselves upright and aloof. The steps were short and precise, and I felt a twinge of distaste as he gripped my hand for the first measure.

'Are you ready for your trial, Princess Wilhelmina?' he asked silkily, and a cold presence began to push at the edges of my mind. 'I, for one, am looking forward to seeing what the Council has prepared for you.'

'I thought you were in charge of the Council,' I said with forced calm, keeping my eyes looking straight ahead, determined not to let him see that he was rattling me.

'We do not share everything with each other,' he replied, 'But I am sure that watching you will provide adequate entertainment.'

'Why do I get the impression that you don't want me to succeed?' I asked through gritted teeth.

'Oh, but I *do*, my dear,' he said smoothly. 'If you manage to succeed you will bring much needed variety into our court.' One finger stretched up and rubbed against my knuckles. Involuntarily I pulled away, but my hand was held fast. 'How disappointing,' he murmured, clicking his tongue reprovingly. 'We will need to tame that rebelliousness of yours, Wilhelmina. Our king will not desire a daughter in law who will not be willing to submit to her Lord's Right.'

I thought for a second that I would faint. My breathing faltered and I almost stumbled mid-step. From the stairway, Aidyn pulled away from Rakael and Erik, cutting through the crowd to make his way towards me.

'Ah look,' the Chief Counsel said, 'the young pup arrives.'

'May I cut in?' Aidyn's tone was cool but firm, asking merely out of forced politeness but his hand had plucked mine swiftly away from the Chief Counsel's grasp, placing it on his arm.

'You need to practise your manners, Lord Aidyn,' the Chief Counsel said icily, 'there is no need to interrupt the young lady and myself.' He waved a hand at Aidyn, who tensed, muscles spasming underneath my fingers. He made no noise, but his breaths came in shorter gasps. 'Luckily for you, young pup,' the older man continued, 'the dance was just ending. Thank you for the *pleasure* of your company, Princess

Wilhelmina.' He bowed to me and departed, returning to the King's Table. As he left, Aidyn relaxed, and it was my turn to steady him.

'Let's go somewhere quiet,' I suggested, eager to get off the dance floor where we were garnering several glances from the Dark Elves. He nodded and led me away, moving perhaps too quickly to avoid attracting attention, but I didn't mind. I needed to get away from the Chief Counsel and his wandering hands and sickening voice. The words he had spoken though lingered in my ear, making me feel a rush of faintness all over again.

Aidyn paused at a sheltered alcove amongst a cluster of stalagmites, which provided a semi-effective privacy screen between us and the dance floor.

'What did he do to you?' I asked anxiously, kneeling beside him as he slumped down against a large stalagmite, which was softened with the strange glowing moss. A lunar moth landed on his shoulder, its wings opening and closing slowly, as it made its way down his arm to his knees, which were clasped to his chest. It paused there, casting a soft pale light around us, almost like a candle.

'Tell me Aidyn,' I pressed, not caring about the dampness and the dirt seeping into the bottom of my skirts. 'What's wrong?'

'It's nothing,' Aidyn muttered, rubbing his temple with one hand, 'the Chief Counsel is rather adept at knowing how to cause pain, that's all. He knows how to twist the mind to make one weep or scream at the click of a finger. Be careful of him, Nina.'

I remembered how my head had pounded with a chilly coldness, earlier on the dance floor and when I was first presented to King Lysander.

'I promise,' I murmured, eyeing him with concern.

'What was he saying to you?' Aidyn asked, 'While you were dancing?'

The whispered words came back to me, and I felt again the brush of his fingers against my knuckles. I clasped my hands together to stop them from trembling and tried to figure out how best to word the question I dreaded to ask.

'He is looking forward to the trial,' my voice was so quiet I could barely hear it. 'He said that I will need to be tamed.' I glanced anxiously through the stalagmites, checking to see that we hadn't been overheard. The dancing continued, my travelling companions however were circling the floor, searching for me. Erik was scanning the crowd, clearly worried to have lost sight of me.

'I must return,' I said abruptly, rising to my feet. The lunar moth was dislodged from its position on Aidyn's knee as he stood too, and together we rejoined the outskirts of the gathering. I felt a touch of cold and looked up towards the balcony overlooking the dance floor. From high above, the silver-clad king and the Chief Counsel looked down at us and I began to tremble again.

Chapter Thirteen

Erik punished me with the silent treatment all the way back to the tunnel where our rooms were. I could tell that he was angry that Aidyn and I had left the dance floor, disappearing from view and, perhaps most importantly, that I hadn't gone to find him instead.

'I am the one who should be protecting you,' he grumbled as I bid him goodnight, sounding like a petulant child. 'Not him.'

Jesse rolled her eyes, 'you need to accept that more people than just you are going to be caring about Nina, Erik. You're not the only one who protects her. Don't forget that she can protect herself.'

I wished that I shared some of her confidence, for mine had been shaken. But I could pretend, and managed to reassure Erik with a quick hug during which I whispered that I was glad he was there, no matter what. That perked him up, and he headed off to the rooms he was sharing with the other men in a relatively jaunty mood. Jesse had raised her eyebrows and bid me goodnight, leaving Rakael behind.

Rakael hovered by the doorway, glancing over my shoulder to see Lisette starting to prepare my nightclothes. I crossed my arms and glared at her, allowing the anger I had felt since that moment in the amphitheatre to finally show. Her gaze met mine and her mouth hardened stubbornly.

'There's no use arguing over the proposal, Princess,' she said with icy calm. 'We need the Dark Elves. You *will* succeed in their trials, and you *will* marry one of King Lysander's children. Your grandfather agreed and signed the wedding contract already. You will not embarrass the High Elven Court, the Resistance or Scardia by refusing to do your duty. We must retake Scardia by any means necessary.'

'My duty?' I asked scathingly, 'how *dare* you speak to me of duty. How dare you make decisions for me without consulting me about them first. You might lead the Resistance, Rakael, but when I am queen…' Something sharp pressed against my neck, just below my chin.

'You might want to choose your words more wisely, Princess,' Rakael snarled, her eyes turning feral. 'A princess does not have to be alive to fuel a rebellion.'

She had gone mad. I was sure of it. I gasped and the blade dug deeper into my neck.

'Do not forget the role you must play,' Rakael breathed, her face inches from mine. 'You will do what you are told and you will *not* disrupt months of planning. I will not let you ruin everything I have worked for.' The blade was preventing me from speaking, so I just nodded briefly. She pulled away, her expression switching from harshness to smiling concern so quickly that I was thrown. 'You will need to make a good impression on Lord Aidyn tomorrow. Get some rest.' With that, she turned and crossed the tunnel, entering the chamber where she and Jesse were sleeping.

I entered my bedchamber, unable to stop my body from shaking. I couldn't quite grasp everything that had happened tonight. My head felt overloaded, my heart was aching from the lies and the deception that I had been completely oblivious to, and my neck stung from where Rakael's knife had been. Lisette came over to me and began to fuss, removing my sapphire necklace and golden diadem, placing them carefully back in their wrappings. The peacock blue dress was lifted away, the sleeves removed, and corset loosened. I noted that the bottom of the skirt was streaked with mud, and my golden slippers were roughened and dirty. Lisette clucked her tongue in disapproval and gestured for me to get into bed. I pulled my nightgown over my head and sat on the bed, watching her as she placed my sullied clothing over one of the trunks and began to set up a small trestle bed.

As she prepared her own toilette, I broke the silence. 'Why didn't you warn me, Lisette? About the marriage proposition, about Grandfather's plans? I felt like an imbecile today. It was humiliating being the only one who did not know what was going on. I shouldn't have been left to fend for myself like that.' I felt tears burn my eyes and crossed my arms, nails biting small moons into my forearms. Lisette stared at me, her eyes large and wide, filled with sadness. 'I should have been told.' I stated, gulping back the sobs that were rising to join the tears. 'Even my mother knew about her arranged marriage before it happened. Why was I not informed about this one?'

She put down a pile of blankets and sat next to me, reaching out and pulling my hands into hers. She gazed at me, and in her expression I saw the regret and the pain, but also the truth.

'Was it because of Markus and I?' I asked, stomach twisting at the thought of him.

She nodded slowly, and then drew me in for a hug.

'I'm still angry,' I said between hiccups. 'You shouldn't keep things like this from me. You're meant to be on *my* side, Lisette.'

She gripped tighter and I realised that she was also crying, silent tears that dripped slowly down her cheeks. We sat there for a while until the tears stopped, then we cleaned our faces at the washstand. I didn't say anything about Rakael, or the Chief Counsel or Aidyn. I wasn't quite sure why. Partially because I didn't want to burden Lisette with anymore guilt or worry, but also because I wasn't sure how to broach the topics; how to express my fears or doubts appropriately. So instead of sharing my additional burdens, I bid Lisette goodnight, rolled under the blankets, and blew out the candle.

It was dark when I awoke. I shouldn't have been surprised, but it was disconcerting. For the first time I was in a place where there was no tracking of the sun across the sky or the moon across the heavens. The lights up high in the ceiling were either the flickering glow worms or the lunar moths, which weren't as constant as the stars. Time was difficult to discern here, and so I could not tell if I slept late or woke early.

Lisette dressed me in one of my more serviceable dresses of deep forest green. I fastened my cloak and bent to tie up my boots. Today I wasn't aiming to impress the king or his court with my appearance which was a relief. She nodded approvingly when I slipped my mother's silver knife down my boot, just in case. I didn't want to be in a position like the night before when I had felt defenceless, despite the training I had undertaken over the past months. Knowing that I had my mother's blade close at hand and my father's cloak around my shoulders provided more comfort than I could explain. It was almost as if they were there beside me, silently urging me on.

'Princess Wilhelmina?' A cool voice spoke from the doorway and I glanced up to see a Dark Elf attendant waiting patiently. 'Lord Aidyn awaits your presence.'

Lisette gave a sharp nod and waved the attendant away, putting the finishing touches to my hair, which had been twisted up into a mountain of plaits and soft curls. In my mind it was a touch too extravagant, but I could tell that Lisette felt bad about the night before and that this was her way of apologising. Looking at my reflection in the mirror I was impressed with her work and the back of my mind wondered what Aidyn would think.

Lisette brushed imaginary dust from my shoulders and then it seemed I was free to go as she stepped back, casting an approving look over me.

'Thank you, Lisette,' I said, squeezing her hand in mine and giving a small smile. 'It's beautiful.'

Her eyes grew watery, and she nudged me towards the doorway after the attendant. As I left the room, I noticed her dabbing at her eyes with a handkerchief and busying herself with tidying the bedcovers. The attendant was waiting just beyond the doorway, one of the pale lanterns in his hand as he led the way through the tunnel and I followed silently, wondering what the day would bring. No sounds came from behind the other bedroom doors as we passed them and my sense of disconcertion deepened, unable to tell whether I had woken late or early. Where was everyone?

I was starting to feel uncomfortable with the silence when the sound of the stamping hooves and soft nickers travelled through the tunnel towards me. I sped up towards the noise and the attendant moved faster to match my pace, the lantern bobbing in his hands.

Soon enough we had reached a point where the tunnel intersected with several others, and I saw Aidyn, adjusting the bridle on his horse, Dolce standing placidly alongside him. He looked up and upon seeing me dropped into a low bow.

'Princess Wilhelmina,' his voice sounded shuttered, unlike his usual self. It was then that I realised that he was not alone, as the light from the lantern flashed off several other masks and silver armour. King Lysander and his Council members were also present to greet me, and I felt a twinge of fear. The king's masked face gazed at me, as though assessing me, and I remembered belatedly to drop into a curtsey.

'Your Majesty,' I said, hoping that the tremor in my voice would not be obvious.

'Princess Wilhelmina, what a pleasure.' The king said, moving over to lift me up. His silver-clad hands were cold and I fought to suppress the shiver they caused. 'You are looking very fine, my dear. I almost regret my son having the privilege of giving you the grand tour. Ah well, perhaps after your trial, I will show you the sights, myself.'

His words were soft, intended for my ears alone and I felt myself pale. I did not like the tone in his voice, almost as if he were wanting to see me react, to see either my anger or fear.

Control your emotions, Nina. Grandfather's voice filled my mind and I took a calming breath, steadying myself.

'You are most thoughtful, Your Majesty,' I said as he lifted me up into Dolce's saddle. Aidyn had mounted already and was sitting rigidly, watching his father's hands linger a moment longer than was appropriate against my waist. I wanted to escape, to urge Dolce into a gallop and flee, leaving the Underdark and its strange inhabitants behind.

'Make sure she is returned before the revels begin,' the Chief Counsel instructed Aidyn coldly. 'The king will be leading her through the first dance.'

'As you wish,' Aidyn's tone was short. 'Come, Princess, we have much to see.'

He urged his dark mount forward, not bidding the Council or his father farewell as he left.

'Enjoy yourself, Princess,' the Chief Counsel said, 'we will be here when you return.'

I inclined my head and let Dolce follow Aidyn down one of the tunnels, grateful for the lantern that was attached to his saddle guiding me after him. I peered back over my shoulder, and saw the Council watching us leave, frozen in a deathly tableau. I shivered and pushed Dolce on, until Aidyn and I were side by side and the tunnel turned, the Council lost from sight.

'Where are we going?' I asked quietly, when it became apparent that he wasn't going to break the silence. 'Aidyn?'

'Come on,' he said, urging his mount to move faster, and I matched his pace. Cool air pushed my hair back, flicking the soft curls into my eyes as the tunnel twisted up and down. It opened onto one of the familiar caverns, but this one was dotted with fields of the strange glowing fungus, and flowers which opened and closed their wide buds as fireflies and lunar moths fluttered from one to the other. Amongst the flowers and fungi, Dark Elves worked, tending to the earth and new shoots of plants.

'This is one of our larger farms,' Aidyn said, leading his horse down a track between fields and navigating his way past the workers. 'It's called the Midos Fields. The plants here are some of the few varieties that grow underground which are edible. A large majority of our food needs to be brought in from the fields out on the mountainside.'

He still didn't sound like himself. His voice was tight, angry and he held himself aloof. The workers around us were staring, following our movement across the fields openly.

'Aidyn,' I began, reaching out a hand, 'what…'

He pulled away, his horse breaking into a canter. Dolce whinnied and sped after the black stallion. My knees gripped the saddle as we plunged on, covering the length of the cavern quickly, following a track alongside a large crevice that plummeted down into the depths of the earth. I kept my eyes fixed on Aidyn's back, forcing myself not to look down. He spurred his horse on, bending low over its neck, the lantern barely managing to stay alight.

'Aidyn?' I cried, 'slow down, please!' Beneath me Dolce was starting to tire. For days she had been travelling and I could feel her muscles straining with the effort of maintaining pace with the black stallion. Aidyn glanced back and came to a halt, breathing heavily.

'What is wrong?' I demanded, out of breath myself as Dolce slowed. 'You're acting strangely. You have been ever since last night.'

'I'm fine, Princess.' He wasn't looking at me now and it made me so angry that I wanted to shake him.

'Stop lying to me,' I snapped, 'tell me the truth. I'm sick of people keeping secrets and not being honest.'

'You're in the wrong place for that,' his voice was hollow. 'It's hard to trust people here.'

'Can I trust you?' I asked pointedly. He didn't reply and I felt my chest tighten. I glanced down at Dolce's reins wound through my fingers, blinking away unexpected tears and said, 'if you have nothing to say, maybe coming here was a mistake.'

'He wants you.' He spoke so quietly that I almost didn't hear it. 'He wants your powers for himself.' I looked up and met his gaze, wishing that I could read the expression in his eyes and hating the mask for hiding that.

'Your father?'

He nodded slowly. 'The Chief Counsel as well. I saw the way he spoke to you last night.'

I felt sick again and swayed in the saddle. In a flash, Aidyn had reached out and was steadying me.

'I didn't expect that my father would want to claim his Lord's Right. But seeing him just now…' His voice drifted off and his grip tightened as he let out an angry sigh. 'I thought you would be safer here, strange as that may seem. But it would appear that I might have been wrong.'

'What do you mean?' I asked quietly. He tried to turn away but I pulled him back to face me. 'Tell me.' I urged, 'Please.'

'I needed to see you again.' He admitted, 'I couldn't think of another way to get around the Chief Counsel's decision. I thought my father would understand, would realise…' He trailed off again and then coughed and said, 'I didn't think he would want to claim the Lord's Right.'

'Tell me what that is,' I whispered, needing to hear the words spoken aloud, although deep down I thought I knew.

'The king may choose to claim a maiden once she has been wed to another,' his voice was bitter and hard, 'it is an old tradition that I thought had died. It hasn't been used since before the Two Hundred Year War. I didn't know he would seek to claim it, you must believe me Nina.'

I did. One couldn't listen to his tortured voice and believe that he had planned any of this.

'I'll contact my grandfather,' I said, 'surely he would not agree to that.'

'By the time a messenger reaches him, it might be too late,' Aidyn said sadly, 'Rakael has a letter bearing your grandfather's seal of approval. If you pass your trial and she wishes to proceed with a marriage ceremony, it would happen within a matter of days.'

My breath caught in my throat. This was too much, too soon.

'Isn't that a bit… precipitated?' Even to my ears, my voice sounded strangled.

'In normal circumstances, yes,' he said, 'but you need an army, and my father would not give one without a signed marriage contract between our peoples.'

'I might not even pass this trial,' I said quickly, trying to hide my rising panic. 'From what you have said, it won't be easy.'

But as I spoke the words, I knew that I couldn't afford to fail. I couldn't let Grandfather down, even if he had gone behind my back about this arranged marriage. And there was Scardia and the Usurper. If I couldn't gather an army, I had no chances of success. The Usurper had been in power for too long now, his Trackers and army were strong and I was sure that the Capital would be almost impenetrable. Without the Dark Elves, my cause was almost certainly lost.

'When I came here,' I said, looking out over the deep ravine, 'I didn't realise I would be bartered and sold off. Perhaps that was naïve of me, but I thought that your father would be convinced to support the Resistance through other means.'

'Perhaps you still might convince him,' Aidyn said, but his tone was skeptical. He nudged his stallion forward and we began to wind our way alongside the ravine's edge, the sound of our horses' hoofbeats echoing far into the darkness below.

'What will the trial be like?' I whispered, 'what was yours like?'

He was quiet for a time, thinking, and then said, 'you have already demonstrated your skills in combat at King Aegis' court. The Council will want to see something else, demonstrations of your other skills and strength. I would be expecting them to test your magic to some degree. And your mind.'

'And your trial?' I pushed, 'Tell me what happened with yours.'

'You are curious, Princess,' he said with mock severity. 'Mine lasted seven days. For part of it I was sent out into the Dark Abyss, left to fend for myself and survive off the land. I had just fought my father's men in the amphitheatre. I was tired, but the Dark Abyss is not somewhere to show weakness. There are creatures in the shadows that prey on those who lose their way, and if you swim in the lakes you are pulled under by the mystera. No matter where you go, there are dangers waiting. And then there was the traditional rite of passage that all Dark Elves must go through.'

'What do you mean?' I asked, wondering why Dylan had never mentioned something like this to me. I thought I had learned a lot about Dark Elf culture but was realising that that was far from true.

'We are left above ground, on the highest peak in the Ombre Mountains for one day and one night.'

That didn't sound too bad, in my opinion.

'It is for Sybilla and Erthor to either spare or sacrifice us,' Aidyn continued hollowly. 'We are bound, our clothing and mask removed, and a flask of water placed just out of reach.

Those who are strong, survive. Others are not so lucky. Some go blind, others burn in the heat of the sun.'

'What happened to you?' I couldn't take my eyes away from his face, wondering whether he had been disfigured or blinded in his rite.

'I did not leave without scars,' he said. 'But I was luckier than most. I broke free from the bonds and sought shelter. As a follower of Sybilla, I was able to withstand the sun's rays to some extent.'

'Did you get in trouble for breaking free?'

He shook his head slightly.

'Once you are bound, there are no rules. You just have to find a way to survive until you are brought home.'

We had reached a point where the path before us split: one track led to a structure built into the cavern wall, another up through the darkness and the other crossed a narrow bridge over the ravine.

'This is where we will leave the horses,' Aidyn said, dismounting and letting out a shrill whistle. From the structure, a wide pair of doors opened and two Dark Elves emerged, one carrying a rucksack, the other a lantern. I dropped to the ground and stroked Dolce reassuringly as they approached.

'Your supplies, Lord Aidyn,' one said, handing over the rucksack.

'Thank you, Gnossus,' Aidyn said, slinging it over one shoulder. The other Dark Elf reached out and placed the lantern in my hands, taking Dolce's reins carefully.

'Thank you Romarin.' He added, handing over his own horse's reins. Romarin and Gnossus bowed and like two silent shadows led the horses away towards the structure, which I assumed had to be a stable of some kind.

'It is easiest to go the rest of the way on foot,' Aidyn said, leading me out over the ravine, the bridge rocking slightly beneath us. I tried to focus on keeping my balance and not looking down, not thinking about how far I would fall if one of the wooden slats broke. Almost as if he could read the direction of my thoughts, Aidyn said, 'it's alright, Nina.'

I wanted to argue with him, to say that nothing was alright. That everything I had thought and believed was being turned on its head and that I didn't like the new direction the Resistance's plans were going. I wanted to say that I felt trapped, and that innate urge to flee was spreading through me, ever since the night before when the Chief Counsel led me out onto the dance floor. Political marriage I could, perhaps, understand and agree to after some time. But the prospect of being married only to be given away to the king, like some weak, mindless chattel? The thought of accepting that blindly, of not fighting and resisting was alien to me. Scardia did not have such laws, and I found it barbaric.

'I can almost hear your anger,' Aidyn said quietly. 'It is understandable.'

'Is there no way you could convince your father to change his mind?' I asked, 'what he plans to do, it seems cruel that a parent would do that to their child.'

He laughed bitterly. 'Indeed, Princess.'

Something in his tone made me pause for a moment and then realisation finally struck, all too late. 'It's you who I'm supposed to marry, isn't it?'

I didn't know why it hadn't occurred to me before, but it all made sense. It explained why he had come to my grandfather's court. The way he had sought me out, his coming to guide us from the Karoni Lagoon. Grandfather allowing him to carry me back to my rooms after the incident with the Tracker. How could I have been so blind? And how did that make me feel, knowing that he was, according to my grandfather's wishes, my intended?

Aidyn didn't answer, but I saw a slight tremor pass through him. He led me on over the rickety bridge, and then took my hand as we made our way down another rocky track. I was grateful for his support here, for the ground was peppered with sharp stones and jagged edges which sought to trip and hurt unwary travellers.

'Are you hungry, Princess?' His question startled me, and I nearly slipped.

'We'll be at the Lake of Tears soon,' he continued, 'we'll pause there.'

'The Lake of Tears?' It didn't sound particularly inviting.

'It is said that the lake was filled by Erthor after Sybilla died,' he said, 'his grief was so vast that he filled the sky with his tears. Wherever they fell, oceans and lakes were created. This lake is supposedly where the first tears fell.'

We began to descend, picking our way around the rocks and coarse shrubbery, which tried to catch my cloak and skirts in its prickly leaves. There was no other sound around us than our breathing and footsteps, and it felt both eerie and intimate. I felt a mixture of emotions, the anger, fear and revulsion at what I had discovered over the past twenty-four hours still churned within me, but now there was also a sweet awkwardness, a catching of the breath and the heart which I had only felt once before. It was strange to feel it again, to acknowledge it and the possibility that such emotions could apply to more than one person. I had always believed that once one loved, it was true and constant. But I was starting to learn that this was not always the case. Markus' inability to forgive my dishonesty and my anger at his betrayal had tainted what had been between us.

'We're here.' Aidyn's voice cut through my thoughts. 'The Lake of Tears.'

To my mind, it looked just like a long dark stretch of water, reflecting the lantern light off its obsidian surface. On the far side of the lake was a small waterfall, a trickle of water tinkling over the rocky cavern wall and down into the lake. It was not loud, like the waterfall we had camped beside. But its sound reached us over the lake, the soft dripping echoing against the walls. The rocky path we had scaled down was replaced by soft moss-covered stones and clumped earth.

'The Lake of Tears is where we come to bid farewell to those who have departed this realm,' Aidyn said, 'it's a holy place, often left alone until someone passes away. Then we will gather here to honour their life and return them to Erthor's embrace.'

I didn't know what to say. The place certainly had a feeling about it, as if a greater being were present, watching over us as we stood by the lake waters. It didn't feel like a malevolent presence, but almost like the being was holding its breath in anticipation, waiting to see what we would do next. It was strange and I glanced around cautiously, half expecting to see other Dark Elves appearing from the darkness.

'We're alone, Princess,' Aidyn said quietly, as he began to unpack the rucksack, drawing out a water flask, some bread and cheese and some pale green apples. He sat down on one of the boulders and drew out a knife from his boot, slicing the bread. I settled beside him and laid the lantern down nearby. He reached over and opened the glass door, snuffing out the light.

'This place needs to be seen when the lights are out,' he murmured, 'look up.'

I blinked, struggling to adjust to the sudden darkness. I raised my eyes, looking up at the ceiling high above where slowly, one by one, tiny dots of light began to glow. They were a soft luminescent green, blinking like miniature stars, their light intensifying across the sky. I gazed at them in wonder, reminded of how they mirrored the Northern Lights that would dance above the Capital on cold winter nights.

'It's beautiful,' I whispered.

'Yes.' He was watching me instead of the glow worms and I felt myself blush, grateful for the dim light that would hide it from his view. I busied myself with taking some bread and cheese, easing my hunger as I tried to avoid the tension. Out of the corner of my eye, I saw him unhinge the base of his mask, placing it carefully on the ground beside him. With short, precise movements, he divided his own bread into smaller pieces to eat.

'Doesn't it ever get annoying, having to wear your mask?' The question spilled out of me before I could stop it.

'Sometimes,' he admitted, 'But when you are raised wearing one, it becomes a part of who you are. I don't think I know who I would be without it.'

'Haven't you ever taken it off?' I asked, slightly horrified.

He laughed, 'I don't wear it when I sleep. We put our masks on when we are around others. When we are alone, or amongst those we trust, then we can remove it. But as many of my kind are wont to kill you as well as aid you, trust does not come easily.'

'I can understand that,' I said, 'sometimes, just when you think you can trust someone, they do things that make you question it. Once broken, trust is difficult to regain.' I was thinking about Markus, about Grandfather, Lisette and Rakael, even Aidyn– who had used trickery to bring me to the Underdark.

'I would like to earn that trust,' he said softly. 'But I realise that it might be unlikely.'

I paused, weighing his words in my mind. I remembered all too well the Winter Spirit's warning, to be careful who I trusted in the Underdark. But she had also said to follow my instincts and right now, they were sending conflicting messages.

'I don't know,' I finally whispered. 'Everything that's happened since I got here has been so overwhelming. It scares me. I thought I knew what I was doing, but now I'm not so sure.'

'You cannot allow yourself to think that way,' he murmured, 'especially not in the trial. You were chosen for a reason, Nina. I sensed it as soon as we met. I knew then and I know now, that you…' His words cut off and he sighed, 'I believe that you will succeed, just like I believed it when you were pitted against your comrades in King Aegis' court.'

'How can you be so sure?' I asked, but then he held up a hand, silencing me. He was tense, listening, one hand pressed against the earth, and then he hurriedly thrust the remaining food and water flask into the rucksack.

'Someone's coming,' he muttered, hastily reattaching the base of his mask and pulling me to my feet. 'Let's go, quickly.'

I barely had a moment to reply before we were hurrying around the edge of the Lake of Tears, moving as swiftly and silently as we could. In the distance, I thought I could hear voices, gradually moving closer.

'Come on, Nina,' Aidyn urged, leading me towards the trickling waterfall. As we approached, I saw a narrow opening in the rocky wall, and we slipped inside. Aidyn was pressed against me, shuffling away, and I slipped as I tried to keep up. The rocky crevice was damp and shadowy, as there were fewer glow worms here to light our way. 'Just a bit further,' Aidyn muttered and then we entered a grotto that stretched behind the waterfall. I could see holes in the wall to the lake beyond and noticed light from a lantern moving steadily closer. Two shrouded figures were walking together to the lake's edge, speaking quietly. From this distance I couldn't hear what they were saying, but it was apparent that they believed themselves to be alone.

'Stay quiet,' Aidyn breathed, his mask flashing in the light from the lantern. The flash reflected across the lake and the two figures paused in their conversation, glancing in the direction of the waterfall.

'Your mask,' I said, 'take it off.'

He muttered a quiet curse and obeyed, stowing the mask in the rucksack. I felt the darkness around us deepen and realised that he was controlling it, effectively shrouding us from view and hiding the opening to the grotto. Before our eyes, the two figures exchanged something– a bottle of some sort– and then one stepped away, kicking a lantern down towards the lake. I felt Aidyn's tension increase beside me and now it was my turn to curse, I hadn't picked up the lantern when we had retreated to the grotto.

One of the figures stooped to pick up the lantern. They both looked around, clearly searching for us, and began to move around the lake's edge, scanning every nook and cranny.

'It's still warm,' one of their voices reached me through the waterfall and I recognised the voice as that belonging to the Chief Counsel. 'Whoever it was cannot be far away.'

The other figure nodded, their features shrouded in a heavy cloak. Unconsciously, I reached back and gripped Aidyn's hand, my own sweaty with fear as the Chief Counsel and his companion drew closer. The darkness around us became thicker and I held my breath, scared that even that sound would alert the Chief Counsel to our presence.

His masked face came nearer, until he was standing on the other side of the waterfall. A blade glinted in his hand, a long, wicked blade that curved upwards like a crescent moon. The lantern was raised and the light tried to pierce the darkness, searching for us. My grip on Aidyn's hand tightened, and I was sure that the Chief Counsel would hear the rapid beating of my heart.

'There's nothing here,' The Chief Counsel finally said, the lantern moving away. 'Bring the lantern with us– perchance we will find the owner on our way out.' The two figures headed back towards the other side of the lake. 'Remember,' the Chief Counsel's voice pierced the darkness, 'two drops and no more. We do not want any long-lasting effects.'

The other figure nodded, and they departed together. As the lantern faded away, the glow worms began to light up the ceiling and the grotto again, and the darkness around us lifted.

I was trembling, frozen with cold terror. Carefully, Aidyn took my other hand and led me to the side of a small pool, a still reflection of the rocky ceiling above. I was gently seated beside the water and he crouched down next to me.

'Why was the Chief Counsel here?' I asked, 'what was he talking about?'

'I do not know,' Aidyn replied gravely, 'but I would guess that it was something he did not want widely known. This place is sacred, the others rarely come here.'

'Why did you bring me here then?' I asked.

'This is where I come to get away.' He gestured at the small grotto, at the glistening walls and wide clear pool. 'Sometimes when it becomes too much, I come here. It is a good place to think, to reflect.'

'A good place to scry,' I murmured, gazing into the pool and feeling the familiar temptation rise in me.

'That too,' he conceded.

'I thought he would find us,' I whispered, 'I was sure he would see us and…'

'He didn't though,' Aidyn said, 'it's alright.' His arms came around and held me close, as if I were as fragile as one of the lunar moths. I leaned against him, grateful for the warmth of his embrace. It felt good, and a fierce yearning spread through me. Gradually, my trembling subsided, but I continued to rest against him, my head pressed to his shoulder.

'How often do you hide away here?' I asked quietly, feeling the need to fill the silence, to avoid the desire that I felt.

'Every few days or so,' Aidyn replied, 'my father and his court can try my patience at times.'

I could imagine. 'It's peaceful here,' I murmured.

He nodded slightly.

'Can we stay a while longer?' I asked, 'I don't want to risk meeting the Chief Counsel and his friend when we leave.'

'Of course,' Aidyn said, 'this was the main place I wanted to show you after all.'

'Have you brought anyone else here before?' I asked curiously.

'Alex, my sister Camille, not many in truth.'

'Will I meet your sister tonight?' I realised that I hadn't been introduced to any of his siblings, that I had been too overwhelmed the night before to even think about it.

'I am sure you will meet some of my brothers,' Aidyn said, 'but not Camille. She was taken to the Breeders when she turned fifteen. I have not seen her since.' His voice was sad, and I could feel his aching loss.

'I'm sorry.' I wasn't sure what else to say, and he gave a low shrug.

'It's the way things are. I cannot undo what has been done, but it is good to know that my sister will be provided for until she breathes her last. The Breeders live in luxury and are well cared for. We said our goodbyes years ago and we can still see each other in the scrying bowl to make sure the other is alright.'

'It sounds lonely,' I said, infinitely grateful that Scardia did not have a similar system in place. He made a sound at the back of his throat and didn't reply, but his grip around me tightened a fraction.

It was not lost on me that I was one of three others who he had brought here. I pondered that for a while as we sat there, and as the silence grew so too did the intensity deep in my blood. The tingling that I associated with magic was thrumming through me, but there was no heat haze rising from my skin. I was hot and cold all at once, both desperate for and terrified of what my instincts were demanding.

When I couldn't bear it any longer, I moistened my lips and said, 'Aidyn?'

'Mm?' It sounded like he was lost in thought, half there and half somewhere else.

'Do you think... would you mind...' Gods this was embarrassing. I felt the blush rise to the roots of my hair and I stammered to an awkward halt.

'What is it, Nina?' His tone was unreadable, and I faltered, the words on my tongue suddenly reluctant to come out. He pulled away and looked at me, his face shrouded in the dim light. I felt his absence like an icy wave of water crashing over me. 'What is it?' he pressed, clearly confused.

'Will you kiss me?' The words were so quiet that, at first, I thought he didn't hear them. If it hadn't been for the sudden stillness then I would have been certain of it.

'Why?' His question was low, as if he were trying to work out some strange puzzle that required an infinitesimal amount of concentration.

I didn't know how to reply, unsure how to express the desire I felt, the instincts that were urging me on. So, in the end, all I said was, 'Please?'

He regarded me silently and I began to feel uncomfortable, the awkwardness taking over. 'You don't have to if you don't want to,' I finally muttered, queasy embarrassment now settling down in my stomach. 'Just forget...' He held up a hand to quieten me and I paused, watching him.

'Are you sure?' His question was weighted, and I felt that I was on the edge of a precipice. My heart pounded, breath caught and I nodded.

'Yes,' I whispered.

'Close your eyes.' He said, and I obeyed. Without the light from the glow worms, all my other senses were heightened and I could feel him moving closer. His gloved hand cupped my cheek and I leaned against it. When his lips brushed against mine, they were cool and soft. I realised that he had removed his balaclava, and reached my hands up around his neck, tracing the planes of his face and twisting in his hair.

He gripped me tighter, and I pressed closer, lost in the moment as time seemed to fade away. Fire flowed through my veins as the kiss deepened and burned, until he gasped and drew away. My eyes opened, confused, and I realised that a shimmering light filled the grotto, rising from my skin. It flickered with the heat I still felt, radiating out into the space around us.

'I'm sorry,' I said, glancing up at him. Aidyn had pulled away from me, shadows surrounding him so that the light coming out of me could not reveal his face.

'I asked you to close your eyes, Princess.' His tone was hurt, pained.

'I couldn't control it,' I said, gesturing half-heartedly at the flickering light.

He sighed, 'I know.'

The longing was rising in my chest again, but this time I didn't want to have to ask. As though he could hear it, he chuckled softly. 'Here.'

The shadows stretched out across the room, and the light around me flickered and faded to a soft glow. I felt a moment of panic and the flames flared again.

'Can you trust me, Nina?' His voice was a mere whisper, and I could hear the same longing in his voice that I felt.

'I want to,' I admitted. 'But…' I bit off my next words. I wanted to trust him, I did, but how could I trust him when it wasn't reciprocated?

'You're scared?' he asked quietly and I nodded. 'That makes two of us.'

The flames around me hovered in the air between us, forming into the firebird that spread its wings and flew around the space. The shadows faltered, receding slightly and I thought I caught a glimpse of him through the darkness.

I stood and moved towards him, stepping over the discarded balaclava and the rucksack. My steps were slow, but my heart raced, heat rushing through me as I approached him in the shadows. When I was on the edge of the darkness, I halted and held my hand out, palm facing upward, hoping, praying that he would meet me halfway.

'Can you trust me?' I said, heart in my throat. 'You cannot ask for it and not return it.'

He paused for what felt like the longest time.

'I…' It was his turn to falter, and I smiled gently.

'Aidyn,' I repeated, 'can you trust me?'

Slowly, tentatively, his gloved hand emerged from the darkness and took mine. As his fingers curled around mine, the firebird beat its wings and soared to settle on a perch high above us. I stepped closer as the darkness drifted away, returning to the edges of the grotto.

'You're so beautiful,' he whispered, and I stared back, taking in his face, the high cheekbones, the deep eyes and wide, generous mouth. For the first time I could read the expression in his eyes as he looked at me and it rocked me. It was as though I were the sun, moon and stars all rolled into one. As though there was no one and nothing else that mattered. It was overwhelming, confusing and addictive at the same time. I couldn't speak but lifted my free hand to the place where his hair curled behind an ear, and raised my lips to his.

Chapter Fourteen

We didn't leave the grotto for a long time. For some time we conversed in soft whispers, and for some I rested in his arms, wondering about what would happen when we left. It seemed that Aidyn too was reluctant to depart, for he delayed as long as possible. We kissed once more before he donned his mask again, and I found myself resenting the loss of connection to his eyes as soon as it was back on.

We didn't speak much as we left the grotto, but my hand stayed in his as we made our way back around the Lake of Tears, up through the twisting passageways and through the Midos Fields. The firebird lit our path until we reached the main track, which was lit with the pale lanterns. The time it took to return to the door of my bedchamber felt surprisingly short, and with it our day together was over. As we returned to the heart of the Dark Elf court, I felt Aidyn withdrawing back into himself, hiding behind the mask once more.

Outside my bedchamber we paused, both unwilling to be the first to say farewell. The door opened and Lisette stood there, her worried expression easing as she saw that the visitor was me.

'Thank you for today, Lord Aidyn,' I said, aware that Lisette was not the only one who watched us from the doorway. Other masked faces observed from the shadows, and I shivered. 'I enjoyed our time together.'

'It was a pleasure, Princess Wilhelmina.' He bowed over my hand, 'perhaps you will save a dance for me at our revels tonight?'

'Of course,' I murmured, wishing that I could hold him to me again. He gave a nod and released my hand, disappearing silently back into the shadows. Lisette clicked her tongue and I entered my room, closing the door behind me.

I sat on the side of the bed, reliving the memories of the afternoon as Lisette bustled around, preparing my washbasin and evening attire. She could tell that something was wrong, for she cast me inquisitive looks, but I didn't share my thoughts. I felt that what had happened that afternoon was something special, something that I wanted only Aidyn and I to share.

I came to myself when I saw the gown she had laid out as I had washed and dried myself. It was made of gold and ivory silk, the square cut of the collar softened by soft lace. The corset was tightened and the gown clung to my body, until it reached my waist and fell in drapes to the ground. The sleeves puffed from my shoulders and stopped at my elbow, with a fine trim of lace resting against my skin. My hair was restyled, curled and twisted up on my head in an elegant knot, with several wisps resting by my temples. The familiar gold diadem rested on my brow and a choker of opals was clasped around my neck. I was helped into my gold slippers again, which were freshly polished and shone brightly.

The young woman looking back at me from the mirror was someone I barely recognised, but she looked beautiful, and I wished I could see the expression in Aidyn's eyes when he saw me.

'Thank you, Lisette,' I said as she handed me perfume to dab against my wrists and behind the ears. She smiled and stroked some errant strands of my hair down, and I wondered if she could tell where my thoughts had been.

'Do you think Lord Aidyn is a… suitable choice for me?' I asked quietly. 'Do you think Grandfather would approve?' Even though I was still conflicted about Grandfather's decisions, I still desired his approval.

Her smile widened and she nodded. I felt a sense of relief spreading through me.

There was a knock at the door and she started, moving away to unlock it. When her back was turned, I reached to my bedside table and lifted my mother's dagger in its sheath and fastened it to my thigh. I didn't want to feel unprotected at the revels tonight.

'I've come to escort Princess Wilhelmina to the King's Table.' Aidyn's voice was quiet as he gave a short bow to Lisette. I rose to my feet and approached the doorway and he paused, before dropping into a lower bow.

'Princess,' his voice sounded strained. 'You look lovely this evening.'

He did as well. His boots had also been polished; his black tunic was embroidered with silver thread. The image of the phoenix stretched across his chest, flickering as it caught the light from the lanterns.

'Thank you, Lord Aidyn.' I dropped into a curtsey and then reached out to grasp his proffered arm. 'Goodnight Lisette,' I called over my shoulder as we moved away, and she waved me off.

'She is welcome to join the revels as well,' Aidyn said, his gaze not leaving me.

'I think she is more comfortable staying behind,' I replied, 'she rarely participated in the dances in Grandfather's court.'

'You look beautiful,' he murmured as we passed other Dark Elves in the hallway. I felt myself smile and moved closer to his side, grasping his arm tighter.

'Do we need to go to the King's Table?' I asked as the boats came into sight. It seemed that we were some of the last ones this time, as only a few boats remained tied to the dock.

'I'm afraid so,' Aidyn replied, 'I don't want to risk angering my father.'

At the mention of his father, I shivered. 'I don't want to dance with him.'

'I know,' he sounded sad, resigned. 'Let's just enjoy the time we can spend together tonight. Tomorrow things will be different.'

Tomorrow my trial would begin. Anxiety grew in me, and I fought to hide it.

'I believe in you, Nina,' Aidyn said quietly. 'You are strong. You could not have survived for so long without it.'

I wished that I had his faith.

The boat rocked slightly as he helped me into it, and I settled down on the cushions as he grasped the pole and began to steer us in the direction of the dancing. I kept my eyes fixed ahead, sensing his slow and steady movements behind me, dreading the moment when we would arrive.

The sounds of laughter and music reached us and by the time we disembarked, the meal was in full swing. Aidyn led me over the dance floor and up the stairs to the King's Table, where he drew my seat out for me. Our appearance had drawn the attention of all those around, and the chatter and laughter died as we entered, silver masks following us curiously.

'You are late, Aidyn.' King Lysander sounded angry. 'I thought I gave you clear instructions to arrive early.'

'My apologies, father.' Aidyn bowed and took the seat next to me, one knee brushing against mine. King Lysander snorted and waved a hand, indicating for the nearby attendants to fill our goblets with wine and ladle food onto our plates.

At the other end of the table, Erik watched me carefully, his eyes suspicious as they flicked from Aidyn to me. At my side, Jesse was speaking to Rakael, who was drinking deeply from her goblet. I met Rakael's eyes and glanced away, remembering too well the sensation of her blade against my throat from the night before.

I didn't have much of an appetite yet forced myself to eat. The food and wine tasted slightly bitter, and I found myself longing for the crisp fresh apple or the crumbling cheese and seeded bread that Aidyn and I had shared by the Lake of Tears.

'I hope that you enjoyed your tour today, Princess Wilhelmina,' King Lysander said in between mouthfuls. 'I trust that my son was a respectful guide.'

'Yes, Your Majesty.' I glanced from father to son and tried to keep my expression distant and detached.

'Where did he take you?' the Chief Counsel asked, voice dripping with false sweetness.

'Uh…' In my mind's eye I saw him approaching the waterfall, curved blade in his hand.

'We saw the Midos Fields,' Aidyn interjected, 'the Devil's Peak…'

'The Lake of Tears?' the Chief Counsel asked.

'No,' Aidyn lied, and I shook my head.

'What is the Lake of Tears?' I asked, with passably false curiosity.

'It is one of Erthor's holy sites,' King Lysander said, 'Aidyn was wise not to take you there. It is not one to be visited often; it is sacred.'

'Indeed,' the Chief Counsel said, and I nodded.

'Then I am relieved we didn't go there,' I said quickly, glancing at Aidyn, 'I would have hated to intrude on a holy place.'

Under the table, his hand squeezed mine and I returned the pressure.

'Hmm,' the Chief Counsel drifted into silence, watching us closely. I kept my expression light and innocent, forcing myself to eat some more. As I reached for my goblet, one of the attendants paused over my shoulder to refill it, the red wine splashing over the brim onto the skirts of my dress. In an instant, the king had risen to his feet with cold fury.

'Imbecile,' King Lysander snapped, 'Apologise.'

'Forgive me Princess Wilhelmina,' the attendant stuttered, dropping to the ground in abject terror.

'String him up,' King Lysander snarled.

'No, there's no need,' I cried, 'it was an accident.'

Behind me there was a guttural cry as vines stretched down from the ceiling and wrapped themselves around the unfortunate servant, lifting him to hang upside down beside the caged musicians. A vine covered his mouth, stifling his cries, and the musicians paused in their music.

'Play!' the king bellowed, and they hurriedly resumed, the sounds of the music covering the soft moans from the dangling servant. 'Your kind heart does you credit, Princess Wilhelmina,' King Lysander said, 'but I will not allow my people to disrespect you so.' He sat down again and returned to his meal, and I stared down at my plate in horrified shock.

'He only spilled the wine,' I murmured, and Aidyn gripped my hand reassuringly.

'There's nothing you can do, Nina,' he whispered. I gave a slight nod and drank from the goblet, trying to keep my hand from shaking.

When the king had finished his meal, he stood again and indicated that I should join him as he descended towards the dance floor. Aidyn's hand convulsed and let mine go, the reassuring warmth vanishing.

'You promised me the first dance, Princess Wilhelmina,' King Lysander said as we left the King's Table behind. 'I noticed last night that you are a gifted dancer.'

'Thank you, Your Majesty,' I replied, forcing myself to smile. The musicians above us struck up the chords of a courtly dance and we took to the floor. It could have been worse, I thought to myself later, as our hands only met intermittently, and I did not try to converse beyond a few polite words.

'What do you think of my son, Princess Wilhelmina?' The king's question surprised me, and I looked towards him to meet his gaze.

'I beg your pardon?'

'My son. Is he to your liking?' the king sounded businesslike and curt, as if discussing the price of grain at a market. 'If he is not, I can introduce you to my other sons. He can easily be replaced. Or perhaps, you do not wish to marry the son when you can have something greater.'

'No,' I said quickly, understanding his meaning, and then paused, took a breath and repeated, 'no, thank you. He is…' How could I describe him? Kind? Surprising? Entirely unexpected? For some reason I didn't think that the king would respond too well to any of those, so instead I just said, 'he is to my liking.'

'Ah,' the king's voice was soft, 'I must admit I am disappointed to hear you say so. I suppose we shall just have to wait until after your trial to discuss King Aegis' proposal further.'

I nodded and retreated into silence, curtseying as the dance ended. The king bowed and returned to his spot at the table, allowing me to dance with a stream of other Dark Elves. Erik led me through a jig, but the pace was too fast for us to speak easily. I spun out, jumped and clapped, before he took my hands again and we skipped down the line of couples.

'We trained with the Dark Elves today,' he gasped as we clapped and returned to our original places.

'How was it?' I asked, slightly breathless from the fast pace of the dance.

'It wasn't like King Aegis' court,' he said, 'they push you harder. They don't seem to need a break, it was uncanny.'

I nodded and then moved out, jumped and spun back to grasp his hands.

'Erik...' I wanted to tell him about the Chief Counsel, about Rakael and the king, but I couldn't find the words. I wanted to tell him about Aidyn and that he shouldn't distrust him as much as he did. Instead, I twirled out, clapped and then the dance was over as quickly as it had begun, and I hadn't found the words to tell him what I wanted to say. Before I could pull him away, another Dark Elf had taken my hand and was leading me away in the next measure. This dance was equally frenetic, and I found myself feeling lightheaded within moments.

I sensed Aidyn standing to the side of the dance floor and saw him approach Erik. The two of them stood on the outskirts of the throng, Erik was gesticulating and talking with more animation than I had seen in a while. They stayed next to each other until the music changed again, the slow strains of a waltz drifting across the floor. When he heard the chords, Aidyn gave Erik a short bow and a clasp on the shoulder and then made his way towards me.

As he approached, I ignored the outstretched hand of another potential partner, my eyes not leaving him. He reached me and bowed formally.

'I believe you promised me a dance, Princess?'

'I believe I did,' I said softly, placing my hand in his and allowing him to sweep me around the floor, one hand on my waist to guide me. It reminded me vaguely of the first time we had danced together, but now his touch made my pulse beat with excitement.

'I was wondering when you would dance with me,' I murmured as I spun out and twisted back into his embrace.

'I was waiting,' he replied. 'Besides, Erik was eager to talk about our training regime.'

'Oh,' I said as I was dipped, the breath squeezing out of my lungs as I dropped down.

I could have sworn he smiled, but the mask ensured it was hidden. As I was lifted back up, my head swam for a moment and I blinked, disorientated. The feeling of light-headedness returned, and the dancefloor spun, it was like all the other dancers were watching me, their masks glinting in the lamplight.

'Nina?' Aidyn's voice sounded like it was coming from far away, 'Nina, are you alright?'

I was struggling to speak now, my throat felt like it was on fire and tiny lights were glittering before my eyes.

'Aidyn,' I gasped, clutching onto his arm, 'I don't think…'

My knees buckled and I collapsed against him. He gripped me tighter, his voice becoming urgent.

'Nina? What's wrong?'

'Nina?' Erik's face appeared beside Aidyn's, eyes wide with worry. They were moving in and out of focus now, and I struggled to keep my eyes open. My grip on Aidyn slackened and I passed out in a crumpled heap on the floor.

When I came to, I was alone. My mouth was dry and my head pounded. I sat up slowly, looking around at my surroundings. I was no longer by the dance floor and my dress had been removed, replaced with the outfit I would wear when training. What had happened? How did I get here? Where was everyone? I began to panic, reaching for my thigh where my dagger had been strapped, but feeling nothing.

I got to my feet and felt something slide against my foot. I reached down and pulled the knife out of my boot and strapped it to my belt. Slightly more comforted now, I conjured a flame into my hand, raising it above my head to see more easily.

I seemed to be in a low-ceilinged cavern, which was scattered with boulders and rocky crags. There seemed to be no one around and the silence was vast and terrifying.

'Aidyn?' I called out, my voice ringing off the walls and reverberating back to me. 'Erik?'

There was no answer, save for the echo of my own voice. A breeze lifted my hair from my cheek and then a crushing darkness filled the space, and a raspy voice filled my mind.

Submit.

'No.' I stumbled to my knees and sensed the movement behind me just in time. I twisted and withdrew my dagger, as the black-cloaked figures circled me. There were five of them, and I struggled to maintain my composure.

This was what I had trained for, I told myself as they lunged at me, and I responded instinctively, deflecting their blows and avoiding their strikes as much as I could. One got the back of my knees with a well-placed kick and I gasped, blinking back tears of pain as another struck my shins. I toppled and rolled, taking one down with me and twisting away.

They pressed on, working as a cohesive unit to strike and push me back until I was against one of the rocks. I was getting tired, my movements more sluggish, but I forced myself to keep fighting back with everything that I had.

Submit. The voice overwhelmed me, and my temples throbbed. I dropped to my knees and my attackers moved closer.

'No,' I gasped, swiping out my blade and meeting flesh. One of the attackers cried out and fell back, clutching a wound in their side. The others began to rain blows down on me with renewed vigour, and it took all my power to protect myself. I focussed my mind, resisting the pain, and breathed out. Flames whooshed out from my raised arms, slicing through my attackers and providing me a moment of reprieve from their onslaught. A trilling cry filled the cavern, and I realised from the light shining through my fingers that it was the firebird, circling me in a protective wall of flame.

There were screams and the smell of burning flesh as the attackers vanished into the shadows, leaving me alone once more. I raised my head and looked around cautiously, wondering where they had gone. It was disconcerting how they had just disappeared, and I took some deep breaths to calm the erratic beating of my heart.

'Nina?' It was Erik's voice, coming from the other end of the cavern, where the shadows were darkest. 'Nina, are you there?'

He sounded lost, terrified, and I got to my feet hastily.

'Erik?' I called, stumbling in the direction of his voice. 'Erik, where are you?'

'Nina?' It sounded like he was drawing further away.

'Erik, hold on. I'm coming!' I began to run towards the distant sound of his voice, the firebird sweeping ahead of me, lighting my way.

'Nina,' his voice broke out in a sob of pain, 'Nina, come quickly.'

'Hold on!' I cried, tripping on the rocks in my haste, searching the darkness ahead for any trace of him but seeing nothing. The firebird let out another call and dove into the heart of the shadows, driving them away to the distant recesses of the cavern. I paused, chest heaving, glancing around in panic.

He wasn't there, but I could hear his cries of pain, his laboured breathing and the sound of something else; a harsh crack and slap as whip met flesh. Erik's screams filled my ears and I covered them, tears running down my face as I spun around, desperately searching for him. There were no entrances or tunnels for me to run down to follow his voice.

'Erik!' I shouted, 'where are you?'

He screamed and the sound of wicked laughter rang through my mind. I was on my knees rocking back and forth, unaware of having fallen, calling for my brother.

Submit. The cold, raspy voice was back, whispering in my ear. I shook my head, trying and failing to evade it.

If you fight, your brother will suffer. The voice laughed. Do you really want that on your conscience as well? You've already been the cause of so much death, Princess Wilhelmina. Can you cope with his blood on your hands as well?

'No, no, no,' I whimpered, curling in on myself. 'No, no, no.'

Submit and he will live. The voice was cajolingly sweet now and I shivered, the words on the tip of my tongue.

The firebird screeched and landed on my shoulder, the warmth from its claws seeping down into me. As it perched there, I felt strength return and looked up again. The cavern was empty. Erik wasn't there. The screams I could hear were in my mind, tormenting me.

'You're not real,' I whispered, 'it's not real.'

Submit. The voice was hard again, commanding and all-powerful. It railed and tore at the edges of my mind until my vision became blurred and I struggled to maintain control.

'Princess?' It was Aidyn's voice now, 'Princess, you don't need to fight anymore. You can give up.'

I froze. Aidyn had never told me to give up. He had always been supportive, believing in me even when I doubted myself.

'Get out of my head!' I snarled, fighting back against the oppressive presence. The darkness swirled around the cavern again and swamped me. I got to my feet slowly, pushing against the shadows, the firebird on my shoulder giving me the extra strength I needed to stand in the eye of the storm.

'I will *not* submit to you,' I gasped, straining against the pressure of the darkness around me. 'I *will not.*'

There was a loud scream, and I couldn't tell if it came from me or the voice in my head. The firebird stretched out its wings and let out another screech, flames cutting through the whirlwind of night, banishing it.

I swayed, one hand pressed against my temple, the other clutching onto the firebird's taloned claws. I had dropped my dagger and I bent to retrieve it, tracing the design of leaves across the flat of the blade. The cavern was silent again and I moved back to its centre, noticing now that there was an opening on the far side. It hadn't been there before, of that I was certain, and so I approached it cautiously, unsure what would happen next.

It was sudden. One moment I was stepping forwards, the next, the earth had swallowed my feet, locking me in place. A figure appeared from the opening and hurried towards me. His face was gaunt and haggard, the rough beard clearly hadn't been shaved in days and his hair fell about his shoulders in a dark tangle. It looked like he had been travelling for a week, and his eyes were dark and anxious.

'Thank the Gods,' he said breathlessly, 'I found you.'

I felt the shock tremor through me, and if the ground hadn't been holding my feet firm I would have stumbled backwards.

'Markus,' my mind was blank. 'What are you doing here? How are you here?'

'I knew I couldn't trust those Dark Elves,' he muttered, dropping to his knees and pulling on my legs, trying to get them out of their bonds. 'I couldn't let you slip away again. I was so stupid, Karliah, so stupid and angry. Can you forgive me?'

It was everything I had wanted to hear on his ship, and my heart skipped a beat. I was on the verge of taking his hands into mine, when I paused. His use of my former pseudonym seemed strange.

'Why did you call me Karliah?' I asked slowly.

He looked up at me, exasperated. 'Help me get you out of this first,' he said, 'then we can get out of here. You can stay with me, we can sail as far away as you want. The Usurper won't be able to find us. You don't have to be afraid anymore. I know it's what you want, Karliah.'

His hands grasped my legs again, pulling until they hurt. 'Come on,' he cried angrily, tugging away.

'Markus,' I said, 'I don't think that's possible anymore.'

'Don't be stupid, Karliah,' he snapped, 'it's what we both want.'

'What about Scardia?' I asked tentatively.

'What about it?' His voice was sharp, angry. 'It doesn't matter too much who's in control of Scardia, Karliah. You have a chance to be free, to live a normal life.'

A normal life. The words drifted back to me as if from a dream. *I wish to be free.*

Suddenly I was seven years old again, sitting beside the wide stone fountain and trailing my hand in the water. Opposite me, a tall turbaned man with skin the colour of umber and eyes that glittered smiled at me with bright, white teeth.

If that is your wish, Princess, then you shall have it. His voice was sweet and warm and in it were all the promises of the world.

'No,' I said. 'I can't.' I was crying silently now, and Markus rose to his feet, his angry face inches from mine.

'You don't mean that,' he snapped. 'You don't want to give up on this; on us. Scardia is not worth it.' He kissed me roughly, his mouth bruising mine and his arms constricting around me. I tried to pull away, but he held me tighter as I struggled. It was wrong. All wrong.

And then I heard his breath catch with pain. His arms dropped away from me and he staggered backwards. Our eyes dropped at the same time to the silver dagger that was impaled in his chest. He reached down and pulled the blade out, dropping it onto the ground at our feet. As it clattered down, the blood in his chest began to spread across the white linen shirt, staining it red.

'Why?' Markus gasped, his eyes meeting mine as unrestrained tears spilled down my cheeks. I was stuck, unable to move as he fell to the ground, clutching his chest. Only when his eyes had gone dark and sightless, was I released from the ground. I collapsed beside him, sobbing, wailing, begging for him to come back, to forgive what I had done.

There was a fluttering of wings, and the firebird landed beside me, resting its plumed head against my side. I opened my eyes and saw that the space where Markus had lain was empty, only the blood splattered knife and patch of stained earth remained.

'Was it real?' I asked the bird, 'or did I imagine it?' The bird gazed back at me without blinking. I sniffed and rubbed my eyes, getting to my feet again and reaching for the bird. It gripped onto my forearm as I picked up my dagger, sheathing it to avoid seeing Markus' blood. I felt sickened, confused about what was reality and what was not.

The path through the opening was narrow and the rocks tore and clung to my clothing, pulling at my hair and scratching my arms as I shuffled through. The firebird took off from my arm, leading the way through the darkness as I followed blindly. It paused and I stopped, teetering on the edge of a precipice that fell away into nothingness.

'Where now?' I asked, and the bird flapped its wings, rising upwards and disappearing from view. I followed it with my eyes, noting how the jagged rock and crystals were embedded in the walls, providing a means of climbing up. I ripped the base of my tunic into two strips and tied them around my palms, pulling them tight.

Then I began to climb. Slowly, painfully, I pulled myself up, forcing one hand in front of another, ignoring the pain as the sharp edges cut through the linen and made my hands bleed– I was grateful for my boots protecting my feet. I froze for a moment, gasping, as one foot slipped off its hold, throwing me off balance. I hung there, desperately scrabbling for another foothold and then continued up. The muscles in my arms and shoulders were screaming, tearing and I pressed my forehead to the rocky wall, gasping.

Something small and white floated down to brush against my hand. I opened my eyes and looked up at the lunar moth which batted its wings and took off again, a pinpoint of glimmering light that helped lead me onwards. It was joined by several others, fluttering around my face, lighting up the way so that I could see that I was nearly at the top. This gave me new strength and I pushed myself up and up, biting back the gasps of pain and the tears, forcing one hand, one foot after another.

When I thought that I was about to collapse and fall back down, my hand found the edge of the top of the wall, and I heaved myself up and over. I dragged my body away from the edge, the moths dancing around me in jubilant abandon. The firebird was sitting nearby, watching my progress, and flew back at me, disappearing into my chest. My breath faltered and I coughed, swaying.

I still appeared to be alone, but I was learning not to trust the darkness. Ahead of me stretched a dark lake. This one was not like the Lake of Tears, with its glow worms and trickling waterfall. This lake was vast and deep, with flashing lights moving back and forth beneath the water's surface. I approached slowly, drawn towards the lights. The lunar moths behind me began to swarm around, trying to lead me away back into the darkness, but I couldn't drag my eyes away from the lake.

As I reached the edge, my toes barely touching the water, there was a swelling, a rush of movement and the bright lights converged into one. A face looked up at me from just underneath the surface, a face I had seen in dreams for so many years, and my heart split with yearning. She was luminescent, her eyes a pale blue and her hair a strawberry gold. She wore a gown of gossamer, which floated around her. She was a being of ethereal beauty, her eyes kind and smile loving.

'Mama?' I whispered, 'Mama, is that you?'

She didn't speak but reached out a hand for me, fingertips just under the surface of the water. I was caught, spellbound in her pleading eyes.

'How are you here?' I asked, 'how is this possible?'

She began to drift away towards the heart of the lake. I staggered after her, water splashing against my ankles as I waded further out.

'Mama, wait!'

There was a flurry of movement around me as the lunar moths swarmed around me, their white wings beating against my face, lights flashing into my eyes. I staggered back a step, confused. When I opened my eyes, my mother had vanished and something silky was stroking against my legs in the water. I looked down and recognised the plant that looked like sea grass. I let out a terrified squeak and splashed backwards, but the mystera had encircled my ankles and held me firm. As I struggled, the water in the centre of the lake began to bubble and churn and my blood went cold.

With shaking hands, I reached down, pulling my knife from its sheath and began to cut at the mystera, trying to ignore the ripples as something large began to move towards me. The grass burnt and stung, but I pushed on, weakening it and pulling away, racing back to shore. The lunar moths led my way, and I kept my eyes on them, praying to the Gods under my breath to escape the creature behind me.

The stones underfoot slipped as I leapt back onto the shore, and I kept running as I heard the sound of something large and heavy sliding out of the water after me. My legs stung from where the mystera had caught me and my chest ached, but I ran on, arms pumping, breath coming out in short gasps as I followed the moths, hoping that they would lead me to safety.

The sounds of the creature behind me began to fade away and then I heard a large, scaly body returning back to the lake. I was crying again, angry with myself for almost falling prey to the wicked trick; for being lured so easily by something that resembled my mother, who I knew to be long dead. But it had been so real, so cruel. I wiped my cheeks with bloodied hands, and one of the moths landed on my hand, its wings opening and closing and its tiny legs clinging onto me.

When I felt safe enough, I paused, slumping down against the wall of the tunnel, the lunar moths hovering around me. By their light I was able to pull the remaining mystera off my legs. The plant had sharp fibres that bit into the skin, leaving behind a burning ache. My breeches were torn, partly from the climb up the jagged slope of rocky crystal, partly from the mystera in the lake. I bit back a cry as I tugged the strands away, tossing them aside and shaking them off my hands. The moth that had been on my hand was now settled on my leg, over the wounds, and I drew comfort from its presence.

The last of the mystera gone, I got to my feet again, knees trembling, and staggered after the moths, trusting in where they led. I moved slowly, holding the wall for support, each step a painful reminder of what I had gone through. A rush of nausea spread through me and I retched, coughing and spluttering. Shaking, I moved on, wiping my mouth with the back of my hand, praying that it would be over soon.

When I couldn't move any further, I sank down against the wall, body racked with tremors and cold. The moths fluttered around my head, urging me to keep going, but I couldn't. I looked up, my vision fading in and out, and I saw her, standing tall in the soft glow from the moths' wings. Her eyes were solemn, watching me.

'Forgive me, my lady,' I whispered, 'I think I have failed you.'

'Far from it, child,' the Winter Spirit said, her voice as soothing as the first fall of snow. 'You have done well. You heeded my advice. There's not much further to go, you can make it.'

'I don't think I can move,' I managed to get out, 'I feel so weak.'

She reached out and brushed a hand against my hair, white on white and I gasped, jolted with a burst of icy cold which pushed the exhaustion to the edges of my consciousness.

'Let me help you, Nina,' she said softly, her hand gripping mine and pulling me to my feet with surprising strength. 'I see that you have got someone else watching over you.' She was looking at the lunar moths with cool interest. 'How intriguing.'

'What do you mean?' I asked, but she was gone in a flurry of snowflakes, which melted against my outstretched hand. The small patches of ice startled me onwards, and I put one foot in front of another, following the white lights. Just when I had caught up to them, they vanished down into a gaping hole in the earth. I paused, uncertain, took a deep breath and jumped after them.

Chapter Fifteen

I don't know how long I fell for, it felt like an age. The wind rushed through my ears and my hair tore out of its knot, trailing behind me in a red and white cloud. My scream was lost, arms flailing as I plummeted down. The moths had disappeared, so everything around me was completely dark, and I squeezed my eyes shut waiting for the moment when I would hit the ground.

There was a loud splash and I was submerged in freezing water, sinking into the depths. My eyes opened in fear; remembering what had happened the last time I had been in the water, I kicked out, reaching towards the surface. I broke through, spluttering and drawing in gulps of air. Above me was darkness, but then the flickering of blue and green lights which began to spread across the ceiling, and I could hear the sound of a waterfall. I struck out for the shore, eager to get out of the water in case another creature was waiting below to catch me in its jaws. There was a flicker of light from the shoreline, a lunar moth was waiting, swaying back and forth. I swam towards it, my tired muscles screaming for relief as I dragged myself onto the mossy shore. I lay back for a moment, gazing up at the ceiling and finally recognising where I was.

I was so tired, but felt too exposed on the shore. My legs shook as I staggered around the lake's edge towards where the crevice to the grotto was located. My strength was waning now, and it took all my effort to make my way through the gap in the rocky wall, the lunar moth lighting the path for me. When I entered the grotto, I was surprised to see that I wasn't alone.

'Aidyn?'

He was sitting cross legged by the scrying pool, his hands resting on his knees, back rigid and muscles taut. The moth settled on his shoulder, but he didn't react, and as I approached I realised that he was staring into the water, unaware of his surroundings as though lost in a trance. He wasn't wearing his mask and his expression was drawn, eyes shadowed and weary with exhaustion.

'Aidyn?' I sank down beside him. His eyes flickered slightly but he didn't respond. It was getting harder and harder to keep myself awake. The Winter Spirit's gift of energy was fading fast. I laid down beside him, resting my head in his lap and closed my eyes.

It felt like only a moment passed, but it must have been longer. I came to when tentative fingers traced my cheek, wiping away the traces of tears, and my bound hands were carefully lifted and kissed. I opened my eyes, looking up into his face and was surprised to see silent tears spilling down his cheeks.

'You're alright,' he murmured, holding me close. 'You're alright.'

I tried to sit up, wincing as pain speared through my legs. 'I think so,' I said, 'but by the Gods it hurts.'

'I knew you could do it,' he said, 'I was sure you would pass the trial.'

I gazed at him, 'You were watching me?'

He nodded, glancing down at the pool. The lunar moth on his shoulder took off and fluttered away. I watched it go, wondering.

'We will need to get back to the amphitheatre,' he said, but he didn't move.

'Do we have to?' I was reluctant to leave too.

'They will start to wonder where you are soon,' Aidyn murmured, 'they were watching as well.'

It was no use asking who 'they' were.

'How are you so sure that I passed?' I asked, 'it felt like I kept making mistakes.'

He gave a lopsided smile, 'trust me, Princess. You passed.'

'Are they going to prepare any more trials for me?' I didn't think I could live through that experience again and was relieved when he shook his head. I fell against him, shaking with sobs as the emotions I had kept in rushed free. 'Is Erik alright?' I gasped, 'Please tell me he's alright.'

'Erik is fine,' Aidyn soothed, rocking me against his shoulder. 'As is that sea captain.'

I froze and looked at him, terrified. He gazed back at me, his features inscrutable.

'I didn't... it wasn't real?' I stammered out, relieved. 'But there was blood, so much blood.' I withdrew my dagger from its sheath, but the blade was as clean as it had been the day before, no traces of blood stained its silver edge.

'The Chief Counsel is skilled in creating illusions,' Aidyn's mouth twisted and his eyes flashed. 'He takes pleasure in causing others pain.'

I reached out and grasped his hands, 'Aidyn, what you saw...'

'All I need to know is whether you want what that man spoke of.' His voice was tight, and I sensed the pain behind his words. 'If he is what you want, then I will not stand in your way.'

I gaped. 'I don't know.' He snorted and glanced away, but he stilled when I tightened my grip on his hands. 'I won't lie to you, Aidyn. There was something between Markus and I, but I also want… I feel…' My voice trailed away miserably, and he kept looking away, towards the scrying pool. I couldn't bear this. I took a deep breath, 'and then you come along and now I feel like a confused mess. I can't forget what I felt for him, but I can't deny what I feel for you too. I think I just need time.'

'Then I suppose I shall need to be patient,' he said, looking back at me steadily. 'I can be patient.'

I smiled and leaned forward, kissing him spontaneously, wrapping my arms around his neck. He kissed me back, gripping me as though he would never let me go. I lost myself in the feel of him, a bubble of happiness tingling through my body.

When we drew apart, he chuckled, 'if you kiss me like that, I don't know how patient I can be, Princess.'

He pulled me to my feet and scooped up his mask and balaclava from a nearby rock. Within moments he looked as he had when we first met, and he held out a hand for me.

'Let's present you to the court.'

'Will you stay beside me?' I asked, 'I don't know how far I'll be able to walk.'

'You cannot show weakness now, Princess,' he said gravely, 'come on.'

The amphitheatre was in an uproar when we approached, and I gripped Aidyn's hand tighter.

'It's alright,' he murmured and then led me across the floor of the atrium, our reflections following us in the mirrors. As we entered the arena, I looked up at the king's balcony and saw a large glass mirror that had been set into the ground.

'They would have seen your trials in that,' Aidyn whispered, leading me around the edge of the dark mirror.

'Where did it come from?' I asked, 'it wasn't here last time.'

'My father has a gift with controlling elements like glass and rock,' Aidyn muttered. 'There, he's waiting.'

Sure enough, King Lysander was standing at the edge of his balcony, looking down at us as we approached. To his side I saw the Chief Counsel and my companions. Rakael was standing rigidly, Jesse was holding onto Erik, who was deathly pale, while Leif, Tobias and Christoff had stern expressions and held themselves apart. Lisette was nowhere to be seen.

When I saw Erik, I quickened my steps, desperate to get to him, to hold him close and make sure that he was alright.

'Princess Wilhelmina Constantina Fiordlasher,' the Chief Counsel's voice rang out across the arena, and I faltered in my approach, watching him suspiciously. Around us, the other Dark Elves fell silent and watched us, masks glittering.

'You have been tried and undergone the rite of passage,' the Chief Counsel declared, 'you have passed your trial and have earned the right to marry one of our own. You may now consider yourself welcome in the Underdark whenever you desire.'

I couldn't speak. I didn't trust myself to say the right thing. All I could do was incline my head and curtsey, which was awkward in torn breeches. Aidyn was silent beside me, as the Dark Elves in the crowd began to cheer and celebrate. On the balcony, Erik broke away from Jesse's restraining grip and sprinted down the stairs, racing over to me.

'Erik,' I cried, releasing Aidyn's hand and hurrying towards him.

There were tears on his face as he slammed into me, the shock almost knocking me to the ground.

'I was so worried,' he sobbed into my shoulder, 'I couldn't do anything. You just keeled over, and the Council took you away and there was nothing I could do.'

'Are you alright?' I pulled back slightly and checked him over, looking for any signs of damage. 'I thought... I heard...'

'I'm fine,' he gave a watery grin. 'And now we can finally go home.'

'She needs to sign her marriage contract first.' Rakael and Jesse had joined us. Jesse pulled me into a tight hug.

'You did so well, Nina,' she said. 'We'll have the Dark Elf soldiers in the Resistance now. You will be able to challenge the Usurper directly.'

I felt giddy with the realisation that reclaiming Scardia was within my grasp, and it was a heady feeling.

'Don't get ahead of yourself, Jesse,' Rakael said grimly. 'Nothing is confirmed until she has signed the contract.' As I met her gaze, I felt a distinct chill. Her expression told me that she knew what King Lysander would expect when the marriage contract was signed, and that it was something I should accept.

'Nina,' Aidyn's arm came around my waist, 'I think you need to rest.'

'She looks terrible,' Erik piped up as we left the arena, Jesse and Rakael watching us leave. 'That mystera looked painful, Nina. How did you get away from the serpent?'

'Serpent?' My voice was thin and reedy. The sound of a large body sliding over rocks out of the lake played through my mind and I was grateful that I hadn't turned around. No doubt I would have been frozen in terror and the snake would have devoured me in one gulp.

'There were these…' Beside me, Aidyn flinched slightly and I amended what I was about to say, 'I thought I saw something back on the shore. By then I had realised what might be in that lake and I ran.'

'But how did you know where to go?' Erik asked curiously and I looked at him, surprised. Could it be that the lunar moths had been visible only to me?

Aidyn's arm around my waist tightened and I said,

'I'm not sure; I was just lucky, I guess.'

Erik fell into silence beside us and I was relieved that he had stopped asking questions. I just wanted to look at him and reassure myself that he was alright, that he hadn't been tortured by the Council. I could remember the sound of his screams all too well and it was a sound that I was determined not to hear again.

The further we walked away from the amphitheatre, the more I struggled to remain upright. My legs buckled, the wounds from the mystera oozing with fresh blood. Erik stared, horrified, and Aidyn picked me up. Apparently now that I had faced the Council and the king it was no longer necessary for me to feign a semblance of strength. I relaxed into his arms, grateful for the assistance.

Before too long, we had reached the tunnel where our bedchambers were located, and Aidyn was knocking on my door. It was opened by Lisette, who looked frantic. Her hair was dirty and she looked as tired as Aidyn, her eyes red rimmed as she took in my appearance. She stifled a sob and let us come in, watching as Aidyn laid me down on my bed carefully.

'I will see you when you are feeling better, Nina,' he murmured, 'I must go and speak with my father.'

'Don't stay away too long,' I whispered. He bowed low and departed, leaving Erik and Lisette to look after me. Lisette rushed into frenzied action, gesturing for Erik to assist with bringing across the washstand and cloths and then unceremoniously pushing him out of the room as well. She stripped away my torn clothing and bathed the wounds on my legs and hands, wrapping them in gauze bandages. As she worked, tears slid down her nose and I patted her hand tiredly.

'It's alright, Lisette,' I murmured, 'I made it out alive.' She gave a choked cry as I pulled my nightgown over my head and settled back into the blankets. She sat beside me, keeping a silent vigil as I fell asleep.

When I awoke, Lisette was sleeping on the palette beside the bed and Erik was perched in one of the nearby chairs, his knees drawn up to his chin.

'Don't wake her,' he whispered, 'she only just lay down. She's been really worried about you.'

'Why are you here?' I asked quietly. 'Is everything alright?'

He shrugged. 'I didn't want to be far away when you woke up.'

I smiled.

'I also wanted to ask about Markus.' His voice sounded flat and hurt. 'I know that the people in the trials weren't real…'

'How did you know that?' I asked.

'The king told me,' Erik said, 'he said that no one would be hurt. But Markus seemed real. And you…'

'He wasn't real,' I whispered, unable to meet the accusing look in his eyes now. 'And besides it was an accident.'

'You killed him,' Erik said angrily, 'you *killed* him.'

'It wasn't really him,' I countered, hating myself for trying to weasel my way out of admitting the truth.

'That doesn't stop the fact that you did it.' Erik said softly. 'I thought that you and Markus…' His voice trailed off.

'Erik,' I began, unsure of what to say. It had been hard enough broaching this topic with Aidyn, I didn't know how I could phrase it so that Erik would understand. 'Please, I don't want to think about Markus right now. I want to try and forget as much about what happened in that trial as possible. They played tricks on my mind in there, I saw and heard things I never want to relive again. I just want to forget it.'

He nodded slowly. 'Alright Nina.'

'Thank you,' I breathed, as my eyes closed and exhaustion took over once more.

According to Jesse, I was in bed for at least a day and a half. Since time was difficult to trace in the Underdark, I wasn't altogether sure.

Lisette fussed over me, rubbing poultices into my wounds and using some of her own brand of magic to accelerate the healing. Erik visited my bedside regularly and kept me abreast of all the news, not that there seemed to be that much. Apparently, Rakael, Aidyn and King Lysander had been drawing up the marriage contracts and there had been many arguments between the three of them. Perhaps that explained why Aidyn had not visited me. All the same, I found myself missing him and as soon as Lisette had given her approval, I slipped out of the bedchamber wrapped in my cloak and went to look for him.

I made my way through the tunnels I knew, past the amphitheatre and the Midos Fields, where the workers paused to watch my passage. I had tried asking some of the Dark Elves at the amphitheatre about Aidyn, but they had not been able to help me and had only stared mutely. It unnerved me, and so I moved on, keeping my head lowered, trying to avoid attracting more notice. My destination was the grotto, the one place where he would go to escape, and since I had no idea where his quarters were and I hadn't managed to find him anywhere else, that was where I would go.

To my disappointment, the grotto was empty when I arrived. There was a flicker of light and I noticed a lunar moth perched nearby. I gazed at it as it fluttered away and sat down on one of the mossy rocks in front of the pool, the cool spray from the waterfall speckling the back of my neck. For the first time in a long time, I was completely alone.

The pool glistened before me, clear and still like the polished glass of a mirror. It drew me in, and I felt the familiar yearning to look into the depths and scry. This was my chance– while I was alone– to check, to guarantee that what I had seen in the trial had really been an illusion. Until I knew for certain, I couldn't rest easily. I closed my eyes and calmed my breathing, slowly releasing it, as I fixed my mind on Markus, praying that he was safe. The sound of the water outside the grotto and the gentle dripping faded away as I gazed down into the shallow pool and the reflected image solidified.

The night was moonless, with only starlight reflecting off the waves. In small groups, men in dark clothing worked together, unloading crates from a rowboat and carrying them up to shore. They acted furtively and I realised that they were smugglers, transporting goods that could not be delivered in daylight. The men kept their eyes lowered, but I could still recognise the one in the rowboat, who was the first to unload the crates, and felt myself sigh in relief. Seawater sprayed up into the boat and he blinked away the salt, methodically passing the crates to his men. He seemed unhurt, much as he had been when we had last spoken, and knowing that eased some of the worry I had felt. When the unloading was complete, he leapt out of the boat and waded to shore to exchange words with another man, whose eyes were flat and lifeless and whose face was scarred with burns.

I leaned closer, recognising the man. I remembered his face twisted in a leer, his coarse voice, his blade slicing Erik's face. It was the Tracker from the forest outside Lowton, the one who had escaped. A sharp breath escaped me as my gaze flicked between Markus and the Tracker. What were they discussing? What was Markus doing with him? What was in the crates that had been loaded onto the waiting carts?

The Tracker nodded and turned, heading back up the sand dune towards the carts, motioning for his men to follow. He paused at the top of the dune and I felt the familiar twinge of unease. Something was wrong, but the sailors down on the beach seemed unaware, Markus had turned to converse with Viktor and the others were heading back to the rowboats.

The Tracker brought his arm down in a sudden slashing motion. On cue, his men threw off their cloaks and charged towards the smugglers, some brandishing knives, others drawing back bows from the top of the dune. Arrows sliced through the night air and I watched as the sailors started to fall, overwhelmed by the sudden onslaught. Markus cried out, drew a blade from his belt and struck out at his attackers. On seeing their leader retaliating, his crew rallied and fought back, but they were significantly outnumbered. My heart constricted in my chest watching Markus deflect a blow that could have easily been his last. He laughed, eyes in his hollowed face dancing with maniacal vigour.

I heard the arrow before I saw it. There was a soft whoosh through the air and I watched, helpless to assist in any way. Despite that I screamed, and as if he could hear me Markus turned, the arrow intended for his heart piercing his shoulder instead. He buckled, falling to one knee in the damp sand. His men roared and fought with renewed purpose, yet their zeal didn't last long. With ruthless efficiency, their attackers cut them down until Markus was the only one left in the blood-drenched sand. His face blazed with pure hate as he was dragged up the beach. When he was in front of the Tracker, he spat,

'What in the Gods' names do you think you're doing? We had an agreement.'

The grey eyes glinted and the Tracker's mouth spread into a wide grin that made my skin crawl. 'His Royal Highness, King Niall of Scardia seeks an audience with you.'

Markus' eyes widened in shock. 'Why?'

'Seems you've not been too honest about who you've been ferrying around,' the Tracker replied, before his fist shot forward and punched Markus in the face, knocking him out. 'Put him in the cart,' he barked, 'leave the others.'

'Nina?' A hand was shaking my shoulder, roughly jerking me out of the vision, and I fell backwards, returning to the present with a shaky cry. Aidyn was tense next to me, a white moth on his shoulder. 'What did you see? What's wrong?'

I wanted to say that everything was wrong. The bodies spread along the beach, Viktor's sightless eyes gazing out at the dark ocean, Markus wounded and taken by the Tracker who had almost caught me. And yet I wasn't sure whether Aidyn would understand.

'I heard you scream,' he murmured, cradling me in his arms, 'tell me what happened.'

Slowly, I recounted what I had seen, keeping my head pressed to his chest to avoid having to see his reaction. When I mentioned the Tracker he went deathly still, listening intently until I finished. He didn't speak for a while and I waited, desperate for him to break the silence.

'Are you angry with me?' I finally whispered when it became apparent that he wasn't going to say anything.

'This Tracker, did he give any indication of where they were going?' Aidyn's voice was hard, and I pulled back, scanning his masked face, wishing that I could read his expression.

'You *are* angry,' I breathed.

'Answer me, Nina.' He sounded unlike his usual self, almost dictatorial. I stared at him, eyes blazing and he sighed, reaching out to take one of my hands. 'I'm sorry,' he said, 'but since he hurt you and murdered Gaelen, this man has not left my mind. I must find him.'

I remembered the strange ritual I saw, the passing of the knife, the blood offering. Once again, I heard Aidyn's cold and solemn words: *blood of my blood, brother of my soul, you will be avenged.*

'I don't know where he went,' I murmured, my hand turning over his palm, tracing the spot where I had seen him cut himself in the ritual. 'I'm sorry.'

He sighed again, heavier this time. 'We need to tell my father and Rakael about this. They will need to know, to send people to dispose of the bodies.'

I nodded blankly and followed him out of the grotto, the memory of the arrows and cries still ringing in my ears. He didn't say anything about Markus as we walked around the lake, but he remained distant. I wanted to break the awkwardness that spread out between us, although I couldn't think of a way to bridge the gap in a way that he would respond to. So, instead, I reached out and took his arm in mine, ignoring the quick glance he shot in my direction, and walked on.

The others were in the amphitheatre, in a small room that was connected to the mirrored atrium. Jesse was sitting in a corner, Erik beside her looking bored. Rakael and King Lysander were leaning over a small table, spread out with parchment and maps. On the other side of the room, the Council watched in silent disapproval.

'We will need to have men come here,' Rakael was saying, prodding at the map deliberately, 'For a full-frontal assault on the Capital…'

'And where will your Resistance fighters be?' King Lysander interrupted, 'my soldiers are valuable. They are not cannon fodder for drawing fire from the Usurper's army.'

'Of course not,' Rakael said impatiently, 'we will arrange for the first wave of assault to be expendable soldiers.'

'Father,' Aidyn interrupted and Rakael glanced around, glaring at the intrusion. 'There's been an incident.'

'What is it Aidyn?' King Lysander asked. 'The Princess looks wan, take her to her rooms to rest, boy.' He waved at Erik who frowned indignantly.

'No,' I said quickly, 'I saw Trackers. They… They…' I couldn't finish my sentence, the memories of what I had seen were too vivid for me to live through them again.

'The ship who brought the Princess and her party to us has been attacked,' Aidyn said succinctly, 'Trackers have taken the captain prisoner and killed the others.'

There was a moment's silence and then the room was in an uproar.

'Trackers found the ship?' Jesse asked, 'How?'

'They took the captain alive?' Rakael said at the same time, 'we need to move. He cannot be trusted to keep our location a secret.'

'Markus is hurt?' Erik said, 'What about Viktor and the others? They can't be dead, they can't be.'

I nodded at him and saw his face crumple. 'But Markus won't die, he won't,' Erik repeated to himself, 'he's strong. He won't tell them where we are.'

'You don't know that for certain,' Rakael snapped, 'torture has a way of making a man talk. Gold will only buy so much silence.' She cursed and slammed a fist down onto the map.

'We have to save him,' Erik was saying loudly, 'we need to bring him back.'

'Nina, where were they taking him?' Jesse asked, 'is there a way you can find out?'

The last thing I wanted to do was to scry again so soon. I felt weakened and shaken after what I had seen, and scared about what I would see next time.

'She needs to rest,' the Chief Counsel interrupted, 'we need to focus on the matter at hand; the betrothal.'

'We need to help Markus,' I murmured through numb lips. 'I can't lose him like I lost Keely.' At the mention of Keely's name Rakael paused and looked at me, expression unreadable.

'The marriage contracts still need to be signed,' King Lysander reinforced. 'Then we might see if we can assist your friend.' From the way he spoke it was clear that he had no intention of doing so.

'The marriage can wait,' Erik retorted, 'Markus is in trouble *now.*'

Aidyn was watching me throughout the whole exchange, noting my reactions and keeping quiet. Now he stepped forward and knelt before me, drawing the eyes of everyone in the room.

'If it is your desire I will find your captain, Princess,' he said quietly, 'if you agree to wed me when I return. We can write it into the marriage contract, a betrothal contract so to speak. You will have the protection of my name and my father's men for your cause, and I will not return until I have found Markus.'

I couldn't reply. My heart was constricting my throat, cutting off the oxygen to my lungs. He waited, one hand outstretched before me, and there was a tearing sensation in my chest.

'An excellent proposal, Lord Aidyn,' Rakael said quickly, and then shooting me a sharp glance, 'Princess?' From beside her, Erik looked at me imploringly.

Mutely, I reached forward and placed my hand in Aidyn's, wondering what I had gotten myself into.

Rakael sprang into action and I let the words fly over me. There was a heaviness falling around my heart and I didn't understand it.

'Excuse me, please,' I whispered and slipped out, desperate to escape. Aidyn watched me leave solemnly and I wondered if he felt the way I did– confused, conflicted, scared. I broke into a run, not caring about the odd glances that I drew, just wanting to get as far away from that small room as possible.

I retreated to my room and sent Lisette away, begging for her to prepare a tisane, anything to calm my raging heart. When she was gone, I paced the room, hands in my hair, feeling trapped. I cried out in anger, kicking one of the trunks and watching as it toppled, clothes and shoes falling across the floor. I crouched down, picking up the items and returning them to their places, blinking back tears.

It was hard to believe that the sailors who had ferried us across the Meridian were gone. Viktor was dead. Markus might very well be dead soon too and it would be my fault yet again. And if Aidyn followed him, what would happen then? I wasn't sure if his desire for vengeance would take over, whether he would return at all. What if he was killed too?

My door opened and I glanced up, wiping away my tears. Aidyn was holding a tray, with two glass cups and a steaming tisane.

'May I join you?' he asked levelly, and I nodded. The door closed behind him and he joined me on the floor, not commenting on my red eyes or the state of my hair which now rested around my shoulders in a messy tangle. With short, precise motions he poured the tisane into the cups and handed me one before removing his mask and drinking from his own.

I didn't know what to say, so I followed his lead, taking a tentative sip of the tisane. It was my favourite, and the dried scent of thyme filled my nostrils as I inhaled the steam.

'Talk to me, dear heart,' Aidyn said quietly. The endearment slipped off his tongue easily and I blinked, unsure of how to reply.

'I didn't expect you to say what you did in front of the others,' I managed, gripping the cup tightly. 'You surprised me.'

'You thought I wouldn't offer to help?' he asked, 'You thought I'd be jealous?'

'I told you that I needed time,' I whispered, 'putting me on the spot like that was not giving me time.'

'I have postponed my father's plans for you,' he said curtly, and his cheeks blushed faintly as he held in his anger. 'I have ensured that you will have soldiers to retake your country without needing to wed immediately. I am also willing to rescue your lover.'

It was as though he had struck me, and I glared at him, smacking down the glass onto the tray. 'How dare you.' I felt my eyes flare and sparks rose. 'Don't ignore the fact that you want to hunt down the Tracker. You want your revenge and are using Markus as an excuse to set about doing it.'

His mouth twisted, 'you are so astute, Princess.'

'Ugh!' I jumped to my feet and began to pace again, trying to control the sparks that flew into the air and to ignore the way he watched me.

'Has it occurred to you,' he said finally, 'that I did what I thought would make you happy? Had that even crossed your mind?'

'Happy?' I cried, 'You think that going after Trackers who show no mercy when they kill is going to make me *happy*?'

In an instant he stood and caught me as I paced, holding me firm as I struggled and then collapsed against him, the tears from earlier returning with a vengeance.

'I hate crying,' I whispered into his shoulder, and he held me tighter. 'I hate feeling like I can't control anything. I want Markus to be safe. But I don't want you to be hurt if you go after him.'

'You have so little faith in my abilities?' he murmured against my hair, and I could feel his gentle smile. 'If I know that you will be here when I return, dear heart, that is all the incentive I need.'

There it was again, the endearment that tore at my heart and confused me even more. It scared and tempted me, promising possibilities that could become realities if I would just let them.

'I'm scared, Aidyn,' I said, drawing away to look at him. It was the first time I had seen him in proper light and I scanned his features, trying to imprint them in my memory. His eyes were a soft lilac colour, framed by pale lashes. His hair was short and spiky, a mixture of white and fairest blond, and I reached up, tracing my hands through it. He looked almost ethereal in the lamplight, and I was struck by how different he was to Markus.

'I will be alright,' he said reassuringly, 'you have no reason to fear.'

My mind was reminded of the massacre on the beach; of how I had heard Gaelen had been killed. Trackers were unpredictable and violent, they could easily cut down anyone, trained soldier or not. As if sensing my train of thought, Aidyn cupped my cheek, the dark leather smooth against my skin.

'I will need you to show me this Tracker, Nina,' he said quietly, 'I cannot scry for him on my own as I have not seen his face. I need you to help me locate where they are going.' I nodded shakily and allowed him to sit me back down on the ground beside the glasses. He picked up the bowl that I used for washing, filled it from the pitcher, and carried it between us. I lifted my cup to my lips, draining the remainder of the tisane, needing the extra burst of calming energy it gave me.

'I'll be here with you the whole time,' Aidyn said, taking my hands with his. 'Show me what you see.'

'I don't know how.' My voice was thin, anxious.

'Relax your mind and allow me to join you,' he said, and I followed his advice, calming my emotions and focussing my thoughts. I gazed into the water as it stilled and envisioned the Tracker. I felt a slight presence at the edges of my mind and the image in the bowl sharpened, much more quickly than usual.

The Tracker was in the hold of a ship, Markus' ship by the looks of it. He was wiping blood off his hands onto a rag, mouth twisted in a sneer.

'You'll talk soon enough,' he promised, 'once we get to Icevale Keep. Those who go in, don't come out alive. You'll never see anything you hold dear again.'

There was a muffled grunt from behind him. Markus was tied and gagged, chained to the wall, one shoulder stained red.

'Oh, be quiet,' the Tracker said, kicking him, 'you'll not be too lonely there. We have a cellmate for you– another young man who thought helping the Princess would be a good idea. It took at least a month before he broke, but he told us that she was headed for the Eastern Lands. Only one ship had sailed for that foreign port in recent times, and sure enough, it had had a female passenger.'

The Tracker struck Markus across the face and he fell limp, unconscious once more.

'Oh yes,' the Tracker leaned back, playing with the clay beads in his beard. 'I am looking forward to making you talk, Captain.'

The image faded and dissolved, leaving me feeling sick and weak. Aidyn released my hands and poured me another cup of the thyme tisane, making sure that I drank it.

'Thank you,' he said quietly, 'I know that cannot have been easy.'

It hadn't. I didn't want to scry again for quite some time, the image of Markus chained in the bowels of his own ship was haunting. I ran my hands through my hair, straightening it in a desperate effort to calm myself.

'Icevale Keep is in Scardia,' I finally said, 'It's where the Usurper keeps his enemies; the ones who are too important to kill outright or to sell into slavery anyway. It's a fortress where the Hoarfrost meets the sea. People say that it's impossible to get into and no one ever escapes. It will be under heavy guard, the Usurper would make sure of it.' I thought for a moment, remembering what the Tracker had said and feeling a thin wisp of hope fill me. 'He mentioned another prisoner, Aidyn. One who told them that I was going to the Eastern Lands, it must be Keely. He must be alive, you have to get him out too. Promise me, please.'

Aidyn was silent as he returned the bowl to its stand.

'If that is what you desire, Nina. If the keep is in Scardia, then I will need to get a small force together and leave as soon as possible.' He was already picking up his balaclava and mask, preparing to put them back on.

'No,' I stood, 'you can't leave yet.'

It was too soon. I wasn't ready to say goodbye.

'You said that you needed time, Nina,' he murmured, 'once the betrothal contract is signed you will have that. From the sound of it, the Resistance will be wanting to move out soon and return to Scardia as well. I will meet you there; you have my word.'

I held him close, unwilling to let him go, knowing that this may well be the last time we would be together alone.

'Kiss me,' I whispered, 'please Aidyn.'

And he did. His lips moved sweetly against mine, setting alight the fire in my blood, and I clung to him. When he broke away, I was left feeling bereft, alone.

'I must go,' he said, 'take care, dear heart.' With that, he kissed me again– briefly this time– and then departed, pulling his mask back on as he reached the door.

Chapter Sixteen

Aidyn left later that day, taking with him a selected group of companions. He made sure to sign the betrothal contract first. We had clasped hands as the Chief Counsel read out the betrothal contract, his raspy voice intoning every component of the agreement. In return for Aidyn retrieving Markus and Keely from Icevale Keep and having a force of Dark Elf soldiers to assist the Resistance from the signing of the contract, I would consent to a marriage alliance with the Dark Elves and marry him upon his return.

There was no mention of the Lord's Right, and I wondered if Aidyn had managed to convince his father to forget about that component of the marriage, or whether it was something that I could avoid in the future. As we signed the document, I felt the steely gazes of Rakael and the Chief Counsel, checking that every 't' was crossed and every 'i' was dotted.

Once the betrothal contract was signed, Aidyn swept a low bow to me and his father and then departed, riding out with his group of soldiers. As he rode away, I couldn't help but feel a premonition that something was going to go wrong.

Days passed but Rakael did not allow me to have much time to think. As Aidyn had predicted, she was determined to make a move, now that she had the army she had been promised. I became more of an afterthought in her plans, having already achieved her purpose for me. Under her direction, several battalions of soldiers had already left the Underdark, each one with separate instructions. I wasn't sure how they would cross the Meridian separately, but Rakael assured me that she had everything in hand which didn't do much to alleviate my concerns.

Dylan had still not returned from his trip to the Archives with Alex, while Erik and Jesse tried to keep me occupied in the training hall, battling it out with the Dark Elf soldiers. I learned pretty quickly that their skill was far superior to mine, and tried not to feel too embarrassed when they evaded my blows and toppled me all too easily. If anything, it distracted me from thinking about what was happening to Aidyn or Markus.

Lisette was also acting strangely. When I had told her about my suspicions that Keely was alive, she had turned pale, clasping onto the wall for support. Since then, she had been preoccupied and distracted, permanent worry marks now etched into her brow as she bustled around, preparing for our departure.

The Dark Elves treated us respectfully, but I didn't like the way the Chief Counsel would follow my movements or how King Lysander found ways to find me when I was walking. With Aidyn gone, it was as though he had remembered about his Lord's Right and was determined to claim it before Aidyn returned. I kept Erik and Jesse close at my side whenever I went anywhere now, just so he wouldn't be able to catch me alone.

It was the night before we were to leave, and King Lysander had organised for the revels to begin early. The wine flowed freely, and the dancing was more frenetic than usual. I was soon feeling sleepy and desperate to return to my room. I was wearing a dress of deep crimson with gold embellishments on the skirt, bodice and sleeves. It was all decoration and no practicality, and I felt more like an ornament for the male gaze than I had in a long time. To make it worse, from across the floor, the Chief Counsel and the king were watching me. Erik was accompanying me in the dance, but I could barely concentrate on the steps.

'Nina?' he muttered, 'what…?'

His question was cut off by screams. The musicians stopped playing, and the dancers on the floor were looking around with growing panic. There was a loud bang and smoke filled the cavern, an acrid burning scent filling my nostrils. Around us people screamed and fled, as men with blazing lanterns, loaded crossbows and curved swords burst into the cavern. Their armour was illuminated by the lanterns they held; the image of the bull's head emblazoned across their breastplates. Erik gripped my hand and we ran, cutting through the crowd, searching for Rakael, Jesse or the other Resistance guards. Neither of us had weapons and we fled; a familiar sense of terror filled me, blocking out all other thoughts apart from the need to escape.

The Trackers attacked, cutting through the crowd with ease at first. The Dark Elves fell, disorientated by the smoke and caught by surprise. When they did fight back, it was with brutal ruthlessness, striking and using the shadows to their advantage, yet the Trackers had weapons available while the Dark Elves did not.

'Princess, come with me.' King Lysander had pulled my hand from Erik's and dragged me away towards a darkened passageway.

'Erik!' I called, struggling to get back to him, but the king's grip tightened.

'Be quiet,' he snapped, 'do you want them to find you?'

He led me down the passageway in a direction I did not know. Gradually the sounds of the fighting behind us began to fade and we paused, breathing heavily.

'I need to find Erik and the others,' I gasped, clutching a stitch in my side. 'We need to get out of here.'

'Let my men dispatch our intruders first,' King Lysander said, his silver armour glinting. I was amazed that he had managed to run in it for so long, it looked extremely heavy. 'We can stay here until they are gone.' The king's hands moved to my shoulders, and I began to feel a different kind of fear.

'Let go of me, Your Highness,' I said, forcing myself to keep my voice quiet and composed.

'You don't have to be afraid, Princess Wilhelmina,' he murmured, 'I will keep you safe.'

'I said let me *go*!' I pushed against him, and his armour lit up with heat, the metal turning white hot. His hands released me and I fled, trying to find my way back to the battle as his screams filled the tunnel behind me. I stumbled and tripped, scraping my hands on the hard ground. I was shaking and then someone pulled me upright.

'Get it together, Princess.' It was Rakael. Her scarred face was stretched tight in the pale light, and she had blood on her tunic. In her hands was one of the curved blades the Trackers had been using.

'Rakael, what's going on? How did the Trackers get here?' I spoke quickly, and she frowned.

'They knew how to get in. They had help from the inside.'

The king's screams pierced the darkness again and Rakael stepped forward, blade raised. 'Who is that?'

'King Lysander,' I whispered shakily. 'He tried to...'

She turned horrified eyes on me, 'what have you *done*, Princess?'

'I just wanted to get away,' I said hollowly as the screams began to fade into agonised, racking sobs and then silence.

'You idiot,' Rakael was furious. 'We needed the king *alive*.' She paused, thinking deeply and then said, 'there needs to be a reason for his death, another way he could have died without you becoming the main suspect.' She was gazing back towards the cavern, the sounds of fighting reaching us easily. 'Unless… yes, there is no other way.'

'What do you mean, Rakael?' I asked, watching her as she came closer.

'I warned you, Nina,' she said with quiet deliberation, 'I warned you not to ruin my plans. But, if a Tracker can be blamed for killing both the Dark Elf King and the troublesome Princess, then getting the support for the Rebellion will be so much easier. There's nothing quite like having a martyr. And then Scardia can become what it should have always been; free of the monarchy and free from the Usurper.' There was a crazed glint in her eyes that scared me.

As she spoke, I felt something pierce my flesh, sinking in deep. Together we looked down at the curved blade that was impaled in my stomach, the blood spreading slowly at first and then more rapidly as the blade was twisted and removed.

'For Scardia.' Her voice was a low hiss, and I clutched my stomach, falling to the ground, watching as she strode away towards where King Lysander lay. My mind was becoming foggy and I tried to pull myself towards the tunnel entrance to the cavern. My energy gave out and I lay in the dirt, breath coming in quick, pained gasps. In a desperate effort, I tried to summon a flame, either to attract someone's attention or to try and cauterise the wound. But nothing happened, no magic responded to my attempts as the cold numbness continued to spread through me.

'Erik,' I mumbled as something small and white fluttered in front of my eyes, landing on the hand that clasped my wound. I tried to focus on it, on the delicate wings that looked like miniature beams of moonlight. 'Find him,' I begged, 'keep him safe.' The lunar moth flicked its wings and lifted into the air, disappearing from view.

I leaned my head back against the wall, the world around me becoming fuzzy, the sounds of the battle becoming more distant. Another light was approaching me now, this one brighter than the lunar moth, and I gasped, struggling for breath as icy coldness enfolded me, leading me from the embrace of darkness to that of the light.

Acknowledgements

The process of writing this second instalment in the Ice Flame Trilogy would not have been possible without the support of so many people. First of all, I would like to thank Ian, Natalie and Brittany, along with the team at the Book Reality Experience for their help with cover designs, editing and the publication process. I am so grateful to have their support and expertise assisting me in this journey.

Secondly, to my family and friends, who have been eagerly awaiting the second instalment and regularly asking for updates at each different event. The demands for Book Two were key motivators for me to keep writing so that some of your questions would be answered.

Lastly, to Jordan and our two boys, Romeo and Gnocchi, who provided all the emotional support needed when I was caught up in the world of Scardia and for understanding how I would closet myself away to write.

About the Author

A booklover from an early age, Rose began writing stories from the age of seven and this passion continued into a life-long dream of becoming a writer.

When she is not reading a new book, jotting down ideas in a notebook or pottering around in her veggie garden under her cats' supervision, she can be found either on the stage in her other passion– amateur theatre– or teaching English and French to high school students.